ESCAPING FIRST CONTACT

T.S. BEIER

Nostromo

This book is a work of fiction. Any references to historical events, real people, or real places are used fictitiously. Other names, characters, places, and events are products of the author's imagination, and any resemblance to actual events, places, names, or persons, is entirely coincidental.

Cover illustration by Jon Stubbington
(https://www.jonstubbington.com/)
Edited by Marthese Fenech. (https://marthesefenech.com/)
"Azomic" freeware font from FontSpace.com

Quotation from *Ozymandias* by Percy Bysshe Shelley, 1791 – 1822.

ISBNs:
978-1-7771295-7-6 (Kindle)
978-1-7771295-6-9 (KDP - paperback)

BISAC:
FIC028090 **FICTION** / Science Fiction / Alien Contact
FIC028030 **FICTION** / Science Fiction / Space Opera

A Note on the Text

Escaping First Contact uses Canadian/UK English during narration, as well as imperial units of measurement. A "u" in colour, for example, is not a typo.

Nostromo

This one is for Sam.
If it bleeds, we can kill it!

Nothing beside remains. Round the decay
Of that colossal Wreck, boundless and bare
The lone and level sands stretch far away.

– "Ozymandias," Percy Bysshe Shelley

ESCAPING FIRST CONTACT

THE BURNT SHIP TRILOGY #1

A NOTE ON THE TEXT

Alien languages would contain their own idiosyncrasies, idioms, and expressions, on top of their culture having a vastly different socio-political-historical context than Terrans (and their colonies). This includes, but is not limited to, race, gender, and religion. As such, when aliens are speaking to one another in their own language, I have elected to use approximate words/phrases/metaphors in English in a way that may not be entirely accurate to the alien culture but creates an easier-to-understand dialogue for the reader. Any anachronism, or cultural improbability, is not an error but a deliberate choice.

Any "alien" words that are similar or the same as those of the real world are used accidentally and not intended to create a connection between the fictional alien culture and that of any human society.

Apostrophes in the middle of alien words denote a sound the English lexicon cannot convey.

CHAPTER 1: RAMMY

The suddenness of the ship's deceleration made Rammy's gut lift and his hope sink. Only his tight grip on the seat's armrests kept him rooted in his chair as gravity dissipated. Other than military drop shuttles, he had never spent time on a ship this small before, and in those situations, he had been strapped in tight until reaching atmosphere. While the P-class commercial towing freighter had the space to store large quantities of goods, it was not large or luxurious enough to house a spinning centrifuge that could generate artificial gravity. Only while accelerating could the vessel maintain a gravitational effect. The captain, who was also serving as pilot, had slammed on the brakes, so to speak, in an extremely risky manoeuvre that had one purpose: a direct challenge to the ship following closely on their six.

Rammy pulled the seat's harness over his shoulders and snapped it in place. He twisted to watch the portside viewscreen, which mimicked a window. The triangular Strenoi ship banked sharply around them, narrowly missing *Starship 330307*. Over the ship's communicator, the Strenoi's hissing language burst forth on the open frequency. Rammy was surprised at how much he understood, then realized it was all swearing and insults, the extent of his knowledge of their main language. He exhaled quickly, unsure whether he should be thankful the captain's "brakes of death" move hadn't destroyed them both or whether it would have been preferable to have died quickly in a massive explosion.

The Strenoi ship slowed outside the bow viewer, then flipped over, twisted, and came at them again. The enemy ship had weapons but hadn't fired them. Yet.

There was a sharp tugging on his left ear as the ship began to move, banking hard to the right to attempt an escape. Rammy used his right hand to grab the wrist of his left, stopping the fingers on his left hand from pulling on his earlobe. He clasped his hands together on his lap. He had experience in active combat. He had passed marine training. He had survived the four battles he'd fought in the war and survived having two fingers shot off (and subsequently regrown). This little incident was nothing compared to that.

So why was his mouth dry and his forehead starting to sweat? Was it because they were being chased by a species that wasn't known for giving up? Or because this mission was far less reputable than he had believed? Or because the alien captain, who could fly, was not a licensed pilot? And because je was hissing and swearing in jer language, dotting spittle on the viewer in front of jer?

"You're fine. The captain has done this all before. This is normal," he whispered to himself.

A choking noise caused Rammy to whip his head to the right. Sitting in the same-sized chair as Rammy but appearing much too thin for it, was the captain's counterpart, a Rip like jer. This Rip appeared positively nonchalant about the Strenoi in pursuit. Jer undone harness was hanging loosely by jer side, jer disconcertingly long and spindly legs were stretched out in front of jer, and curved feet hung over the empty co-pilot's chair. Rips didn't have feet or toes; hundreds of tube-like cilia descended from their ankles which propelled them along.

Despite having been in the ship for two days with the alien, Rammy took a moment to stare at the Rip. He'd fought them in battle from a distance but never hand-to-hand. He'd seen them at the marine base, as they served as mercenaries or assassins on both sides of the war, but he had never spoken to one before signing up with this mission. The Rip's arms were almost as long as jer legs, with five fingers like a Terran, but fingers that were double the length and had three sets of knuckles. Sharp, curving wine-red nails protruded from the Rip's fingertips. Jer torso was slender with a gentle curve to the hips that would make any model jealous. This was the only feature of the Rip physiology that wasn't a complete nightmare.

The Rip, whose name was Wind, had an oversized mouth, thin lips, long skinny teeth, skin the colour of ink, and bright ruby eyes with slanted pupils. Wind had no hair on jer head and wore a tight many-pocketed vest and equally tight pants. The Rips were biologically determined as hermaphrodites by Terran scientists and sported no external genitals or secondary sex characteristics. Terrans, of course, had non-binary people, and the Dirge species were entirely gender-neutral, but the Rips had no concept of gender or different sexes until they met the other species in the galaxy. As such, they insisted the other races use "je/jer" to describe them, rather than "they," as a marker of their physiological difference.

After glancing at the viewer to see the Strenoi were now flying directly beside them, as if to suggest they could not escape, Rammy frowned at the Rip. "What are you laughing at?"

While Rammy prided himself on being open to new experiences and new people, the Rips were hardly a species he was willing to settle down with. They sold themselves out to the highest bidder, and their physical appearance was, well, creepy. Had Rammy known when he showed up with the corporal on his shore leave that the captain of this mission was a Rip, he may have left Kosa to this expedition on her lonesome.

But then again, where else would he have gone? Back to base, where everything reminded him of AJ? Back home to Terra? Back to his parents where he'd have to explain why another relationship failed? Perhaps being here with the Rips was preferable. And perhaps he was being a bigot. Just because the Rips looked like something from a horror film didn't mean they were what the rumours said.

"This is not normal," the Rip clarified in response to Rammy's previous whispering.

"You speak English!?" Rammy demanded. Any attempt to be accepting flew out the window. He and Corporal Koharu Saito, nicknamed Kosa, had been on this flying death trap for two days, and no one thought to mention the Rips could speak a lick of English, Mandarin, or Spanish, Terra's three official languages. The captain had simply pointed at jerself and said, "Captain Stares."

At first, Rammy hadn't been sure what je meant, but nodded anyway. Kosa had explained later that the captain's full name was translated to "Stares at the Stars," as all Rips had descriptive names rather than family or surnames.

Many times during this journey Rammy had wished he had joined up with renegade Strenoi instead, as at least the reptiloid aliens weren't completely different from Terrans. They had a similar naming convention to Terrans, two discernible sexes, and their antagonism made sense, given the almost ten-year war Earth had fought with Strenovast. They were militaristic, honour-bound, and had sticks up their asses, but Rammy could understand those traits, as his father had those characteristics too. No wonder the guys he dated tended to be free-spirited and spontaneous.

The other two aliens on the ship, a mated Pir-An couple, hadn't bothered to talk to Rammy that much, though the navigator spoke all three languages quite well. Perhaps she was sick of being a translator, as that tended to be her primary function after plotting the course.

Stares, the captain, let out a similar chortle to jer compatriot, waving at Wind to join jer upfront. As Wind stood and lifted jer long leg to step over the chair, rather than go around it, Rammy found himself staring at the alien's body again, much like one is compelled to view a horrifying scene in a movie. While Rammy was Black in ethnicity, his skin tone was umber. Wind was truly black as pitch, jer skin reflective and shiny, like metal or tar.

As though je felt the Terran's eyes on jer, Wind turned jer head 180 degrees, like an owl. Rammy gaped at the movement, unaware they could do that. Yet another reason why the Rips were off-putting as hell.

The Rip opened jer mouth in a wide smile, showing all jer teeth.

Rammy tried to look casual but only succeeded in causing the Rip to smirk. As the Rip joined the captain at the front of the ship, the two Pir-An entered the cockpit. If the Rips were terrifying, the Pir-An were the opposite. At barely five feet tall, they were squat with thick, shark-like skin, bulging eyes reminiscent of fish, gills along their necks, and three-tiered lips. The pair were distinguishable from one another in that the female, Klen'ai'bagra, had sky blue skin and a curving fin on her back. The male, Flug'ger'alaio, was indigo and his fin was much shorter.

Rammy had overheard the couple refer to one another as Klenni and Flugger, and as such, that's what he called them. Klenni began to speak to the Rips, moving her tendrils expressively. The Pir-An communicated with words and some hand gestures, like the other species, but they expressed emotion with two thin tendrils that exited their body at their wrists. The tendrils reminded Rammy of slightly thicker red string licorice. The Pir-An could not smile or move their faces much. Rammy had worked with Pir-An during his studies at university, so he understood some of their emotive gestures. Given how violently the tendrils were waving about, the Pir-An was angry.

The Rips looked at one another, then chortled their laugh again. The captain waved a hand dismissively at the pair, as if they need not worry about the Strenoi fighter. The Pir-An, bodies still as statues, watched the triangular alien ship on the viewer. Rammy followed suit. As much as he could tell, the Pir-An were as perturbed by this situation as he was. The Strenoi ship, of military design and much faster and more powerful than their simple freighter, dropped behind, then approached from the port side.

What the fuck did they want?

The Strenoi language barked from the comm. The Rips stared at it. Wind translated for the captain as the female Pir-An locked eyes with her partner. Wind turned to the Pir-An, saying something to them in Rip. In response, Klenni began yelling louder at the Rips, pointing outside, pointing at Rammy, and then pointing vaguely towards the back of the ship, where Kosa spent most of her time.

The captain turned and looked at the Pir-An for a moment, then stuck out jer skinny blood-red tongue, twisting it slightly at the end. Clearly it was an insult far graver than it would be coming from a Terran, as the male Pir-An pushed past his partner and grabbed the captain by the shoulder. The captain hit auto-pilot and was instantly on jer cilia, towering over the Pir-An, mouth open, drops of saliva splatting onto the Pir-An's shoulders almost two feet below. To his credit, the male Pir-An backed up only slightly, but his fish-mouth bobbed open and closed as if he were gasping for air. Despite his thick, shark-like hide, he had no natural defences against a Rip's teeth or claws. It wouldn't be a fight but a murder. Rammy stayed frozen in his seat, hoping the resolution was not violent, as he had seen Rips in combat and didn't want to intervene.

Wind maintained a constantly creepy air, usually standing in dark corners or sharpening jer knife, eyes always watching everyone. On the other hand, Stares was intense in jer unpredictable moods; sometimes, je would be laughing with the Pir-An or poking in admiration at Kosa's muscles and tattoos, but then would snap with anger at what seemed like a small issue. What set jer off this time, Rammy couldn't figure out.

Stares' skin was shining silver, so bright je glinted, but jer eyes were black, the pupils blending into the irises. Je dressed in a manner Rammy had never seen on the usually practical Rips: flowing silk-like garments. Unlike Wind, who wore bottom-less hanging Kevlar socks over most of jer cilia to afford jer protection and movement, Stares wore no protection for jer cilia. When je stood, as je did now, je appeared to be hovering on the two-inch tubes.

After a terse moment of glaring, the Pir-An backed away. Stares sat with a snort, pressing buttons on the com, and nodded at Wind to reply to their pursuers: two curt words.

The Pir-An couple sighed collectively and made their way behind Rammy to strap themselves into their seats. Rammy undid his harness so he could turn and look at the pair.

"Raptors want us to stop," Flugger explained, using the slur for the Strenoi created by Terrans, his English barely discernable. He was a doctor, a field medic, so he had a Terran vocabulary limited to medical phrases and basic words.

"Stop what?"

Klenni explained, "They want to stop our expedition and claim the ship for Strenovast. You know the Strenoi – they're not ones to share."

"That makes sense, I guess. Doesn't Stares want to claim the ship for jer people?"

Klenni shook her head. "No, Stares has been hired to investigate, as far as je told us, though je could be lying. Rips don't claim stuff. They don't care. All Rips want is to kill things, to fight. To live on their dank planet. Perhaps they think this ship will give them more weapons. Who knows? Rips are … not like the rest of us."

Ripplia was a dark world with swampy, desolate bogs and scant vegetation. The Rippliagnos hadn't evolved to be the dominant life form on the planet. Nomadic, they were constantly hunted by large amphibians. The animals, called *Borkas*, hadn't gotten hold of a Rip since the latter had signed a deal with first Strenovast and then Earth in the war five years ago; the bulk of their payment for becoming mercenaries for both sides was weapons and technology to fight off the *Borkas*. No job was too dirty for them, no fight too challenging. The first time the Strenoi used Rips in battle, the battle had been a decisive victory. Given how terrifying the Rips were in physical appearance and mentality, Rammy doubted either side would have agreed to elevate them scientifically if the war hadn't forced their hand. The last thing you want to do is give chaotic nihilists weapons. Unfortunately, the Rips were armed now and unwilling to give the weapons and other technology back. The other species reacted to this by pretending to ignore them. They allowed a few to settle on various other worlds, but only enough to placate them. Neither of the four other species believed the Rips were capable, or even willing, to rise up *en masse* against the aliens in the peace treaty they called the Accord. Still, they didn't let the Rips have nuclear technology.

Wind's ability to speak Strenoi was rough, and the reptiloids replied with their word for "repeat." Wind tried again while Klenni rolled her eyes.

"Rips should not be captains. They're too risky," she said in English, her accent strong, putting emphasis on the wrong syllables at times, but quite understandable. Klenni had mentioned she had spent time on Terran and Strenoi ships, often helping them with Pir-An upgrades to their systems as well as navigation.

The Strenoi voice came through the comm; their language was guttural but elegiac, even with the harshness of the tone. Wind looked at Stares, who nodded.

Flugger tightened his wife's harness, then his own. Rammy fumbled with the straps. Klenni's left tendril wrapped around Flugger's right. Wind spoke again, and Klenni's gills contracted as she translated.

"The Rips told the Strenoi to shove their ship up their ass. Hold on, Terran!"

Rammy was thrown from his chair as Stares gunned the engine and banked right, accelerating from hundreds of kilometres an hour to thousands. Rammy rubbed his elbow as he sat up, annoyance overtaking his trepidation. He watched the rear viewer from his position on the floor as the Strenoi ship got smaller and smaller. A few seconds later, as he expected, it grew larger again as they accelerated to match speed. A bright pink light bloomed on the tip of their ship. Oh shit, they meant business.

"Evasive manoeuvres!" he yelled. Wind turned jer head when Rammy spoke, then barked something to Stares. The captain let out a shrill noise that was part howl and part cackle and sent the ship "up." The pink blast of concentrated plasma whizzed past the ship, and Stares jabbed a finger into the comm controls so je could send another insult to the Strenoi. Or at least Rammy assumed it was an insult since Wind laughed yet again. Rammy stood, legs shaking, and positioned himself behind the captain's chair. A harness wouldn't save him if the Strenoi scored a hit. Besides, looming in the distance was the reason why the Strenoi were attacking them. Aside from the insults, of course.

The mystery ship was immense. More than five times the size of a Terran A-class dreadnaught, the ship lacked a resemblance to any spaceship Rammy had ever seen. Terran ships were bulky and extraneous, with rounded corners, many individual compartments, and gigantic engines. Pir-An ships were elegant and shaped like a teardrop, as sleek as a bead of mercury, with no doors or openings while in flight. Strenoi fighters, like the one chasing them, were triangular, with no ostentatious pieces or visible thrusters. Strenoi ships of this class were designed to link together around one of their battle cruisers, thousands of ships strong, so to channel power through interconnected conduits to create a massive plasma beam. Rammy had seen a beam attack only once, and the way the small triangles had performed a synchronized dance around the battle cruiser reminded him of bees. The beam had pierced the *USS Lusitania* for only a moment, but the result had been to explode the Super Lumen engine as well as the fuel for impulse flight. Nothing had been left of the *Lusitania* aside from charred metal detritus.

The Rips boasted no ships of their own. The other aliens in the galaxy, the Dirge, kept mostly to themselves. Rammy had more than a passing interest in alien technology and knew their ships were circular with a central courtyard. He would love the chance to check one out.

This new ship was rectangular – it could easily have been a slab cut from something larger, like a brick chiselled from a wall. It had doors, bays, windows, and weapons. To Rammy, doors and bays suggested the occupants moved as individual units, windows meant the aliens had eyes, and the existence of weapons could mean anything from self-defence to outright aggression.

Regardless, it was wholly alien. Rammy had seen ships designed primarily for use in space that weren't conducive to flying in atmo, but they still had to be built on the ground and therefore retain some aerodynamic capability. This ship could never leave a planet unless it were sent to space inside something else. But to carry this ship, the rocket would have to be over ten kilometers long and five high. Had it been built in the vacuum? It resembled an apartment building more than a ship. It was so awe-inspiring it distracted Rammy from the aliens pursuing them.

"Jesus," Rammy breathed, leaning forward. His hand came close to the captain's shoulder. Je snapped jer teeth at him, and he backed up. Wind chuckled.

"Don't worry, there's no one on the ship I'd prefer to touch less than you," Rammy muttered. Clearly, the Rip had a thing about personal space.

Their current speed made finding a place to land a challenge, despite the perception that they had slowed to a crawl. The dash read two hundred kilometres per hour.

The Strenoi's voice resounded through the comm again, making Rammy jump.

"Final warning," Klenni said in English, her voice wavering. Rammy wasn't sure whether he was happy to know what was going on. Ignorance is bliss and all that.

"For what?" he asked.

"They want us to go away."

Stares snorted as if je'd understood, reversed the throttle, and jammed the directional level at the same time. The ship groaned as if in pain.

Wind swore in jer language, and Rammy was thrown off his feet again, only to float before he hit the ground. They had spun but weren't moving forward. Rammy pushed himself so he floated towards the viewer, twisting over in mid-air so he could see the Strenoi ship barrelling at them, pink plasma beam building in concentration.

The captain's mouth opened in a wide smile. Rammy had enough time to wonder what it was like to be Stares, to live entirely at the two ends of the bored/excited spectrum, when the captain pressed a button. The freighter shook violently from below. Thanks to Zero-G, Rammy floated in place, but the smell of ozone permeated his nostrils. He sneezed as the Rip let loose a volley of railgun fire at the oncoming ship – staggered bursts. Rammy wanted to turn and ask the Pir-An whether they had known this ship was secretly weaponized, but his eyes remained glued to the viewer.

"What the fuck is going on?" Corporal Kosa demanded, propelling herself into the room. Beads of sweat floated off her shoulders. A small liquid filter along the wall, which activated whenever the ship was in Zero-G, sucked up her perspiration. Kosa's floating A.I. robot accompanied her. Both stopped beside Rammy to watch the scene outside. The Strenoi ship artfully sidestepped the first bolt, then the next, dropped below the third, jumped axis to avoid the fourth, and bypassed the final two tandem-fired bolts with an inverted side-twist that made Kosa swear in appreciation.

"That raptor-face can fucking fly," she admitted.

"They want us to leave the derelict to them," Rammy explained, "and I think they're about to make us."

"There!" Kosa said. She smacked the Rip lightly on the shoulder, ignoring the baring of teeth, and pointed to the starboard viewer. "Computer, enhance quadrant C-6!" The viewer zoomed in on what looked like an open bay door.

The Rip needed no encouragement. Je jammed on the throttle and directed the ship at the bay. The Rip's eyes moved back and forth from the front viewer to the smaller one above that showed the view behind, much like a rear-view mirror in a car. The Strenoi recharged their weapon.

"They only have enough juice for one more blast," Kosa said definitively. Rammy had heard her lie to boost morale on previous occasions and wished she hadn't bothered.

"All they need is one hit," Wind commented dryly, jer feet up on the dash as if this were a casual country drive. Stares gnawed on jer lip as je flew. Rammy gave jer credit. Je was not a pilot by trade, but je was keeping them alive—at least for a few more seconds.

"It was a pleasure, Corporal." Rammy nodded at Kosa. Her eyes darted from the viewscreen to meet his as he gave her a shaky marine salute. Before she could reply, the ship was slammed by the weapon, and the viewscreen met Rammy's face with a thunderous crack.

CHAPTER 2: FLUGGER

He was unable to open his eyes. He tried to lift his lids, but it was as if someone had stitched them shut with wire. Flug'ger'alaio raised his tendrils frantically to his face and then his body, probing for injury. *Ah, I'm intact.* He leaned his head back and rolled his eyeballs a few times in his head; they were stuck closed because they were not lubricated.

While Pir-An slept, their eyes moved, but when they were unconscious, the body sent more fluid to the more critical organs. Pir-An in a coma or under anesthesia had to have a nurse practitioner lubricate their eyes every few hours. No one had found a more practical method for this, either with robotics or a synthetic liquid.

After a few moments of self-lubrication, Flugger was able to open his gummy eyes. After wiping away a sticky build-up of fluid, he glanced down; his body was unharmed, held in place by his harness. There was gravity, which he had not expected. A little lighter than it was on Bubble, his homeworld, something the short-legged male did not mind. His eyes quickly moved to his partner. Klenni was blinking hard, waking up. He extended his tendril towards hers, wrapping them together.

Hurt? he asked telepathically, probing her. Klenni shook her head. Flugger, as a doctor, had more training in tendril-induced telepathy than his navigator wife, as doctors could use the skill to assess the pain and damage a person might not know they had. Flugger was not a natural at tendril-telepathy like some of his peers, but he was able to determine that Klenni had a mild concussion and would be fine. He let out a sigh of relief. Pir-An lived two centuries, and the couple had only paired twenty years ago. He consciously thought back to their ceremony to calm himself. How he had waited in the surf of the ceremonial lagoon as she swam to him, her long fin decorated in traditional ribbons. The sun had been warm on his face, the air cool, and the water lapped gently against his legs. Her fin had cut through the water like a beam of sunlight through thick fog, making the witnesses sigh at her beauty.

"What happened?" she asked aloud, her voice faint. "The Strenoi blasted us?"

Flugger nodded as he reached forward and undid his harness. Klenni undid hers as well, shaking her head to clear it. "They must have only skimmed us with the blast, or maybe they hit the mystery ship, and the blast knocked us into it. I have no idea why we aren't dead."

Klenni's tendrils waved slightly, suggesting she was thinking. "Should we assess the rest of the crew? Find out where we are?"

Flugger nodded, glad she was awake not only because he loved her but also because he did not want to explore their surroundings alone. The viewers were broken. One was shattered, the other two black. Klenni's tendrils were sticking straight up now, suggesting confusion.

"There is no power, but the oxygen is working, and there is gravity?" she commented.

"Are you sure there is oxygen being generated, and we're not just breathing in the last of it?"

She shook her head, eyes bobbing slightly with the movement. "No, look. These dials are simple sensors – they don't connect to the ship's power systems in case of a ship being dead in space." She pointed at three small dials near the pilot's seat. "Oxygen is normal, gravity is normal, no toxins in the air."

"Are we on *dilapa*? Are we having a bad trip?"

Klenni twisted her tendrils at him and gave a small laugh as she moved to assess the two Rips. "I wish we were. Remember when we did some back on –"

A groan interrupted her inappropriately timed reminiscing.

"It's the Terran. The female," Klenni said, pointing her tendrils at the Terran lying on the floor. "You tend to her. I'll assess these idiot Rips."

Corporal Koharu Saito, Kosa, was lying prone in the middle of the floor, having been thrown backwards by whatever force had shaken the ship. She was moving her head and uttering noises of distress, much like a beached *landoo* back home, albeit ten times bigger. Were he home, the *landoo* would have made a decent snack, but Flugger had no interest in eating a Terran.

"Alive?" he asked.

The Terran rolled onto her stomach and pushed herself onto her elbows. She stared at him, her eyes adjusting to the dim light in the ship.

"Apparently," she replied. "What happened?"

"No knowledge," Flugger said, wishing she spoke his language, as he hated speaking Terran, or whatever their main language was called. "I medic. Let me …" he struggled to think of the word. "Check."

The Terran nodded wearily but sat up and crossed her legs. Flugger stared down at them. He'd worked with Terrans throughout the war but had never lost his awe at their flexibility. Granted, their skin tore like paper, they bled everywhere, and they had disgusting fur on their heads and other places, but their bodies had a grace to them when they moved. Strenoi were elegant, with their smooth scale-like skin, but Terrans were fluid when in motion. Both Terrans here were in the pinnacle of health, but he had no idea whether they would be considered attractive by their own people. Their skin tones were very different, as was their hair. And they had no fins. The Pir-An could be turned on by other body parts (like butts – every species in the universe appreciated a well-formed ass), but fins were the marker of sexuality and attractiveness to the Pir-An people. Terrans, in lacking a fin, were very ugly to Flugger.

He wanted to ask about Terran races, why they had such variance in eye shape and fur texture as well as skin tone, but he didn't have the vocabulary. His people had varied colours of skin, but all Pir-An had very similar eyes and lips.

He extended his tendrils towards the soldier, and she did not move as he touched her temple. Given her comfort with his movement, she clearly had been ministered to by Pir-An in the past, probably during the war, and knew their methods. As usual, when he touched Terrans telepathically, he was awash with the sound of their organs. It took a few moments for him to mentally categorize all he was sensing, enough to acknowledge that she was not internally injured.

He did not offer her a hand to help her stand.

"Thanks, Flugger," she said as she pushed herself to her feet. "Ah, there's Rammy." She approached her companion and knelt beside him. Whether they were a mated pair, Flugger did not know. She put two fingers to his throat. His hand shot out and grabbed her, twisting it backwards. The corporal instantly chopped her free hand down on his wrist and he dropped her. She gently slapped his face.

"Rammy!" Her voice took on a deeper, stern tone as she ordered. "Private First Class Ramone Delaney!"

"What is Ramone Delaney?" Flugger asked.

"His full name," she replied without glancing back. Rammy sat up quickly, eyes wide and darting from side to side.

Kosa's thin lips tightened, impatience washing over her face. *She could never be a doctor*, Flugger mused.

"Flugg!" Klenni was calling him. Flugger eyed the other Terran. Rammy sucked in a deep lungful of air. He was alive, at least. Flugger could ascertain whether the Terran suffered any injuries later.

Both Rips were out cold, thin limbs draped over their chairs, heads resting on their shoulders. They reminded Flugger of a dead spider hanging from a web but inverted.

"I didn't know how to check their vitals, so I tried to start the ship," Klenni explained.

"When did you learn to fly a Terran ship?" Flugger commented, impressed.

Klenni shook her head. "You know I can only fly Strenoi. But I know how to turn it on and run a diagnostic. But it won't even start. I can't even retract the viewers so we can look out the windows; they're stuck or broken." When the Terran ship was in atmo the viewers retracted into the ceiling, and the panels behind them opened, allowing the crew to see outside without the need for cameras.

Flugger snapped his fingers, the Pir-An equivalent of a shrug. "Let's deal with these monsters first."

He had never attempted to heal, or even touch, a Rip before. They either died in the field or were left to die. He had heard of a sympathetic Terran who had attempted to carry an injured Rip back to base during one battle but had been bitten in the neck for her trouble. Whether this was unfounded rumour or fact, he did not know, but he wouldn't have been surprised if it were true.

He tentatively stuck out his tendril, placing it gingerly against Stares' temple. He closed his eyes, which wasn't necessary but helped with his concentration. If accessing Klenni were as natural as breathing and accessing the Terran was a rush of stimuli, accessing this creature was like being pulled into the Dark Sea back home on Bubble. When he was a child, he and his cousins had dared one another to dive past the sandbar near their vacation home. It had been fun until the current nabbed him. As like back then, in attempting to link with the Rip he struggled to swim against the flow, then tried to get out of it altogether. The Rip's mind was like the Dark Sea. It wasn't drowning that was the problem but getting lost. The ocean was immense and filled with large, carnivorous creatures. The Rip's mind was a jungle with live vines coming towards him. Like a Terran child lost in the woods, he started to panic. In the water, he had flailed, kicked, and tried to scream. Now, his mind reacted as his body had those years ago.

He forced himself to remember what happened in the ocean. He'd felt a tug on his leg. He tried to kick whatever creature had already nabbed him, but it was his eldest cousin's hand around his ankle, pulling him out of the current.

This time he'd have to save himself. He was stronger now; he could handle this. He let his mind relax and the pressure against his mind eased, letting him navigate. He felt it. A pulse. Jer dual hearts. Three quick beats each in tandem, then one slow. Jer other organs were moving normally. Jer brain was functional. He paused, then probed a little deeper – maybe he could access jer psyche, see where the dark current that was jer mind truly led.

A mental slap sent Flugger reeling backwards into reality. He opened his eyes to find the captain glaring at him with jer black eyes, mouth in a snarl.

"Fish for dinner?!" Stares snapped in broken Pir-An, a common Rip threat to his kind.

"I was checking to see if you were alright!" Flugger exclaimed, also in Pir-An, forgetting je did not speak his language.

Je merely laughed, then turned and touched Wind on the shoulder quickly and decisively. Je did not react. Stares leaned forward and pressed jer tongue firmly against Wind's cheek, then ran it up jer face, leaving a faint trail of glittering saliva. Flugger glanced back at Klenni and twisted one of his tendrils around his pointer finger. She did the same, sharing his expression for disgust.

"Are these two paired?" he asked his wife.

Stares did not react to the question. Je clearly did not understand (or seem to care) that they were talking about jer literally behind jer back.

Klenni shrugged. "I don't know. I never served with Rips, only Terrans and Strenoi."

"Same," Flugger replied, though they had both known that already.

After the lick, Stares sat back. "Alive," je croaked.

"How the hell can you tell that from giving him a gross lick?" Flugger could not keep the disgust from his voice.

Klenni translated what Flugger assumed was a more polite version of his question. Stares extended jer tongue out of jer mouth and ran it slowly over the front of jer teeth, then replied.

Klenni turned to Flugger. "Stares says je has receptors in jer tongue that allow jer to identify viable food. If a fellow Rip is hurt, they lick jer, and if je are alive they are, therefore, I guess, not food."

"They're cannibals?"

"Are you surprised?"

Flugger shuddered. "No, not really."

Wind stretched and sat up, clearly no worse for wear. "Hungry," je said in Pir-An, grinning menacingly at the Pir-An pair. Je wiped the saliva off jer face, then turned to jer captain, asking jer a question in jer rasping language. Stares grinned and laughed in response. Je said something and snapped jer teeth at Wind.

"Meeting," Stares said loudly in Pir-An. Je was staring at the Terrans, who were conversing at the other side of the room.

"What did they say to one another?" Flugger asked Klenni.

She opened her gills as she followed the Rips. She let out a little bubbling noise, signalling amusement that wasn't quite laughter. "Wind asked Stares why je licked Jer. Je said je wanted to make sure Wind tasted as good as je looked."

"Was je flirting or being legitimate?"

"I have no shelling clue, love. These people are crazy."

CHAPTER 3: STARES

Captain Stares gathered jer team in the centre of the ship. As much as this situation was frustrating in the extreme, because je had no idea whether those lizard-breath Strenoi were out there stealing jer giant derelict alien ship, Stares couldn't help but grin. Je glanced over at As Silent as the Wind but je clearly did not share jer excitement. Je was picking at jer teeth. Then again, je was merely backup against these idiotic aliens and their patronizing ways. The aliens were interesting though, je'd give them that. Stares, though je positioned jerself to the others as a battle-hardened mercenary, was not that. This was jer first real job for the Upper Echelon, and je wanted to perform exceptionally. Jer people deserved it. Je deserved it. These aliens were so full of themselves, what with their technology and their fancy, ten-year war. Stares' real agenda was proprietary, and the crew's being unaware of jer motives would not change the situation.

Je studied them as they moved closer to jer. There was a clear divide between the two other species and jer and Wind. The Pir-An were a mated couple, but je was not sure about the Terrans. They did not look alike, but je was unsure whether that was required for Terrans to mate. Jer people did not consider skin colour in that regard. When you spent most of your life fighting to survive, things like whether you were red, black, or silver were minimal to fuss over. Yet, it would be handy to know whether the two Terrans were, what was the phrase? Penetrating one another? In truth, je wished je had done some more research on Terran and Pir-An cultures before sending out the ad for this job, instead of only watching a few examples of their pornography. The fact that Wind was the only other Rippliagnos on this expedition was not jer ideal crew at the outset, but now that je thought about it, it worked out better. Other, less nonchalant Rips might be able to taste out jer secrets and steal the ship for themselves, which was not productive to Stares' mission. Je glanced over at Wind. If je could keep Wind occupied, perhaps je wouldn't figure it out either.

Or maybe Stares could convince Wind to join jer plans?

Stares grinned at the group. All this unknown danger invigorated jer senses.

"What are you so happy about?" Klenni asked in Rip.

"This is an exciting time for us," Stares replied. Klenni translated for the Terrans and her partner.

The stronger Terran, the corporal, spat out a word, then a question. *Female. Like the Pir-An and Strenoi, these aliens usually identify themselves based on reproductive lines.* Je had to keep reminding jerself that, but the concept was so strange. Stares didn't have Wind's background working with the other species, so this was all new to jer.

"She wants to know why you think it's exciting," Klenni said.

Stares cocked jer head to the side and studied the confounding Terran. They were in a life-or-death, unknown situation! How could it be anything but exciting? Je glanced at Wind. Je was standing impassively, still picking at jer teeth. Je resisted the urge to snarl at Wind; je was supposed to be helping jer with these people. But, if Wind were like most of jer people, je had spent most of jer life skulking in the swamps of

Ripplia, trying to both hunt for food and avoid being hunted jerself. No wonder je had been a mercenary in the Strenoi-Terran War. Wind had the personality of someone who grew up in a small community, perhaps with fewer grandparents than was needed to maintain the property and defences. Je was probably out in the bogs contributing to the hunt when Stares was still sequestered in the fortified zone of jer community, learning to think instead of merely survive.

"It's exciting because we are going to discover something new!" Stares replied to Klenni, who translated.

"How do you know we're not trapped in the middle of space? The ship will not turn on. The Strenoi could come back at any moment," Rammy asked. Klenni translated.

What was wrong with this Terran? Stares scoffed. "The Strenoi aren't going to come back. If they didn't finish us off, they are likely dead."

"What is your plan?" Klenni asked, then translated again. Having to talk through the bubble-eyed Pir-An was getting old fast, especially since Stares understood far more Terran and Pir-An than je let on. Luckily, years of training had prepared jer to hide jer reactions until je pretended to hear it first from Klenni. It was interesting what she left out when she translated.

Stares paused before je replied. Everyone waited. Je was not used to this. Normally, no one waited on jer to make decisions. But who else was going to do it? Wind, a sniper who didn't give a shit what happened? Klenni, a navigator? Flugger, a doctor? Rammy, a grunt? Kosa, a military lifer if Stares ever saw one? Of course, they were all waiting for Stares' orders; je was the leader, and they were jer troop. Pride swelled in jer chest. True, they were a motley crew at best, but je commanded them.

Stares would admit to anyone that staying on task was never jer strong point, but je made up for that with jer ability to think on jer feet. Je glanced around the room.

"There." Je pointed at Kosa's A.I. Unit. The robot hovered at Kosa's eye level and resembled a bowl turned over onto a plate. As far as Stares could tell, the corporal only used it to play Terran exercise videos. Stares had left the freighter on autopilot throughout most of the journey, and as there was nothing else to do but talk to Wind, which was hardly stimulating, Stares had taken to watching the Terrans, especially Kosa. Terrans were the "pretty ones" of the galaxy. The Strenoi were aristocratic but too scaly, their faces were too squat, and they had those off-putting legs that could bend forwards and backwards. The Dirge were big, hulking brutes with smelly fur and ugly snouts. The Pir-An looked like food.

But the Terrans could move like no one's business. And they were always modifying their bodies in painful ways for superficial reasons, which Stares respected and rather envied. Kosa had an entire arm devoted to art, with pictures set into her skin from her shoulder to her wrist. Stares admired her ability to withstand pain simply to ornament herself. When Kosa had been "working out" in the near-empty storage compartment the day before, Stares crawled up onto an old crate to watch. Kosa moved like a *Borkas*, with quick movements fueled by the strength in jer muscles. Stares had no interest in touching the Terran, but je did enjoy watching this particular one move. When the Terran had noticed Stares enter the room, had stared at Stares pointedly, clearly wishing jer to go, but when Stares brought out a fish bar to eat, the Terran had simply sighed and gone back to her workout. She practiced attacks with her knife, she pushed her body on her arms, she performed actions that were clearly intended to strengthen her muscles. Stares had attempted to join in yesterday, curious whether je could modify jer own body, but the Terran had stomped away.

Kosa narrowed her eyes at Stares and asked a question to Klenni.

"She's asking why you want her A.I. Unit."

Stares put jer hands on jer hips, a position of dominance back home on Ripplia. Wind's lips twisted when je saw jer doing this as such a pose was something only community leaders did. Hopefully, Wind would assume Stares was doing it here to try to maintain control. If je had a problem with jer posturing as a leader, well, je was welcome to try and fight jer over it. Stares would doubtlessly win.

"We are going to use the A.I. Unit to scout. We'll send it up through the vent to the exhaust panel. If it gets sucked away from us as soon as we open the door, we'll know we're in space. If it makes it through, we might be inside the ship. I was aiming for the bay when we were struck, so I hope we were pushed inside by the Strenoi blast."

After Klenni translated, Kosa crossed her arms over her chest. "Fine."

Stares nodded. The Terran took the A.I. Unit and spoke to it while Wind, the tallest in the group, flipped the mechanism to open the hatch that Stares recommended. The A.I. Unit flew up into the opening in a controlled manner and was gone.

They waited. Stares kept jerself poised as the leader, hands-on-hips, head thrown back. Wind sidled over to jer.

"You don't need to posture for them. They don't understand what you're doing."

Stares snorted. "Body language works wonders."

Wind shook jer head but returned to jer position against the wall, picking up a knife to clean jer claws. The Terrans were silent. The Pir-An were silent. Silence reigned for a full two minutes.

Finally, Kosa frowned at the group and left them, making her way towards the crew quarters. She pushed on the door. It was stuck. She pushed some more, then called for Rammy, presumably to assist her. They both took turns pushing on the door, then shoved on it together. Stares approached. Kosa began to complain in her language to the captain, flailing her arms and huffing air from her nose. She spoke too fast for Stares to understand, but the word "fuck" came up a lot.

"She needs to change her clothes," Klenni explained. "She says she cannot wear her 'workout' clothes in a potentially hostile situation."

"Why not? They expose her muscles and artwork," Stares replied. The Terran was wearing a tight piece of clothing that held her mammary glands close to her body, exposing her stomach. She also wore skin-tight, dark blue leggings that tapered at the ankle, tucked into her combat boots. When Kosa heard Klenni's translation, she turned and faced the Rip. She asked Klenni a long question with her brown eyes narrowed.

Klenni's sky-blue scales deepened to light purple. Embarrassment, Stares believed was the emotion. Je had never experienced it. Shame was a close approximation, but Stares had only suffered that once.

"What did he ask?" Stares asked.

"She," Klenni corrected. Stares shrugged, though made a mental note to try and remember their gendered pronouns. "She was asking whether you were, ah, interested in her. She says you keep watching her and that you tried to work out with her yesterday."

Stares wasn't sure what the issue was. "Of course. She's an alien who is clearly the strongest one here."

Wind pushed jerself away from the wall, approaching.

"I thought I was the strongest, after you," Wind said.

Stares cocked jer head to the side, bending it almost ninety degrees. "You think you could take this Terran in a straight fight?"

Wind looked at the Terran, who stared back once Klenni reluctantly translated. Kosa was far shorter than Wind, almost a foot and half so, but she had taut muscles and more weight. Rammy was taller, wider, and far heavier than his corporal, but Kosa was clearly more skilled in fighting. Wind and Rammy would be an interesting fight, but Kosa would knock Wind on jer ass in a heartbeat, despite jer claws, teeth, and thicker skin. Je was a sniper, not a hand-to-hand fighter. And gravity was much stronger on Terran worlds.

Stares blinked hard when Wind opened jer mouth at Kosa in a snarl of challenge; Wind would likely lose. Whether it was a matter of personal pride or species pride, Stares was not sure, but je crossed jer arms over jer chest, waiting for the inevitable fight. To jer disappointment, the Terran shook her head at Wind. She said something to Klenni, then nodded at the Pir-An to tell Stares. The Pir-An would not meet Stares' eyes. Instead, she kept hers trained on the floor.

"She says she's not interested in fighting your lover for your affection. She says she has no sexual or romantic interest in you at all and that you should forget about it before she makes you forget. Captain or not."

Stares paused, then laughter bubbled up inside of jer. Je gripped jer thighs and laughed heartily. Je felt saliva trickle off jer teeth and drop to the floor. Je wiped jer mouth as je stood up. Kosa appeared unmoved, but Rammy tried to hide a look of disgust by turning his head. Terrans were weird about saliva. Wind did not appear amused. Jer lips curled off jer teeth and jer shoulders were hunched, as if je were trying to make jerself disappear.

"What's funny?" the female Terran asked. Klenni translated.

"I'm not mated with Wind! We Rippliagnos don't do that like you people until we're old. And I never thought about non-reproductive sex with a Terran before! I don't even know how that would work! I do think she is an interesting specimen for all her strength. I want her to be my second-in-command."

Klenni paused before relaying the information to Kosa, as if she were trying to remember all the facts. The Terran pursed her lips in consideration after hearing the translation, then asked a question.

"She's asking how she can be second-in-command if you can't speak to one another. And why you were too … ah, cheap to provide translation devices for this job."

Before they could discuss the matter further, the A.I. returned. It beeped twice at Kosa, who pressed a button on its interface. The A.I. settled onto the floor and projected an image. Except for Wind, who remained at the wall, the rest of the crew huddled around the Terran so they could see. The A.I. showed them its journey through the vent and its foray into what appeared to be a landing bay, given the immensity of the space. The A.I. flew towards a wall a few hundred feet from the ship, then spun so they could get a view of their ship, half of it in the bay, the other half presumably outside in space. The doors of the bay had sheered off the cargo hold, sleeping quarters, and engines.

"Good thing I came in when I did," Kosa muttered, her expression tight. Klenni translated, and Stares nodded.

"What is that door made of that it could cut through our ship like that?" Rammy asked. Klenni again translated.

"Diamonds? Lasers?" Klenni suggested sardonically, saying it in Terran and Rip in succession.

Stares' teeth were clenched so tight that jer jaw ached. The council had assumed that the ship was dead in the water, that it was a piece of ancient alien technology that had been discarded or damaged and floated into known habitable space from somewhere else. Stares had been sent to document it, to take parts of it if necessary – preferably weapons. Now je had other ideas. But how were they to leave?

"Our engines are gone …" Rammy trailed off. Klenni repeated what he said and added more.

"Yes, we are trapped here."

“Something either captured us or saved us.” The thin, furry black lines above Kosa’s eyes came together. Klenni translated.

“The question is,” she said, “which is it?”

“We need to investigate,” Stares decided. “Did the A.I. take readings?” Klenni posed this to Kosa.

“Yes,” Kosa replied, Klenni translating after. “It does that by default. The air is breathable, and there is gravity. We’re fine to leave the ship.”

“Then I propose we leave *Starship 330307* and try to find a new ship inside this other ship.”

Je didn’t expect an enthusiastic cheer, but something other than mild grumbling would have been nice.

“Why do you call it that?” Rammy asked. Klenni forwarded the question to Stares.

Je turned to look at the Terran. “Call what?”

“The ship. You keep calling it *Starship 330307*. Why not give it a name?”

“That is its name. It’s a designation.”

“Yeah, but it’s … a little …” he pulled on the hanging bit of flesh on the side of his head, his oratory sensor. He did not finish his thought, but Stares thought je understood after Klenni translated.

Stares laughed. “It is silly to name objects. Do you name your guns?”

“Yes,” Rammy and Kosa replied at the same time.

Stares stared at the Terrans then looked at Wind. Je met jer eyes and they both broke into laughter. Terrans were so weird.

CHAPTER 4: KOSA

Corporal Koharu Saito of the Terran Space Force Marines frowned at the room, trying to think up contingency plans for an unknowable situation.

"I'm not leaving without a weapon," she stated. "Despite what Allie showed us, we have no idea what we could be dealing with out there. Stares, unlock the weapons … please."

"Allie?" Klenni asked after she translated for the captain.

Kosa gestured with her head towards the A.I. Unit. She called it Allie, because it was faster than calling it "A.I. Unit". Besides, the unit looked like an Allie. It was cute, given how its camera lenses looked like eyes and its charging port a mouth. Klenni's normally static lips turned upwards as far as they could go, which wasn't a lot. A smile of understanding.

Kosa took deep, slow breaths. She remained calm, unlike Rammy, who was clearly distraught, given his damn ear pulling and nervous glancing around the room. Kosa had run enough missions with her private to tell when he was worried. Kosa wasn't anxious. She was *pissed*. She never should have left the base. She should have worked off her suspension at the gym, drank with friends, slept with some attractive men, and maybe taken a trip back home. Komorebi, her home planet, had been colonized by Japanese refugees after the tidal wave of 2147. She'd lived there her whole life before military service.

She brought her thumb up to her mouth and nibbled on some dead skin around her nail. She lowered her hand but continued to gently chew on the flesh that remained in her mouth, working it over and over until it was gone.

Stares made a big show of opening the armoury with a key je wore about jer neck. Rips were like children at times, eager to show that they were big people like the other species. Where Kosa could get behind Wind's calm, albeit creepy, personality, Stares reminded Kosa of a new recruit eager to shoot off rail guns before je was even in uniform. Those were the recruits you kept an eye on, the ones who tended to go AWOL – the ones who didn't work well with authority.

Stares opened the cabinet, and Kosa pushed past the other Rip and the Pir-An to get to her shotgun first. She carried the case over to the defunct navigational console and held her eye over the retinal scanner. The case opened with a hiss that was her favourite sound in the world, after her best friend's baby's laugh. She wished she had her tablet with her so she could re-watch a couple of videos of Yeva, the little girl she referred to affectionately as her niece. The tablet was probably spinning away towards another galaxy, along with her real clothes.

"Bringing out Airi, eh?" Rammy asked, a smile gracing his face for the first time since they had taken off in the Rip's ship. While he wasn't particularly moody, his recent breakup with that loser AJ had dampened his generally positive outlook to sullen. He was a huge nerd who preferred his books to his gun, but his smile made him handsome. If she didn't have a personal rule against fucking subordinates, she wouldn't have ruled out a few drinks and an overnight session with him. But, along with her rule, to which she stuck hard and fast, he was gay.

Unfortunate, since they were off duty now. Not like this was the time or place for sex.

She smiled down at the gun. "Airi has been bored lately. She needs to come out and play."

Airi, the shotgun, was a modified Remington 870. It had started its life over one-hundred and sixty years ago. The tactical model had become the standard shotgun for colonists on planets with aggressive wildlife. Kosa had inherited it from her grandmother, who had been a firearms fanatic and had lived on the edge of civilization until her death. She had modified it with a tight choke and increased capacity. Kosa always brought it into battle, in addition to the standard S2 hand-held rail gun issued to the Terran Space Force Navy marines. Sometimes you had to go old-school. The raptors never expected it on the field, as they had never developed that type of firearm.

We aren't at war with the raptors anymore, Kosa reminded herself, but it rang hollow. She had fought the damn lizards her entire military career – enough to respect them as combatants. She had successfully commanded combat and recon missions. She had killed nearly one hundred Strenoi with weapons, and a dozen hand-to-hand. Why she had been passed up for promotion to Sergeant over that weak-willed, desk-jockey Caroline was beyond her. Kosa turned her thoughts from that, knowing it would only raise her blood pressure, and she inspected the weapon for damage. Airi was good.

"Why do you call it Airi?" Klenni asked, approaching. Kosa glanced at the Pir-An. The guppy seemed like a bit of a pushover with her medic husband always fawning over her, but Kosa knew when someone was part of the tougher-than-they-looked crowd.

"Airi Nakamura was a hero for my planet."

"A war hero?" the Pir-An asked.

"You'd assume so, but no. Though, she was a fighter pilot. When I was ten, there was a catastrophic failure on one of the F-Class frigates in orbit around our planet. They're still not sure what happened, but something caused an explosion, and one of the thrusters went haywire and sent the ship on an uncontrollable descent. Airi was performing a routine orbital bypass, so she turned her fighter towards the ship and flew straight at it. She launched all her ordnance at the engines, exploding the frigate. The manoeuvre killed her, but rather than an entire ship screaming down, which would have taken out a good chunk of the coast, she broke it up enough that the defence cannons could pick off most of the debris.

"I call this gun Airi, after her. Some pieces of the ship are embedded in the fields near my home. We leave them there as memorials to her sacrifice."

Kosa smiled slightly, picturing the jagged piece of metal that had thrust its way into the earth on the edge of her town. It resembled a cartoon lightning bolt, though it was dull gray. The farmer took pains to keep it rust-free, and Kosa always dipped her head towards it when she walked by on a rare opportunity to go hiking. The ship would have turned her home into a crater.

Klenni nodded but said nothing. Kosa didn't know or care whether the alien approved of her story.

Luckily, Kosa's strap for the shotgun, her regulation 9mm pistol, and her bowie knife were also in the case. Her S2 rail gun, which she had insisted to Stares that she needed to keep out of the locker and at her bunk, was likely out in space now, along with her tablet, clothes, and the rest of her personal effects. She glanced down at her body. At least she was wearing her boots. The trip to this place with no one to talk to but heartbroken Rammy or the boring Pir-An had left her pacing the halls. And then, when the damn Rip tried hitting on her yesterday, it had cut her workout short.

She glanced over her shoulder at Stares. The silver Rip was surveying the group as if je thought je was their general. Technically, je was captain, but Kosa was not going to let some primitive alien freak tell her how to survive this situation. She'd play nice for now, but the instant Stares got out of line, Kosa was going to blast jer. Whether the blast would come from words, fists, or her shotgun, she hadn't decided.

Kosa slung the strap over her shoulder, frowning as the shotgun butt smacked into her tightly covered ass. She attached her armpit holster for her pistol. She slid the knife into her boot, having no other place to put it. She draped both ammunition belts across her chest, crisscrossing her breasts. She frowned as she glanced down at her body; she looked ridiculous in only a sports bra and leggings, like an under-clothed heroine from early twenty-first century movies. Normally Terrans wore full combat armour in battle, which had shielding and Kevlar to take the brunt of a distanced projectile attack. But both Kosa's and Rammy's armour was military property and back at their base. They had both brought personal armour, but it had been in the hold, now out in space. Rammy wore cargo pants and a black shirt, which provided no more protection than Kosa's outfit.

She glanced at Klenni. No. And there was no way she was wearing Pir-An clothes, as they were far too small, and their puffiness would impede her ability to fight.

Rammy and Klenni brought out their weapons. The former had his military-issued S2 rail gun, and Klenni sported a small "plasma" pistol of Pir-An design. Kosa had fired one before, but it wasn't her weapon of choice. It didn't actually fire plasma blasts but a specialized bullet that encased a small bit of plasma. Upon release from the chamber, the plasma was activated inside the bullet and, after a few seconds, would burst. This made it an expensive short-range weapon, but it could penetrate most armour and could stop an enemy in its tracks; the bullets were hollow points on steroids. It also had a stun setting that fired a jolt of electrical current at an enemy that incapacitated them momentarily.

Wind retrieved jer battered, black sniper rifle of Strenoi design (with a modified trigger) from where it had fallen beside his seat; Stares had let jer keep jer weapon out because it was too long for the case (which was not an armoury in truth, but a cabinet for chairs). Wind didn't bother to check it over or even look at it before je slung it over jer shoulder. There were notches carved in the stock very similar to those that Kosa's previous boyfriend, a sniper himself, had made on his own rifle. Kosa rolled her eyes. All snipers were the same no matter the species; if she were to notch her gun after every kill, she would have no stock left, but snipers felt the need to brag about their minor contributions to the war effort.

Stares also carried an S2, though where je got it, Kosa didn't want to ask. You couldn't buy one through regular channels. Looting battlefields for weapons or items of worth from either side was not something Rips shied from or apologized for.

The hatch opened easily enough, and Rammy exited with his weapon aimed and body hunched in an attack position. Kosa slipped after him, with Allie floating behind her right shoulder. Wind left the ship, but instead of moving forward, je turned and lithely climbed on top of it, crouching with jer scope to jer eye. The Pir-An and Stares exited last, the two guppies standing behind Stares, though the captain was so thin a bullet would likely bypass jer and hit the other two. No attack came.

Rammy glanced at Kosa. She signalled that he inspect the left and she'd go right. The room was barren, as Allie had shown, but the immensity was heightened when experienced in person. The bay was roughly the size of a football field, but there were no other ships in it. The stillness of the space had an eerie, funeral-home vibe, and

Starship 330307 was the only coffin in attendance. Kosa glanced up at the ceiling that was shrouded in shadows. Embedded sconces hung every five feet, seven feet off the ground, giving the room a soft glow. Her gaze climbed the wall another twenty feet to the ceiling.

Kosa sniffed. Her experience indicated the air was recirculated, but it lacked any other scent — no trace of the oils, lubricants, and chemicals that she would expect to find in a bay. If this was even a bay. It could be a place to park a ship, like a garage. It could be a warehouse. Or a bedroom for an extra-large creature who did not require bedding. Or maybe an empty room with no purpose yet. Classifying the room based on her own assumptions was foolish. Many times Terrans had been caught off-guard when raiding Strenoi buildings and ships by assuming they followed the same purposes as Terrans. The raptors were similar to Terrans, as both species were bipedal mammals with the need to eat, sleep, and shit, but the raptors had some weird design ideas sometimes. And they loved dark purple.

"The only door appears to be here," Rammy called. The Pir-An translated.

"Advance," Stares hissed in English.

Rammy glanced at Kosa, who nodded for him to continue. Good, he still thought of her as his leader. There was one ally she could count on. Then again, Rammy hated making decisions, so he would never try and take charge.

Stares let out a barrage of words. Both Terrans turned to stare as je strode up to them and began poking Rammy in the chest with jer long finger. Kosa stepped forward, not ready to raise her weapon on the captain yet, but was preparing to.

"Je says je is the captain, not Kosa. You don't look to her for confirmation," Klenni explained, racing up to the trio, her husband on her heels. Wind hadn't moved.

"Sorry, Captain," Rammy replied. "It won't happen again."

"Are you clear, too?" Klenni said to Kosa after the Rip turned to her and spattered out more words, finishing with baring jer teeth. "Je says you signed up knowing Stares was the leader."

Kosa raised her eyebrows at Stares and blinked a few times, attempting to convey innocence. "Oh, I thought I was jer second-in-command now. In the Terran marines, the leader tells us what to do, and then the second sends out the orders." It was a lie, at least in these circumstances.

Stares' black eyes narrowed, but jer lips receded over jer bright teeth. "From now on, you are only to give orders when I'm not here," je said, which Klenni translated.

Kosa nodded. She had a lot of experience with inept but demanding commander officers, and it was best to let them think they had you cowed.

Stares sniffed, satisfied. As je backed up, Wind's rifle retorted through the empty space, the flat crack reverberating through the metal walls.

"What the hell!" Kosa yelled at jer. The Rip nodded towards the door behind Rammy. Je had hit the control with jer bullet, causing it to slide open.

CHAPTER 5: KLENNI

Klenni was a navigator. And while she had been in dozens of tense ship battles, she didn't travel into dark hallways. She didn't carry a weapon with any real intention of firing it. This mysterious, apparently abandoned but functioning alien ship left tremors in her gut and parched her throat. Yet, despite her terror, exhilaration swept through her. She hadn't felt this alive since the war, though she'd never admit that to Flugger.

Some days, she wished the war was still going on. The Terran-Strenoi conflict had been good for the Pir-An. While they were technologically advanced, they were not a militant species. They'd had their wars in the past, on their own planet, but not for centuries. Bubble was a large, water-rich world with plenty of resources. Klenni had never visited Earth, but there was a reason why the Pir-An considered Terrans rather … stupid. They had destroyed their home with civil wars, environmental devastation, and greed. The only thing that had saved their species was space-flight – when their world was dying, and subsequently their people as well, they put all their effort into finding a new world a little over a century ago. The Pir-An had met them a few years after, in the Terran year 2130. Just as they had with the Strenoi, who were stilted as a species but in a different way, the Pir-An traded with

Terrans the technology to clean their air and oceans, to save their old world but also to terraform a new one. Most Terrans acted as if the Pir-An were saviours. However, others realized that the Pir-An were not working out of humanitarian rationale but were getting the Terrans to do their manual labour. The Pir-An could send expensive robots or machines to mine and gather other resources on desolate planets, but they'd let the Terrans do that in exchange for cheap tech that was new to them but decades or even centuries obsolete to the Piscine species.

The Terrans caught on, of course, and while relations between the two cultures weren't hostile, they weren't as friendly as they could be. While not as honour-bound as the Strenoi, the Terrans could not understand how Pir-An society functioned economically. It wasn't capitalist but wasn't entirely socialist and was also a monarchy; Terran universities had begun to teach political science courses focused on the Pir-An socio-political system. For the Pir-An, being a repairperson for food production units was viewed as just as socially valuable as being a doctor, scientist, or musician. The Pir-An did not place value on tasks or careers the same way the Terrans did. Some Pir-An loved learning, some loved menial tasks, some loved swimming, some loved scientific discovery, some loved science, and some loved anything else you could think of. Klenni loved navigation. She loved plotting a course. She loved sailing (as much as her people did not need boats to traverse the seas). She loved adventure.

This adventure, though, might be a bit more than she had ever asked for.

She glanced at her husband. Flugger didn't appear too off-put by the situation, but he had seen battle. Only as a medic, true, but this wasn't the most dangerous situation he had been part of. He wasn't a doctor to save lives, but because biology was his passion. His newest interest was healing aliens, to see how they functioned internally, though he preferred it when the aliens were unconscious or dead. He was a bit speciesist at times, almost as if he saw studying aliens the same way an archaeologist studied old buildings – as something inert. This job had seemed perfect. Klenni could navigate to the outer edges of cultivated space, a place she had always been interested in seeing. Flugger, at the same time, had the chance to study alien physiology. Indeed, the mission was more to her liking than Flugger's, and she'd had to convince him to go using one of her only remaining trump cards in their marriage, but now it seemed Flugger might have more chances to heal aliens he had bargained for.

The longer they walked, the more her shoulders began to relax, and her grip on the pistol softened. The ship was a mass of long hallways separated by a bulkhead every one hundred feet, some bends, and even more long hallways.

"Are we going to go back to the ship?" she called in Terran, then in Rip. She didn't mind being the translator. In fact, it was fun to make subtle changes to meaning. While she wasn't trying to create discord in the already fractioned group, the only person she liked, other than Flugger, was Rammy. Kosa and Stares were both arrogant, demanding people. And Wind was terrifying. Je reminded her of a species of eel back on Bubble that hung out in shallow seaweed, waiting for an unsuspecting leg to brush past so it could strike. They shared the same set of teeth.

Kosa, who had taken point, glanced back at Stares for confirmation about returning.

"Of course, idiots!"

Klenni rolled her large eyes.

The hallways were barren – no artwork, no differentiation. Their only accompaniment was the soft light of the sconces and the sound of their footfalls. No one talked. The ceilings were ten feet high and the halls six feet wide, allowing them to travel in groups of two. Instead, their group mainly went single file: Kosa, Stares, Rammy, the Pir-An side-by-side, and Wind.

They travelled for an hour, seeing nothing of interest. Klenni's stomach clenched slightly, warning her that she would soon be getting hungry.

"Flugger and I can't travel indefinitely," she called, her voice ringing loud and hollow. She hated how apologetic she sounded.

As Stares turned to glare at her, a sharp clacking and slapping reverberated from the next hallway. *Clack slap, clack slap, clack slap*. Kosa raised her shotgun and cocked her head to the side, listening. It sounded familiar to Klenni as well.

"Pir-An, stay behind me," Stares ordered. "Rammy." Je pointed towards Kosa. Je told Wind in Rip to get a bead on whatever came down the hallway. Klenni glanced behind her quickly to see the Rip on one knee, rifle balanced, and scope to jer eye.

Clack slap, clack slap, clack slap. The sound grew louder. The group was in the middle of the hallway, twenty feet of free space between them and the entrance to the next turn. Kosa's body was the pinnacle of martial skill: she was slightly crouched, muscles ready to react, shotgun butt propped to her shoulder, and mouth set in a firm line. Rammy's grip on his gun was steady, but sweat beaded his forehead despite the cool temperature of the ship. His eyes were wide and unblinking as he watched the hallway.

Clack slap, Clack SLAP, CLACK SLAP. The sound grew in intensity then stopped as a pair of Strenoi rounded the corner and skidded to a halt. The noise had been the alternating sounds of their large, exposed third claw and their sandaled soles hitting the metallic floor. The Strenoi were slightly bigger than Terrans, with their average height being six feet and some reaching seven. They were similar in body structure to Terrans, in that their arms and legs were proportionate. Their body mass was heavier, as their bones had more density.

Kosa chambered a round into her shotgun. A warning. One of the Strenoi raised a rifle, the other a long melee weapon resembling a pike.

If the Strenoi with the gun opened fire, Klenni would have nowhere to hide. More importantly, the one who would carry her eggs was also in a precarious position. She raced past the startled Stares and Rammy, to throw herself in front of Kosa. She held one hand towards the Strenoi and the other at Kosa, hoping both wouldn't shoot through her.

"Move, guppy," Kosa ordered. Klenni ignored her.

"Were you in the ship?" she asked the newcomers in High Strenoi, their official language.

Of the two, the male Strenoi appeared in command. He snarled at Klenni and shook his weapon at her as if to indicate he would not hesitate to shoot through her.

"We were chasing a Terran vessel. Was that you?" the other Strenoi, the female, asked.

"Yes, we were in that ship. It was destroyed."

"I don't give a shit," the male spat. "We asked you politely to back down, but your infernal Rips insulted us. We had every right to attack."

"That may be so," Klenni spoke slowly, calmly, as she eyed the six-foot-tall reptiloid's teeth and claws, not to mention the rifle. "But we are in the same predicament as you. Was your ship destroyed?"

"Yes! Thanks to you! We barely survived." He raised the gun again, pointing it past Kosa at Stares.

"Do it. Die," Wind spoke clearly in High Strenoi from jer position behind the pack. The Sternoi glanced over at the other Rip. Wind trained jer gun on the male Strenoi. The alien in question raised his thin lips clear off his teeth, baring them at the Rip. Wind chuckled.

"Look. Look. Let's work together," Klenni soothed. "The war is over. We both lost our ships. We're both stuck here. We have no idea what is going on."

"I would be fine with a truce," the female Strenoi said, lowering her weapon quite quickly. "Crenkleost?" Klenni did not understand the word, so assumed it was the male's name or perhaps a rank she wasn't familiar with. He glared at his companion and threw down his weapon. It swung by its strap against his side. Klenni had never seen a Strenoi pout before.

"How dramatic," Stares quipped in Rip. Wind snickered.

"Do you want to be torn limb from limb!?" Crenkleost bellowed. He lowered his chest and opened his arms wide. He likely had no idea what Stares said, but anyone could tell it had been an insult. Klenni translated the threat to her captain, hoping it would get Stares to stop antagonizing the angry reptiloid.

"Sounds sexy," Stares replied with a grin. Klenni suppressed a nervous giggle and did not translate that. Flugger wrapped a tendril around her wrist.

Kosa had not lowered her weapon. "What is going on?" she demanded in English. Klenni explained. Kosa shook her head. "No way. I'm not teaming up with some lizard-face raptor fuck."

How much the Strenoi understood, it was hard to tell, but at *raptor,* they both hissed, baring teeth. Kosa hissed back mockingly. *Shells, did she have nerves of steel.*

Crenkleost raised his arms in a T-shape: a challenge. He pulled the gun off his shoulder, dropped it, and strode purposefully towards the group. He stopped three feet in front of Kosa, glaring at her. The Terran was only five foot five inches and half his weight, but she calmly passed her shotgun to Rammy, removed her ammo belts and holster, and stepped to meet the large and quite formidable alien. Luckily for Terrans, Earth had a much higher gravity than the alien homeworlds. As such, Terrans were naturally stronger than the other species, despite having less mass. And Kosa was from Komorebi, a planet with a gravity of 10.5 meters per second squared, meaning she was even stronger. She was also apparently fearless.

No one tried to stop them. The rest of the group, including the female Strenoi, encircled the pair as Kosa and Crenkleost met in the center of the room. The Strenoi extended his long arm forward to either punch or grab Kosa, but she bent her body backwards at the last second and delivered a kick to his gut. She fell to the floor, but the angle of the kick caused Crenkleost to stumble back. Kosa rolled to the right as he recovered and lunged for her, then swung her body 180 degrees. She shot her legs upwards, making contact with his ribs.

The Strenoi grunted but refused to show pain. Instead, he reached out and snagged the Terran's ankle, lifting her a few inches and slamming her to the ground. She gasped as her hip struck the metallic floor. He prepared to lift and slam her again.

"Bastard!" she swore, pushing her body upwards from her elbows, striking him under the chin with her free foot as he pulled her towards him. He dropped her and took two steps back, reorienting himself and rubbing his jaw. Clearly, he was as surprised by Kosa's skill as Klenni was. Kosa leaned back on her hands and flung herself forward, landing on her feet in a crouch. The Strenoi female clapped her hands twice in appreciation, to which Rammy laughed.

"Show-off," Crenkleost muttered in his language. He made to grab Kosa again, but she dodged, leaning forward for another attack. The Strenoi's grab had been a feint, allowing him to use his other arm to slam into her left shoulder, sending her into the wall. The impact wasn't hard enough to truly hurt her, but she stumbled. Crenkleost grabbed her right shoulder, but Kosa bent the fingers of her right hand and grabbed under his wrist, then leaned forward and used her elbow to force his hand off her. She used her other hand to simultaneously grip his left tricep muscle, blocking an attempt to grab her from that side too. She thrust her face at his, baring her teeth at him like a baboon. It was the same gesture the Rips and Strenoi used for defiance or challenge, and the Terrans were slowly adapting it. The Strenoi glared down at her.

"Strong for a Terran," the female Strenoi commented in English. Crenkleost's eyes narrowed, and he turned his head and glared at the female. He yanked his right hand back, expecting Kosa to resist. Instead, she let go and used his surprise to pull his left hand across her body, forcing him to take a step toward her. Kosa didn't try to grab his arms but instead let go again, crouched slightly, reached around him, and placed her right hand on his right thigh, just under his ass, and her left under his kneecap. As she did so, she sank to the floor, her right knee braced behind his right foot, her foot flat. She locked her left knee behind her. She pushed forward with all her might, and the Strenoi flopped, landing on his back with a tremendous thud. Klenni blinked. It had to be a matter of leverage, not strength. Kosa couldn't be that strong.

Rammy whooped, and Stares laughed. Before Crenkleost could recover, Kosa launched onto his chest and headbutted him in the forehead.

Strenoi have thick skulls. Her headbutt would have knocked a Terran opponent down for the count. Crenkleost hardly felt it, grabbed her waist and flipped her over, pinning her to the ground.

"No disrespect!" he spat in rough English. It took Klenni a moment to realize he was saying that he refused to take disrespect from her, not that he didn't mean any disrespect to Kosa by straddling her.

"Raptor-face," Kosa snorted and kneed him in the crotch. While the Strenoi males did not have external genitalia like Terrans (theirs retracted into the body when not having intercourse), they were not immune to damage in that area; like a Terran vagina, it was still sensitive. While Crenkleost froze, letting the pain subside, Kosa leaned back and slammed her hands forward, attempting to shove him off her. He was so heavy she only succeeded in pushing him to kneeling, his pelvis still on her thighs.

"Get off!" she ordered in English.

"I win," Crenkleost declared. Kosa's face darkened to the same shade of burgundy as Crenkleost's scales. The Strenoi leaned forward, holding her down. Klenni heard Rammy chuckle. Why was he happy to see his corporal bested?

In several deft simultaneous movements, faster than Klenni could really comprehend, Kosa grabbed the Strenoi's right wrist with her right hand and placed her left on the right side of his head, gripping behind his neck. She slid her right foot under his stomach and used the pressure he placed against her to spin her body to the right. She lifted her right leg around his shoulder, then wrapped her other leg around the same shoulder, crossing her ankles. He had a millisecond to understand what was happening, but too late. Her knees were braced against his elbows as she rocked forward, throwing the Strenoi onto his back yet again. She straddled him, triumphant.

"Kosa has won every grappling contest in our unit," Rammy commented.

"And I've won again," Kosa declared.

"Fuck you," Crenkleost swore, but it was more sulky than angry.

"Yes, please," Stares exclaimed, closing in so je was staring down at the brawlers. "I've never heard of a Terran-Strenoi bonding, but it would be interesting to watch. Would they make a half-breed?"

"No, that's idiotic, you stupid Rip!" Flugger exclaimed, having understood the gist of jer comment. Klenni had not translated Stares' statement for the rest of the group, knowing it would only cause more tension (and not the kind Stares was hoping for). As Crenkleost tried to flip Kosa again while she crossed her arms over his chest to try and hold him down, Flugger took Klenni's pistol from her hand and fired the stun blast at the pair. The attack dazed both combatants, and they froze like statues. Kosa fell off Crenkleost and onto the floor beside him, both immobilized for three seconds.

Klenni stomped over to stare down at them, tendrils waving. "Are you done?" she asked in both languages. "We can worry about Strenoi and Terran arrogance later."

"Yes," Kosa whispered, sitting up. The Strenoi nodded, also sitting up. Kosa pursed her lips slightly as she got to her feet, as if in thought. To Klenni's surprise, she extended a hand down to Crenkleost. The Strenoi looked at her hand, glanced at the female Strenoi briefly, then accepted. Kosa pulled him to standing and let go but looked up at his face, considering him. He looked down at her, also contemplative.

If there had been anger before, the fight had dissipated it, leaving what looked to Klenni as grudging respect. *Primitives,* Klenni thought, but part of her wished her life were as exciting. Then again, she was trapped on a mysterious ghost ship with a bunch of psychotic aliens.

She exhaled, stepping away from the pair as the rest of the group crowded in for what was likely to incite a lot of translation on her part.

CHAPTER 6: WIND

The undulating pulse started as a minor headache – a pressure behind the eyes, the unsettling sensation that the world was too bright. Wind stretched jer neck, wondering why jer head suddenly felt as if je had just woken up hungover after jer community's annual hunt festival. Nausea, an uncommon sensation for Rips, made jer heave. As je rested jer palms on jer knees, jer mouth open, je managed to glance beside jer; the others were in similar positions.

Kosa let out a string of expletives that Wind understood the basis for – if sound could be a bullet, it was piercing jer temples. Jer brain was fizzing underneath jer skull, wanting to boil out from jer ears. Wind's hands began to shake, and je sunk to the floor; je was too overcome to even stop jerself from falling over on jer side. Jer eyes remained open; je couldn't close them if je tried. The Pir-An couple lay crumpled on the ground, arms around one another, tendrils flaccid. The Terran Rammy rocked back and forth on his knees, clutching his head. The female Strenoi curled into herself, her teeth baring and unbarring, her eyes wide. Crenkleost and Kosa had fallen towards one another, gripping each other's arms, both apparently unwilling to show weakness to the other by falling. And Stares … je had jer mouth open in a silent scream, jer claws digging into jer legs, claws cutting into the fabric.

Wind's body was on fire, jer skin sizzling. Jer mouth overflowed with saliva.

Then it was gone. Wind sat up. Je felt fine, aside from residual shakes.

The rest of the group looked at one another. The Pir-An helped one another stand, Crenkleost and Kosa shoved one another away, the female Strenoi shook her head, Rammy blinked heavily, and Stares let out a laugh that did nothing to hide jer unease.

"Well, that was fun," je said in Rip.

"Whoa." Rammy turned his head to look at Stares. "Hey … I understood that. Like, my brain translated it for me. Unless … are you speaking English?"

Stares stared at him. "No, I'm speaking Rip. But I understand *you*."

"What the fuck?" Kosa demanded.

"It was that pulse, that pain. Whatever it was," the female Strenoi suggested. "It wouldn't make any sense for it to be anything but that."

"Wait, so you're saying that when we all suffered that pain, it gave us the ability to understand one another?" Rammy's face twisted into an expression of disbelief.

"What else could it have been?" Klenni asked.

"But how would it work?" Kosa demanded. "I've never heard of anything like that."

Stares shrugged. "Maybe it's a virus."

The female Strenoi snorted. "Too instantaneous for a virus. More likely, it was a frequency designed to penetrate the area of our brains that focus on language. Perhaps these mystery ship aliens have mastered wavelength frequencies and were able to alter our brains with it."

"I wish they'd mastered 'come out so we can fight you' frequencies," Kosa muttered.

"True, that," Crenkleost agreed.

Despite being able to speak to one another without Klenni's input, the conversation petered out; everyone was simply staring at one another as if this were a first contact situation. The two Strenoi had moved to stand side-by-side. Wind had never seen a female Strenoi up close. While there were female soldiers, most of the females stayed back on Strenovast, leading the government and businesses as je understood it, as the Strenoi population naturally produced twenty percent more males than females. She was taller than Crenkleost, but he was wide for a Strenoi male, with uncharacteristically stocky shoulders. The Terrans called the Strenoi *raptors*, which Wind understood to be a reptile from their planet. The Strenoi were not reptiles, merely reptiloid in appearance; they were not cold-blooded and did not have tails. Their faces were shaped closer to a Terran's than a lizard's, as they lacked a protruding snout, but their eyes were tear-shaped with an internal and external lid. They had no external ears but flaps they could raise to increase their auditory senses. Their noses were similar to both Terrans and Rips, but with larger nostrils. Their mouths were wide, spreading almost the entire width of their faces, with thick lips and small teeth. Their legs were long and had double-jointed knees that could bend forward and backwards. Hailing from a planet with a harsh sun, their bodies had developed scale-like skin, and these scales came in various colours. Crenkleost's scales were burgundy, rich as wine. The female's was a lighter shade, almost lavender. Wind had seen green, brown, and even blue Strenoi before, though reddish hues were more common. The female was built much like the male but had a single protrusion at the front of her chest, presumably for child-feeding. Wind knew Stares was fascinated by the breasts of Terrans and Strenoi, as their people did not feed their young in such a manner and thus had none. The female Strenoi lacked the distinctive ridge bone that rose off the male's skull like a small mohawk.

Both Strenoi were dressed in the black, skin-tight under-armour they typically wore beneath their full armour. Wind wondered if they had lost their armament and other clothes in the same way Kosa and Rammy had, but je wasn't going to ask. Such problems were why je carried everything je owned on jer person.

"After we escaped, what happened to you?" Stares asked the Strenoi.

"We aren't sure," the Strenoi female said. "Your ship made it to the bay before we could strike, and the door closed on your vessel, sending parts of it flying towards us. Crenkleost dodged the larger pieces and banked around to see if we could ascertain whether you were alive. As we slowed to look, all our electronics went black, and our viewscreens turned off. The ship began shaking violently, and we passed out. We woke up in a large, abandoned bay, our ship completely dead. We couldn't even get auxiliary life support to function."

"We decided to try and find another ship," Crenkleost added, "and then we ran into you."

"Are you the pilot?" Kosa asked.

Crenkleost nodded. Kosa nodded back but clearly refused to compliment his ability further.

"Who is your pilot?" the female asked.

"We don't have one," Stares admitted. "I was flying the ship."

"You? I didn't even know Rips could fly." Crenkleost snorted.

"Well, I wasn't aware Strenoi could do anything but die on the battlefield, so I guess we're both learning something new today."

Crenkleost scoffed at the petty insult. It was not one of Stares' best.

"What were you doing out here?" the female asked.

"I was hired to form a crew and make a survey of this ship," Stares replied. "These people all signed up."

"Military?" Crenkleost asked, gesturing towards the Terrans.

"Corporal Koharu Saito and PFC Rammy Delaney," Rammy clarified.

"Senior Pilot Crenkleost of Ris'anact," he replied, giving the name of his Estate and not his last name, as was common for his people. He turned to the Pir-An. "You. Science, I'm assuming?"

"I'm Klenni, the navigator, and my life-mate, Flugger, is a doctor. Rammy is Terran military, as he said, but he is also a scientist – in what, again?"

"Classical mechanics. Physics. I'm finishing a stint in the military so that they'll fund my Ph.D. I've been working part-time on my Masters while serving. I study alien technology. I must say, I'm fascinated by the design of this ship. It's both drastically different yet oddly similar to ours. I wonder how its power source operates?"

"Maybe you'll be able to help us understand what's going on." Stares turned to the female Strenoi. "What is your name and function?"

"I'm Dr. Ow'llent of Estate Dig'nele. I'm a scientist myself, a biologist mainly, but I also have experience in other fields."

"Are you mated?" Stares asked, eyes gleaming.

"Pervert," Kosa muttered as Wind rolled jer eyes. Stares was obsessed with the mating practices of other species. Such a useless thing to care about. While sex was not something je was opposed to, je didn't go out of jer way to seek it out. That would mean more interaction with others than je deigned worth the effort of an orgasm and the potential risk of fertilization.

Ow'llent and Crenkleost both laughed at Stares' suggestion. "Mates?" Crenkleost shook his head. "She is far too old for me." He chuckled as Ow'llent smacked him on the arm.

"Yes, I am past my ability to mate for breeding," Ow'llent admitted, "but that doesn't mean I couldn't give this young *grutyk* an entertaining time." Crenkleost made a face of mock disgust. "The Strenovast High Council sent Crenkleost and me to do a cursory investigation of this ship. I suppose it's now a more thorough investigation if we even make it out of here to report on our find."

"How come there aren't any Pir-An or Terrans investigating?" Kosa demanded.

"As far as I know, the Pir-An are unaware of the existence of this ship. I didn't see anything about it on our news feeds before we left," Flugger explained. "Unless our government has managed to hide it and are sending an expedition as we speak."

"It must be the same with our people," Rammy added.

"How in the name of *kuso* do the Rips know about it?" Kosa asked.

Stares flashed teeth at Kosa. "We aren't creatures lolling in the mud, you know. We have intelligence operatives and have acquired many long-range satellites."

Wind hid jer surprise behind a well-practiced mask of indifference. Jer people had I.O. and satellites now? Just whom did Stares work for? Stares claimed je was a mercenary, but je was too knowledgeable for that—brash and arrogant to be sure, but clearly formally educated. Stares' teeth snapped together audibly as if je had said too much. Perhaps je had. What was jer game? Wind shrugged internally; as long as je got them out of this mess, je didn't care. Though, Wind would admit, je could have been stranded with a much worse Rip than jer; at least je had a sense of humour and jer skin was dazzling under the right light.

Ow'llent sighed. "Who cares about any of the politics? What matters is getting out of here. Now, who is your leader? Corporal Koharu?"

"You can call me Kosa," the Terran clarified.

"No!" Stares pushed past the woman in question and pointed at jer chest. "I'm the leader. This is my mission."

"You?" Crenkleost laughed. "Give me a break."

"Excuse me? I could kick your ass into next week."

"You sure?" The Strenoi took two steps towards jer. Wind wouldn't have been surprised if Stares backed away. Instead, je doubled down by closing the gap between them and opening jer mouth as wide as it could go. Stares was taller than Crenkleost, but only a quarter of the weight. Saliva dripped through jer spiky teeth and dribbled onto the floor. Wind blinked hard; je must really be angry if je were salivating that much. Then again, Stares didn't seem to have much room in jer personality for emotional nuance.

"Unlike the Terran, I have claws and teeth too, lizard. I'm happy to fight you for real."

"We were fighting for real," Kosa cut in.

"Well, technically …" Crenkleost began, never taking his eyes off Stares.

Kosa put her hands on her hips, glaring at the alien who was not looking at her. "I'm not an idiot. I knew we weren't fighting to kill – your claws were retracted. But I usually fight dirtier than that."

"Sure."

"I've killed fourteen of your people in hand-to-hand combat," she retorted, "*while* they were wearing your fancy-ass armour." At this Crenkleost turned his eyes from Stares, who snapped jer teeth together in triumph. Wind wasn't sure what Stares thought je had won.

"Truly?"

"Yes, truly."

"Kosa has been in service since she was eighteen, over eight Terran years before the truce," Rammy explained. Kosa raised an eyebrow at him as if amused he knew this about her.

"How long is your year again?" Klenni asked. Wind admired her ability to come up with ways to distract people from fighting. She had worked on Terran ships, she had said, so there was no way she didn't know this already.

"Three hundred and sixty-five days, twenty-four hours per day."

Crenkleost scoffed. "What! Why not something that divides more cleanly?"

"We can't help how Terra rotates around our sun! We use Earth time as our standard on Terran Space Force ships," Rammy said.

Klenni nodded. Wind pursed jer lips. Ripplia's time markers focused less on years than on the *Borkas* migratory mating season. The days on Ripplia were thirty-two Terra-hours long. Je had to adapt to it when je worked for their military in the war.

Klenni sighed. "If all our people are going to work together, we need to come up with a unified way of tracking time."

"Age *is* just a number after all," Ow'llent kidded.

"How about this?" Stares suggested, still wanting confirmation that je was the leader. "I hire you both for my mission."

"It's not so much a mission as an escape," Flugger cut in.

"Yes, but this way, we have a leader."

"How about you only get to use your *leadership* when we can't agree by consensus?" Flugger suggested. "That way we all get a say in this unique situation, but we aren't sitting around arguing for hours over whether to go left or right."

"Do these halls even have that option?" Rammy asked. "We've been walking in a straight line."

"Same," Crenkleost said.

"We were lucky we didn't go opposite directions," Stares mused.

"We could only go one direction," Ow'llent explained. "We brought all we could carry with us that might be useful." She gestured to her backpack, which bulged slightly.

"You make the old lady carry the stuff?" Kosa took the chance to snort at Crenkleost this time.

"She's not *old*, just past breeding age. And she's carrying it to protect it; I'm the first line of offence."

"Shouldn't you be the last? You're the pilot. She's trapped without you."

Crenkleost glanced at Ow'llent. Her shrug was surprisingly close to the Terran version.

"You raptors give all your smarts to the ladies, eh?" Kosa grinned but kept her lips closed, so as not to suggest antagonism, though it was clear she enjoyed riling up the Strenoi. Crenkleost narrowed his eyes at her, his second eyelid blinking steadily.

"At least *we* dressed appropriately for the mission," Ow'llent cut in.

Kosa made a face. "I was working out when you attacked us. All my stuff was lost."

"She's lying. She loves showing off that *fine booty*," Rammy joked. His grin faded when Kosa's head snapped towards him, her expression fierce. "Uh, Corporal."

Wind was glad Kosa hadn't accepted jer challenge earlier.

Kosa was now frowning at everyone else. "Yes, because my goal here is to get laid. I guess if I got desperate, I could try for the gay dude, a threesome with a pair of married guppies, or I can make it with a couple of raptors, a species with whom I've been fighting since I was old enough to buy a drink in a bar." She sniffed in an exaggerated, dismissive manner.

"What about me?" Stares asked, leaning forward, the claws at the end of jer fingertips wriggling slightly. Wind raised an eye-ridge. Stares must truly be interested and not just provoking the Terran. But from what Wind could tell, Stares was the most curious person je'd ever met. Je would be the type to try anything just to see what it was like. Including having sex with an alien.

Kosa blinked rapidly. "I told you before. I'm not interested. You look like something from a horror movie."

Rammy took two steps closer to his corporal. Wind guessed in case of an inevitable attack.

"Thanks!" Stares beamed. "I've worked hard on cultivating an aura of malevolence."

"I'm here for it," Wind said from jer position just outside the group, behind Rammy. Je grinned as Stares threw back jer head and laughed.

"And who is that one?" Ow'llent asked, pointing at Wind.

CHAPTER 7: OW'LLENT

Ow'llent had never been interested in fighting the Terrans – it was a waste of money that could be used for better things, like healthcare, research, and scientific innovation. During the fighting, she volunteered and donated to a group that generated and disseminated anti-war propaganda. While some of the arguments her fringe group served up were conspiratorial in nature, she believed there was at least a morsel of truth to it all. She wholeheartedly believed the High Council (which governed Strenovast and the colony worlds) had encouraged the war to proceed longer than it needed to control the agitated Worker population. The only way for upward mobility if you were not High Born was to join the military or move off-world. It also helped that the Workers simply didn't own capital or property. They were paid in "Estate Chits," which they could only use at Estate-owned stores. No one had questioned this way of life for centuries, at least not on the scale the population had begun to in the last two decades. Ow'llent, as one of these nobles from a mid-level Estate, saw the disparity and disagreed with it. Her wife, Corcalla, saw the disparity and was organizing a revolution.

Ow'llent looked hard at Rammy. The Terran was of the darker-skinned variety of Terran, with dark brown eyes. He had curly, black hair and was taller than most Terran males, but not freakishly so. His muscles were not as pronounced as his corporal's, and it was clear he cared more about his brain than his body structure. Watching the female grapple with Crenkleost had been amusing, as Ow'llent had not expected the Terran to hold her own for more than a moment, let alone succeed. Perhaps gravity worked in her favour, but it was more likely that this woman was just extremely fit – her abdominal muscles were taught and pronounced, as were the ones on her arms and back. Her eyes were small and close to her nose, and her cheekbones pushed against her skin. She had colourful pictures etched into her flesh from her right shoulder to her right wrist, though Ow'llent could not recall the word for them.

Ow'llent had determined in her studies that the Terrans shared a distant genetic ancestor with her people. Most scientists believed the species' similarities resulted from convergent evolution. All five sapient races in their known universe were bipedal, had two eyes, and breathed oxygen. Ow'llent was a biologist and, upon studying Terran DNA for weapons research at the start of the war, discovered that their people shared a very minute, single genetic marker. She almost missed it, which was likely why no one else had seen it before – it only showed up under certain conditions. Yet, because she had been able to prove it wasn't an isolated anomaly, this suggested fascinating ideas about their history: perhaps their homeworlds were both colonized by the same bacteria or perhaps they were both designed by a higher intelligence that had died out millennia before. Strenoi and Terrans were far more similar on a reproductive and biological level than the Dirge, Rips, and Pir-An put together. But Ow'llent's argument (contested wildly at any summit she presented it to before she was forced to stop) was that Terrans and Strenoi evolved from the same last universal common ancestor at the cellular level. Their differences were on the surface due to the dissimilarity in the environments. How they got on two planets light-years from one another was not something she had gotten to yet in her research, as her funding from the High Council had dried up a few years ago.

"What are you staring at, raptor?" Kosa demanded of Ow'llent.

"Stop calling us that," Crenkleost hissed.

"I'd say it's a compliment more than an insult, really," Rammy said. "I mean, it is intended as an insult when we use it, but velociraptors were fearsome, intelligent hunters. At least as far as our movies depicted them, eh?"

"What the hell are you talking about?" Crenkleost frowned. "Aren't raptors just lizards?"

Rammy shook his head. "No, we call you raptors because of that big claw on your foot. A raptor was a dinosaur."

"What's that?" Ow'llent asked. She had studied animal life on Terra as part of her research but had never heard of this type of animal. If she were able to secure some specimens, it might help her research further!

"A dinosaur? It's well … holy shit. I mean, okay … so before humans evolved on Earth, hundreds of millions of years before, there were these other creatures on our planet we call dinosaurs. Some were bigger than seven metres."

"Bullshit!"

Rammy ignored that. "An asteroid wiped them out. We were able to find skeletons of the dinosaurs buried in the ground and pieced them together. We have a whole field of vertebrate paleontology to study them."

Crenkleost shook his head. "That's ridiculous."

"If it is true, it's awesome," Stares exclaimed. "What else?"

"Shouldn't we be moving on?" Flugger asked. "We've been standing here chatting about useless stuff like we're at a cocktail party!"

"I want to hear about these lizards too, love," Klenni admitted.

Rammy grinned widely, then quickly lowered his lips over his teeth. It made him look ridiculous, but Ow'llent appreciated his understanding of how the Strenoi reacted when they saw fully bared teeth. She had read that Terrans showed teeth in such a way to be extra friendly or very happy, where the Strenoi kept their lips closed to smile in all instances but a challenge.

"The dinosaurs were from long ago and existed for millions of years. Our scientists had to break their existence into eras of time based on how far below the Earth's surface their bones were located. They are such a fascinating part of our history – all kids love dinosaurs. Even now, with alien races around, kids still love them."

"My friend's toddler is obsessed with them," Kosa added. The A.I. rested on her left hand as she keyed commands into it with her right.

"I really think we should –" Flugger began, but Klenni put a hand on his arm to silence him.

"Anyway, there's a huge entertainment industry devoted to them. Back in the late twentieth century, a movie about dinosaurs started the whole thing; it was actually based on a novel. The screenwriters modified the look of the dinosaurs, specifically the velociraptor, to make it more vicious and bigger than it was in reality. It was distinctive for its clawed back feet with one large claw, like yours. That's the impression of the creature that is stuck in our Terran collective memory. Anyway, that's why you're called raptors."

Crenkleost snorted. "Humph. We just call you *encims*."

"I've heard that." Rammy nodded. "What does it mean?"

Ow'llent glanced at Crenkleost, who chuckled in response. "There's this creature on Strenovast called an *encimstrani*. It's a bottom feeder."

"It eats its own shit," Crenkleost added, laughing.

Kosa crossed her arms over her chest. "Raptor is what we call you when there are children present. We have plenty more nicknames for you. Allie, show'em."

The A.I. projected a hologram of a velociraptor.

Crenkleost cocked his head to the side. "Ok, I see the claw."

"You have those walking around on your planet?" Stares asked. "Can I buy one?"

"No! Didn't you listen, you stupid, shelling Rip?" Flugger exploded. Everyone turned to stare at him. Flugger's outburst clearly surprised Stares as je only snarled slightly. "They're *extinct*. Like *we* are going to be if we continue hanging around in this corridor, *jibber-jabbering*."

"It's funny how my brain translates expressions too," Kosa replied, ignoring the distress in Flugger's voice and his dancing tendrils. "I'm assuming my mind is simply choosing an equivalent."

"It's really quite odd," Ow'llent added, "because colloquial expressions or concepts unique to our cultures would require contextual understanding. And I seem to understand all but a few words. I wonder if the pulse somehow tapped into the Pir-An telepathy as well?"

"PEOPLE!" Flugger whined. "Seriously. There is –"

"Flugger, shut up," Stares snapped. "I hear something."

The group fell silent. Flugger glowered at everyone while Klenni rubbed his shoulder with hers. Had Ow'llent not been listening so hard, she would have chuckled. The Pir-An, for all their technology and economic strength, were the universe's nerds. And this was coming from someone who spent the last twenty years in a university lab.

The noise Stares had pointed out was growing in volume and clarity: the slamming of naked feet and clicking of claws on the floor, the buzzing drone of humming and groaning. It was not one thing coming towards them but a collection of things.

"What do we do?" Rammy asked, eyes darting towards Kosa, then to Stares. He tightened and retightened his grip on his rifle.

Stares took a moment. "We run. We regroup back at the Terran ship."

"What? No. We fight." Crenkleost picked up his fallen rifle.

"I'm the leader! I say we go!" Stares ordered. "We have no idea what's coming! It could be a tank!"

"No, je is right," Klenni exclaimed. "We can use the doorway to the bay to funnel whatever it is! Let's go!"

Kosa glanced at Crenkleost, then at Stares.

"That's a direct order!" Stares opened jer mouth wide and threw jer hands to jer hips. "We are retreating! NOW!"

Crenkleost growled low in his throat but turned away from the noise.

"Let's go! Run!" Stares exclaimed. The wheezing, hissing, and raspy breathing grew cacophonous. Ow'llent began to run, pausing to scoop up the Pir-An female on her way.

"You're too slow," she muttered when the Pir-An began to protest being slung like a sack of *durlags*.

She craned her neck behind her to see Kosa and Crenkleost standing their ground; it was clear neither of them wished to be in front of the other.

"Crenkleost!" Ow'llent demanded. "Now!" Stares, Wind, and Rammy already made it to the end of the corridor. Flugger struggled to keep up. Kosa and

Crenkleost raced past Ow'llent, now competing to see who could run fastest – Crenkleost had longer legs, but his claws slowed him down, making it a tight race. Ow'llent gritted her teeth and muttered under her breath about pride, stupidity, and smashing heads together. Klenni murmured agreement.

Crenkleost paused in his race to grab Flugger and fling him up onto his back. The other Pir-An did not argue about being carried.

As she turned the corner, Ow'llent twisted her head behind her. Humanoid shapes poured into the hallway.

"Holy shit!" she yelled. "Move!"

They ran. The other group had taken their time when they had first left the bay, partly from caution and partly because of the Pir-An's short legs. The Rips, with barely any body fat and longer legs than the other species, had already left the next corridor when Ow'llent reached it, breathing heavily. The Pir-An, despite her diminutive stature, was not light. Crenkleost clearly had no issue with his burden, already passing Rammy with Kosa just behind him, but Ow'llent cursed her older body and choice of vocation. Corcalla was always chiding her for not exercising enough. She took deep breaths, willing her arms to lose their fatigue, willing her legs to move faster.

"Put Klenni on my back!" Rammy fell in step beside her.

"No time!" she grunted.

"You can't keep this up!" Rammy exclaimed. She glanced at his muscled arms.

"Fine." She stopped. Klenni willingly climbed onto Rammy's back, gripping his shoulders. Kosa fell back to take Rammy's weapon from him.

"I'll take a turn if you need it," she ordered as they began to run again.

"I … can … handle it."

"I'll take rear guard then."

"Multiple beings. Chasing us." Ow'llent struggled not to wheeze. They entered the next corridor to see the Rips darting away. Crenkleost was halfway down the hall, glanced behind, saw the stragglers were fine, and continued moving.

Ow'llent focused on Kosa's steady breathing. It was obvious the woman could have caught up with Crenkleost and maybe even the Rips if she had chosen, but she kept her word of guarding their backs. A very honourable thing to do, something Ow'llent had suspected Terrans were capable of, despite all the war news claiming Terrans would kill their own children to further their success in battle.

Ow'llent had the typical defence training given High Born Strenoi but had never served in the forces. Many women didn't, but they were not barred from it. One of their top generals was a female of breeding age. Every day in the news, there were speculations of whom she would choose as her first brood mate since she was already in a love match.

Forcing herself to focus on this meaningless drama from home distracted Ow'llent from not only the fear of the things chasing them, but the growing pain in her chest and stitch in her side. Her lungs burned, her legs felt like lead blocks, and her heart grew tight beneath her ribs. The metallic surface of the floor provided no give for her large toe-claws. They jarred against the floor with each step, forcing her to clench her feet to prevent it from happening. She could retract the claws on her hands, but not the ones on her feet. She could not allow herself to trip.

They ran for ten minutes. Ow'llent knew her tongue was hanging out of her mouth but couldn't hold it in. Rammy was drenched in sweat. Kosa was slightly red in the face but kept casting worried glances at her companions. Klenni's constant apologies for being a burden did not help the situation.

The corridors began to bend towards one another, just as Ow'llent's vison grew fuzzy around the edges, an indication that her body was craving more oxygen than she was inhaling. The hissing, growling chorus of the creatures persisted, evidence they had not given up their pursuit, but she was so tired she almost relished their attack so she could stop running. She would gladly succumb to their violence if she could rest.

"Here!" Crenkleost called from a doorway. Kosa ran past and stood outside it, shotgun at ready. Crenkleost aimed his rifle down the hallway. Rammy burst into the room, struggling not to stumble as Klenni dismounted. Ow'llent followed them in, allowing herself to fall to her knees so she could take deep breaths.

"That … was … fun," Rammy managed to say, sharing her gasping intakes of oxygen.

"No time to rest!" Crenkleost called. "Ow'llent, you're with the Pir-An."

"Like hell," Ow'llent muttered. The Pir-An had moved to the back of the bay, where the remains of the Terran vessel sat. Klenni had a pistol out. Flugger was shaking slightly – he was the medic, Ow'llent recalled. Klenni was calmer. Stares hovered inside the door frame, a long leg bent up against it as if je were waiting for friends to arrive at a party. Ow'llent cast about for the other Rip – ah, je was on top of the Terran vessel, jer dark skin blending in with the ship itself. Je was prone, sniper rifle pointed at the door.

Kosa began barking orders, fast and loud. "OK, people, good hustle." She slapped Rammy on the shoulder as he joined Stares at the door. She passed him his S2 rifle. "Crenk and I –"

Crenkleost cut her off by sputtering an unintelligible word as Ow'llent's eyes widened. Using a short form of a name was something Workers did, not High Borns. Even if you were from a struggling rural Estate like Crenkleost, it was an insult to use a diminutive version of his name.

Kosa glared at him, obviously not caring what he was annoyed about. "*Crenk* and I are going to take the first wave. If we can't take them all down, we're going to lure them into the room. Delaney, you head ten feet into Port, Stares to Starboard. Wind!" she called behind her. "You wait for Crenk and me to get clear before you start firing. Delaney, Stares, you let Wind fire at will before you start firing – conserve ammo and only take the second line if Wind can't break it. Pir'An, Ow'llent – you engage only if the creatures approach you. Leave the fighting to us."

Stares began to speak, but Kosa raised a hand. "Let me do what I do best, Rip!"

Stares nodded, to which Ow'llent gave the Mystics a silent thank-you. Kosa flicked her gaze from Ow'llent to Crenkleost, who, to Ow'llent's surprise, raised his fist to his temple, a salute. *Oh, right, in this moment Kosa is his CO.* Crenkleost was a decorated pilot, but everyone from an Estate had combat training. He likely enjoyed a skirmish, as did the Terran corporal presumably, given the two exuded the same excited energy. Rammy's face was wan with fatigue and Stares was clacking jer teeth together. The hissing and stomping grew louder and louder. The four warriors at the door stood their ground, all of them steady. None of them appeared to have their stomachs in the throats, as Ow'llent did.

"Ready, here they come! Ow'llent, get back!" Kosa ordered.

CHAPTER 8: CRENKLEOST

The Terran woman clearly had the most experience leading a team in battle. Though a patriot, Crenkleost was not an idiot. While he could beat her in a *real* fight, Kosa had surprised him with how much she had held her ground against him. Not only that, but she had risen to his challenge. And with a gun, it didn't matter how much bigger you were than your opponent, but life or death could depend on who called the shots. As such, their best chance of survival came from following Kosa's lead. He knew more about the Terran ground forces than he suspected they thought he did; he knew a corporal was an officer who commanded a team. Kosa was a corporal. That meant she had, and could, lead in battle. Crenkleost had never led a team on the ground or a squadron in flight.

Even Stares, for all jer attempts to assert control, allowed the Terran to do what she did best. Crenkleost, while still annoyed at her for shortening his name, glanced at Kosa as they stood ready, the creatures approaching. Her face was tight, but her dark brown eyes gleamed – he understood that look; she wanted to prove herself, she wanted to win. He had been shooting Terran fighters down his entire career but never once stopped to think that maybe he could share anything with one, let alone an emotion. Ow'llent's rambles about their similarities and the sham of the war during their flight here started to make an odd sort of sense.

The tumult of unholy noises reached its peak. The creatures rounded the corner *en masse*. Had someone asked him to explain what they were, he would have struggled to define them. They were alive, that was clear, but various limbs and torsos were spliced together with machine parts. And the limbs were Strenoi, Terran, Pir-An, Rip … even Dirge. They were a horrific medley of creature and machine. The legs and arms were disgusting enough, but the humanoid heads let out hisses and moans. Were they robots melded with severed parts? Or were they sentient or even sapient creatures that had been horribly disfigured with bionic elements? Crenkleost snapped his mouth shut and opened fire.

Kosa's shotgun blast took the first creature in the chest, sending it screeching backwards, arms flailing. Crenkleost's rail gun fire tore others apart, leaving a groaning pile of blood, white fluid, and what looked like black oil. Other creatures stepped through or over their dead to try and reach their targets. Kosa's shotgun blasted out again and again, but Crenkleost could barely hear it over the *blat-blat-blat* retort of his own rifle. He squeezed his oratory flaps tight.

"I'm out!" he exclaimed.

"OK, head in!"

Crenkleost paused, not wanting to leave Kosa alone.

"I only have three shells left in the chamber! Get in there!"

She fired at one who got too close, splattering brains and bionic components over the wall. As Crenkleost raced into the room, he heard the second blast, then the third in quick succession. He pulled out his large knife, which closely resembled a Terran golok with its curving tip and handle. He stood ten feet in front of the Pir-An and

Ow'llent, protecting them from the creatures. Kosa raced into the room, yelling, "Wind!"

She slid on the ground as she spoke to give the Rip a cleaner shot. She made it to Crenkleost's feet, and he extended a hand to help her up without thinking. She didn't pause before accepting. Meanwhile, Wind had released shot after shot in an almost robotic sequence.

"Holy shit," Crenkleost breathed. Every shot the Rip took was a headshot. Every one. Je didn't miss. Je was so fast, so accurate, je created a pile-up of bodies in the doorway.

"Ok, let them in," Kosa called. "Stares, quit staring at Wind! Rammy, be ready."

Wind took three more shots, then let the remaining creatures climb in over the bodies. Stares and Rammy took them out with careful three-round bursts from their rifles. Soon, there was nothing left of the creatures but a stinking pile of death.

Stares approached the door, rifle in front of jer. Je leaned out the door, looking in both directions.

"All clear. Should someone go to the end of the hallway and make sure there aren't any stragglers?"

"You're the leader," Kosa muttered.

Crenkleost snorted softly.

"Well, then, I'll do it. Be right back." The Rip took off, climbing over the viscera as if it were something innocuous, like a mound of unfolded linen.

"What are they?" Klenni asked. The group advanced towards the pile at the door in the manner of a distraught driver approaching the deer they had just turned into roadkill. They stared down at the bodies in silence. Flugger raced to the corner to throw up.

"Hybrids." Ow'llent used her pike weapon to poke at a mechanical arm attached to a Terran shoulder. "Whoever is running this ship has managed to merge live beings with mechanical parts. Fascinating."

"Also disgusting. And unethical," Klenni said.

"I didn't think that needed to be said," Ow'llent added.

"Well, good work taking them out, everyone." Kosa nodded. "I think we retained as much ammo as we could, given the circumstances."

"No one else is around," Stares called, jumping lithely over the bodies to join the group. "Just a bunch of dead things in the hallway. I dispatched a few that were still breathing. If you can call it that." Je slid a short billhook knife into a hidden sheath under jer flowing red garments.

"I'm assuming they aren't the ones running the place?" Rammy asked.

Ow'llent shook her head. "I would be very surprised if that were so. These … modifications … appear to be experimental. The stitching is rather crude, wouldn't you say, Pir-An?"

Flugger had returned from his jaunt to the corner, his normally indigo skin a pale lilac. He nodded.

Ow'llent prodded at a different creature. "It seems like the robots were paired with one being but with different parts. There's, what, thirty creatures here, but the body parts melded to the mechanical seem to match up. One of each of our species."

"How …" Rammy began, then jumped back when one moved. In a fluid motion, Crenkleost unsheathed his golok and stabbed it in the head. Flugger ran to throw up again when Crenkleost pulled the blade from the brain with a squelch.

"I would presume that they kept the sapient beings alive while they removed parts to place onto robots. Then they used what was left and added robotic parts. I'm hoping the subject was anesthetized." Ow'llent spoke softly, retracting a claw and itching the underside of her jaw.

"Regardless if they were put out or not, that's fucking sick." Kosa's face twisted, her cheeks a deepening shade of burgundy as her voice rose. "We should stop them. What if this is their goal? To do this to *us*? To all our peoples?"

The group, who had been holding side conversations, fell silent.

"Why would they send such a small force if they intended to kill us?" Rammy asked.

"They're testing us," Klenni suggested. "Maybe they wanted to see what we could do."

"Or these escaped, and we murdered them," Ow'llent suggested.

"I'm pretty sure I didn't hear them calling for help," Kosa replied. "Truth is, we probably put them out of their misery."

"Anyone we know?" Stares asked Wind, poking at a Rip leg.

"Hopefully, someone I didn't like."

Stares raised an eye ridge. "There are people you like?"

"My grandparent. My parent. My cluster-cousins. I like you, sometimes."

"Aw, how sweet. And I thought you were a cold, hard killer."

"I'm a hunter, not a murderer."

"What are we going to do now?" Crenkleost asked, trying to break up the inappropriate Rip flirtation. How could they be so callus amidst the death and disturbing implications of the state of the bodies? Goddamn Rips were so primitive they couldn't even feel empathy. He stifled the growl that rose in his throat.

"I vote we stay here," Klenni suggested. "Push the bodies into the hallway somehow. Get our bearings. Make a plan."

"In my medical opinion, that is the best option," Flugger added. "We need to rest and eat. This ship, if you haven't noticed, is immense. If we leave this room, we likely won't be coming back. There's room enough here for us to all sleep on the floor, and we can post a guard rotation on the top of *Starship 330207*."

"Why do you not name your ship properly?" Ow'llent asked.

Rammy rolled his eyes. "Ask the Rips."

"I'd rather not," she replied.

"I like this plan," Stares cut in, ignoring or not caring about the jibes at jer expense. "We can inventory our weapons and ammo too."

"If Kosa doesn't mind," Klenni began, "I can modify Allie's location tracking to function as a rudimentary map. That way we can at least tell if we're moving further into the ship or following alongside the outer edge."

"Do it," Kosa agreed.

"I'll give everyone a medical check," Flugger offered.

"Piss in the starboard, shit in the port," Stares said. "Of the bay, I mean. The bathroom facilities in *Starship 330307* are gone."

"Just like basic training," Rammy joked, to which Kosa and Crenkleost laughed. No one else got it. It felt odd to laugh with Terrans, but the events of the day had proven utterly inexplicable.

The three soldiers moved the bodies using a large piece of *Starship 330307*'s plating that the bay door had sheared off. They shoved the sheet of metal at the corpses and pushed them out the door, then used it as a barricade. Kosa wiped her hands on her pants, though she hadn't touched the creatures, and headed back inside. Crenkleost felt the other Terran staring at him, so he turned his head to look down at Rammy.

"What?" he asked. "Worried I'll fight your corporal again?"

"She can handle herself. I've just never been so close to one of your people before. I mean, I've passed you at various docks and in battle, of course, but, well, it's interesting to meet you, I suppose."

"Did you say that to the Pir-An and the Rips?"

Rammy scoffed. "I worked with Pir-An in university – got drunk with more of them than I can count. And Rips … who wants to get close to them?"

Crenkleost laughed. "On that, we agree, Terran."

Crenkleost and Ow'llent were the largest physically of the group, so they settled near the back of the ship where there was more space. The Rips claimed the captain and pilot chairs, at the front, their cilia-toes on the dash. The Pir-An had first watch, as they had done the least amount of physical activity, so Rammy and Kosa settled in the middle of the room after throwing the table out into the bay. The Strenoi had two ration bars in their pack, which they ate for dinner. The crew of *Starship 330307* found two stores of similar easy-to-eat food. No one attempted to use their food producer machines.

Ow'llent unwrapped their producer to check if it was damaged in the run. It was fine, so she set it aside. She patted a blanket she took from her pack and looked at Crenkleost expectantly. Crenkleost stared at it blankly.

"Give her my blanket." Ow'llent nodded towards Kosa, who was lying down on the floor beside Rammy, her head on her arm. The Pir-An and Strenoi were nearly as unclothed as Kosa, with exposed arms and legs, but they had physiological advantages against cold. The Strenoi's nervous system boosted heat-producing cells more effectively than Terrans. The Pir-An could consciously regulate their body temperatures within a specific range, though they burned more calories doing so. No one worried about the Rips.

"Who?" Crenkleost asked. The older Strenoi cast him a glance commonly used to admonish a whiny teenager. Crenkleost grumbled. "I don't see why."

"To mend the rift. We are stuck with these aliens for who knows how long. I know you and she have a rivalry borne from years of encouraged hatred, but this is not the time, or place, to focus on that. When we get out of here, you two can fight to the death if you wish." She paused. "After you fly us home. I don't want that Rip flying me anywhere."

Crenkleost snorted. "This is dumb."

"You're dumb."

He sighed and stood, glanced down at the blanket.

"This is your breeding blanket!" He protested. "Why do you have it with you? Also, I can't give her this!"

"Well, *I* obviously can't. Also, she has no idea what it is. Just make sure I get it back."

"Why? You don't need it anymore." Crenkleost grumbled, then noticed her hurt expression. Shame washed over him. "I'm sorry." He sighed, bowing low to her in apology. "That was very rude of me. I've had a hard day. Lost my ship. Have to work with Terrans."

Ow'llent blinked her inner eyelids three times in acceptance of his apology. "It's ok. And you are right; I don't need it. But, that doesn't mean I don't value it."

Crenkleost nodded. He knew that. Damn his impetuous nature. He was never able to think before he spoke.

Crenkleost stood over Kosa, intentionally making himself appear as if he were ready to attack. To see the Terran startle would be worth this whole exchange. Instead, she opened her eyes and yawned, looking up at him. She stretched slightly, then rubbed her lower back as she sat up. The muscles on her thighs were impressive, he had to admit.

"You trying to scare me, raptor?" she asked, resting her elbows on her knees and her cheek on one of her hands. He and she both knew her nonchalant posture was intentionally telling him she did not find him a threat.

Crenkleost almost turned back around, but he could feel Ow'llent staring daggers at him. Respecting your elders was a strict tenet of Strenoi society, especially respecting women, and Crenk had no notion of disobeying her request.

"No, I'm not trying to scare you." He dropped the blanket unceremoniously on Kosa's body. "Here."

"What's this?" She picked up the gray material and admired the elaborate embroidery.

"A blanket. You Terrans don't have them?"

"Har har. I mean, why?"

"You're a good fighter. Can't have your frail body dying of hypothermia in the night."

"Why don't you warm her up?" Stares suggested from the front of the room. Wind's chuckle followed shortly after.

"Shut up, you disgusting nightmare," Crenkleost retorted. *Gross*. He turned to Kosa and rolled his eyes in the direction of the Rip. The Terran wrinkled her nose in the same direction. They agreed on one thing, at least.

"Thanks for the blanket," Kosa said, wrapping it around her body and lying back down.

Crenkleost sighed and headed back to his own section of the ship. He tried to wrinkle his nose like the Terran, but his physiology wouldn't let him, pushing his lower lip out instead. Ow'llent saw him contorting his face but said nothing, though he knew she was laughing at him on the inside.

CHAPTER 9: WIND

Wind and Stares sat beside one another on top of *Starship 330307.*

"Watch is almost done," Stares pointed out. Wind glanced at jer. Stares was leaning back on jer hands, gazing up at the ceiling.

"And?" Wind asked. Je knew what was coming. Stares had been harassing jer like a post-birthing *Borkas* needing to feed all night.

"And I think you should let me hold your gun for a little bit."

"If I were a Terran, I would think that was a euphemism," je replied.

Stares laughed, chomping jer teeth slightly at Wind.

"Nope, I plain want to hold your gun."

"Why? It's a regular Strenoi sniper rifle."

"Where did you get it?"

"Where do you think I got it?"

Stares paused, tapping jer chin with jer long fingers. A purring sound escaped jer throat, a Rip's version of saying *Hmmm.* "I would suggest you took it off a battlefield, but –"

"No, you're right."

"Dammit, As Silent as the Wind Over the Open Plain! Don't you have anything interesting about you whatsoever?"

"No."

Stares exhaled sharply. "Even your stupid name is boring. Let me guess; your grandparent gave it to you because you're good at being silent while hunting?"

"Yes."

"Big surprise!" Stares threw up jer hands. "You see, it's that mentality which keeps us Rips under the *Borkas'* foot. We need to think bigger, think *galactically*."

"I think I understand your name now." Wind studied the captain. Je had dramatically flung jerself onto jer back, closing jer black eyes. The silk had settled against jer body, clinging to it. Despite the rest of the aliens thinking the Rips looked the same except for skin and eye colour, Wind noticed the minute differences between jerself and Stares. Jer legs were longer, the cilia on jer feet curled in further, jer eyes were further apart and had a sharper incline at the sides. Not only that, but jer silver skin was the rarest of the three colours. It didn't mean anything in their culture, as the most important thing about a person was whether they could survive, but Wind had to admit to jerself that Stares was a rather fetching specimen when je was lying still. Not that je wanted to risk fertilization with jer. Wind turned away. Neither spoke for a moment. The ship emitted the same ambient hum of any other large spacecraft.

"Are you going to enlighten me or sit there like a fucking stump?"

Wind looked over to see Stares now staring at jer, the other Rip's mouth slightly open, jer eyes bright. Wind fiddled with the gun, turning away from jer arresting gaze.

"Well, Stares at the Stars too Long and Forgets Where Je is From, I have a feeling your grandparent named *you* such because you would climb to the top of your hut and watch the sky instead of doing chores. I would bet that you're a great fighter but not a good hunter. I would think you were better suited to running a community than food detail. I think you get bored easily. And I bet you left Ripplia as soon as you could."

Stares sat up quickly, gawking at Wind with jer mouth open.

"Accurate?" Je asked.

Stares narrowed jer eyes. "In most regards, yes, but I would not consider my tendency towards boredom to be a character flaw. Don't think you have me all figured out, Wind. It ruins the mystery."

Stares stood, stretched, and climbed down off the ship to wake the rest of the group.

"What mystery?" Wind whispered to jerself before je climbed down after Stares.

"Okay crew!" Stares called as Wind entered the ship and leaned against the doorway. Flugger raised his head slightly, then lowered it back to where he had been sleeping on Klenni's chest. Kosa and Rammy were under a blanket, and Crenkleost was sleeping on his stomach, his head on his arms. His large back moved up and down slowly with his breathing. Ow'llent was awake, sitting cross-legged and fiddling with her food producer.

"Wake up! The creatures are back!" Stares yelled.

Kosa lifted her head. "Not true."

"Aren't you a marine? Aren't you used to waking up and getting to action right away?"

"I'm on sabbatical," Kosa muttered.

Rammy rolled away from Kosa. He stood and stretched, then walked past the Rips and headed outside, presumably to relieve himself. Kosa sat up, wrapping the blanket around her shoulders.

"Need coffee. That was not a fun night. Rammy smells." She rose and cracked her back.

Ow'llent's wince was almost audible. Wind recalled that Strenoi hated the sound of cracking cartilage, but whether it was due to the noise itself or in reference to a cultural taboo, je wasn't sure.

"I managed to mod the A.I's programming during our watch," Klenni said as she slid out from under her husband, her tendrils twisting together; Wind wasn't sure what emotion that conveyed. "Wherever we go in the ship, it should create a map based on what it knows about where we are now. Or, at least it knows that we're on an outside wall at the moment. And I was able to hook it up briefly to the computer. I can't get the ship to turn on without an engine, but the battery backup in the black box allowed Allie to access the data. It gleaned an approximate length of this mystery ship from it."

"Mystery ship? More like *misery* ship, am I right?" Stares joked. No one laughed. A few seconds later, Wind coughed.

Stares exhaled, eyes narrowing. "We don't have any proof we're on the outside wall. Who knows how *Misery* operates? Maybe the bays rotate."

"Wouldn't we have felt it?" Ow'llent asked.

"Again, who knows how *Misery* operates?"

"I'm not calling this ship *Misery,"* Kosa exclaimed from her position in front of the Terran food producer. She pressed a button, and the black liquid the Terrans called coffee spurted into a surprisingly intact white mug she held beneath it.

"Regardless of what we call this place we're trapped in, let's get moving," Stares said.

Rammy returned during Stares' last sentence, doing up his pants. Terrans took forever to void their bowels. "I agree with the captain. I want to see what this ship is all about. Oh! We should give it a name."

"*Misery!*" Stares exclaimed.

Rammy thought about it. "I like it. Kind of like mystery, right?"

"*Baka*!" Kosa cursed.

"Why didn't my brain translate that?" Ow'llent asked.

Kosa looked at her. "I wasn't speaking English. My first language is Japanese."

Ow'llent used her large fingers to activate what Wind had thought was a wrist guard on her right arm; je originally assumed it was a medical instrument. Instead, the wrist guard glowed light green as she brought up a holographic keyboard – oh, it was a civilian form of a Strenoi Dev. She began typing quickly.

"What are you doing?" Crenkleost asked, waking up.

"I'm making notes about this translation program in our heads," Ow'llent explained, "I'm trying to log any inconsistencies and variables."

"How much battery do you have on your phone?" Kosa asked. For the life of jer, Wind had no idea why the Terrans always referred to their communication devices as "phones." Every Terran he'd ever talked to or overheard had referred to their communication device, which was usually built into armour with a holographic interface, as a "phone." The other aliens in the galaxy called them Devs, a derivation of "task device."

"We all lost ours in the crash. If yours works, why haven't you used it to send a signal?"

"It's like your Allie. It doesn't have any connection out here! It's just my research tool. No long-range transmitter. It can scan objects, take data, make notes, and take photos."

"Ooh, take one of me." Stares struck a pose, raising one arm in the air and the other towards the ground, throwing back jer head.

"She doesn't want to break it," Crenkleost grunted.

"Very funny, you overgrown *samdu."*

"What's that?" Crenkleost asked with eyes narrowed.

"It's a scaled, slug-like creature," Wind explained. "We also call them shit slugs because they look like turds."

Crenkleost growled slightly. Stares laughed, clearly unafraid. Wind wondered how long it was before the Strenoi, who was used to being intimidating, was driven to the point of attack by all the nonchalance towards him.

"I suppose we should make some sort of a trolley," Flugger began, "to pull our gear?"

Kosa snorted. "What, like luggage? No, if we get attacked, we'll need all our important stuff on our person. Rammy and I can take the Terran and Pir-An FPs in our packs."

The first invention each culture had created after they developed prolonged space flight was a molecular assembler to feed their crews without the need for hydroponic bays or chefs on board. Most starships had hydroponics to provide plants for their occupants to enjoy, as Terrans got depressed without vegetation around them, and most ships grew enough produce for at least one meal a day. The molecular assemblers, aka food producers or FPs, provided most nutrients. When the Rips joined the war, the Pir-An quickly manufactured and sold a Rip version to both sides. They made a killing when the Rips started buying them and sending them home to their communities. No one had bothered to do a study on how this impacted Rip society, but had they considered it a viable inquiry, they would have noticed a decrease in migration and an increase in reproduction. Perhaps someone from the Accord worlds should be paying attention to what was happening on the small backwater planet.

The machines were small, about the size of a Terran drip-coffee machine, with a slot on the top, a twisted spout for liquids, and a tray on the bottom. Wind retrieved jer hunting bag from jer locker and slid jer machine into it after producing a small meal for Stares and jerself. Kosa produced two meals as well, then wrapped the machine in Ow'llent's blanket. As she slid it in, she cast a glance at the Strenoi, as if to question whether the alien wanted her blanket back, but was waved off. Ow'llent was too busy typing.

When everyone had eaten, gathered all supplies they could find (including first aid kits for Flugger), and used the makeshift bathroom facilities, Stares gathered them around in a circle.

"OK, so say goodbye to *Starship 330307*. *Misery* is our new home. We'll go the opposite direction the Strenoi came from, as we know that way is a dead end. Sound good?"

"All except the part about calling the ship *Misery,*" Kosa mumbled.

When everyone else nodded, Stares walked over to the captain's chair. As the aliens began to chat amongst themselves, je unzipped the upholstery. From between the fluff in the seats, je pulled out a modded MP5-PL99 submachine gun. A portion of Wind's eyeballs that had never felt air before grew cold when jer eyes widened. The basic shape of the gun was standard, but the stock and forearm were silver-plated, matching Stares' skin perfectly, and the trigger itself was dark blue. There was an amplified laser sight and a pistol grip. Stares caught Wind gawking at it and shook it at jer.

"*Bh'rith'jikx*, right? I somehow completely forgot I'd stashed this here until we were talking about guns last night." Je rummaged in the upholstery and pulled out seven rifle magazines. Je lifted the flowing silk around jer stomach and slid the magazines into clips on a belt designed to hold them.

"Where the hell did you get that?" Kosa demanded, approaching.

Stares sniffed. "This one I bought myself."

"They don't sell those to civilians."

"Yeah, on dumbass Terran colonies. On Ripplia you can buy whatever the hell you want. Where do you think I got the guns mounted on the bottom of *Starship 330307*?"

"Wait, Rips are running around with MP5s?"

"You think we'd fight in your stupid ass war for five years and then crawl back to our sludge pile and eke out an existence? *Borkas* are going to be extinct!" Je pointed a finger at Kosa, then at Crenkleost, who had crept up behind Kosa to check out the gun too. "Your people introduced us to space flight. Or, as you so call it, *elevated* us. So, thanks for the gift, *yurtl-nakers*. I think I'll keep it."

Kosa and Crenkleost exchanged a look of shared horror that would have made Wind laugh if je wasn't so insulted by their reaction. Why did the other species think Rips were children who couldn't be trusted with anything sharp? No, that wasn't it. The Accord species treated the Rips like they were born criminals. Je looked at Stares, bolstering jer suspicion that je wasn't just some bored mercenary. Je had an agenda and monetary backing from someone. But who? Or what? And why?

"Why were you bothering me so much to hold my sniper rifle when you had this beauty?" Wind asked, deciding to keep jer more concerning questions for when they were alone.

"We had to talk about something," Stares replied. "Here, I'll be the nice one. You can hold mine."

Je passed the weapon over. Wind ran jer hands over it, inspecting it. The militaries had only ever let Rips buy outdated hand-me-down rifles. And Wind never bothered to fight over the loot of the dead – je'd found the Strenoi sniper rifle by accident. Je directed the MP5 away from the other people and sighted down it. Je gurgled saliva in jer throat, jer people's way of whistling in appreciation.

Je faced Stares and nodded deeply to express what je was going to say next was entirely serious. "I will mouth your cilia if you let me use it. You can have my rifle."

Stares snorted. "You have to do a bit better than that. But you can carry it for a while if you promise not to make a mess all over it."

"Mouth your cilia?" Kosa began.

"Don't. Don't ask. Just don't ask," Klenni interjected with a shudder. "And don't try to think about it."

Wind ignored the further insults as je played with the SMG.

They walked for hours through endless hallways. All were the same dull gray and held the same faintly glowing sconces. The halls never altered in shape or size. The Pir-An, though they barely carried any gear, kept the team walking at a slower pace than the long-legged Rips preferred, but Wind didn't mind. Stares hadn't asked for the SMG back yet, and je couldn't keep jer eyes off the beautiful gun.

"You keep caressing it like that and I'll get jealous," Stares said from beside jer.

"Of me or the gun?" Wind asked, surprised by jer own retort.

Stares laughed. "Finally loosening up, I see."

"How far have we gone?" Kosa called to Klenni. She and Crenkleost had argued over who would take point, so Stares had ordered them to walk beside one another. Behind them strode Ow'llent and Rammy, who had been chatting about their theories on the translation program. The Pir-An trailed behind the odd pair, tendrils intertwined as they walked. The Rips followed after. Wind didn't mind being at the back. Stares claimed it was the best spot to direct from, though Wind was skeptical whether je had commanded anyone in jer life.

The group stopped as Klenni called to Allie. The A.I. flew with a lazy sway towards the Pir-An, who typed code into it when it hovered by her fingers.

"If any of you want to access the mapping program for some reason, you need to bypass the administrator controls and then run a command to parse location fragments. I couldn't get the code to do it automatically. The memory protection is too complex without a hardwired bypass system."

Kosa wrinkled her nose, which Terrans usually did when they smelled something bad. "I use this thing to show me workout videos."

"Klenni has a secondary career in computer science," Flugger explained, the hint of pride in his voice unmistakable.

"Maybe she can tell us what these symbols mean," Crenkleost said. "I thought it was flakes of dust in my eyes, but look!" He pointed at the wall to their right, near the end of the corridor. Wind blinked as if to reset jer eyes. At five feet off the ground shone the faintest of symbols. Everyone except Ow'llent took a step closer. The Strenoi had the best eyesight of the bunch and the Pir-An the worst. Their eyes were composed in a way that allowed them to see in saltwater without irritation, but nature compensated by making them near-sighted. Despite jer people's lot in life, Wind was thankful je was not born a Pir-An.

"I can't see a thing," Flugger said. Klenni shook her head, turning back to Allie.

"Eh! I see it!" Rammy exclaimed. "It's like a *fleur de lis* with the petals moving."

"A flower is what I see," Ow'llent said.

"Yeah, sorry, what I said is another Terran language. I see a flower, but a stylized one."

"Me too," Kosa agreed.

"It looks like a sucker plant," Stares commented. "Like it's going to open up and snag an insect."

"Do you have any pleasant creatures on your planet? Anything aside from shit slugs and killer flowers and whatever those Borks are?" Kosa asked.

"*Borkas*. And no. Why do you think I'm so tough?"

Crenkleost snorted. The Strenoi did this so much Wind wondered whether his nostrils were growing sore.

"Is it the same on every corridor?" Ow'llent asked.

Kosa pointed at it. "Allie, take a picture and mark this on your map."

The A.I. beeped slightly, its noise for acknowledgment.

CHAPTER 10: KLENNI

Since noticing the patterns at the ends of each corridor, it was hard not to see them. Klenni had Allie take a photo of each one, even one that was the same as a previous version and had the A.I. run a simple comparative analysis that wouldn't tax the robot's battery too much.

Klenni intertwined her tendrils with Flugger's, sending him love and support. Her husband was not the most physically active of Pir-An, but she had married him for his mind, not his legs or arms. She was glad he had those, of course, but she didn't think any less of him for not being a strapping brute like the Strenoi, a slightly smaller Terran brute, or a weird Rip. In fact, Klenni was extremely thankful he was not a Rip. She did not like having the Rips behind her.

Me either, Flugger told her, in her head.

I don't like this place at all, she pulsed back. *I don't understand how everyone else is so calm.*

She and Flugger did not exchange actual sentences telepathically but thoughts and emotions. She could not explain it to someone who did not have telepathy, but to her, it was as if she received images, words, and emotions from Flugger, and her brain reordered it into a language – she was aware she was not hearing him speak, but at the same time it felt as if she was. The Pir-An, with their ability to breathe underwater, had evolved this mind-linking as a way to communicate while submerged. Most Pir-An could have full conversations with others if they wrapped their tendrils together, and some, like Flugger, could delve into the minds of those he simply touched. Some Pir-An could do neither. While these people weren't shunned in society, they were the first to accept posts on alien worlds, to work beside others who did not commune this way. Klenni did not envy these disabled Pir-An, as communicating with Flugger without speaking was intimate. She assumed it would be the same for a Terran who could not whisper or a Strenoi who was unable to blink their inner eyelids, which they sometimes did to communicate affection.

I'm very glad we are still able to talk together without them understanding, Klenni said. *I was probably the only one not happy when that pulse made us understand one another.*

No, I felt the same way. I don't want to get to know these aliens.

Rammy and Ow'llent are ok.

Terrans are like amsuns, Flugger communed. *They fly around and get into everything, causing trouble. And those Strenoi will eat us first if the food producers break.*

Shells, husband, you worked with both for years. You know they don't eat sapient beings.

The Rips do.

Rips are barely sapient. To cement their alliance in the Accord, the Terrans and Strenoi should attack Ripplia and wipe them out.

Flugger twiddled the tendril on his free hand, suggesting agreement, though Klenni had only been making a dark joke. This had been happening lately, before this mission. She and Flugger hadn't been seeing things the same way. They bickered more often than not, and little things about him had begun to irritate her disproportionately. This situation had thrust them back together, but how long before they started to fight again?

Klenni stared at Rammy's back, but she couldn't think about Flugger with the two Rips behind her saying suggestive things to one another. Were they a couple? Shells, why did she care?

"Another crab-thing," Kosa said, peering close to look at the symbol. As Crenkleost leaned forward to also examine it, Kosa pointedly moved away. Klenni held in a giggle. The Terran and Strenoi were so similar they should be friends. Then again, if the Terrans and Strenoi species did eventually team up on a galactic scale, they would be a hard force to stop. While Klenni agreed with Flugger that both races were aggressive and often rash, she didn't think the Terrans would stoop to attacking Bubble or other Pir-An worlds simply for resources. At least, she hoped not. She also didn't think the Strenoi would allow it, as they only attacked races that could fight back. It had something to do with honour, which Klenni thought was a waste of time but beneficial to her people's security. She imagined her parents and friends back home on Bubble. Picturing them under attack, getting shot, made her tendrils ache.

"That's three crab-things so far?" she asked.

"Three crab-things, six *fleur de lis*, four bubbles, and two images of a tower," Ow'llent intoned.

"It's a dick," Kosa said. "The tower thing looks like a dildo."

"What's that?" Stares asked, bounding over. Kosa let out an exasperated sigh.

"A Terran sex-toy," Rammy explained.

"Ooh," Stares clapped jer hands together. "Right! You … *men*, right? They have hanging things, and the *women* have holes."

To everyone's surprise, Kosa laughed loudly.

"Yes, I guess," Rammy admitted. "I mean, we also have people who don't identify with the sex they are born in and –"

"Can I see it?"

"What? My dick?"

"Yes."

"No!"

"Why? I won't touch it." Stares gave the Rip version of a saucy grin, which looked more like a demented leer, jer teeth on display. "Unless you want me to."

"Jesus, no!" Rammy recoiled backwards two steps. "I mean, un, no thank you."

Stares pouted.

"You can touch my cilia," Wind suggested to Stares.

"What's the point of that?" Stares sighed dramatically.

"Alleviate boredom?"

"Are you two going to have sex or what?" Crenkleost demanded. "Your shitty flirting is driving me insane."

Klenni shuddered. "Don't even say that! You don't want to see that – it's like two *lavegs* ripping each other apart."

"What's a *laveg?*" Stares asked.

Klenni wished she had could make the exasperated facial expression Kosa often gave to Stares. Ow'llent typed something into her wrist device; the *laveg* popped up holographically. It was an amphibian from Bubble with dark blue skin, teeth so large they were always exposed, and a darting red tail. Its mating consisted of a fight to the death.

"Ooh, pretty." Stares smiled.

Klenni caught Kosa and Rammy sharing an expression of disbelief.

"How do you know what Rip sex is like?" Stares asked Klenni, jer expression innocent but jer eyes denoting mischievousness. Flugger's tendril wrapped around Klenni's.

"Don't engage!" he cautioned telepathically.

Klenni took his advice.

"I think we found Klenni's pornography preferences!" Stares sang when Klenni offered no explanation. Klenni couldn't stop her face from turning light purple.

"Ignore them," Flugger urged. *"We'll be out of here soon enough."*

"How do you know that?"

"We have to be, or I'm going to kill them myself."

"Just Stares."

"No promises."

Though Klenni had spent years on Terran and Strenoi ships as a navigator, even the tersest of ship battles was never as bad as this situation. Perhaps it was because if a ship were attacked, they would be dead instantly – there was no rending of flesh, no suffering. She could not comprehend how the rest of the group was not unnerved; even Ow'llent, who was not a soldier, didn't appear frightened but intrigued by the mystery of the symbols. Klenni didn't sleep a wink the night before; visions of those creatures bursting into the room permeated every thought. Not only that, but seeing how everyone but she and Flugger were able to fight was frustrating. Sure, she had a gun and knew how to use it, but she would be completely vulnerable if a creature made it past her weapon. And these larger, stronger, and more seasoned warriors with claws, teeth, and agility meant she and Flugger would be the first sacrificed for food or as cannon fodder. And while the others had carried the Pir-An on their backs, how long would this benevolence last? True, they couldn't navigate without Klenni if the ship they found had no way of finding home, but they were dumb aliens – they wouldn't think of that. They'd fill their guts and then realize their mistake. They also had no real need for Flugger; Rammy fidgeted and pulled on his ear a lot, which indicated he had nerve damage, at least by Pir-An standards, the Rips were born clinically insane, Crenkleost would be too proud to ask for help even if his arm were hanging off, Ow'llent was old and probably dying, and Kosa had purposely damaged herself by digging needles into her flesh to decorate her arm with pictures. And one of the pictures was a fish! Klenni was afraid to ask what it represented.

There was a reason the moniker "Fish Food" was a common insult directed towards Pir-An. Every species in their galaxy had fish in their waters and ate them. Even the Pir-An ate lesser fish. And while Klenni knew the difference between her species and a fish for consumption, now that their situation was getting worse, she was convinced the other species saw her people as one step off the dinner plate.

They continued walking. And walking. And walking. There was no end to the corridors, no change except for the symbols. Eventually, it seemed like the group entirely forgot where they were. The Rips made more flirtatious jokes to one another, Kosa and Crenkleost got in a heated discussion about tactics in war, and Rammy and Ow'llent discussed their Ph.Ds. Klenni was interested to hear that Rammy had joined the military to help pay for his education. He had almost enough saved to cover his upcoming Ph.D. studies and planned on being honourably discharged in six Terran months. He was already accepted into a university back in Canada, a country on his homeworld of Terra, and was just wrapping up his Masters. Ow'llent complained about the rigidness of the Strenoi academic structure – it seemed they shared the same problems relating to tenure as the Terrans and Pir-An. Klenni wanted to join in and talk about her time in Computer Science, but Flugger, sensing her desire, urged her not to. She pulled her tendrils from his in annoyance but did not interject all the same.

They walked all day, except for a few breaks for food and water. Stares halted their progress.

"Alright, let's stop for the night," je declared. "I'm hungry."

Kosa took off her bag and set it against the wall. She reached inside and pulled out the Terran food producer.

"What have we got?" Rammy asked, passing his bag to the Pir-An on his way to his corporal, as their FP was inside.

Kosa pulled out a couple of pill bottles that contained the recipe, so to speak, for the machine. "Wraps or sandwiches?"

"Sandwiches." Rammy sat on his heels, rocking back and forth. Kosa dropped in two pills, and after a moment of dull whirring, the machine produced two square pieces of food, which Rammy scarfed into his mouth. Kosa ate slower but with big bites. Klenni refrained from asking what type of sandwiches they were eating, fearing it was tuna.

She waited while Flugger readied their food, a stew of mussels, cockles, and seaweed in a thin broth, the bowl edible. The Strenoi's food was more carnivorous, consisting of meat and a few vegetables in a pile they held in their hand. The Rips produced a thin wafer and what looked like jerky.

The group masticated in silence. Klenni watched the rest of the group as they ate. Wind played with the SMG between bites, Stares leaned back on one hand looking at the ceiling, Ow'llent fiddled with her Dev again, Crenkleost and Rammy concentrated on their food, and Kosa stretched her legs. Her muscles flexed as she placed one leg in front of her and extended her torso over it so it was nearly parallel to the floor. Sure, the Terrans might be flexible, Klenni admitted, but they were dumb as shell. They couldn't even make a plasma weapon before the Pir-

An showed up. She glanced at Rammy. Well, *he* was smart. She sighed; her anxiety over being trapped here was making her jump to all sorts of specieist conclusions.

"So," Stares began. "We're not tired yet. Let's go around and introduce one another again."

"No way." Kosa shook her head from where it lay on her leg. Her hair swished back and forth, just skimming the floor. "I'm not doing this."

"Doing what?" Stares demanded.

"I'm not getting to know all of you and then we become friends and two people fall in love and one of us dies. It's not going to be like the movies. We're doing a fucking job here. We're not *bonding*."

"Fine. Let's talk about how many of one another's people we killed in the war. You go first, you snarky bitch."

Kosa's eyes narrowed. "You really want to know, you stupid Rip? I've killed dozens of your people. Dozens."

"What do you Terrans say? All is free in love and war."

"Fair," Rammy corrected.

"Yeah, it's a fair assessment. One thing you Terrans got right," Crenkleost said. "War and love *are* freeing."

Kosa snorted. "Love, eh? You have a brute of a woman back home?"

"What do you mean by that?" Ow'llent asked calmly, but her lips rose off her teeth slowly, deliberately. Kosa looked at her, then snarled. Ow'llent snarled back.

"Corporal …" Rammy began.

"No, I don't care if I made a shitty, specieist joke. This mission is hard enough without walking on eggshells around everyone."

"It would be easier if we could call the Terrans *encims*, which is what they are. Bottom feeders that breed like insects and live in their own filth," Crenkleost cut in, glaring at Kosa across the hallway.

"No one needs to fight," Klenni broke in.

"Shut up, fish food," Crenkleost snapped. "You two are lucky we're letting you tag along. You don't think I can navigate?"

"I won't be beholden to you!" Klenni stood, wrenching her hand from Flugger, who tried to hold her back. "You Strenoi and Terrans think you're so strong and so tough, well, guess who owns you? *We* do! All your economies filter through *us*. At the press of a key, we could render your inflation through the roof. We can lower or raise your interest rates based on our whims. You're so indebted to us you should be giving us your children as slaves to move big rocks around. Which is what you're good for!"

"What did you say to me?" Crenkleost demanded, standing up.

Klenni stuck her chest out at him, raising her gills off her neck, which is what she would do if a large predator approached her in the sea. "I said: keep the peace, you big dumbass. You too, Kosa, you … what did Stares call you? Snarky bitch."

"If you weren't so beneath my level, I would squash you like a bug." Crenkleost glowered, his wide mouth settling into a thin line. His large head was lowered, his body crouched, his teeth exposed, and his claws extended.

"Keep it in your pants," Kosa muttered. "Can't you tell you're being goaded?"

"I have half a mind to finish where we left off!" he barked, turning to her.

"What, under me?" Kosa snorted. "I don't care about your claws or teeth. 'Half a mind' is correct on your part."

"Corporal," Rammy said softly. Crenkleost had begun to growl low in his throat, his hand opening and closing over his large knife.

"Calm your shrivelled balls, Delaney." Kosa took a small knife from a pocket on her boot and began cleaning her fingernails.

"You think you're so … cool," Rammy turned on her, standing up. "But you know what everyone calls you? Crazy Kosa. And not because you're a beast on the battlefield, which you are, but because you are so goddamn intense. All you do is look for fights or someone to hate-fuck. Grow up."

Kosa looked up at him after a long moment of continuing to clean her thumbnail. "What did you say to me, Private?"

She was giving him a chance to take it back, Klenni realized. The group waited. Even Crenkleost seemed interested in what was going to happen. Rammy's mouth hardened. His jaw tightened.

He did not apologize. "I call you corporal as a mark of respect, but, in truth, I report to Stares in this situation, so I can say whatever I want to you."

"Not if you want to keep breathing."

"Oh, please," Rammy crossed his arms over his chest. "There's Crazy Kosa again."

Kosa lunged to her feet. She took a swing at Rammy, who blocked it at the last second. Kosa swung again with her other arm, a wide haymaker, and Rammy ducked. Kosa's aim was wild, her cheeks flushed. She focused and took another shot at Rammy, striking through a block to hit his gut hard enough that he stumbled. He held his stomach as she took a step back, her eyes wide.

"Fuck sakes," she said, rushing back to the wall opposite and sitting down, placing her head between her knees.

Klenni took small backward steps towards Flugger, watching as Rammy looked at Kosa, then turned and went to sit beside Ow'llent. Crenkleost looked at Ow'llent and Rammy, then Kosa, and sat down on the floor between them, saying nothing to anyone.

"That was great!" Stares clapped jer hands. "Now we know each other a little better."

CHAPTER 11: RAMMY

He woke first. Ow'llent snored beside him on the floor, and Crenkleost lay in the middle of the hallway. Kosa was curled up under Ow'llent's blanket, away from everyone. He watched the slow rise and fall of her back for a moment, unsure whether or not she was feigning sleep. Had he been too harsh? The stress of the situation caused him to lash out; he was sure of it. It had nothing to do with Kosa's being very much like his father, right? Rammy sighed.

His assignment to Kosa's unit hadn't been as worrisome to Rammy as it had some other PFCs. He was content to have an intense CO because her leadership style made sense to him. She shared his father's demanding, overconfident personality. Of course, there were differences, as Rammy's father didn't have a temper, but Rammy had a feeling his father would have taken Kosa's side in most things. And now he didn't even have AJ to complain to. AJ would have let Rammy vent, then downplayed the entire argument. He would have put on his "Kosa expression" to make Rammy laugh. Then he would run his wonderfully deft fingers through Rammy's hair, down his chest …

He shuffled into a sitting position to shake away those thoughts. What brought *that* on? He was trapped on this crazy spaceship with a bunch of aliens, and he was worried about his father? He was ruminating on the man who had unceremoniously dumped him? Didn't he have bigger issues, like being murdered by Frankenstein-creatures? Then again, what did it matter if he were killed if he couldn't please his father or AJ? It's not like someone else couldn't take his Ph.D. candidacy to study ancient alien ruins.

He rested his wrists on his splayed knees and studied the rest of the group. The Pir-An resembled two pill-bugs squished together, as usual. The Rips slept flat on their backs with their heads against the floor. Wasn't that uncomfortable? More importantly, weren't the Rips supposed to be on watch? Wait, did the group even set a watch? He couldn't remember. He couldn't remember anything past his argument with Kosa.

He stood so he could get a better view of everyone. He picked up his rifle. Despite the emptiness at both ends of the hallways, the hairs on the back of his neck rose. Someone or something was watching him. He walked over to the symbols. They were glowing now, a faint green. He leaned closer. He glanced back at the others. Still sleeping. He slipped into the other hallway and jogged to the end. The symbols here weren't glowing. He returned and stepped gingerly around the others to make it to the hallway they came from before they stopped. The symbol here wasn't glowing either, and it was the *fleur de lis*. He licked his lips as he tried to recall what it had been last night. He returned to the group and picked up Allie, who was conserving power next to Kosa.

It was easy enough to project the photos. The last one was of the crab. Not the flower. He dropped Allie. The A.I. unit sank slowly down to the ground.

Why would it be different? How could it be different? He ran his hands down his face, pressing hard into his skin. What do the symbols mean? Rooms? Directions? A flower was what … hydroponics? The crab – food?

Water? Bubbles – no, that would be water. Or it could be cleaning. The phallic object … he was at a loss. But these were alien. A crab to them could mean engineering for all he knew. Why was it glowing? He crossed to it again.

While his BA and MA were in Classical Mechanics, he harboured a deep interest in alien technology and was tying the two together for his Ph.D. A thrill ran through him – what a puzzle this was! What if this ship functioned entirely different from anything he knew? What if it used High-Temperature Superconductivity? Or applied quantum science in a new way? Or maybe it was macromolecules? He took a step back. No, let's simplify. If it were glowing, that would mean it had power. Or maybe it was a connection? Maybe … he went back to Allie. He managed to bring up the map the A.I. was plotting as they walked. It looked like they were travelling in an angled spiral. That would make sense. They had reached the end of the hallway, at least according to the map. The next hallway was the last one before it turned back into itself.

"It doesn't make sense!" he whispered. "There were no doors. No indication of doors. Nothing but the hallways!"

He slumped to the ground, running his hands over his face again. He pulled on his lobe, hard. It was like that final exam question in fourth year that had stumped him and still plagued him to this day. While the other students wrote or typed, he had stared at the tablet, stylus held over it, for almost five minutes, trying to figure out where to start. He had blanked. The same vexation from years ago bubbled inside the kettle that was his gut, threatening to geyser out a scream of frustration from his throat.

Four symbols. One glowing. Wait. Things that glowed on Terran ships were indication lights. They were switches. Toggles. No one had thought to touch the symbols yesterday. What if the symbols weren't specific places but routes? It made no sense to design a ship that way, but these *were* aliens. Maybe it made sense to them.

"Hey, Stares!" he exclaimed.

"What?" je asked, instantly awake, lifting jer head off the ground to look at Rammy.

"Want to do something foolish and crazy?"

"Why, Rammy, I thought you'd never ask." Je rose to jer feet the way Dracula emerges from his coffin, using jer cilia to rise straight up without bending jer knees, and walked in jer strange hover towards him.

"Push that," Rammy said, indicating the symbol.

The others began to wake.

"Is this wise?" Flugger asked when he saw what Stares was about to do.

Crenkleost snorted. "You don't get credit for waiting."

"Fortune favours the bold," Kosa muttered after. The Strenoi looked at her.

"That is a better saying," he admitted after a moment.

"One of our greatest generals said it over twenty-five hundred years ago."

"It's a good one. No wonder you kept it."

Kosa pushed herself off the floor. "Is Stares going to blow us up, Private?"

Rammy glanced at her. "No, I don't think so."

Stares fidgeted at if impatient, jer hand hovering over the symbol. Rammy nodded, and je pressed jer hand against it. Everyone braced themselves for something, anything.

Nothing.

"Way to get our hopes up for a quick death," Ow'llent said as she rose to stand.

Rammy sighed. "I was certain … wait. Stares, don't touch anything else."

Stares hand, which had been ready to push the symbol again, dropped to jer side, dragging jer shoulders into a dejected slump. Rammy bolted into the next hallway. This time, at the end of it, was a door.

He returned, skidding into the room. "There's a door, guys!" He pumped his fist in the air. "I knew it! This place reconfigures!"

"It what?" Klenni asked.

"It reconfigures itself. Just the inside, I'm assuming. I was looking at the map Allie had created, and we were spiralling into our original path. These hallways all must rotate somehow, which is why we have been walking forever with no change. Allie's plotting is correct, but the map isn't – the ship has been moving hallways around on us, behind our backs, so to speak. It's been keeping us in very subtle circles."

"That seems … extravagant," Ow'llent said. While her wording was neutral, her tone suggested 'insane' was the word she wanted to use.

"I would agree, but how big is the ship? It looked to be dozens of levels tall. It's possible just one or two levels shift. Perhaps it has something to do with energy dispersal or –"

"How do we get out then?" Flugger asked.

"We have to get to another level," Stares suggested.

"Have you seen any stairs?" Flugger demanded.

Stares' lips rose off jer teeth. "I said what we had to do, not how we do it, fish face."

"Ok, no more arguing," Rammy declared. "And no more mean-spirited comments. We all know the Rips are crazy. We all know Strenoi are arrogant. We all know Terrans are emotional. We all know Pir-An are stuck up. So let's accept our cultural flaws and move on. Let's work as a team."

He expected the most opposition from the one person who provided immediate support.

"Yes," Kosa agreed, her face hard but her eyes contrite. "Rammy is … not wrong. I … I'm sorry for my actions yesterday and what I said … to everyone. We need to work as a team if we want to escape this fucked-up place."

Ow'llent nodded. "Fine by me."

The Pir-An nodded as well.

Stares shrugged, and Wind said nothing, as per usual. Crenkleost looked at Kosa and Rammy.

"I'll fight with you like I fight with my own people," he said, then paused. "Wait, what I meant was that I would fight alongside you."

"We got it, shit slug." Kosa grinned with a hint of teeth.

"Glad you understand, sucker flower." Crenkleost gave her the same 'smile' back.

Rammy considered their sibling-like bickering to be better than active antagonism.

"Wait, that was awfully easy," Ow'llent said.

"What was?"

"All of us getting along, especially after last night's episode. Who kept watch last night? No one woke me for my turn."

"When I woke up, you were all asleep," Rammy said.

The tip of Ow'llent's tongue flicked out of her mouth. "I'd say we were drugged."

"Maybe they wanted us to press the symbols?" Stares suggested. "Maybe they put us to sleep so we'd get a good rest and reset our brains? On the other hand, if they are watching us, maybe they're getting as bored with our walking as I am?"

Flugger took a small instrument from his pack. Rammy, who had watched a few episodes of *Star Trek: The Original Series* in an undergrad Media Studies course, compared it to a tricorder. Flugger held it against his wrist and pressed a button, which triggered the machine to take a few drops of blood.

"Nothing residual is in my system," Flugger said after looking at the readings. "Should I test everyone?"

“Don’t touch me,” Stares hissed and backed up a full five feet. Rammy had forgotten the Rip’s dislike of physical contact. Stares and Wind’s odd flirting seemed to contradict jer personal bubble preference since all their jokes were sexual.

“Yeah, fuck it,” Kosa chambered a round in her shotgun. “Let’s see what’s in that door you found.”

It took them a few minutes to figure out how the door even functioned. Stares volunteered to open it, pushing on the left, then the right. It didn’t move. In the centre was a round orb. Je pressed jer hand to it, and nothing happened. Je pushed it gently, and it swung away from jer like the flap on a dog door but moved only three inches above the ground before returning to its original position. Je turned to look back at the group, then shrugged and gave it more effort. The door rose and hung parallel to the floor. Rammy peeked his head into the room and looked upwards; a hinge suspended it. He finished entering and waited for the others, eyes on the door the entire time.

“Odd,” Ow’llent commented when they were all in. “I wonder if this is the normal way they open doors or if it is special to this room?”

“What is this place?” Kosa whispered.

The room was large, about fifty feet in diameter. The circular shape threw Rammy off, as he had expected another square or rectangular room. How did this fit with the map? Before he thought to ask Allie to show it, his surroundings distracted him. No, distracted was hardly the word. The expressions on the faces of his companions ranged from mesmerized to horrified, except for the Rips. Wind appeared jer usual bored self, though je had let the SMG fall to jer side. Stares’ eyes shined with interest.

The room was organized like a museum with themed displays in five areas against the wall. The middle of the circle contained a large table, but the controls along the side indicated it was likely a workspace. There were no chairs. The table was not what everyone was staring at. They were looking at the bodies strung up on the walls.

Clockwise from where the group stood, mounted so their feet hung three feet off the ground, were two Pir-An, two Strenoi, two Terrans, a Rip, and a Dirge.

"It's like a ghastly art gallery," Ow'llent breathed.

"More like a fucked-up butterfly box," Kosa replied.

"What's a bitter-flea box?" Stares asked.

Kosa replied without looking at the captain. "Back in the olden days on Earth, people would catch beautiful insects called butterflies, kill them with gas, and mount their bodies in a glass box. They would often have signs beside them indicating species. It was a messed-up hobby."

"They caught some big ones here," Stares replied, approaching the Rip on the wall. "Anyone you know?" je called to Wind. The other Rip looked closely at the person and shook jer head.

Rammy and Kosa slowly approached the mounted Terrans.

"Are they dead?" Kosa asked.

Rammy took a step closer. "I hope so."

Someone had hung the bodies naked, arms and legs akimbo. The man was of Earth-Arabic descent, the woman Caucasian. They were in their late twenties if Rammy could posit a guess. For some reason, the man's flaccidly dangling penis was the hardest thing for him to look at; it lay against the man's thigh, drooping sadly. The woman's breasts sagged as if deflated.

"Are they … like … embalmed?" Kosa narrowed her eyes as she attempted to discern what had happened. "They look … flat."

"Someone will die for this dishonour!" Crenkleost roared. Rammy jumped, and Kosa spun to face the sound. The Strenoi male stalked back and forth in front of his suspended people, words issuing from his mouth for which no translation came into Rammy's mind. Crenkleost must be speaking a different Strenoi language, like when Kosa swore in Japanese. Ow'llent's face was tight with her lips pulled back in a snarl.

Rammy turned his eyes to the mounted Strenoi, internally berating himself for finding it morbidly fascinating. The dead female's reproductive system was similar to a Terran's, from what Rammy could tell, but hairless. The male's genital region was almost entirely flat, except for a large slit.

Oh right, Rammy recalled, *their dicks descend.* Their urethra exited somewhere else, almost like a Terran woman's. He wanted to inspect them more, from a scientific angle that bordered on voyeurism but wasn't sure he wanted Crenkleost's anger directed his way, given the Strenoi's extended claws. His chest rose and fell so quickly it bordered on hyperventilating.

"They have removed the insides," Flugger said from where he and Klenni were examining their people. He held out his tricorder-like instrument. "My tool can perform rudimentary x-rays – there is nothing in there to x-ray. They are skins. No organs and minimal bones."

Crenkleost roared again.

"I hear you, *mikata*," Kosa said, her voice low. Rammy glanced at Kosa sharply. She usually reserved that Japanese word, meaning ally, for those in her squad. She slammed her hands against the wall beside the Terran female body. "This is fucking disgusting. Tell you what? Let's smash that table over there. Then we'll find who did this and pin *them* to the walls." Her eyes gleamed with the desire to destroy.

Crenkleost nodded briskly, pulling his gun off his back and readying the butt like a club.

"They're studying us," Stares interrupted their approach.

"What?" Kosa demanded, eyes still on the table, her shotgun held above it.

"Look!" Stares pointed at the screen mounted beside each corpse. "For the Rip, it lists our stats, you know, average height, weight, gestational growth." Je used jer finger to scroll through the information. "It has everything! It talks about how the roamer Rips move from camp to camp based on the *Borkas* mating patterns." Je frowned, then bared jer teeth, rising on jer cilia and leaning over the screen like the grim reaper. "What the hell!? It says we're a nomadic society barely functioning in civilized terms. You know what, I'm going to smash the table too!"

"But that's true," Klenni pointed out. "Ripplia *has* a nomadic system with no formal or central government and no democratic process. Aren't the Terrans and Strenoi helping you create a unified government?"

Stare paused on jer way to the table. Je looked away as if ashamed. "Yeah, ok. Helping. Sure." Jer tone turned sour.

"You can't expect everything to be perfect overnight. It took Bubble centuries after civilization to create the constitutional monarchy we have today," Klenni pointed out.

"You guys have a royal family?" Kosa turned to her.

Crenkleost grumbled at the delay of table destruction.

"Yes, a ceremonial royal family and then elected officials."

Kosa nodded, pretending not to care.

Rammy couldn't help it; he chuckled. "You are interested in royalty, Corporal? Are you following the royal wedding back on Earth? The English one? Do you have a weird hat to wear on the big day?"

Kosa crossed her arms over her chest. "So what if I do? It's fascinating. My best friend and I were going to travel to England to watch it, as it corresponded with my next shore leave. Did you know the English royals have been around since the year 1100?"

Rammy smiled like a fool to picture tough-as-nails Kosa sitting in front of her vidscreen in her bunk, wearing her military garb but also a bright blue fascinator, her eyes glued to the Royal Wedding.

"1100? What year are your people on?" Crenk asked.

"2243."

"I thought it was longer?" Ow'llent probed.

"It is! They're liars – they started tracking time three thousand years ago!" Stares pointed. "You can look at all the races' info on the charts if you swipe upwards."

"Before I explain our ridiculous system, how can you read that?"

"It's in Rip," Stares replied.

Rammy approached the Terran chart. "There are options to read it in all our official languages! What! Why? Why wouldn't it be in the Alien language?"

"They're messing with us," Wind said from jer position near the Dirge display. Je was leaning against the screen holder, watching the group. "I don't believe this is for their benefit. This is for us. To fuck with us again."

"Have you ever been fucked, Wind?" Stares asked.

Rammy heard Klenni's exasperated groan and agreed with her sentiment.

Wind shook jer head. "No. I don't want to risk pregnancy."

"Wait, what?" Kosa asked.

Rammy scrolled through the charts. "You Rips don't have birth control?"

Stares shrugged. "No. We have a low birth rate. Any baby born is needed to make the clan stronger."

"What if the person doesn't want to or can't raise the baby?" Ow'llent asked.

"It's similar to your family units," Stares explained. "We're raised more communally than Terrans or Pir-An. But Rips of breeding age give the baby to their parent as the primary caregiver. They are usually old by then and thus turn from hunting to raising the young. When we get old and can no longer make kids, we'll settle down, maybe find a partner or two if we feel like it and raise our kid's baby. It makes perfect sense."

"You know what makes more sense? Birth control!" Kosa exclaimed.

Stares shook her head. "No, it's doesn't. Besides, how would that work?"

"A condom."

Stares cocked her head to the side. "What's that?"

"You know, when the male ejaculates …." Kosa began but stopped when she saw Stares' eyes were wide and jer head still cocked to the side. Rammy wasn't sure whether Stares was interested or confused or a mix of both. Kosa looked at everyone else. "You all … orgasm, right?"

"If they're good enough," Ow'llent joked. Crenkleost snorted. Klenni nodded vigorously while Flugger refused to engage.

"We orgasm too!" Stares exclaimed, placing jer hands on jer head. "I don't understand!"

Rammy had been reading while Kosa conducted her inquisition. "Oh, I see. Kosa, everyone else, the Rips … this is fascinating. They're true hermaphrodites – what happens is when they orgasm, it triggers their body's attempt to self-fertilize. It's a form of parthenogenesis."

Kosa frowned. The word clearly didn't help her understand what he was saying.

Crenkleost blinked hard. "Every time they orgasm, they get pregnant?"

Rammy scrolled further. "Well … yes, but most of the pregnancies don't take. This is very confusing, but it looks like their DNA undergoes a mutation sequence upon implantation; if the DNA of the zygote is too close to that of the parent, it self-aborts. This explains why Rips don't have a lot of differentiation in their appearance!"

Crenkleost repeated himself. "Every time they orgasm, they get pregnant?"

Rammy nodded. "Yes."

"Even when they jerk off?" Kosa asked.

"We don't masturbate." Stares sniffed. "Our sexual urges don't work that way. It's … it's hard to explain."

"I don't want to know," Klenni said.

"Sure, you don't." Stares winked.

Klenni sighed.

"Hey! I didn't know I could only get pregnant a few days a month!" Kosa exclaimed, looking at the Terran chart.

Rammy looked at her. "No shit, Sherlock."

Kosa ignored him. "It says here my body releases different hormones based on my cycle, and only during a certain time can I get pregnant. Weird! I just get the NoPreg shot every five years. I never really asked what it was doing to me."

"How do *I* know more about your body than you do when I've never even *seen* a vagina? Didn't you go to sex ed?" Rammy asked, unable to keep the disdain from his voice.

Kosa raised an eyebrow at him. "You think I was paying attention in sex-ed, nerd?"

"How about you, raptors?" Stares asked. "How do you have sex?"

"The normal way," Crenkleost replied. "Insert something into something else."

"That's not very inclusive," Rammy noted.

Crenkleost raised his eye-ridge and chuckled salaciously. "I didn't say where things were going or what things were being inserted. I'm pretty sure my comment includes everyone at some point."

"But not Stares," Klenni joked. Rammy and Crenkleost turned to look at her. Flugger's cheeks were dark purple in embarrassment, but Klenni's tendrils were waving gently. Rammy wasn't sure what that meant, but he laughed to encourage her – she seemed to want to be part of the group.

"Good one, Klen," he added.

The Pir-An's tendrils entwined around one another, so they now resembled Twizzlers licorice.

Ow'llent laughed. "If you're asking everyone about breeding, Stares, I'll spare you the reading. Our women decide who they want to breed with, given we have so many more men than women. They select the man, hopefully get pregnant, and raise the child in the household with their partner who usually is not the father. We often have three or four households in one house, at least amongst the High Born. Generally, one woman is the household 'Mother' whose job is to raise the children; sometimes it is a man too, but not as often. The others oversee different Estate responsibilities, work for the government, or are in academic positions like me. The Workers have a similar setup, but they don't track their bloodlines as we High Born do. At least officially."

"We can find out who our father is in the records," Crenk added. "But we aren't supposed to acknowledge it or act differently around him. We call all the men in the household uncle and all the women aunt, except for the House Mother or House Guardian if they're male. The House Mother is often the birth mother of at least a couple of us, sometimes not."

"Why?" Kosa asked.

Ow'llent shrugged. "That's how we do it."

"No, I mean, you have babies with someone you're not partnered with? Why?"

Ow'llent listed off reasons, using her fingers. "Strength, intelligence, virility. Or if our women are what you call lesbian – we don't have specific words for sexual orientation like you do – they simply pick a male for breeding purposes. Or they go to the clinic for implantation if they'd rather not do it the fun way. It's hard to explain to a non-Strenoi; it's rather nuanced."

"What do the men think of this selection process?"

Crenkleost's chest inflated slightly. "It's a great honour to be chosen to breed."

"Are you allowed to breed with someone you love?"

"Of course!"

Rammy and Kosa exchanged glances. "Sounds kind of nice, actually," Kosa admitted.

Ow'llent leaned on her pike while she skimmed the screen in front of her. "What do you do?"

Klenni giggled. "The Terrans are crazy. The males choose the partners."

"That's not true!" Kosa exclaimed, insulted. "Ok, maybe centuries ago, but now it's equal. For the most part."

Ow'llent chuckled. "Listen to this! *It took the Terran race centuries since civilization to become space-born due to their divided continents, but equally due to a unique patriarchal system based on the domination of one another. Racial division, dichotomies, multitudinous religion, and restricting female access to breeding choices created war after war. Since condemning racism and sexism, their scientific process has quadrupled in development, allowing them –*"

"Wait, we're the only patriarchy?" Rammy asked.

"Pir-An have always been entirely egalitarian," Klenni explained, her tone just shy of boastful. "Your social system fascinated us when we first met. Based on what Ow'llent said, I suspect it's because we Pir-An cannot create young by accident. I fertilize eggs, and the male will carry them. It's never an accident."

"Do you have sex, though?" Rammy asked.

"Oh, of course, but it's entirely for fun. Reproduction is separate."

"If you don't have … what we have … how do you do it?"

Klenni blushed lilac. "We have orifices, and our tendrils and fins are very sensitive."

Rammy glanced at Ow'llent, the biologist. She grinned as if enjoying how awkward the conversation had gotten. Clearly, this topic was nothing new in her studies as a biologist and geneticist. Klenni was handling it well, but Flugger was hiding behind her. Rammy stepped this way and that, trying to get him to look at him – he was a doctor, he should be able to answer the questions. "But if those body parts weren't designed to encourage reproduction, why are there –"

"I don't get the Terran system," Crenkleost interrupted. "Why wouldn't the breeders have control over their own bodies? And over who fertilizes their egg? Again, I don't get it."

"It's because Terran men are horny all the time and equate power with fertility," Ow'llent explained.

"Hey!" Rammy protested.

"Oh, come on. You guys will fuck *anything*."

"That's not true!"

"It says it right here!" Crenkleost pointed to the screen in front of him. "*Any object in existence has been an attempted sex toy by at least one Terran.*"

"That's an alien's perception!" Rammy protested though he couldn't keep the laughter from bubbling up in his throat. "Where are they getting this information?"

"Our porn, probably," Kosa said, unoffended. She wasn't known as Crazy Kosa simply for her temper and skill on the battlefield. Gossip about Kosa's one-night stands was a common topic in the corps. After every battle, she was known to hit the het-bars to look for someone to blow off steam with. Then again, with the

STI-shot being mandatory and free, most soldiers generally weren't sitting around reading most evenings like Rammy. Kosa had a couple of steady boyfriends throughout his time on her squad, but never for longer than a few months.

"What about the Dirge?" Rammy asked, glancing over at where Wind was still standing in the same spot, near the dead, furred alien.

"Dirge don't have babies," Wind said simply.

"I know that, but I never learned why," Rammy admitted.

"Dirge are older than the Pir-An," Klenni replied. "They were in the stars before we ever left the sea."

The group approached the hanging alien skin. It appeared less floppy than the others, possibly because of the fur. The Dirge was a large beast, as tall as the Rips and wider than the Strenoi. They had stocky, powerful, furry bodies, resembling that of a Terran bear, but with long fingers and opposable thumbs on both sides of the hands. The Dirge did not lope when they walked, like an animal of that size would, but moved with the grace of a species much thinner. The Dirge's head was bovine, with a long snout, square teeth, and large eyes. But Dirge, unlike cows, had long Terran-like hair, their main vanity, and they often wore it long or braided. Not quite minotaur, not quite bear, the species also was not unintelligent. Far from it.

Klenni continued speaking. "The Dirge were masters of genetic manipulation centuries before even we met them. Then they had a war. I'm not sure what it was about, but they ended up launching a bio-weapon: a virus that sterilized their entire species. Even by implantation, they couldn't reproduce; all the sperm lost its potency, all the eggs shrivelled. All Dirge have been vat-grown clones for the last few centuries. They are engineered with a universal sex organ. They have sex, but only recreationally, like us."

Rammy stared up at the Dirge. He had always assumed they were simple brutes one step up from animals. That a deep intelligence could be housed in that cow-like skull made him wonder. Were Terrans on the same path? Would their hubris one day be their undoing?

The group stared up at the Dirge in silence, all considering what Klenni had said.

The creature let out a massive roar that filled the room with undeniable rage and despair. Everyone screamed in response. Even the Rips.

CHAPTER 12: KOSA

After the initial shock, everyone's heads darted back and forth, desperately trying to see whether the Dirge's scream had been in response to something specific or just general agony. Nothing about the room appeared different, and silence surrounded them.

There was something warm under Kosa's palm and fingers. She had gripped Crenkleost's arm in her alarm, as one would in a haunted house. Her eyes widened, and she let go quickly as if his skin were scalding. It made her feel better that the Pir-An were still holding onto one another, Wind was retrieving jer dropped SMG, and Ow'llent and Rammy were pressed against one another, still looking around. The Dirge, after their outburst, had drooped, chin to chest.

Crenkleost looked down at Kosa. His chin raised slightly, and his eyes twinkled.

"Don't be embarrassed, Corporal." His magnanimous tone set Kosa's lip curling. "It's natural to go to the strongest in the room for protection." He gently tapped his upper teeth with his tongue, which she had seen him do earlier talking to Ow'llent. She decided to believe it meant he was teasing, the equivalent of a Terran wink. The anger rising in her chest receded with the gesture.

Kosa snorted. "What my body does involuntarily has nothing to do with my strength."

"It was only by luck you grabbed onto me?"

"Go fuck yourself, *Crenk*."

Crenkleost laughed loudly, then fell silent when the rest of the group looked their way; Rammy was glaring and Ow'llent frowning in disapproval. Crenkleost leaned towards Kosa, as if he were going to say something else. His natural odour reminded her of the sea back home. It wasn't fishy, but a scent of salt and sandalwood mixed with iron. She hadn't noticed this during their initial spar. Kosa sniffed at him in a manner she hoped was dismissive, but she couldn't keep the right side of her mouth from raising in a gentle smile at the thought of the waves crashing against the shore. Komorebi was blessed with unique sand that was so white it resembled snow, though not many people visited because the temperature was less than ideal for swimming. But Kosa had always enjoyed walking the beach, the wind ruffling her hair, the scent of the ocean washing over her. It was where she had felt the calmest growing up.

Crenkleost tapped his tongue to his teeth again and turned back the Dirge.

As soon as his gaze left her face, two wrinkles grew between her eyes. How was this raptor growing on her? She had been fighting his people for her entire career, had seen them as the antagonists of her entire adult life. She looked at the others – Rammy and Ow'llent had moved to inspect the Dirge, the Rips were standing together watching, and the Pir-An were looking at one another but not talking, their tendrils intertwined. Other than Rammy, Crenk was the only competent person here. And even Rammy was the most basic of soldiers, uninterested in continuing his career after the monetary boost that service provided him. While Kosa couldn't blame Rammy for pursuing other goals, she also considered it a waste. Still, she was glad he was here rather than some others from her squad. At least he obeyed orders without question. Wind proved jerself a good sniper, and Stares made up for lack of skill with jer no-holds-barred enthusiasm, but the Pir-An were a pair of dorks, and Ow'llent was old. Slim pickins in terms of soldiers. Moreover, since accepting Kosa's leadership in combat situations, Crenk had become respectful and downright chatty – he was easy to talk to. He was a good soldier, and based on what she'd seen previously, a brilliant pilot, although a little impetuous – what was he doing here in the middle of uninhabited space with Ow'llent? She glanced at him.

"They're unconscious," Ow'llent said, disrupting Kosa's thoughts. "But very much alive. We need to get them down."

Kosa went to the screen. The writing was gentle sloping symbols that reminded her of home, though it was far from Japanese. It was the Dirge lexicon.

"I got this," Stares said and jumped. Je soared gracefully three feet up and over onto the screen. Je balanced on jer cilia like a ballet dancer and reached towards the Dirge. Kosa dipped her head to peer at the Rip's digits. The cilia resembled long, thin ivory fingers with suction cups on the bottom. She leaned closer. The suction cups contained thousands of even smaller cilia moving frantically. These minuscule tendrils held up Stares' entire weight. Kosa wasn't one to show her awe, preferring to keep her cards close to her chest, but the way the Rip balanced on these thin tubes was nothing short of fascinating.

Stares, oblivious to how Kosa was staring at jer feet, placed jer mouth against the leather-looking clasps holding the Dirge to the wall.

"What are you going to do?" Rammy asked. He'd only just finished speaking when the Rip bit down on the clasp and snapped it in half with jer teeth. Ok, so Stares had a good idea for once.

"Remind me never to make out with Stares," Ow'llent remarked.

"Not interested." Stares laughed, then moved on to the other side. Crenkleost and Rammy moved to brace the Dirge from falling as Stares bit the other strap. The three-hundred-pound alien fell forward with a groan, Rammy and Crenk barely catching and balancing them on their shoulders.

As they laid them on the ground, the Dirge moaned, head moving from side to side. The group stood around them, unsure whether to try to move the Dirge and where they would move them to.

"Alright, people," Kosa began. "Flugger, give me a medical assessment of our friend here. Crenk and Ow'llent, help Flugger if he needs to move the Dirge. Rammy, you go scout the door."

"Klenni, care to join me?" Rammy asked.

Kosa had to keep herself from scoffing as the short Pir-An followed quickly after Rammy, her tendrils floating. Did the fish have a crush on Rammy? Kosa shook that thought from her brain – not important.

"What should we do?" Stares asked.

Having two idle Rips was asking for trouble. Kosa pointed at the two of them, then at the other side of the room. "How about you try and see if you can remove those screens from their holders? See what powers them."

"I'll fiddle with the table," Wind suggested.

"How about I fiddle with you?" Stares laughed.

"I don't give a shit if you jerk each other off while you're doing this; just get it done."

Stares chortled, skipping over to the screen while Wind headed towards the table. As they left, Kosa realized she should have sent Rammy to assess the table, given his obsession with alien tech. He sometimes spent his evenings fiddling with any Strenoi or Pir-An device he could get his hands on. Dammit. Well, no one challenged her, and she wasn't about to admit to a mistake.

Flugger extracted his medical scanner from his bag and began a sweep of the Dirge's body.

"Nothing physical aside from likely starvation and the beginnings of dehydration," he said definitively after a few minutes. "Dirge are hearty, but I have no idea whether they are infected with some sort of disease or whether the aliens have done something to them my basic tool can't determine."

"Could it be PTSD from being mounted on the wall?" Crenkleost suggested.

"They have that in Strenoi culture?" Kosa asked.

"Unfortunately," Crenk replied. "My, ah, my best-cousin, he –"

"Incoming!" Rammy called.

Crenkleost dropped the story without hesitation and hefted his rifle. Kosa pulled the shotgun from her back.

"How many?" she yelled.

"Dozens!" Rammy exclaimed, removing the mag from his gun and checking the rounds before reinserting it. "ETA twenty seconds!"

"Ok, we're going to hold them off here!" Kosa ordered. "Flugger and Ow'llent – guard the Dirge. Klenni, behind the table – guard Wind, who is sniping. Rammy, Crenk, and I will take opposite sides – every third creature if you can handle it."

"What about me?" Stares asked.

Kosa glanced at jer. "You, with that SMG, you go front and centre. Mow them down, and we'll take the stragglers."

"But I want to use the SMG," Wind whined.

Kosa took a precious second to send Wind a glare so vicious jer mouth opened in a hiss. "Do as you're told."

Wind closed jer mouth as everyone moved into position. Stares smirked as je took the SMG that Wind reluctantly held out. Wind snarled, and Stares snapped jer teeth in response. Stares positively bounded to jer assigned spot.

Kosa moved to stand across from Crenkleost, near the doors. "Protect the Dirge! They are our best chance of finding out what the hell is going on in this place."

As the clanking and moaning of the creatures approached, the cacophony of their howls reverberated through the metallic hallway. The forced allies in the laboratory waited with tense composure. To their credit, no one was freaking out, not even Flugger. Kosa's chest swelled with pride. The pent-up frustration in her soul dissipated as she looked at the crew; her *raison d'etre* was to lead people in battle. The best years of her life had been when she had been given her first command, when she was tasked with bringing a group of disparate people together to succeed in a goal, whether it was simply staying alive through a battle, destroying a particular Strenoi stronghold, or providing backup for another squad. Kosa's teams had always performed above average, which was why it grated on her so hard that she was overlooked for the position they gave to Caroline, that desk jockey.

But now, she was grinning as the creatures raced through the doors. She continued to do so as she opened fire on the monsters that were rushing to rip her to shreds.

The whine of Wind's shots and the subsequent splatter of the bullets hitting organic material broke through the rapid-fire of Crenk's rail gun and Stares' SMG. Klenni's small plasma handgun packed a powerful punch, the resulting sizzle of the weapon's discharge reminding Kosa of bacon on a skillet.

"I'm out!" Crenk called, flipping his rifle in his hands to use the butt as a club. Kosa's shotgun was quickly running out of ammo too. Based on numerous sims and real combat situations, Kosa decided not to reload but to save twelve slugs for later. She slung Airi onto her back and brought out her big knife, the bowie.

"Klenni, fall back to the Dirge! Wind, only take shots if you have a definite kill. Stares, with us!" Kosa called. At that moment, a creature with the head of a Terran man, a Strenoi arm, and a robotic body lunged out of the group at her. It clasped her around the throat. Kosa brought her knife up and sliced through the arm; it severed easier than she expected. Black viscous blood splashed down onto her exposed midriff. The blood was hot like fresh coffee – not boiling but scalding enough to make her gasp. The nauseating combination of burnt cooking oil and heavy iron filled Kosa's nose. The blood oozed over her skin, as thick as used motor oil.

She broke the creature's hold by shoving upwards on its remaining elbow, then lunged forward with her knife, stabbing the monster through the eye. As she did so, two more reached for her, their long nails raking across her exposed skin. She kicked one and shoved the other. As they stumbled backwards, Wind's sniper rifle let out two sharp retorts, and both their heads exploded, splattering Kosa in more viscera.

More and more came through the doorway. Kosa readied the knife, licking her lips and spitting when she tasted the salty blood. Crenk and Rammy were fighting creatures back-to-back, the Strenoi's fists stunning the creatures and then slicing them with his claws. Rammy had always been good with a knife, so he was dancing around the outstretched and grasping arms of the creatures plaguing him, jumping forward for quick slices.

Stares, the insane being that je was, matched the creatures claw for claw. Je leapt forward, wrapped jer legs around a creature's waist, and rammed jer jaws into its neck, vampire style. Je spat out blood as je jumped off the creature, who flailed on the floor as it bled out through the jugular.

Ten more creatures poured through the door. Kosa gritted her teeth, tossed her knife to the other hand, pulled out her service handgun, adjusted her stance, and released six shots in short succession, hitting five of the creatures in the head and the sixth in the shoulder. Crenkleost leapt for the wounded one, bashing in its Pir-An head with his fists as it mewled pathetically. As the creature crumpled, three more jumped on the Strenoi.

Ow'llent let out a feral howl as she leapt into the fray, slicing at the creatures with her pike. Ow'llent had the forms down, but she moved with jerky, stilted movements that betrayed her inexperience in the real-world application of her formal weapons training. Still, she lopped off limbs and gave much-needed relief to her fellow Strenoi, allowing Crenkleost to crawl out from beneath the pile of bodies and begin his fight anew. Klenni followed Ow'llent's lead, rushing towards the battle and firing into the crowd of creatures still entering the door.

"Fall back!" Kosa called. They weren't going to win this if they didn't regroup. It wasn't her first choice, but if the creatures tried to rip her apart or drag her off to be the next fixture on the wall, she would shoot herself in the head. The group backed up, using melee weapons to keep the creatures at bay. A furious howl sounded behind them.

How did they get behind us? Kosa had time to wonder as a mass of dark brown fur rushed past and grabbed Klenni away from the creature that had her captured by her large head. Klenni was tossed backwards to relative safety.

The Dirge tore into the creatures, massive limbs knocking them senseless, large hands dismembering those which survived the beating. The rest of the team didn't let them do all the work. As six creatures piled onto the Dirge, mouths and fingernails and claws digging into their thick hide, Kosa, Crenk, Rammy, and Ow'llent attacked from behind. Klenni used her pistol to keep them away from herself and Flugger as Wind dropped his rifle and raced towards the group, the knife je used to clean jer claws now applied to its proper purpose.

In a similar manner to the first time they fought off the creatures, the crew was left standing in a pile of body parts.

CHAPTER 13: STARES

Stares inspected jer red silken garments in dismay. One of the long sleeves appeared as if it had been attacked by scissors, and one of jer pantlegs was matted to jer thin thighs with the dark blood of the creatures. "My clothes!"

"You're better off than me," Kosa grumbled.

Rammy, who was also sporting splashes of blood on his shirt and several thin scratches down his arms, laughed at Kosa.

"Damn, Saito, you look like you were mud-wrestling the things."

Kosa's stomach had blood running down it, some of it her own from a gash near her collarbone. Her sports bra was splattered inky red, and her legs had rivulets quickly drying on them. Her pants had received a massive splash on the front. She glanced down at herself.

"Looks like I got my period early," she joked.

"How can you laugh?" Ow'llent protested.

"It was a good joke," Stares said. "Now that I understand how Terrans reproduce."

"No, it's not. It's crass to joke right now. These poor creatures were once Strenoi, Pir-An, Terran, Rip, and Dirge. My people. Our people."

"If we don't laugh, we go mental," Crenkleost said, his voice subdued. Ow'llent appeared to want to argue more, but the look on Crenkleost's face stopped her. His expression was pained, morose. Stares wasn't sure what was going on between the two Strenoi, but it was clear Ow'llent had struck a nerve. Stares wanted to ask for an explanation, but the Dirge was stirring. They had fallen to the ground again when it was clear the wave of creatures had receded.

"Klenni," Kosa ordered. "Go scout the hallway. Make sure no more are coming."

"That's not going to happen," Flugger said. His voice was stern, but he approached tentatively, his skin as pale as it had been the first time they fought the creatures.

Instead of agreeing, Klenni waved a tendril at Flugger, her wide eyes narrowing at him before she flounced off.

"We all have to pull our weight," Kosa said, staring at Flugger. "And since we don't need any navigation at the moment, Klenni can scout. And you can patch our wounds."

Flugger muttered something under his breath but did as commanded. He began with Rammy.

The Dirge pushed themselves to sit, looked around with blurry eyes, then fell forwards, catching their large head in their massive hands.

"Are you okay?" Ow'llent asked.

The Dirge groaned, then a thick tongue extended from the cow-like snout and licked dry black lips. "Yes," they said, head still resting between their knees. "I'm okay. Thanks to you."

"Why are you here?"

"Long story."

"It's doesn't look like we have anywhere to go at the moment," Stares pointed out.

The Dirge lifted their head and met Stares' gaze. The Rip had never met a Dirge before. Je had seen them from a distance, but je was struck by how soulful their eyes were, how intelligent. Like most of the sapient beings in the universe, at first glance, they equated the big brutish race of Dirge as just that – dumb hulks. Stares, generally not one for self-reflection, registered that if je wanted jer own race to be taken seriously, je should start by not making assumptions about others. Perhaps what jer people needed to make their case as an independent world was to learn from the other races already in existence. Without them knowing, of course.

"Please," je added.

The Dirge nodded. "Give me a moment to order my thoughts. I'm rather discombobulated by the rescue and subsequent altercation."

"I'm going to try and get that table working," Rammy announced. Flugger moved to wave his medical scanner over Wind.

Klenni returned. "We're good for now. I went all the way into the other hallway, and nothing."

"Good work." Kosa nodded as Klenni's tendrils wiggled with pride. Stares made a face. The female Pir-An had morphed from a standoffish, shy thing to a kiss-ass. Stares wasn't sure which was worse.

"Do you need anything?" Ow'llent asked the Dirge. "Some water? Food?"

"If you could assist me in moving to someplace without dead bodies, that would be ideal," the Dirge replied.

Kosa and Crenkleost immediately moved to help the Dirge stand, one on either side of the furred alien. Stares raised an eye ridge. Of course, once the Dirge joined the fray, the Sternoi and Terran loved them. Comrades-in-arms and all that. Stares had not fought in the military, was too young for the Strenoi-Terran war, but je understood the bond-by-blood mentality, primarily because je was starting to develop it for jer comrades. Je wasn't going to sacrifice jerself or jer goals for their lives, but je was beginning to see them as more than expendable.

When they slid down the wall to sit, a large sigh emanated from the Dirge. Klenni approached with a cup of water from her food producer. The Dirge took it gratefully as the group, Rammy excluded, encircled them. Flugger continued to scan and apply healing and antibacterial salve to those who needed it, moving on to Kosa's wound.

Ow'llent reached into her pack and pulled out a small box. Stares watched intently, wondering what was in it. Was it recording equipment? A bomb? No, wet cloths. Of course, the woman of grandparent age carried such a dull thing. Ow'llent passed two to Crenkleost, then three to Kosa, who accepted them with a nod of thanks.

Crenkleost said to Kosa, "You have blood on your back." She did indeed; it smeared there when she helped move the Dirge.

"Can you get it?" she asked. "I'll wipe you too."

"Ooh." Stares couldn't help jerself. "This is like the start of one of those porn holovids."

Kosa and Crenkleost's shared expression of exasperation made jer laugh. "Oh, your faces. I love it. You act like the worst thing in the universe would be if you two hooked up."

Crenkleost and Kosa exchanged glances of dismay.

"Get your weird xenophilia fantasies out of here, Rip." Crenkleost snarled. "We're adults. Even if we *were* interested in one another, which is weird to think about, joking about it is immature."

"Yeah, Stares, you're just jealous because you're the last person here I'd ever fuck," Kosa added.

Stares pretended to pout as Crenk began to wipe Kosa's back free of blood. Inside, je was laughing. Their pride made them both so easy to tease.

After a long drink, the Dirge cleared their throat. "Ok, let me tell you what I know. There were five of us. Asuun'sana. Rynveld. Sarah. Hunts Better at Night. And myself."

"What's your name?" Klenni asked.

"Hynd. I was abducted off a new planet we Dirge were studying. We call it 737C. An ice planet on the outskirts of our space."

"Why did they take you?" Kosa asked.

"I was the only one there. I was on a cursory assignment that isn't usually in my prevue; I was filling in for a colleague. I was to land in various locations, plant transmitters and trackers, and we would use the data to extrapolate on the stability of the planet for terraforming and study. But that's not important. One moment I was returning to my ship after placing a transmitter. The next, I woke up in this ship."

"We call it *Misery*," Stares cut in.

The Dirge blinked, then a ghost of a smile touched their lips. "Good name. Makes sense."

Stares beamed. Kosa sighed.

"When I woke, there was this Terran staring at me. A soldier she looked like from her outfit, with two arms covered in black tattoos and the palest skin I've seen on a Terran. She said her name was Sarah, and she had no idea how she got there; she had been on a training mission on Hartfield, one of the moons of Austen. The Strenoi woke next, and we had to subdue him by force before he would calm down. He was Rynveld, a diplomat from Strenovast. He had been heading to Harmony for an Accord conference when they were attacked by a ship that hadn't appeared on their scanners. All he recalled was his ship received a large jolt and lost gravity. He assumed the rest of his crew were taken or killed. Asuun'sana was a student on one of the Pir-An worlds, taking a walk in the woods. I forget which world. And Hunts was on Ripplia."

"What!" Stares exploded, spittle flying from jer mouth. "They abducted someone from our homeworld?"

"You only have *one* world," Crenk pointed out.

Stares hissed at him. "That's beside the point, dumbass. If these aliens know where our homeworld is, they sure as hell know where *your* worlds are! *Misery* could be an early scout ship. Their main fleet could be heading to our planets right now!"

"Given the number of creatures that have attacked us, they must have abducted many, many people," Klenni commented softly, her eyes wide. "How come we haven't heard of people going missing?"

"They're spacing it out by taking people from different planets," Flugger suggested. "People go missing all the time."

Klenni glanced at Rammy, still working on the table, then left to join him.

The Dirge turned to the rest. "We experienced a head-splitting translation mind-modification. I'm assuming you did as well?"

Ow'llent nodded. "I have some theories about what it did."

The Dirge nodded. "Me too."

"Enlighten us, please," Flugger asked, putting away his medical scanner, having finished his tasks.

The Dirge shrugged. "A brain sync? That's the only way I imagine it was able to translate colloquial terms. Either that or they have been monitoring us for a long time. Long enough to obtain a database of our idiomatic words and translations in all languages."

"I'm not sure what's worse," Kosa muttered.

"Once we could talk to one another, we began to wander the halls, searching for a way out. Other than Saran and Hunts, we weren't military. And we were hardly the cohesive unit your team is. Were you together before this?"

Crenkleost and Kosa chuckled while Stares erupted in a hefty belly laugh. "No! I had hired the Terrans and Pir-An to assist me in studying this ship. The Sternoi attacked us. *Misery* took us both in. We teamed up after fighting a first wave of the creatures."

"The creatures attacked us, but instead of killing us, they herded us to another room," the Dirge said. "Sarah and Hunts tried to fight, but there were too many. They must have gassed us then because we woke up as you found me. We were hung on the walls like meat for sale at a market on a backwater world. They injected us with various syringes, took samples of our blood, and eventually killed us."

The Dirge fell silent for a moment, staring at the floor.

"What did they look like?" Kosa demanded.

The Dirge shook their head. "I don't know. Every time they did something, they turned out the lights. It was pitch black, making it all the more terrifying because we weren't sure what was going on, could just hear the pleas and cries of the others. Their feet … they … they scuttle. They don't sound like any of us."

"They can see in the dark – that's something. And that means that bright light might be able to blind them," Crenk suggested.

Kosa nodded. "Good point. Is there anything else you remember, Hynd?"

"They never spoke to us, but they did speak to one another, a chittering language."

"How did the others … die?" Klenni asked.

"We knew it was coming. The others, the male Terran, female Strenoi, and male Pir-An, were on the walls when we arrived, already dead. They didn't murder anyone in the room. They turned out the lights, and we heard screaming – Asuun'sana. When they turned the lights back on, she was gone. The next time they turned out the lights, we heard shuffling, and she was back, in the state she is now." Hynd gestured towards the hanging bodies, their eyes wet.

"Sarah and Hunts put up a fight when it was their turn, but Rynveld simply called out that he wished us to die with honour. I thought I was to be next – I'm not sure how much time passed between what I call the drainings. Not only was hanging on the wall uncomfortable, but it was also exceedingly boring. I tried so hard to break the bindings, but eventually, I was too tired. At least we could talk to one another. Until I was the last one … insanity began to overtake me. And now, all I want is to see the sky again."

Hynd sighed again, head drooping.

"Hey, you're with us now," Ow'llent said, placing a tentative hand on the Dirge's shoulder. Her long fingers buried themselves in the coarse fur, squeezing. "I know you don't know us, but we have weapons. And a plan."

The Dirge raised their head to look at her. "I don't want to sound like a fatalist, but we're doomed. They're playing with us. The only reason you're all alive is that they want you to be."

"That might be true," Rammy called from the table, "but I bet they didn't expect us to have a xeno-mechanics researcher and a computer scientist here. We've discovered something that might give us an edge."

"Does it involve moving?" the Dirge asked. "Because unfortunately, I need to recuperate before I can go anywhere. I should be okay in a few hours." They paused. "You're not going to leave me, are you?"

"Of course not!" Kosa exploded. "We would never." She paused, looking at Stares, "Well, we might leave Stares if je doesn't stop being annoying."

"You can never leave me. When I die, I will haunt you."

"Do they have ghost stories on Ripplia?" Kosa asked.

Stares nodded. "Oh yes, it's rumoured if we die by a *Borkas* hand, our souls are trapped in the bog until we are avenged. If no one kills the *Borkas*, our souls are trapped forever."

Kosa pushed out her bottom lip. "That's a pretty cool myth."

"I know, right?"

Kosa smirked. "Ok, team, we're going to take a break here and recover for a few hours. At least here we can funnel any attackers. Rammy and Klenni, you tell us what you found. Wind, since you won't contribute much to the conversation anyway, you keep watch. Flugger, you have the next shift after jer."

As Klenni approached the group, she looked tentatively at Kosa. "I'm sorry if this is rude, but if we are going to die in the near future, would you mind if I touch your hair? I've always wondered what it felt like. I never got up the courage to ask any of the Terrans I worked with. We didn't really mingle after hours."

Kosa, sitting on the ground beside the Dirge, looked at the Pir-An. Her shoulder-length black hair had been pulled back in a tight bun for most of the trip on *Starship 330307*, but her elastic had snapped in the first fight. Now that her hair hung free, her strict face appeared softer.

"What?"

"I'm sorry." Klenni's face turned lilac, and her tendrils dropped. "I just, um ... Never mind."

"No, it's ok. Here. Feel away." Kosa stood and approached the Pir-An. "See? I'm not that crazy."

Klenni reached forward and gently caressed the Terran's hair, cooing. "So soft."

Stares glanced at the door, where Flugger was staring at his wife with his tendrils waving. Angry. Klenni glared back then turned back to Kosa.

"Want to feel mine too?" Rammy offered his short mass of black curls. "Can I touch your skin?"

"Okay, whoever is willing, while we wait for Hynd to rest, let's just have a touching free-for-all," Kosa said, somewhat sarcastically. Everyone joined in aside from Flugger, who stood back, arms crossed over his chest, and Wind, who was on guard. Terran hands ran down Strenoi and Pir-An skin, Pir-An hands touched Terran hair and

Strenoi scales, Strenoi touched Pir-An gills and Terran hair. Stares stood off to the side as jer companions assessed one another physically. When Crenkleost ran a finger tentatively over Kosa's tattoos, admiring the stylistic canyon running across her forearm, Stares darted forward and placed a hand on each of their shoulders, then retracted quickly. Kosa and Crenk turned to gape at jer.

"What?" je said. "I'm starting to like you guys, ok?"

CHAPTER 14: HYND

Though they didn't let on to the others, Hynd was in a great deal of pain. Being suspended for so long on the wall had made Hynd's limbs ache as if somebody had stretched them past their limit. And tapping into their adrenal reserve to fight, a conscious process not unlike a Terran consuming caffeine or cocaine, left their entire body incredibly sore. Shivers of pains constantly radiated from shoulder to elbow and elbow to wrist, as if targeted by an electrical shock. Their hips, knees, and feet shook. Their three stomachs churned with a throbbing combination of hunger and nausea, and their two hearts seemed to be thudding against one another, leaving their chest constricted. Hynd longed to lie down and sleep, but that was dangerous. Like a Terran with a concussion, it wasn't wise for a seriously injured Dirge to sleep – their body required conscious healing. It wasn't a sure thing they would die if they were to sleep, but it would prolong the healing process. If they suffered through two hours of conscious pain now, it would allow their circulatory systems to recover. Then they could sleep. They lowered their head as the other aliens talked around them.

These people seemed competent. And the Rips, as inscrutable as the race was, seemed less peculiar now. Perhaps it was because they had been around these other aliens who were closer in societal mindset to the Dirge.

Hynd let their head rest against their knees as they took deep breaths. In the days they had been suspended on the wall, they had often wondered: *why me*? What had prompted these unknown aliens to abduct them from the planet, to do this to them? There was nothing special about them. A typical tank gestation, a typical three years in the training and growth centre, and a typical school and workplace assignment. They were a mathematician and an engineer, but they loved the outdoors. The worst part about being on the wall was knowing they would likely never see a sky again, would never inhale the scent of pine and lavender on the breeze. They would never feel the brisk air of an ice planet ruffling their fur, would never again experience the delight of seeing a curious animal approach their camp, intent on discovering who the interlopers were on their land. Hynd resisted the urge to look up at the crew as they chatted amongst themselves. As curious as they were about them, about their relationships, they knew it was futile to get to know them.

No one was making it out of this *Misery*.

The crew settled down, using their food producers to generate a meal.

"Can you eat something?" the female Pir-An, asked Hynd. Like when you're incredibly hungover, the mere thought of food made their stomachs clench. The Dirge shook their head.

"No."

"But you need to build your strength back up," the Pir-An protested.

Hynd sighed. The Pir-An was correct; while the thought of eating was enough to make Hynd wince, they knew a small meal would indeed be beneficial. "Yes, alright. I can eat most Strenoi and Terran food. Something light."

After a few moments, the Pir-An returned. "Here – Ow'llent had some protein derivative."

"Ow'llent is the female Strenoi?"

"Yes, I'm Klenni. My partner is Flugger, the medic. Crenkleost, the other Strenoi, is a pilot. Our leader is Corporal Koharu Saito, but we call her Kosa. The Rip, Stares, was our captain back on our ship. Wind is the other Rip, the sniper. And Rammy is another marine, a private."

Hynd could only nod wearily, taking the proffered strip of jerky and nibbling at it. After a few minutes, it appeared the Pir-An had given sound advice; the food lessened the angry throb in their guts into a dull ache. Half an hour after that, they had raised their head and began to watch the group.

Klenni had moved back to assist the male Terran, Rammy, at the workshop table. They were talking animatedly, though Hynd, who had inferior auditory senses compared to the other races, could not hear their words.

Ow'llent typed into a Dev, though what she could be documenting, Hynd couldn't say. Flugger sat against the wall, eyes closed, away from the group. Kosa and Crenkleost leaned against the wall where Hynd had recently hung. The straps dangled above their heads, and Hynd had to force themselves not to stare at the fastenings. To help distract them, they focused on the aliens' voices: Kosa was explaining to Crenkleost about a Terran beer-drinking festival, of which Crenkleost appeared quite interested. Upon finding their eyes returning to the straps unbidden, Hynd forced themselves to watch Stares and Wind guarding the door. Stares' high-pitched laugh cut into the room at random intervals.

"Corporal, can I upload some data into Allie?" Rammy called.

Kosa nodded. "Yes, of course. Have you two discovered something?"

"It was Klenni. We think she's cracked their system's operating parameters. If Allie can run a translation, at least enough to determine a Y/N contingency, we'll be able –"

"Do it, please." Kosa sighed. She glanced at Crenkleost as Allie floated over to the worktable. "Nerds, am I right?"

Crenkleost chuckled. "They have their purposes."

"We heard that!" Klenni protested, her tendrils flailing while Rammy flipped them off. Hynd grinned to themselves. The amusement was fleeting but a welcome respite from the pervading dread that the others didn't seem to feel.

"Incoming!" Wind called, jer voice ringing through the room like an asteroid proximity siren on a space station. Behind it, Hynd could hear the growing clatter of running feet.

"Holy shit, they're fast this time!" Stares cried, turning towards the door and firing jer SMG into the hallway. Wind had already slung jer sniper rifle over jer shoulder and was retreating, unable to get off a single shot.

"Klenni!" Flugger called as Kosa and Crenkleost jumped to their feet and raced towards the door, knives out.

Hynd could only stagger to their feet, then fall to their knees. They hadn't had time to recover fully. And they were tired. So, so tired.

A group of creatures set upon Kosa, controlled attacks having replaced their shuffling gait and clumsy grappling. She began yelling orders.

"Flugger, Ow'llent cover the Dirge. Stares, get –"

"They got my gun! Help!" Stares cried. When je had stopped firing to change the magazine, one of the creatures had grabbed hold of the gun and wrestled it from jer just as je pulled back the bolt to load the bullet into the chamber. Stares attempted to wrench the weapon back to no avail.

No one could help Stares. Kosa could barely keep the three creatures hassling her at bay with her bowie knife, and Crenkleost was too far away.

"Hold on just a few minutes, Kosa!" Rammy called. "I'm opening an exit!"

As Hynd watched, powerless to do anything, the little Pir-An, Klenni, left Rammy and raced towards Stares. The Rip pulled on the SMG harshly, ripping it from the creature's grip, though je pulled too hard and ended up launching the gun sideways. It landed with a clatter five feet away. As Stares' head naturally turned to follow the course of the gun, the creature, with a red Rip's head and Dirge body, dove for jer, pushing jer to the ground and attempting to bite jer with its large teeth. Stares raised jer claws and jabbed them into the creature's neck, trying to either kill them or push them off. Despite jer no-holds-barred aggression, the hybrid was too heavy. It held jer down as Stares swore in its face and dug jer claws even further into its flesh, trying to sever the head.

Klenni, meanwhile, had reached the SMG and scooped it up.

She opened her mouth in a silent scream as she braced the stock against her shoulder and let loose on the creature on top of Stares. She cut it to ribbons with the powerful barrage of bullets, narrowly missing Stares jerself.

"Down!" Klenni screamed. The Terran, Strenoi, and Rip swung in her direction, saw Klenni armed with the SMG, and simultaneously shoved themselves off or away from their opponents and dropped to the floor. Klenni opened fire, spraying wildly, striking the creatures almost as much as the walls behind them. Black goo and blood geysered from the backs of creatures as bullets slammed into torsos, arms, and heads. As the gun ran out of ammo, Stares hoisted the dead Rip-Dirge up enough to roll out from underneath.

"Gun," je said to Klenni, holding out jer hand.

"I can see why Wind likes it so much." Klenni's lips rose slightly, but her tendrils twisted in the equivalent of a grin.

Stares cocked jer head to the side, studying Klenni. "You know what? Keep it for now. But you and I are going to have a lesson on aiming with big guns."

Klenni opened her mouth to reply, but nothing emerged from her lips.

Stares laughed.

"Ugh, I'm covered in blood again," Kosa muttered, rising.

"Looks good on you." Crenkleost laughed, also getting to his feet.

"Oh yeah? What if I said the same about you?"

Crenkleost leaned against the wall on his elbow, sticking out a hip. "Oh, I'm not considered very attractive by my own people, because of my big shoulders, but don't Terrans like these on their men?" He flexed.

Kosa raised an eyebrow. "That's a matter of –"

The clambering of footsteps and familiar groaning from the hallway cut her off.

"How many of these *yurtl-nakers* are there?" Wind grumbled.

Rammy rapped sharply on the table to get their attention. "Everyone over here! I've found another exit, but we're going to need to make a quick getaway. I think the door will only be open for a few moments."

Kosa listed off orders, yet again. "Hynd to Rammy. Ow'llent and Crenk, help them get through as fast as you can. Klenni, Flugger, you're after the Dirge and Strenoi. Wind, Stares, with me. Rammy, do your thing."

As ten more creatures clamoured over the dead bodies to get into the room, Hynd made for the door, wishing they could propel themselves with more than a stumbling gait. A headache blossomed behind their temples; bright spots burst like fireworks at the corner of their eyes. Two sets of scaled and strong arms braced them up, one under each arm, and they were propelled towards Rammy.

"Go! Go! Behind me!" Rammy exclaimed, waving a hand through a holographic orb projected over the worktable. On the wall behind him, between the hanging Terran and Strenoi skins, a doorway opened silently in its disconcerting way. Was it there the whole time? So close to where Hynd had been hanging, waiting to die? A skein of sanity snapped in the Dirge's brain.

The creatures attacked. Despite being faster now, they still employed brute force over skill. Kosa, Wind, and Stares met their charge with their melee weapons. Kosa and Wind stabbed and slashed while Stares used jer claws and teeth. Stares had perfected throat biting, leaping towards jer targets. Blood sprayed the room like a burst hose when je ripped out their jugulars.

"We're in, Kosa!" Rammy called. Hynd continued to watch as the three fighters dispatched the rest of the creatures, though not without sustaining damage. Wind sported a long gash in the leather of jer shoulder, dark purple blood seeping through, and Kosa had several gouges on her arms and stomach from claws.

Roaring and hissing erupted from the hallway as six more creatures entered the room. Stares was the closest to the hall door, and as je turned to escape, a Dirge-headed creature with Strenoi arms backhanded jer across the face. Stares fell to the ground.

"Kosa!" Rammy called. "The door!"

"Wind, take jer!" Kosa called and jumped towards the large creature, using both hands to block the downward strike that would have smashed Stares' stunned face in.

Wind didn't hesitate – je grabbed hold of Stares' silken shirt and dragged jer towards the others. Crenkleost rushed to help, stabbing a creature that had pursued Wind. As Wind moved past him, dragging the unsteady Stares, Crenkleost paused to watched as Kosa kicked the Dirge-

Strenoi in the stomach. When it hunched, Kosa slammed it in the nose with the heel of her palm, sending it sprawling backwards with a howl. Another raced towards her, and she settled back on her haunches, arms raised with fists guarding her face. She punched the Terran-headed creature in the nose with a fast jab, blood spurting down its face as it stumbled back. She spun in the same movement and threw a round-house kick at another creature. As yet another approached, Kosa yanked her knife from her boot and stabbed the creature through the neck, ripping the blade through skin to unleash a torrent of blood. More monsters rushed into the room, snarling and pushing at one another in a bid to be first.

"Kosa! Ten seconds!" Rammy cried, staring at Allie, who had a countdown projected on its interface. Kosa didn't seem to hear, too busy turning her knife on yet another creature.

"Koharu!" Crenkleost bellowed, his deep voice penetrating through the room. Kosa glanced back, taken out of the fight by Crenkleost's roar. She shoved another advancing creature backwards, then turned and bolted towards the door.

She made it with two seconds to spare, breathing hard as the door slid closed.

Hynd, breathed a sigh of relief despite not knowing the woman. Kosa and the male Strenoi appeared to be their best fighters. Stares lay prone on the ground, though je rolled over and clutched jer head.

"Where are we?" je groaned.

"Some kind of utility closet," Rammy explained. "Klenni and I managed to use Allie to translate the computer's code into one it could understand. It's not much, but I was able to use that to bring up the door codes for the room and discovered this area."

Klenni carried a screen from the other room. "I discovered that the screens are connected to the same network. As such, we can route Allie through one of them to open doors. I'm trying to find the system with the floorplans, but it's hard when the writing is in a different language. Allie is helping translate, but it's not designed for that, and it's sluggish. The battery is also getting low."

Kosa sighed. "Well, we're making progress at least."

"Thank you, all," Hynd said. They knew the group wasn't expecting a thank you or that they needed one, but without these people they would still be mounted on the wall, waiting for the moment when the lights would go out, and their unknown adversaries would enter to finish their life. Did Sarah or Hunts or the others see the aliens before they were killed?

"You're welcome," Wind said, nodding politely.

"Check out my hat!" Stares exclaimed, having wandered away during Rammy and Klenni's explanation. Je returned with a small metal bucket, which je had placed on jer head. The area of the room Stares came from was stocked with cleaning supplies, though why did the aliens need a bucket with all their technology?

The group stared at the Rip, then Kosa let out a braying laugh, sinking to her butt on the ground.

"Flugger," she said, her voice heavy with weariness. "Medical checks."

As the Pir-An stood, Ow'llent brought over her and Kosa's packs. The Strenoi had grabbed all of them before assisting Hynd in escaping. Hynd slumped down across from Kosa.

"Let me clean you up, again," Ow'llent offered to Kosa, reaching for her wipes.

"Why do you carry those?"

"I've never birthed children, but I have them on my Estate. You always need wipes."

Kosa's grin was warm. "Oh, I understand. My best friend's daughter, Yeva, is a toddler and always a mess. I call her my niece."

"Children are one part mess, one part sweet, and two parts beast." Ow'llent smiled the Strenoi close-lipped grin, but her eyes were warm.

"That was something to see," Crenkleost said to Kosa. Hynd turned their head to the pair. Interactions between Terran and Strenoi soldiers were always volatile and therefore interesting, but this was more curious than a fight because the Strenoi's tone lacked the typical resentment when speaking with a Terran. Crenkleost's voice held something else – respect.

"What was?" Kosa asked as Ow'llent used the wipe to clean the blood off the Terran's face.

"You took them out so quickly with your fists. I'm impressed."

Kosa's look was at first calculative and distrustful but softened. From Hynd's angle, the Strenoi's eyes held an earnest compliment.

"If you two are going to talk, then I'll tend to others," Ow'llent said, placing the cloth in Crenkleost's hand. As she left, Crenkleost leaned forward and dabbed at a three-inch cut running from Kosa's collarbone down towards her chest. Kosa looked up at the Strenoi face close to hers, and their eyes locked. Crenkleost paused in his ministrations, the cloth hovering over her flesh. Hynd blinked hard, intrigued, despite their fatigue.

Stares approached Kosa, removing the bucket from jer head and twisting it in jer hands.

"Thank you," je said quickly to Kosa, bowing jer head deeply.

"For what?"

"You saved me from having my head bashed in."

Kosa blinked hard. "Oh. Well, of course I did. You're on my team."

"Rips aren't used to being part of the Accord team," Stares explained.

"No problem, Stares."

Stares reached out tentatively, then squeezed Kosa on the arm, where she didn't have any cuts.

"Uh, thanks," Kosa replied to the gesture.

"What je did was equivalent to a big hug," Crenkleost explained.

Kosa blinked hard again. "Well, don't I feel honoured."

"Want me to show you how we kiss?" Stares grinned, leaning closer. Je opened jer mouth to reveal the fangs of an anglerfish.

"Ah, there it is." Kosa rolled her eyes but followed the gesture with a brief laugh. "I would have thought you were truly hurt without some weird comment."

Stares leaned back. "Nope! I'm as happy as a sucker flower during the drier season. By the way, is there anything you can't do, Corporal?"

Kosa paused as Crenkleost began to dab at her wounds again, moving on to the one on her jaw. Hynd couldn't keep their eyes off this strange trio. They had never seen the three races working in such harmony before. There were rumours of alien friendships on the aptly-named colony world of Harmony, but Hynd had never witnessed them. In truth, they had never been that interested in the treaties, formally called The Accord, between the sapient beings in the universe, preferring to do their work with their own kind or independently. Hynd hated politics, and the war had been one big political pissing contest. It had started over the most asinine of reasons: trade and resources. There were skirmishes over and on various planets for a decade until war had officially been declared after one particularly bad fight. And now that peace was declared, it was still the same old complaints about who "owned" which planet and trade taxation.

Kosa frowned, but not at the aliens. "According to my aunt, there's a lot I'm a failure at. But I'll admit I can't cut a bagel for the life of me. It's always weighted too far to one side, so I have a really thin piece and a really thick one."

"What's a bagel?" Stares asked.

"It's like a thick bread, in a circle. With a hole in the middle."

"What's bread?"

"What?" Crenkleost and Kosa intoned together.

"Rips don't eat complex carbohydrates," Hynd explained, despite their weariness. "That's why they're so skinny – their bodies only burn proteins and other vitamins. Carbs would likely sit in their guts like a rock, and they'd retain no nutrients from them."

"You never know unless you try!" Stares exclaimed. "Do you have any bagels in your FP? Can I try one?"

"How about you can have one when we get out of here? I don't want to piggyback you around this ship when you get indigestion or a blockage," Rammy called out.

Stares pouted; it appeared to be jer new favourite expression. Hynd almost smiled, picturing the Rip riding on the shoulders of the Terran. They may have been slightly off on the idea of what a piggyback was, but knew it was a form of rudimentary transport.

If we get out. Hynd's worry overtook their amusement as they watched Crenkleost pass the cloth to Kosa so she could clean his wounds in return. Flugger hovered near, waiting for her to finish so he could spray their cuts with a disinfectant and a cauterizing agent.

CHAPTER 15: THE CREW

The rest of the group let Hynd sleep, trying to be quiet, unaware that the Dirge's poor hearing made their efforts unnecessary. Unlike the other times they were forced to share a space, instead of splitting up by species and avoiding conversation, they intermingled.

The room was four feet wide and eight feet long and stored only the chemicals and Stares' "hat." There was not much space for nine people, especially with one that was three hundred pounds and almost seven feet tall. It also didn't help that Hynd was passed out on their stomach like a drunk, arms and legs splayed, snout pressed against the floor. Ow'llent sat with her back against the door, with Rammy and Klenni beside her. The three scientists whispered their theories on the aliens that held them hostage and what their "draining" was for. It was macabre but working through the situation helped calm and occupy their analytical minds.

It was clear Flugger was annoyed with Klenni, as he sat to the left of the Dirge, eyes closed. Klenni knew he was not asleep, that he wanted her to go to him and ask him what was wrong, that he wanted her to comfort him and tell him she was sorry, but she refused to comply. When they first met, Flugger was a stick-in-the-mud, a quality she had found cute. He had become far less rigid over the years, but it appeared this situation had brought it all back. As much as she wanted to console him, the other aliens were starting to like her, and Flugger should recognize that their best chance of survival in this situation was ingratiating themselves to the strongest people. Besides, she liked *them*. Kosa and Crenkleost, not as much, but Rammy and Ow'llent were scientists like her. And they were nice, normal people. While the Rips were still downright scary, she was beginning to rely on Wind's quiet seriousness. And Stares owed her one after Klenni had saved jer ass with the SMG.

Flugger kept his eyes closed but listened to everyone talk. He wasn't physically strong like any of the others, but he didn't understand why Klenni would latch on to them in such a way. They weren't to be trusted. He didn't assume they were going to turn on the Pir-An at any moment, but he knew that if it came down to it, these people would save their own kind over someone else. She didn't see he was only trying to protect her, and it only deepened his frustration. When he realized she wasn't going to sit with him, he slid further down the wall and began fiddling with his medical tool to distract himself.

Stares had been watching Wind for a full minute, but je never moved. The other Rip sat to the left of the chemical cabinet at the back of the room, watching everyone with jer red eyes, hardly blinking and body still as the wall behind jer. Wind had entered what the Rips called the Hunter's Trance, a deep state of meditation. Stares jerself had never been able to master it. Many times in jer youth je had been threatened by jer elders to practice it and had been told je was worthless if je couldn't hunt. Instead of buckling under the pressure, Stares spent more time on the roof of jer home, looking upwards, making plans. At the moment, je was studying all the chemicals on the shelf, admiring the labels with their fascinating alien lexicon.

Crenkleost and Kosa had no interest in hypothetical scientific inquiry or chemicals. As there was nowhere else to sit, they were relegated to sitting across from the Dirge, beside one another.

Kosa put her back against the wall, resting her wrists on her knees which were pulled up to her chest. It was the only comfortable position with the Dirge splayed out on the floor. Crenk slid down next to her. His double-jointed legs crossed at the knees, but his thighs were pushed tight and his calves were crossed under them. His shoulder brushed hers accidentally. Instead of snapping at him to keep his scaly skin away from her, as she would have a day ago, she thought nothing of the contact. In fact, she was glad he was here with her, and she wasn't stuck with only the Rips and the nerds.

They watched the Dirge. Hynd snored, their bovine lips fluttering. Drool inched out of their mouth, pooling on the floor.

The pair looked at one another, then broke into laughter. They quickly tried to stifle it when the Dirge shifted.

"Not to be specieist, but I hope I'm not that ugly when I snore," Kosa commented.

"Terrans are the least ugly of all the races. *After* Strenoi," Crenkleost replied.

"Oh really? You don't fancy getting down with a Rip? Or a Pir-An?"

"Can't say I haven't thought about it," Crenkleost joked.

Kosa wrinkled her nose. "Pir-An may look like," she lowered her tone "… food, but their planets are generally beautiful. If you like manicured beauty, that is." Besides the oceans, Bubble was a perfectly coiffed planet, down to the trees and even the grass. The Pir-An liked symmetry and order. They had machines that combed the beaches at all hours, and their cities were organized in symmetrical spiralling streets.

"I prefer a wild planet." Crenkleost looked straight ahead, his thoughts bouncing over memories of the worlds he had flown over and in during the war. "A planet where people haven't ravaged the land and tried to sculpt it."

"You'd like Komorebi then," Kosa said. "I was home six months ago for only a week, but after seeing my mother and my niece, I spent a day in the canyons. It's very serene. Terra is crowded, and we had destroyed most of the environment before the Pir-An showed up to help reverse some of it. On the colony, we wanted to work with nature. When we built cities, we made sure the trees and plants had their spaces within them and left giant preserves surrounding each. My ancestors were known for this iconic tree from Earth, the cherry blossom. We had festivals every year when they would bloom. It was very important to our culture, a symbol of focus on impermanence. We brought cherry tree seeds with us to Komorebi, to continue the tradition."

"You grew up on a colony world?"

"Yes – I've only been to Terra once for my military induction. Are you from a colony?"

"No, I hail from Strenovast. A smaller province. Unlike your Terra, we only have one continent. I'm from the middle – it's very hot there. There's not a huge Worker force, so we don't have a great deal of industry or money, but it's an Estate. Ris'anact."

"You don't like it?"

"Oh, I love it, though the heat is sometimes unbearable. But being a pilot was my dream, you know? The war … it was never about fighting you people – I just wanted to fly."

Kosa was surprised to hear this, given the abject antagonism from him when they first met but maybe that was based on Strenoi honour or even just the situation. Hell, she had snapped at Rammy only last night. For her, everything *had* been about fighting. Captain Airi, her role model, the one she had named her shotgun after, had been her impetus to join the corps when she realized dancing was not going to be her career. But had she truly *hated* the Strenoi? Or were they the target she had been pointed towards? Knowing Crenk and Ow'llent now, she could no longer say the Strenoi, as a people, were all her enemies.

This was … frustrating.

"What does the name mean? Kumurobi?"

Kosa turned to look at Crenkleost. He was leaning towards her, his voice low to not wake the Dirge. She met his gaze. Today was the first time she had been close to a Strenoi without being involved in hand-to-hand combat. His dark blue eyes reminded her of a husky – the iris filled the entire eyeball, a slightly darker blue along the outside, deepened by his burgundy skin. His pupil, slightly elongated but nowhere near that of a cat or a Rip, was dark purple. His eyes were lovely, she realized with surprise, breaking her gaze away.

She corrected his pronunciation. "Komorebi doesn't have a direct translation, but it describes sunshine filtering through the leaves of trees. Our world is very lush with a bright sun. The name makes sense. We only have a few pockets of civilization. The rest of the world is large, deep canyons. Not badlands exactly, but hard to farm. We terraformed the places we wanted to build on but left the rest to its natural state."

Crenk nodded. "That sounds pleasant. Strenovast is over-populated. Since the war, many workers were allowed to move to the colonies, but I've always thought about finding a smaller, less-populated planet when I get old. At the moment, I'm all for society, but as an old male,

I wouldn't mind a bit of peace and quiet." He paused. "If we get out of here."

Kosa's face hardened. "Oh, we will."

"I admire your determination," Crenk said. Kosa glanced at him. He was looking at the Dirge. Maybe he had been speaking to them instead of her?

"People!" Stares interrupted, approaching Kosa and Crenk. "I don't think these aliens have hands like we do. These bottles open weird. Look!"

Like the doors, the bottles opened a different way than they were used to. The bottle "broke" in half to open, but there was no liquid. Instead, there was a mesh that kept small pellets from falling out unless they were shaken.

"Strange," Kosa agreed. "But maybe they don't like having their chemicals in liquid form."

Stares shrugged. "Maybe." Je sat down beside Kosa. "I'm *bored*," Je complained.

Ow'llent was the first to notice the Dirge shuffling. It had been three hours since they had fallen asleep. Hynd pushed themselves to sit. "That is so much better," they said, stretching. A shoulder audibly popped, and the Dirge sighed. Both Ow'llent and Crenkleost shuddered.

"Yeesh," Rammy agreed.

Hynd laughed, a deep *gwuh-fah*. They pushed themselves to their feet and rose. "What's the plan?"

The group had discussed it while they waited for Hynd to wake.

Kosa, as usual, took charge. "Klenni and Rammy have modified Allie, our A.I. Unit, to work as a key. It can scan for openings and send out a ping on the alien's frequency that opens doors. Our plan is still to get off this level. Try to find a ship."

"I still don't understand why we aren't going to try and stop the aliens," Crenkleost said.

Kosa shook her head. "No, our priority is to escape."

"But if we can stop them, we can prevent others from getting captured and killed. It would be the honourable thing to do."

"And if we die in the attempt?" Kosa answered her own question. "If we die, everyone still gets captured. If we escape, we can let our governments know what is going on. That will prevent more deaths."

"They won't believe us," Flugger pointed out.

"Agreed." Ow'llent nodded. "We should escape and say nothing."

"If that's the case, if there's a chance we can stop them right here right now, we should take it!" Crenkleost said.

"That's stupid!" Kosa spat. "We have no idea what we're up against. You saw those creatures, how they were faster than last time. There are only nine of us. We are losing ammo fast and, eventually, we will run out of food tablets and water pellets. Our top priority should be escaping. Then we can argue about telling our peoples."

Crenkleost grumbled to himself. Ow'llent agreed with Kosa but had no interest in returning to her people. Instead, she needed Crenkleost to fly her to safety, somewhere far from Strenovast.

"I agree!" Stares enjoined. "I need to get back to Ripplia and tell them about my people being abducted from our homeworld!"

"Your only world," Crenkleost muttered.

"Oh, shut up," Stares replied, putting on a deeper voice. "Honour, honour, whine whine whine. Who cares about that?"

Ow'llent hid a smirk. Crenkleost tried so hard to be the "perfect" Strenoi it was clear he never would be. His Estate was too small, his shoulders too broad, and his manners unrefined. Though older, he reminded her of a lot of her students who just wanted to be accepted by their peers. He never mentioned a romantic partner. It was likely hard to find someone if you were from such a small Estate as he was.

Crenkleost's shoulders arched as his head dropped and his mouth opened in a snarl. Stares strode up to him and hissed in his face, saliva dripping from jer chin.

Kosa crossed her arms over her chest, jutting out her hip. Rammy rolled his eyes.

"How about this?" Hynd suggested. "We attempt to escape. If we encounter the opportunity to sabotage or otherwise damage the aliens on the way, we amend our plans? That being said, we don't have to remain as a cohesive unit, do we?"

Crenkleost turned his head to look at Kosa. Rammy and Ow'llent shared a glance.

"Yes, we should split up," Flugger suggested. "Klenni and I will –"

"No," Klenni said, her tendrils clapping together. "We are not splitting up. We all have skills that the others need. We're a team."

Kosa nodded. "I agree."

"Me too," Crenkleost and Rammy said.

Ow'llent nodded.

Hynd huffed air from their nostrils. "Okay. I see you are a tight-knit group."

"No, we're not," Kosa replied.

"Could have fooled me."

"Let's go."

The door opened to another hallway, no different than the others they had previously encountered.

"I'm getting real sick of this colour grey," Stares pointed out.

"Allie indicated there is a large open room coming up in two hallways," Rammy said. "It can't translate the label on the ship's schematic, but a large room should have ventilation, so perhaps we can send it through to scout?"

“Do it.” Kosa nodded.

No creatures harassed them, though everyone strained their auditory sensors for the sound of feet charging towards them. The room opened via two doors with overhead hinges, revealing a large area much like the common room on a space station.

“What the hell?” Kosa whispered, having taken point. She lowered her handgun as she surveyed the room, then waved everyone else to enter. Weapons were stowed quickly. What could only be an overlarge, beige sectional couch lay against the back and right walls, opposite a love seat. Coffee tables, throw pillows, a large dining table with gravity-defying one-legged stools, and large armchairs occupied the rest of the space; it was a lounge.

“This is so freakin’ weird, eh?” Rammy muttered. “There is something off-putting about it.” He snapped his fingers. “It’s a simulacrum of a living room.” No one else agreed, as no one else knew what that meant.

“I’m not worried,” Stares said, skipping towards the couch and lying down on it. “Ah. Finally. Proper treatment.”

“What is this room?” Crenkleost asked.

“Aliens gotta party too, I suppose,” Klenni joked. “Maybe it’s for the creatures.”

Rammy shook his head. “Do you think they let them enjoy themselves if they are even capable? This is meant for us, but there’s something strange about it.”

“Now that you mention it, it feels like we’re on some kind of alien spaceship,” Ow’llent quipped.

Rammy cast her a disapproving glance. “I don’t know how to describe it, but it feels like they’re trying to disarm us, trying to make us feel comfortable.”

“Maybe they were testing us all along, and we’ve passed. Perhaps this is our celebration area?” Klenni suggested.

Rammy frowned but didn't reply.

"What do we do?" Hynd asked. "Stay here? Leave?"

Wind spoke up. "We can accept that this room is part of the alien plan to disarm us or trap us. Or we can accept that we've simply stumbled into an alien janitor's break room. We should – what the fuck!?" Wind slapped jer hand to jer neck and brought it away to stare at it. "Something bit me!"

Stares laughed. "Was it the realization that – *Yurtl-nakers*!" Je also slapped jerself.

Rammy clapped his hands over his neck to protect it, but the base of his spine felt a sharp sting. Kosa was next. Crenkleost dove under the table and growled when it hit him too. Ow'llent and Hynd stood still, accepting the inevitable. Flugger tried to shield Klenni, and the sting struck them at the same time.

The group stared at one another. No one dropped dead. No one fainted.

"What was that?"

"Bugs?"

"Bugs? Are you stupid, Stares?! That was far too precise for bugs!" Flugger shook his head. "Let me get out my medical scanner."

"Did they turn up the heat?" Rammy asked, a sheen of sweat appearing on his forehead.

Kosa, too, had started to sweat. The Strenoi body temperature adjusted to compensate for the growing heat. Hynd's mouth opened, and they began to pant. Like a dog, the movement expelled hot air to bring in cooler air, which helped the moisture in their mouth evaporate quickly to reduce their body temperature. The Pir-An looked at one another, shrugging; they felt fine. The Rips also did not notice a temperature change. Instead, they both began to waver on their toes, eventually having to sit down. Flugger turned his scanner on them.

"My cilia no longer support me!" Stares exclaimed, staring at jer feet.

"I'm so dizzy," Wind muttered.

The Pir-An's tendrils began to wave gently, like seaweed in water. They could not control them.

"Oh shit." Klenni giggled. "Flugger, it's like *Frili.*"

Flugger took a moment to think, to try and assess what his body was doing. He set his scanner aside and leaned against the couch, watching his tendrils floating of their own accord up by his face. As Rammy watched, both the Pir-An's pupils grew so large as to encompass their entire eye and stayed that way. "Yes, I think you're right."

"What's *Frili*?" Kosa demanded. "Some kind of heat … thing?"

"No! It's a drug. It turns off your inhibitions, and it makes you feel … happy."

"A drug? Wait, Klenni, you do drugs?" Rammy asked.

Klenni laughed. "Yes, I do drugs! I *love* drugs."

"She loves them too much," Flugger said, chuckling.

"Am I going to sweat myself into dehydration while you two are over there having a blast?" Kosa demanded.

Flugger shrugged, taking off his backpack. "I have no idea." He was the most relaxed the crew had ever seen him. His shoulders actually dropped an inch.

"They injected us with a drug? A stimulant drug?" Hynd asked.

"Looks like it," Ow'llent said. "Speaking of this room – it's starting to look different. Nothing is changing, but everything is kind of … hazy."

"It reminds me of an old movie," Rammy said, sitting on the edge of the couch. "One of those really old ones from the 1900s. *Singing in the Rain*."

Kosa shook her head. "I've never seen one of those. This is terrible. I don't want to be drugged! I've never done drugs in my life."

"What? Really?" Rammy stared at her. "Nothing? Not even weed?"

"Ok, yes, I've done weed a few times. But I've never done anything stronger."

"Me either," Crenk replied. "Us Strenoi don't really use them," he boasted.

Ow'llent pealed with laughter. "Oh, my dear, sweet, *grutyk*. They are very strict about drugs in the navy, especially when you're a pilot, but when you're a civilian ..." She turned to the rest of the group. "Crenkleost is also from the equator province, where they're a little more … conservative. You could call him a … country bumpkin. He's probably never even *seen* hard drugs."

Crenk began to frown, but he was not angry. It was funny, actually. He laughed. Ow'llent joined in. They couldn't stop.

"For me, the room is very defined. It looked like everything is more three-dimensional than usual," Stares tried to explain over the bellowing Strenoi laughter. "Oh good, my feet feel better."

"I love your weird feet," Kosa heard herself admit, almost as if she couldn't hold it in. "They are so interesting."

Stares lifted a leg and waggled jer cilia at the Terran, causing Kosa to laugh. Kosa extended a hand down to the Rip to help jer up. Stares paused, then took it, allowing Kosa to pull jer to jer feet. Kosa stared down at the long, skeletal, silver fingers in her hand, marvelling at how brilliant they seemed to shine, how they sparkled. If it weren't for jer overlarge, arresting black eyes and terrible spike-toothed mouth, Stares could be a nymph. Stares pulled jer hand out of Kosa's grasp, stepping back a few feet. But je didn't hiss.

"For some reason, it doesn't feel like we're on a ship anymore. It's like we're at a party," Rammy admitted. "I know it's the drugs, but I'm not worried about anything right now. I think the aliens are giving us a break."

"I think so too!" Klenni smiled, staring at her bobbing tendrils. "For some reason, I don't think this drug will give me any paranoia, either."

"You people are all crazy," Hynd said, but they were smiling and moving side-to-side. A faint sound resonated inside their head, reminding them of *trulu* birdsong. They were aware the others did not hear it. Nevertheless, it did not bother them, as it would in other circumstances.

"I feel great!" Kosa exclaimed, her face flushed but her rare smile beaming. "This is what drugs are like?"

Rammy laughed. "Not all drugs feel the same. This feels like … it feels a little like Molly but also not. I'm assuming the aliens dosed us based on some study of our body chemistry."

"You know what's weird? That doesn't bother me one bit!" Kosa declared.

Flugger moved his hips – it was a jerky dance, but Klenni began to giggle. "Don't do that!"

"What is it?" Rammy asked.

"It's his mating dance!"

Flugger continued to jerk his arms and legs; it looked to the Terrans like he was trying to disco. "I've been so fucking worried this whole damn time. And I know the worry is going to come back as soon as I'm sober, but I'm going to enjoy this damn drug!" Flugger declared.

"Go, Flugger, go!" Kosa called. "Dance that fish ass!"

Flugger shook his hips even more wildly as Klenni giggled uncontrollably.

"It's so inappropriate!" She blushed at the same time as she laughed.

"I can't let him dance alone!" Rammy declared and stepped forward, falling into a graceful gyration of the hips and waving his arms over his head.

"Do you hear music?" Ow'llent asked.

"I thought it was in my head," Crenkleost replied. There was indeed music, growing in volume. It wasn't a song from any of their planets. To the Terrans, it sounded like an attempt to create Electronic music by someone who had only been told the basic concept and had never heard it themselves. There was a pulsing bass and quick rhythmic synthesized sounds that morphed into other sounds, with stabs of other synth accents. To Kosa and Rammy, it was familiar but weaved into their ears in a different way than they were used to. It had a similar effect on the Strenoi and Pir-An, who were from musical cultures too; they could recognize the attempt at melody and rhythm. The Dirge were an unmusical race, preferring background noises to be natural (such as running water), so Hynd was overwhelmed by the sounds – only their poor hearing kept them from putting their hands over their ears. The Rips, who had no time in their live-or-die society for frivolities like culture, confined music to singing; they didn't use instruments. Still, the Rips began to sway to the music, Stares' flowing red robes billowing around jer. Wind danced stoically, jer eyes closed and head held back almost parallel with the floor. The Rips did not touch one another.

Hynd continued their side-stepping dance, a slow off-beat polka.

Kosa pumped her fist in the air and grabbed Klenni by the hand. She spun the Pir-An, making Klenni laugh even harder. Kosa let her go and began to swivel her body in a sexual manner, how she would dance at clubs and bars to attract partners. Her tight ab muscles contracted, and she raised her arms over her head, closing her eyes and exposing her throat. Rammy glanced at her, grinning. It was nice to see the corporal let loose – they didn't frequent the same bars unless it was a squad member's birthday. AJ strayed into Rammy's thoughts. They had met at a bar on Toronto Space Station, named for his home province's capital despite being hundreds of light-years from Earth. The memory of AJ's dyed blond hair and easy smile made Rammy's heartache. No, Rammy wouldn't think of him. That wouldn't be good in this state; it would only cause a spiral of doubt and longing and self-pity. He turned his gaze to the Strenoi, who were standing off to the side watching everyone else.

"Come on, you big lizards!" he called. "Or do you guys not dance?"

"We're not lizards!" Ow'llent laughed. "We're mammals like you! In fact, I was working on a theory that we share –"

"Yeah, yeah!" Rammy replied, holding out his hand. Ow'llent didn't pause before taking it and letting Rammy pull her in.

Kosa opened her eyes to see Rammy and Ow'llent attempting a strange slow-dance like at a sixth-grade mixer. The Strenoi was a foot taller than Rammy, despite his above-average height. They both overstepped and laughed in each other's arms when they stumbled.

"I wish I were able to make friends so quickly," she said aloud. She snapped her mouth closed, then let out a sigh. "Damn this drug! It's like I have no filter."

"That's the point!" Klenni said. She was dancing with Flugger now, their tendrils intertwined to either side, their bodies pressed close. "Just let it happen – you'll enjoy yourself more. Believe me, I know – I've coached many new users through their first time."

"It's like her hobby," Flugger said sardonically but with affection.

Crenkleost stood outside the group. Everyone was dancing but him. His body wanted to dance, but he wasn't good at it. He did not enjoy it and did everything he could to avoid it at social gatherings. He had no rhythm. His best-cousin was the better dancer, the one to drag Crenkleost to parties. Crenkleost would stand around the food table and watch while Guermun stole all the attention. Crenkleost didn't mind, as he wasn't a showboat, but going places with Guermun guaranteed Crenkleost would be overlooked. His cousin had inherited dark cherry-coloured skin and a cascading ridge bone that stood a full two inches taller than Crenkleost's. He was slim and tall, with the wiry body Strenoi culture deemed the most desirable. Guermun had received three breeding requests already and always had a romantic partner, though he didn't keep them long. Crenkleost had a few partners over the years, but Guermun was the family heartbreaker. And the brains. The only thing Crenkleost had over his cousin was his military record. And now that was tarnished. All for Guermun too.

Thoughts of his cousin, his dishonour, Ow'llent, and his orders circled in his brain like predators on the offensive. He put his hands to his temples, but he couldn't stop the thoughts. He felt a sting against his neck – did the aliens shoot him again? Why? Were they trying to drive him crazy?

He took deep breaths. As he did so, the thoughts of Guermun melted away, replaced by an intense desire to dance with someone, to have bodily contact. It wasn't sexual, at least not entirely, but he couldn't touch *any* of these people. The Rips would lose it, the Pir-An were together, and Rammy and Ow'llent were dancing and talking animatedly. Hynd was … he had no desire to get that close to the Dirge who had been in this ship for a week without washing. That left only the corporal. He had no opposition to touching her, having already been on top and below her when they had sparred. The blurry effect of the drug framed the area around her in a dull fog as if she were dancing on a beach after a storm. Her hips and body moved languidly, opposite to her take-charge personality. Her legs seemed to start the movement, and it would wind up to finish at her neck, then spiral back down. Despite her being a Terran, he wanted to touch her. But she would shove him away. All he wanted was physical contact – he wanted to hold someone, to feel them against his body. If he could do that, he knew he would share the euphoria the rest of his friends felt.

Friends? He blinked. They were temporary comrades-in-arms, not friends. Right? True, Rammy was genial, Ow'llent was funny, Klenni was sweet, Flugger was cantankerous in a way Crenkleost found amusing, Wind was reliable, and he never knew what Stares was going to do next. And they were already at a sort of party together, like friends would be. He knew he should be wary of an attack by the aliens. He knew dancing in this room was the stupidest thing they could ever do, but he closed his eyes, took a deep breath, and let the drug's effects take him over. He stopped fighting it.

He approached Kosa from behind and took her hips in his large hands. She jumped slightly in surprise, then looked up at him over her shoulder and smiled in a dreamy way. He moved his body closer to hers, bringing her against him. The heat from her Terran core was intense, but it reminded him of home, of the driest of the dry season. Trees shed their heat-curled leaves. The wind ripped down the long pathway to their Estate, causing the shrubs to shudder, but brought no relief. The water in the cavern pools was cool. A rare flower bloomed, but only at night.

The craving for contact increased. He tightened his grip and lowered his head, so his cheek was against hers. She didn't pull away. He closed his eyes, revelling in the smoothness of her skin. How could it be so silky?

Sensations flooded his chemically stimulated cerebral cortex. The Terran smelled of perspiration and dried alien blood, but her soft hair let off a floral scent as it brushed against his chin. She had her hands above her head, dancing as if he wasn't directly behind her. Her well-shaped butt brushed his thighs and her swaying shoulders skimmed his chest. He stepped backwards slightly, his need for contact satisfied. But instead of dancing on his own, he left his hands on her hips. He could feel every bone move under her skin. He let the music dictate his movements.

The drug lasted for three hours. When its effects began to wear off, the group dispersed to the couches and chairs. The Pir-An settled into one of the large armchairs together, their marital tension from earlier apparently forgotten. Ow'llent and Rammy sat on the couch, filling Hynd in on their speculations about their alien captors. Wind found a chair slightly apart from the group while Stares moved around the room, inspecting the various shelves and furniture.

The music, still pulsing, began to lessen in volume, though Crenkleost and Kosa continued to dance. They were facing one another now.

"I take it you love dancing?" Crenk asked as he moved a hand from Kosa's waist and took hers in it. He attempted to spin her, and while he did so awkwardly, she turned the movement from fledgling to graceful.

"My aunt offered to pay for dance lessons when I was a child," Kosa explained. "I continued with it until I joined the military. I performed in competitions and shows. My mother and my aunt wanted me to be professional, but while I do love it, I didn't want to do it as a career. By eighteen, I could tell that while I had talent, it wasn't enough to take me to the top. And, quite frankly, I was tired of the dance drama and wanted something different. Much to my aunt's anger."

"I'm not fond of dancing as I'm a bit of a klutz."

Kosa smiled. "I think you dance fine. Besides, you're just here to support *my* dancing. If we had the time, I bet I could teach you some proper lifts. We could be stars!" She laughed, imagining bringing Crenk to a competition. Her mother, not to mention her aunt and cousins, would have heart attacks, though if it got her dancing again, Kosa was sure her mother would be overjoyed and welcome Crenk with open arms. Wait. Why was she thinking about having Crenk meet her family? What was *in* that drug?

"Is that a threat?" Crenk asked, spinning her again, but too quickly. She stumbled, and he stretched to catch her, his large hand at the base of her spine. "Being a dancer sounds like torture to me."

Kosa raised a brow teasingly as she looked up at him; for someone who didn't like dancing, he had her in a dip. She let him support her weight as she lifted her hand from his shoulder and poked him in the chest, letting out a small half-smile as she did so.

"You teach me to fly, and I'll teach you to dance," she said.

Crenk looked down at the Terran he was holding. The warmth from her body had dissipated somewhat, but her hand was still hot in his, as was her back under his other hand. There was a faint sheen of perspiration on her forehead and a trickle of sweat running down her neck. Her intense, dark brown eyes were no longer severe. Her jaw, which was usually set in a defiant, upward position, was relaxed. Her neck was long and slender, smooth.

"You can call me Crenk," he said.

"What?"

"Shortening names is not something those from Estates do; it's an insult, really, but I'll allow it if you want. If it's easier for you."

Kosa smiled. "Well, that's great because you've been Crenk to me since I learned your name."

His reply caught in his throat. She, too, appeared reticent to continue speaking. Wait, why was he holding a Terran in such a manner? Clear, rational thoughts broke through the optimistic fog that had bedevilled his brain.

"So, that was drugs," he said, setting her upright and stepping backwards. The stiff tension returned to her face as if she had just remembered they were in *Misery*. She shook her head as if to clear it.

"I guess so."

"That was an extremely intense high," Rammy said as Kosa and Crenk joined the others on the couch. They chose not to sit together.

"I loved it!" Klenni called. "I wish they would sell me some." She turned her head up to the ceiling. "Hey! Aliens! Can I buy some of that shit?"

"Klenni, you are a riot!" Rammy laughed. He sniffed. "Guys? Do you smell that?"

Flugger glanced at everyone in the room doing their equivalent of sniffing and broke into laughter. "You people look ridiculous."

"You don't smell it?" Kosa asked.

"Smells like weed to me," Rammy said. "But also not exactly."

Kosa sighed as the room began to fill with visible smoke. "More drugs? Are we their guinea pigs now?" She didn't bother trying to cover her mouth and nose as if out of spite.

"Shells, people! Maybe they've been drug dealers all along!" Klenni began to giggle.

Flugger and the Rips joined in. Being smaller in mass, the hotboxing of the room hit them quicker. Eventually, everyone was stoned, even Hynd. They sprawled on the couches, staring at the ceiling or one another.

Rammy was telling a story, "… one of my friends, back in undergrad, he got this bad pain in his mouth right before exams. We all thought he was faking it to get out of the tests, but when he went to the dentist, they found that one of his baby teeth had never come down and had fused to the bone and needed to be removed – it was causing him nerve pain."

"Wait, what do you mean by baby teeth?" Ow'llent asked, leaning forward.

Rammy laughed. "You guys aren't born with your adult teeth, right?"

"Yes, we are." Crenk snorted. "What are *you* talking about?"

Kosa laughed. "Terrans are born with no teeth. By the time we're two, the teeth grow in. Then when we're like six, we start to lose them, and our adult teeth grow in by the time we're ten or so."

"That is too weird for words," Klenni breathed. "I never heard that before."

"Oh, come on!" Rammy said. "It's not that weird! What about you guys? Everyone tell us one weird thing. We'll see if there's something that can top baby teeth."

"Ok!" Klenni exclaimed, sitting up. "Ooh, I have one. For us Pir-An, the men can tell when their eggs are fertilizing."

Flugger nodded. "I haven't felt it, *yet*, but apparently, it's very obvious that the eggs are developing." The way Flugger said *yet* to Klenni with such insistence put Kosa's back up.

"Our women feel that too," she said, almost to knock down his point.

"Not fertilization! Women don't feel kicks until about twenty weeks." Rammy laughed. Everyone stared at him. He laughed again. "My mom is a midwife, so I know a lot about fetuses and birth. Every night at dinner, it's babies this and pregnancy that."

"And you paid attention in Sex Ed." Kosa grinned at him. He pointed his finger and thumb at her as if it were a revolver, then winked as he clicked his tongue at her.

"Strenoi have tails until we are twelve," Crenk said.

"I always wondered about that," Kosa said. "I saw a few children during Operation … I mean, when I was on duty, and the first time I saw a tail, I didn't know what to think."

"We lose the tail at puberty," Ow'llent explained. "That's why a lot of our insults about whining or being a coward reference tails. It implies that they are still a child."

"What do you do with it when it falls off?"

"Give it to a doctor. They do tissue screening, and then they use the rest as samples for genetic testing or other experiments."

"Do you have a scar?"

"No, it doesn't fall off at random one day!" Crenk laughed. "Can you imagine? You're playing a sport or sitting in school, and then your tail falls off?"

"It begins to go gradually, and children are given a special brace for it until it detaches," Ow'llent explained. "But children often worry about their tails embarrassing them."

"We have that too," Kosa said. "Girls worry about getting their periods and boys about getting boners."

Crenk laughed. "Terrans and their boners."

"They are useful for some situations." Kosa grinned.

Crenk laughed harder.

"Dirge can't swim. We're too head-heavy. We just sink." Hynd said solemnly. The group fell silent until Klenni let out a shrill giggle. Once she started to laugh, the rest joined in, picturing Hynd slowly sinking in a pool, then sitting at the bottom, a sad look on their face.

"What about the Rips?" Ow'llent asked. "You guys have any weird shit about you we don't already know?"

"They're cannibals!" Rammy pointed out.

Stares crossed jer arms over jer chest. "Only in dire circumstances."

"And when someone is particularly tasty," Wind chuckled. Kosa groaned at his joke, and Klenni grimaced.

Stares frowned. "Everyone always focuses on the bad stuff. What you might find interesting is that to take control of a Rip clan, you have to hunt and kill a *Borkas*. You are allowed a small team, usually your supporters. If you can bring back its head, you can take over the clan."

"Is this common?"

Stares shook jer head. "No. Maybe once a generation, you hear about a clan leadership switch based on the ritual hunt. Most people don't attempt it."

"Would you?"

Stares blinked. "If I thought I needed to, I would."

Wind snorted.

Stares whipped jer head around, *Exorcist*-style, to stare at Wind. "What? I couldn't win?"

Wind shrugged. "You're not the best fighter – you're too reckless."

Stares stood, hissing. "Taking down a *Borkas* is not about martial skill. It's about leadership! It's about having the best team to listen to your commands. It's not a one-on-one fight, dumbass *yurtl-naker*!"

"Oookay," Ow'llent said, "that escalated quickly."

"Hey, Stares!" Rammy called.

Stares continued to glare at Wind. "*What*?" je barked.

"Terrans have tons of other useless body parts, did you know that? We have these things called tonsils and a part called the appendix, which does nothing but can rupture and kill us if we don't get it removed in time."

Stares' head swivelled back to the group. "Really? You have a little bomb in you?"

Rammy nodded. "Yep. We still don't exactly know what it's for."

Stares nodded. "That's super cool. Is it in your brain?"

"No, it's in our stomach."

"Speaking of stomachs," Crenk said. "I'm starving. Should we get out the food producers?"

Stares pointed towards the opposite side of the room. “There’s food on the tables! Look!”

The long dining room table was loaded with food for all five species though no one noticed it arrive. The group, even Wind, walked over to look at it. Collectively, their stomachs grumbled.

Flugger sighed. “Goddamn munchies.”

“Oh look, they have *chorgans*.” Klenni sighed. The *chorgans* were similar to Terran anchovies. “I love *chorgans* when I’m high. The salt is divine.”

“Jeez, you really are a pothead, aren’t you?” Kosa asked, not hiding the amusement on her face.

“Just because I’m a little shy doesn’t mean I’m some goody-goody!” she protested, tendrils flailing.

Kosa held up her hands in mock fear. “Sorry, sorry.”

Klenni’s fish lips twisted in a frown, one of the only expressions her people could do. Flugger took one of her tendrils in his. *Don’t worry about them, love; they aren’t important anyway.*

Klenni’s right tendril snapped like a whip out of his grasp, and she did not reply telepathically or vocally. Flugger stared at her, his heart sinking.

“Looks like the food was delivered by this area, eh?” Rammy ventured, the excitement restrained in his voice but still noticeable. Everything the aliens did was so precise; the more they travelled through the ship, the more Rammy wanted to learn about them. There were faint lines on the wall they had not noticed before, two feet tall by eight wide – enough to slide out food onto the table.

“How did they get our food?”

“If they were able to abduct someone from Ripplia, it wouldn’t be hard for them to get our food from somewhere. Or synthesize it,” Stares said.

“How did they know our *favourite* foods?” Kosa asked, pointing at the chocolate chip cookies.

“Cookies are your favourite food?” Rammy asked.

"Why? You think it would be salad?"

"Well, yes, or something else healthy."

"I eat healthy food to keep fit. What I would eat on my deathbed would be cookies."

Rammy's face twisted in chagrin. "Oh. Yeah."

"What's your favourite? You're Canadian, right? You like poutine?"

Rammy nodded. "Yes, actually. I would die for poutine right now."

"There are a bunch of popular Strenoi snacks here, as well," Ow'llent joined in. "But not my favourite, unfortunately. Perhaps it was just coincidence they had Kosa's."

The group stared at the dishes in front of them. Those who had been stoned before in their life understood the craving for sweet or salty (or both), but this was stronger than usual. Kosa's mouth flooded with saliva when she imagined how sweet the perfectly cooked oatmeal batter would taste on her tongue, the welcome bitterness of the semi-sweet chocolate chips, and the bite of sea salt from the dusting on top. The others shared the same craving but for different foods.

"Are those Sun Day rounds?" Wind asked, staring at a small plate in the Rip section. Jer voice was soft and tone subdued, as if je had witnessed a particularly moving scene. The small, brown, round balls were the compressed brains of a solitary and reclusive squirrel-creature from Ripplia. Once a year, the squirrels left their burrows to mate. That day, if the Rips could find them, they made Sun Day rounds. Wind had only had one in jer life, back when je was a child.

Stares shrugged as if they were common where je lived. "Looks like it."

Wind grabbed the plate and stuffed one into jer mouth. Jer long teeth made ribbons out of the dried meat. Je let out a moan of satisfaction.

"Don't get pregnant over there," Crenk joked. The rest of the group laughed as Wind tossed another in jer mouth while flipping Crenk off in the Terran manner; it was a gesture the Rips had been quick to adopt.

Klenni reached forward and took one of the *chorgans* by the tail. Then, she leaned back and dropped the small fish in her mouth.

"Yum," she said. Flugger stared at her, his exasperation apparent in his stance, if not his face. She caught his look. "Live a little, Flug."

"Fine," he said, taking what looked like a soft macaroon. He ate it with a decisive chomp. Klenni ate another *chorgan*.

Ow'llent glanced at Rammy.

"When in Rome," he said with a shrug and picked up a chocolate cupcake with glistening chocolate icing. Ow'llent chose a dish resembling steak tartare.

"Is there anything to drink?" Hynd asked, squinting. Their eyes were still dry from the smoke and as a residual side-effect of the previous drug.

"There's a bottle of something," Kosa said as she passed it over. Hynd examined the unreadable label closely, then used one thumb to pop off the cork of the swing-top glass bottle. Hynd upended the bottle into their mouth, chugging it back. It looked like milk.

Crenk moved to stand beside Kosa. "Do you also think everyone is crazy to eat this shit?"

Kosa nodded. "Yes. One hundred percent."

"You guys aren't eating?" Stares asked, throwing little yellow balls into her mouth one-by-one. They were the Rip version of candy: small, desiccated eyeballs of Ripplian eels. They tasted like lemon by Terran standards.

"It could be drugged!"

"Drugged?" Stares asked if je hadn't considered that. "Great! The last two drugs were awesome!"

Having eaten all but one of the Sun Day rounds, Wind passed the remaining piece to Stares, who accepted with a flick of jer tongue as a thank-you. Stares reached down and picked up another Rip snack. "Don't be a … what would you call it? A tailed Strenoi?"

Crenk glowered. Kosa put her hand on his arm.

"Don't listen to them. We're the smart ones."

Crenk nodded, and she removed her hand.

"I don't think it's drugged. I feel totally normal," Stares said.

"I'm not taking a Rip's assessment of normal as an indication of anything," Kosa muttered.

"What's that animal you Terrans use?" Stares pondered, forgetting that je was supposed to be unaware of how to speak Terran without the alien interference. "Ah, yes, a chicken."

"What now?"

"Don't be one."

Kosa's mouth dropped open. "Are you calling me … chicken?"

Stares smiled. "Yes."

"Do you have a death wish?"

"Of course. I wish to die in a warm bed with medals of my achievements around me."

Kosa pursed her lips and was about to explain the true intention of her question when Stares started to giggle.

"Ugh, stop that," Kosa ordered.

Stares' giggle rattled in jer throat like rusty pipes rubbing against one another – it was a grating, irritating noise. Je only increased in volume when Kosa tried to get jer to stop.

"Koharu …" Crenk began, noticing Kosa's cheeks growing red with frustration. It was obvious to him that Stares was goading Kosa, but whether the woman in question knew this was the case, it was clear she was unable to accept a challenge to her courage. Crenk understood that more than anyone, but he hoped Kosa would settle down. He didn't want to be the only one not eating the doubtlessly poisoned food.

"Fine! You want us all to join you? Great, we're all dead!" Despite her better judgement, Kosa picked up a cookie and took a bite. She had been in battle and never lost her head, had withstood the news of her lack of promotion with a stoic expression, she had gotten them this far on the ship, she had been polite to her hated aunt because she paid for the dance lessons her mother couldn't afford, but upon eating that cookie, Kosa let out a lusty sigh full of pent-up emotion. Usually, only dancing, fighting, and sex brought out that much relief.

Crenk eyed her. This was so stupid, but he didn't want her to think he was a coward. He reached forward and picked up what he considered the hardest thing to poison: a skin-on fruit close in appearance to a Terran apple. He took two tenuous bites, then finished the entire thing when the flavour compelled him.

"Those look good," Kosa said. "Can I try one?"

Crenk laughed. "This isn't my food. Eat what you want."

Kosa picked up one of the Strenoi apples, then took a small bite.

"Wow," she said. "I was expecting apple, and I got a very sweet grape. I'm calling these grapples from now on."

Crenk snorted, then took another bite. "I guess we were too cautious."

Kosa shook her head. "I'm sure we are idiotic for doing this."

"You think we're like Persephone?" Rammy asked, coming up between them.

"What?" Kosa turned to look at him.

"The Greek myth. Persephone ate six pomegranate seeds, and she was stuck in the underworld for six months and –"

"She needed a better lawyer," Crenk cut in.

"You guys have lawyers?" Kosa asked.

"Of course, every civilized culture has mediators. How do you think we got the Accord written up? My best-cousin is a lawyer."

"I'm sorry," Kosa joked.

Crenk grinned. "Good to see some jokes cut across cultures."

Rammy tapped his foot. "Excuse me? I'm still here, telling my story. Whoa." He held up his hand and stared at it for a moment, the other two people forgotten.

"Private, your pupils are very wide," Kosa remarked. The cookie in her hand began to shake. She let go of it, startled, but it hovered at nose-level, spinning slowly on its axis. She glanced at her companions, but they did not notice what was going on. She closed her eyes briefly in resignation – they didn't see it. Rammy was explaining how the fingers on his hand looked like they were melding together and coming apart again.

Of course, the food was drugged.

CHAPTER 16: FLUGGER

The lights were too bright. Flugger's eyelids were tacky when he tried to open them as if his eyeballs were sticking to his lids. Pressure grew behind his temples. He exhaled and pushed himself to a seated position. His head fell forward onto his hands, and he let out a groan. He'd suffered this before, this drug hangover. He took slow breaths as his eye fluid returned to normal viscosity. He opened his lids to see his inner thighs and his genitalia. What the …? Why was he naked? Despite the pain it caused, he shot his gaze over the rest of the room. He exhaled heavily in relief. Only he and Klenni were naked. They were together in the corner of the couch.

Hynd was lying on their back, snoring, as Ow'llent used the Dirge's furry stomach as a large pillow. The female Strenoi, whom Flugger always considered rather refined before now, had her arms around the Dirge as if she were a child and Hynd her comfort doll.

Rammy's feet hung off the coffee table where he lay upon it, his shirt missing, his shoes off and pants undone, six cupcake wrappers strewn around his body. His chest rose and fell.

The Rips were across from Rammy on the same couch as the Pir-An, on the other side of the L. They were entangled, their limbs so twisted around one another it was hard to tell what was an arm and what was a leg. Given

Stares' aversion to physical touch, this struck Flugger as odd.

Where were Kosa and Crenk? Flugger slowly turned his head towards the table where all the food had been. Only empty plates, cups, and a few bottles remained. Kosa slept underneath it with her head on a throw pillow from the couch. Several of the cushions were leaned up around the table, enshrouding her within. Across from her, surrounded by his own cushions, was Crenk. He had fallen asleep slouching against the wall, his head hanging down as he snored. Throw pillows lay between the two forts, suggesting the two had engaged in a siege. Flugger would have snorted in amusement if it hadn't threatened to tear his brain in two.

Klenni stirred, then moaned.

"Shells …" she muttered.

"I hear you," Flugger agreed, returning his head to his knees.

"Why are we naked?" Klenni asked. Flugger heard her moving and assumed she was rescuing their clothing. He was right; she dropped his onto his shoulders. She shuffled into her clothes and then lay down beside him again. He risked lifting his head to look at her.

Her sky-blue skin was as beautiful as ever, her fin gracefully arced. He reached forward and ran a hand down it. The fin rippled with the sensation. Klenni opened her eyes.

"We should have guppies when we get out of here," Flugger said.

Klenni closed her eyes.

"What? Why don't you want to?"

"I want to someday, but not yet. I'm not ready."

"But you don't have to do anything! Just fertilize my eggs."

Klenni scoffed. "Oh yes, because having a clutch is no work at all for me. Once they hatch, there goes our life as we know it."

"What life? Taking on dubious missions that turn into death-defying escapes? Wait … are you *enjoying* this?"

Klenni refused to reply. Flugger felt his mouth drop and quickly snapped it shut. She *was* enjoying this! At least, some aspect of it.

"It's those aliens, isn't it?" he hissed. It must be that. They must be controlling her somehow. Who knows? Maybe they were in on the entire thing! Why would she trust them?

"What aliens?" she whispered.

He gestured to the room. "These aliens! I don't want you hanging around them unless there is fighting. You talk to me only, ok? It's not safe." As soon as the words left his mouth, he wanted to take them back.

Klenni's eyes hardened. "Excuse me? Why are you telling me what to do?"

"Because you are acting irrationally! As a medical professional, it seems like you're under the influence of something."

"Yeah, freedom."

"Excuse me?"

"Maybe you're a scared little guppy, but I happen to have faith that these people, and me, are going to help us escape."

"You?"

"I have combat training, Flugger. I killed those creatures with that huge gun while you cowered in the corner."

"Is that it? Being around these meatheads has sullied me in your eyes? I'm no longer worthy? Would you rather fertilize one of *their* eggs?"

Klenni laughed at him in response, a harsh, grating laugh he'd never heard from her before. "Don't talk to me for a while, Flug'ger'alaio," she said, pushing herself with a grunt of effort to her feet. She headed across the room to the backpacks, retrieving their food producer. She fumbled with the pillboxes, dropping them. She cursed as she picked up the one for water and made herself a glass. She guzzled it.

"Ugh, Klen. Keep it down, would you?" Rammy murmured from the table. He sat up slowly. "Wait, wait. Where are we? Oh my god."

Flugger watched the Terran's bloodshot eyes take in the room. Rammy gingerly lay back down, then rolled slowly off the table to lie face down on the area rug. He coughed a few times, then closed his eyes.

"Get off me, Wind!"

Stares was up. Flugger glanced at the Rips. Stares struggled to extricate jerself from Wind, who was not resisting but not helping. Je probably considered it safer to lie still.

Stares berated jer. "What were you thinking? Wrapping me up in your arms like we're some Terran or Pir-An mated pair?"

Wind sighed. "From what I recall, you were the one caressing me last night."

Stares scowled. "I did not! I would never compromise myself that way!"

Wind snorted.

"Stares, please stop yelling," Ow'llent said, her face buried in the Dirge's fur.

"Doesn't that smell?" Stares asked as je moved to sit a few feet from Wind.

"I heard that," Hynd rumbled.

"We all smell," Ow'llent pointed out. "We haven't bathed in days."

"I smell magnificent," Rammy mumbled from the carpet.

Ow'llent chuckled, then placed a hand over her eyes. "By the Mystics, I'm plumb knackered. I haven't had a night like that since my grad school days."

"Does anyone remember anything from the last part? After we ate the food?" Klenni asked, bringing her FP to the center of the table. She had rooted through everyone's bags to bring over their water bottles or cups. Despite his annoyance, Flugger was in awe of her considerate nature. He would never have thought to offer water to others, even if they were all Pir-An. But that was why he loved her. Dammit, why did he say those things to her? He didn't deserve her. But that was why he had to protect her from these aliens, from herself. She wasn't in her right mind.

Rammy used the table to pull himself into sitting.

"Thanks, Klen." He took a sip. "All I remember is eating that cupcake."

"You mean all these cupcakes?" Ow'llent asked, gesturing to the litter.

Rammy laughed feebly.

"I remember everyone dancing," Klenni commented.

"That was before the food."

"Oh, right. I guess I don't remember much." She narrowed her large eyes. "Well, I remember laughing a lot. I remember someone … someone running their hands over my fin. And something like …" she paused, then laughed. "I do remember something. Rammy, you were really frustrated – I think it was about the end table. You kept saying that it was moving, and it felt like it was alive under your hand. You were so mad because you claimed its 'life level' was higher than it should be. You couldn't figure out what it was made of."

"What?" Rammy laughed softly.

"You kept saying something … oh right. You were angry because you couldn't tell if it was wood or metal."

"I remember that. He claimed that wood has a higher life level than metal, but since the table was metal, its life level was too high for it, and it should be wood," Stares added, but it was hardly a clarification.

"Yeah, the *table* was too high. That's what happened," Ow'llent joked.

"Goddamn it, Ow'llent," Crenk muttered from across the room. "How do you guys enjoy drugs when this is the result?"

Klenni shrugged. "It's fun to open your mind to new perceptions."

"Even if you can't remember them?"

"I remember most of the time. I'm not sure why we blacked out."

"Maybe it was because of the *alien* drug?" Wind suggested, just a hint of sarcasm in jer tone.

"What I want to know is, what was the point?" Kosa ventured from her fort. "Were they testing us somehow?"

"Our physiology, maybe?" Ow'llent suggested. "I'd love to know whether we all had the same dose or even the same drug."

"Maybe it was to try and force us to bond?" Rammy offered. "I mean, not to be presumptuous, but I'd consider you guys my team now. I might have already, but when you share drugs like that with people, it has a way of uniting you."

"Are you saying it's like we took a *trip* together?" Ow'llent grinned again.

"One more of those jokes and you're no longer allowed to use me as a pillow," Hynd grunted.

"Oh no." Ow'llent cuddled down. "I'm taking you home with me. You're my new bed."

"Is that allowed?" Stares asked.

"What?"

"Cross-species relationships?"

Ow'llent merely laughed. Hynd chuffed air.

"You're obsessed. You need to have sex and get it over with," Rammy suggested. "You're like a horny fifteen-year-old looking at porn. Once you do it, you'll realize it's great, but it's not this big mystery."

Stares pouted. "It's not my fault you guys are throwing all these ideas into my head."

"Ah yes, we're poisoning the virgin minds of the Rips." Crenk snorted.

"Well, *you* were anyway. You and the corporal getting all frisky last night."

Crenk's eyes darted towards Kosa, who met his startled stare with a look of wide-eyed, unabashed concern.

"What do you mean?" he asked.

"Your dancing. Couldn't keep your hands off of her."

Crenk scoffed much too loudly in Flugger's perception. "Give me a break. We were dancing. That's how you do it. You're the only race that dances like it's the *Orandark* era."

"What's that?" Klenni asked.

Ow'llent explained. "An era of our history where societal norms around sex were very rigid. It lasted about fifty years before people grew frustrated by it and it went back to normal. It's very complicated to explain how it came about. Regardless, it's hard to track bloodlines when you can't talk about sex."

"We had an era like that too, but much longer," Rammy said.

"I know. I've studied some of your history. Much of your past has been about controlling sexuality. It's fascinating."

Flugger couldn't take it anymore. "Instead of Terran social history, maybe we could talk about what we're doing next?"

"First, we're going to take these pills," Klenni said, shaking out enough for everyone. Flugger sighed. Those pills weren't cheap. Also, why had Klenni brought hangover pills on the mission?

"More drugs?" Kosa shook her head, backing up.

"You don't have to hide in your fort. This is a cure for a hangover. It's a very mild medicine – it'll calm you down and take away your headache. Settle your stomach."

"Like smoking a joint when you're hungover. Nice," Rammy said, picking it up.

"Stick it under your tongue, and it'll dissolve. You'll feel better in about five minutes."

"Thanks, Klen, you're the best."

Only Flugger understood how her tendrils twisted up with happiness. His began an agitated dance, and he thrust them behind his back so his partner couldn't see.

The crew sat on the couches facing one another in a circle. Flugger had debated declining the mild relaxant but decided he needed his brain and body working correctly. He watched everyone while perched forward on the edge of the couch, his feet planted and his hands pressed to the upholstery by his thighs. Klenni had made a point not to sit beside him after handing out the pills, squeezing between Ow'llent and Rammy so he couldn't follow her. Flugger tried not to watch her, but his eyes moved to her form no matter how much he willed them to stop. He knew he was being irrational, that he was being selfish, that he was clinging to her, but as much as he was aware of that, he accepted it as necessary. He was being irrational because she was being stubborn.

Flugger wanted Klenni, he wanted guppies with her so badly, but these aliens were twisting her thoughts away from where they should be – on him and their future. Hadn't he been wonderful in postponing kids so she could go off on adventures? She was the one who argued that they spend a year or so in space. He had agreed, as long as the crew were mainly Pir-An. She had accepted his compromise until this last job. She had promised him they'd go back to Bubble early if they could first take this strange mission into deep space with the unorthodox Rip captain. Throughout the journey, he knew she was regretting her choice – the Terrans were aloof, the Rips insane. But she refused to admit he was right. This worked for him since he knew she was realizing that his sensible plans were the best ones. But now these infernal aliens had morphed from threats to colleagues, and Klenni got what she wanted after all: adventure. And like most addictive things in her life, she would only want more.

"Chill out over there, Flugger," Kosa said. "Your angst is making me uncomfortable."

"When Kosa tells you to chill, that means you really need to." Rammy laughed.

Kosa deposited a glare on Rammy that he returned with a hearty grin. Her glare softened into a smirk of begrudging acceptance.

"Yeah, Flugger, what are you worried about?" Stares leered. "That some aliens are going to barge in here and kill us?"

Flugger wasn't usually a violent person, but if he had to choose between throttling one of the mysterious aliens and throttling Stares, he would have picked Stares.

"I don't understand you people at all – are you not concerned? We are going to die, most likely."

Kosa shrugged. "Of course, I'm concerned, but fretting about it only raises your stress and makes you react in panic."

"You're soldiers, most of you. You're used to this."

Rammy laughed, but it had an edge to it. "None of us is used to *this* ship."

"I'm not a soldier," Ow'llent said, flashing her teeth.

"Me either," Stares and Hynd replied in unison.

"There are only three soldiers here, Flug," Klenni replied with a sigh, "but I think everyone is sick of your depths-damned whining."

Her comment struck him like a slap. Clearly, everyone else was just as surprised as he was by the vitriol in her comment, as they all turned to stare at her. She had her head resting against the back of the couch cushion behind her, eyes closed. Precisely why she didn't react when the world suddenly went dark.

CHAPTER 17: WIND

A split second after darkness descended, Kosa began shouting orders.

"Wind, grab your rifle – get to the back and cover the door. Those who cannot see in the dark get to the floor. Stares, you're going to take my arm – don't complain – and lead me to our packs. I have a light in mine."

Once in position, Wind watched as Stares took Kosa's hand in jers and led the Terran towards the pile of packs. While Wind accepted that je had a growing affection for the aliens, je wasn't yet as comfortable with them as Stares clearly was. Je was *touching* them; something Stares was reticent to do even with Rips. Granted, in this situation it was required, but Stares hardly seemed put out by it. Stares was as fascinating as je was annoying. Wind was on the misanthropic side of the Rip social participation spectrum, which was why je was a great hunter and an even greater sniper, but Stares was *overly* social. Je wasn't meant to be a hunter, that was for sure. Wind could see how Stares was the sort to lead a community if je could settle jer shit for five minutes.

"See anything, Wind?" Crenk's voice whispered from the floor. Wind started, glad none of the others could see how jer rifle had been dipping as je watched Stares' hips in jer red silk.

"Not yet," je whispered. Je waited, covering Stares and Kosa as they made it to the packs. Je kept jer sight focused on the rectangular entryway. Je practiced deep breathing so that jer shot would be more accurate. Je licked jer lips slowly, a habit from jer hunting days back on Ripplia.

Stares passed Kosa her pack, and Kosa blindly rifled through it with one hand as the pair made it back over to the group. The Terrans' eyes had adjusted to the darkness enough for Kosa to avoid hitting the couch with her knees.

Kosa pulled her light from her back and activated it. Wind's nose itched when the film over jer eyes, the natural liquid that descended when je was in darkness, receded. The lights proper came back on.

"Power outage?" Crenk suggested as the group picked themselves off the floor. Kosa frowned as she switched off her portable light. She pulled a zip tie from her pack to attach the light to the strap on her shoulder. Her adaptability would make her a great hunter, but Wind suspected she was a bit too impatient to wait in the shadow of a *toura* tree for hours. She could probably handle an hour. Stares, less than five minutes. Je glanced at the rest of the group, though je kept jer rifle trained on the door. Ow'llent was probably the most patient of the group, though it was likely she would be distracted with her Dev or contemplating the wildlife and would miss the target's arrival if she went hunting.

"Possibly, but somehow I don't think so," Klenni suggested regarding the lights. "It looks like fun time is over."

"If the aliens are messing with us, why did they not steal our weapons?" Crenk asked as he checked the rounds in his rifle.

Kosa shrugged as she opened her backpack to take inventory. "No idea, but I'm not complaining."

"You don't complain, do you?"

Kosa paused and looked at him, bag hanging idly in her hand. Their eyes met and stayed with each other's for a long moment as if Kosa were deciding how to respond. Was she under the impression Crenk had insulted her? Wind couldn't tell.

"No," she said. "Complaining is not useful. I bitch at people when they mess around, but I don't complain about my situation." She gave a small smirk. "But if I need to let off steam about something, there are two methods I tend to employ."

Crenk's eyes widened, but he did not ask her to clarify.

Kosa began directing the team to various positions across the room.

"Are we doing a last stand?" Stares asked. "I've always wanted to be part of a last stand!"

"Yes, every time something odd happens, the creatures show up. I'm expecting them."

"Corporal, what if they don't show up?" Rammy asked.

"Then we move on."

No one disagreed.

The creatures did not show up. The crew waited an hour. Stares was fidgeting so much beside jer that Wind breathed a sigh of relief when Kosa said they were moving out.

"If the creatures won't come to us, then we'll go to them!" the Terran declared.

"Maybe there are no more creatures. Maybe that party last night was a congratulations-you-survived party," Klenni suggested.

"You want the aliens to be friendly so you can buy drugs from them," Ow'llent teased.

Klenni gently fluttered her tendrils at Ow'llent. Wind assumed the movement was a gentle "screw you," like the kind je would say to jer cluster-cousins when they teased jer.

"Come on, come on," Kosa urged.

Allie's schematics suggested they head to the right. Kosa and Crenk took point. Klenni walked behind them with Stares. Flugger trailed the two. Even Wind could tell he and Klenni were fighting about something. Probably something ridiculous like who used the last of their fin lotion. From what je observed during jer time during the war, couples were always fighting about something stupid. Je took rearguard with Rammy and Ow'llent in front of him.

"I have a theory." Ow'llent leaned towards Rammy, but Wind could hear her just fine. By the way the Terran's eyes darted towards his corporal when Ow'llent spoke, he was more worried about annoying Kosa than alerting the aliens. Ow'llent ignored his discomfort. "I think this ship is not entirely mechanical. I've been scanning it with my Dev, and what limited data I could collect shows organic matter in high concentration."

Rammy's eyebrows came together. "What do you mean?

"This ship, it's alive."

"It's a giant space slug?"

Ow'llent sighed. "No. You know how we use A.I. in our ships to manage certain functions? Life support, waste dispersion, etc.?"

"Yes, we do that too."

"We all do – the Pir-An invented it. You people got it from them."

"Yes, well, go on."

"I think this ship uses biological organic components to do the same thing. That's why Allie can hack into only certain parts of it; it can only access similar systems. I think these walls are armour. And it's also why and how we are being led; we're being controlled."

"What!?"

Wind glanced at the walls. Je didn't wholly discount Ow'llent's discovery, but je couldn't begin to fathom how that would work. Then again, je had no training in anything but hunting, cooking, and mending jer clothes. A spaceship technician je was not.

"Incoming!" Kosa called. Klenni let out a small shriek, Flugger swore, and Stares cackled. "Wind, any movement back there?"

"No, hunt leader," Je replied without thinking. Stares only had time to turn jer head to glance at Wind in surprise before Kosa was snapping orders. The group instantly obeyed her instructions as the creatures careened around the corner.

They were fewer creatures, ten in all, but they were bigger than before. No longer were they simply hacked together hybrids of all races, but mechanical parts were adhered to their limbs, hands, and heads – they were armoured.

A pale red light blinked twice by Wind's eye where jer rifle scope was positioned – five shots remaining. Wind used two, both headshots, evening the odds of the fight. The rest of the creatures howled in response and stormed towards the group. They moved too fast for Wind to risk wasting a bullet, so je threw the rifle over jer shoulder and pulled out jer knife. Everyone was engaged in a battle. Rather than attacking mindlessly as before, these creatures were more cunning. Three cordoned off Kosa and Crenk so the rest could make it to the others. Kosa took out one with her shotgun before it reached the pair.

"Behind me!" Hynd roared to Flugger as a drooling creature with a Terran head and Rip arms reached them. The doctor made no heroic stand, diving behind the Dirge. Hynd slammed the creature in the head with their massive paws, raking their claws into the creature's flesh for good measure. The creature's Rip arms were long, and they used them to jam their curved nails into the Dirge's neck even as it stumbled from the blow to the head. Hynd roared and head-butted the creature, sending it sprawling to the floor. Klenni shot the creature in the skull.

As she did so, another creature leapt for her from behind, grabbing her backpack and slamming the Pir-An to the floor on top of it. Luckily, the creature had a Pir-An body, so it wasn't very agile when it jumped on top of Klenni, but it had Terran arms, which it used to pin the Pir-An down. Klenni struggled to move, kicking at the monster and whipping it with her tendrils to no avail. The creature ignored her attacks and arched its Strenoi head forward. Klenni managed to roll with all her force at the last second; the teeth missed her neck but sunk deep into Klenni's exposed fin. The Pir-An screamed, and her eyes rolled back in her head.

"Klenni!" Flugger yelled as Hynd brought their paws together and slammed the creature in the temples. The creature pulled back from Klenni's fin, leaving wounds that bled profusely. The monster stumbled, dazed. Hynd wrapped their large arms around the already flimsy neck and broke it.

Ow'llent and Rammy were fighting their own adversaries. Ow'llent kept one at bay with her pike-like weapon, swinging with determination if a severe lack of skill. Rammy chose to save his last magazine for later use and was exchanging punches with a half-Terran half-Dirge. Rammy was taking a beating; the fourth hit to the face split the Terran's lip, and he stumbled in pain. The top half of the creature he was fighting was Terran and grinned with the derision unique to their species. The creature's eyes moved to the Terran's fallen pack, and it raised a huge Dirge foot and slammed it down on the bag. Something splintered. Rammy balled up his fists again as

Wind strode forward into the fray, grabbed the monster by the shoulder, reached around it, and slid jer knife across the creature's throat.

Rammy spat blood. "Thanks, pal." He winced after speaking, his split lip oozing.

Wind nodded. Ow'llent let out a bellow of triumph as she ran her creature through.

The sharp retort of a shotgun overtook Ow'llent's cheer, followed by the crunch of something against a wall, then a scream of rage. In front of Wind, a bloody-mouthed Stares stood over a dead creature that was now missing most of its throat, Crenk was bashing in the head of another, and Kosa was staring at her broken shotgun. Clearly, she had fired on the creature, but it had fought through the pain of the slug to reach her. Given it was a Dirge-Strenoi with a Rip face, it had wrenched the beloved weapon from its owner and slammed it against the wall. Kosa had taken her revenge, launching herself towards the creature and stabbing it repeatedly in the chest with her bowie knife. When she picked up what remained of her shotgun, despair replaced the victory on her face.

"Everyone aside from Airi okay?" Kosa sighed, running a hand over her face. Wind had seen Terrans cry before, and given Kosa's red eyes, wrinkled forehead, and pressed lips, she was trying not to.

I'm fine," Crenk said. "The *encim* creature smashed my Mystic's-damned pack, though!"

"I need some bandaging," Rammy said, gingerly touching his lips.

"My neck is bleeding," Hynd offered.

"My leg hurts," Stares groaned.

"Klenni needs attention first!" Flugger snapped. The other Pir-An lay on the floor, blood still running from the wounds on her fin. Her eyes were closed, and she appeared to be unconscious.

"Looks superficial," Ow'llent commented.

The glare Flugger administered made the much larger and stronger person back up. "No, it's not. Our fins are extremely sensitive! Take all the nerve endings in the Terran clitoris and times that by a million. The pain must have been intense, enough that she passed out."

"Stupid design if you ask me," Crenk muttered.

Kosa held up a hand to prevent anyone else from commenting on Pir-An physiology. "Be that as it may, Rammy, Hynd, Crenk, and Stares – guard Flugger as he patches Klenni and tries to wake her up. I'm going to scout this way a bit with Allie. Wind, you go the other way. Two minutes, then turn back." Kosa's voice trembled. She took off at a jog.

Wind nodded, heading out. Je found nothing. On jer way, they had passed a few doors, but now there were none. Je placed jer hand against the wall. Organic? Didn't seem so.

When Wind returned, Flugger was using Rammy's knife to gently shave some hair from Hynd's neck to see to their wounds. Klenni lay unconscious on the ground, opaque sealant on her fin wounds. The areas of skin je could see were rust-coloured and puffy.

"Allie found another room we can access," Kosa declared as she rounded the corner. "Let's go there now and finish patching everyone up. Regroup." Her face was wan, and her hands were fists. A tendon in her neck pulsed.

Flugger stepped back from Hynd, and the Dirge bent down and lifted Klenni into their arms. The Pir-An stirred but didn't wake. The dark red, almost purple, blood from the Dirge's neck wound was finally beginning to slow, the trickle running in thin rivets onto Klenni's stomach. Flugger had used up the last of the sealant on Klenni at Hynd's insistence.

"Why are your most sensitive areas on your back?" Stares asked Flugger.

"Fuck off, you piece of shit!" Flugger replied, his tendrils flailing so fast they were a blur. Wind hissed at him, unable to hold it in. Stares, for once, was taken aback and slightly stumbled.

"Watch it!" Kosa whirled around. Wind thought she was about to berate jer for hissing, but, instead, she turned on the Pir-An. "I don't care if Klen is your life partner. We've talked about remarks like that. We're a fucking team, and I'll not have you disrespecting anyone in it for no reason. Je asked a logical question."

Flugger stood his ground. Wind had to give the guppy some credit because je wasn't sure je would be able to withstand the Terran's glower.

"It was trying to goad me into an argument!" Flugger protested.

Kosa's glare intensified. "First of all, calling Stares *it* is extremely rude. Second, I was also wondering how your people evolved in that manner."

Flugger sighed. "It's because the fin holds the central nervous system of our tendrils. It's like we have a second brain in there. It's sensitive as a defence mechanism. And if we're doing something dangerous, like fighting in battle, we generally have fin armour. There! You happy, you shells-damned *kringle amers*?!"

"*Kringle amers*?" Rammy asked.

"Lesser life form," Stares translated.

"How do you know that?" Flugger demanded. He must have been using the second official Pir-An language to swear, given it hadn't translated for Wind. How *did* Stares know it?

Stares shrugged. "Call me that again, and we'll see who the lesser life form is, my tasty friend."

"Are you threatening me?"

"That depends. Are you going to get off your high horse? Or do I have to eat that too?"

Kosa moved to stand between them. "Alright, alright, enough. We have Klen, Rammy, and Hynd to patch up still. Let's move."

The dimly lit space was a utility closet of sorts, at least to Wind's understanding. The lighting was lower than the other species preferred, but the area was roomy enough for the group. It had panels on the walls at four-foot intervals, and machinery stood impassive and inexplicable in its function.

"It's a maintenance room," Rammy explained, peering at a large machine that was connected to the ceiling with what could only be piping and conduits. Growing on the metal or composite material was a light orange moss. "This appears to be a sort of heating coil. It must be what provides temperature to this level of the ship. Ow'llent, look at these here … I think you're right about the organic fusion."

As the scientists marvelled at the alien design of the ship, Wind settled towards the back of the room, sinking to jer butt. Three shots remained in jer rifle. Je took the respite to notch two more headshots into the stock with a claw. At this rate, je would need a second stock. Wind's grandparent would be proud.

Flugger finished patching up Hynd, then handed Rammy a bio-clamp for his lip. The Pir-An grunted in response to any attempt at conversation.

"Are we going to talk about that fight? How different the creatures were?" Stares asked, claws clacking together.

"Don't sound so excited, Stares." Kosa sighed, sitting against the wall in a very uncharacteristic slump, staring at the shotgun pieces she had taken with her. She suddenly tossed the remains into the farthest and darkest corner of the room. Their clatter resounded like a tray of plates dropped in a near-deserted diner. Everyone looked at something other than Kosa, unsure what to say.

Except for Stares. Je stopped clacking jer claws and looked down at Kosa. "You loved that weapon, yes?"

Kosa rubbed her eye. "My … it had sentimental value. My grandmother gave it to me." She grimaced. "And don't say something of sentimental value shouldn't be brought into battle."

"I wouldn't," Stares said, jer tone soft. Wind raised an eye-ridge.

"I just … I just … it just doesn't seem fair that my damn shotgun, which made it through the *war*, is now a hunk of shitty metal. It's garbage. It shouldn't bother me so much, I guess, but it does. I … identified with it." She sniffed, wiping away a tear that had escaped her left eye. Crenk set down his backpack and turned towards Kosa, likely to bolster her spirits as a good second-in-command should.

Before he could, Stares opened jer mouth and began to sing, jer voice directed at Kosa. Wind sat up sharply, uncaring that jer eyes were likely as wide as jer head.

It was a very common Rip song – an elegy – but it was also used to soothe the young. Stares' voice was lilting and strong, with perfect pitch. It all made sense to Wind now. Stares was not some Rip from the swamp. Je was Upper Echelon. While most Rip communities were nomadic tribes, they had a small upper class: Rips who had made a stand four generations ago and carved out a base in a mountain where the *Borkas* couldn't reach. They built walls and farmed. They conducted surveys of the various settlements. They were the first to trade with the other species, and they had some technology, agriculture, and the time to devote to singing and art. And politics. The nomadic tribes called them Heretics because they abandoned the old ways, though jealousy played a big part in that moniker.

Wind narrowed jer eyes as je slumped back down. Stares had lied to jer the whole time. Je was not a mercenary like je was – je was here for some other reason, some *political* reason. Je had to be. That was why je wasn't the best fighter, why je was so concerned with discovery more than escape. There was a reason Rips like Wind didn't even try to join the UE: the UE Rips were flighty with Rip traditions, too risky, too demanding in their devotion to the UE cause, which was to elevate the Rips from what they viewed as their base state. Wind never thought je'd meet one in jer life. They didn't let many people into their base, and they didn't spend time in Ripplia proper. They called the other Rips "roamers", and it wasn't a compliment.

Stares' voice was beautiful, Wind had to admit. As was jer deception. Wind would never have been able to pull that off. Stares was so crafty. Was jer frantic and overly-enthusiastic personality a front? Who was the real Stares? Would Wind ever know? Wind's other cilia, the ones not on jer feet, flexed within jer pants. Je blinked, glancing down. Nothing was pressed up against jer, nothing was around that would cause … je let out a sigh of defeat. Je could not longer ignore this thing that had been building in jer since the two of them talked on top of the ship the first night they were here. Je wanted to mate with Stares. Of course, je did. Stares was Upper Echelon. The rare skin colour, the singing, the scheming, jer unabashed lack of fear. How could Wind not want to get with that? *Dammit.* And until Stares helped jer out, je would have the distraction of what the other races called "being horny," but in a manner that was as strong as an addict needing a hit. Je would start to lose concentration and jer hands would shake. At least, that's what jer grandparent had explained. Wind had never experienced it before. They called it the *Thrum*. Why did it have to be on *Misery* of all places?

As Stares wrapped up jer song, Kosa stood and approached the Rip. She reached forward and took Stares in her arms, pulling jer close. Stares hissed slightly but tolerated the hug.

"Oh, shit," Ow'llent said. "We have a problem."

CHAPTER 18: OW'LLENT

"What?" Hynd and Rammy asked in unison, turning away from the odd scene of Kosa embracing the volatile Stares.

"Our FP is broken."

When Crenkleost set down their pack, Ow'llent had opened it to find that their machine had been smashed to bits.

Rammy snatched up the Terran's pack and let out a groan. "Ugh, ours is broken too! I guess we're stuck eating Pir-An or Rip food."

"No." Flugger shook his head. "I noticed earlier but didn't have a chance to say anything. Ours was broken when the creature attacked Klenni."

All eyes turned to the Rips. Having escaped the hug, Stares opened jer bag and let out a droning hiss that lasted five whole seconds. "Ours is *Borkas* shit."

"Wait, all the food producers are destroyed?" Hynd asked, bovine eyes blinking steadily. "All in the same battle?"

Ow'llent sighed. "You think it wasn't accidental."

"Is anything on this goddamn ship accidental?" Rammy asked.

Kosa exhaled sharply. "We have to make do. Frankly, I thought we were getting a little complacent here. With our food producers, we could have wandered around here for weeks, maybe months. But now we must escape."

"I was never complacent," Flugger muttered. Ow'llent resisted rolling her eyes. Flugger was such a tail-keeper.

"Why would they do this?" Crenkleost asked. "Why would they wait until now to destroy the food producers? If they had sent in those bigger creatures when we were in the lab, or even at our first attack, they could have killed some, or all, of us." He slammed his fist into the wall. "I hate not knowing their game!"

"Such a pilot," Kosa remarked, though she softened the comment with a rare half-smile.

"What do you mean by that?" Crenkleost bared his teeth, though with less menace than usual.

Kosa stuck out her hip and crossed her arms over her chest. She hadn't yet dropped the smile. "Pilots. Once you're in the air, you have a target, and you go after it. Us marines, we need to think on our feet."

"Oh please!" Crenkleost snarled, but his tone dropped to mild irritation. "You wouldn't even get to the battle without us!"

Kosa poked him on the shoulder with her finger, then twiddled her fingers before his eyes as if waving goodbye as she spoke. "Sure, you drop us off, but then you fly above, watching us do all the dirty work."

"Stars are in the sky, and dirt is on the ground," Crenkleost replied, his tone haughty.

Kosa crinkled her nose. "What does that mean?"

"It sounds better in our language," Ow'llent cut in. She had been watching Crenkleost with the Terran female since their escape from the lab. While she was relieved the two weren't fighting anymore, as their constant one-upping had been getting on her nerves, something about their still-continuous banter was starting to rub her the wrong way. Why couldn't they stop talking to one another if they disliked each other so much? It was like cousins.

Then again, thinking back to the drug-induced party, where Crenkleost and Kosa had been dancing together long after everyone else had retired to the couches, it was decidedly *not* like cousins. It reminded her more of when Corcalla had picked fights with her back when both of them were vying for the same grant funding before becoming a couple. There was an antagonism, but it was from being too similar rather than too different. Ow'llent frowned at the pair, not wanting to admit what was right in front of her eyes.

"I have an idea!" Rammy suggested. He had been studying the heating mechanism. "I think Klenni and I can override the controls on the maintenance shaft here." He pointed to a large square access panel in the ceiling. It was located in the corner of the room that didn't have any machinery.

"And?" Stares asked. Rammy pushed on the square. It rose upwards to rest perpendicular to the floor. He pointed inside.

"We go through it. It's huge – I bet it's designed for transporting either a team of people or perhaps machinery."

"Klenni can't do anything until she's feeling better," Flugger warned.

"Shells, Flugger, I'm fine!" Klenni burst out. She'd been stirring since Stares' serenade. She sat up and winced. "Rammy, if you sit down here with me, I can help you with Allie."

"Are you sure?" Flugger asked.

"You gave me painkillers!" Klenni's tendrils began a wild dance Ow'llent had learned expressed anger. Flugger said nothing, merely slid to the ground, his fish-face contorted into as much of a frown as he could muster.

"Wind, guard the door. Hynd, you relax. Ow'llent, Crenk, Stares, and I will inspect this hatch," Kosa ordered.

"What about me?" Flugger asked.

"Just take five."

Flugger grumbled.

"Lose your tail," Ow'llent said as she passed him. "You're acting like a newborn wanting his milk."

"Our guppies don't drink bodily fluid like you savages," Flugger replied, glaring. Ow'llent bared her teeth at him, and he looked away quickly.

As Ow'llent moved to join Stares and Kosa in the hatch, she noticed Crenkleost in the far corner. He reached down and picked up Kosa's shotgun pieces, sliding them into his pack.

Ow'llent opened her mouth to ask him what he was doing but closed it again. Kosa hadn't noticed what Crenkleost had done as she and Stares were gazing upwards. Ow'llent joined them, and Crenkleost slid into the smaller room shortly after.

The shaft was indeed large, wide enough for Hynd's bulk and Crenkleost and Ow'llent's shoulders to fit comfortably. Unfortunately, it was blocked by a thick, dark-green grate that resembled a net. Ow'llent reached up to tug on it. It was warm. She withdrew her hand quickly, wiping it on her exo-suit as if it were slimy.

"If everything else on this ship is so advanced, why is there a ladder?" Kosa asked. Ow'llent had no idea. The foursome stared up for a moment.

"This is an emergency hatch, isn't it?" Stares suggested.

"What's what Rammy said."

"Maybe they don't use technology because of that?"

"What?" Crenkleost asked. "Oh, wait, I know what you mean. An elevator could break down, but a ladder doesn't."

"Unless you smash it!" Stares laughed.

Crenkleost let out a guffaw and shook his head. "Rip, you are crazy."

"You know it, Shoulders," Stares replied. "You get a lot of action with those?"

"Stares!" Kosa laughed.

"Oh, come on. No one can deny that Crenkleost is attractive. For a Strenoi."

"Stares!" Kosa laughed again but with less ferocity.

"Actually, Crenkleost is considerably wider in the chest than most of our males," Ow'llent added, enjoying the discomfort on Crenkleost's face. "A slender chest is generally a more desirable trait in males than in females. If you're going by our societal standards of beauty, of course."

Crenkleost rubbed the back of his neck with his hand. "Yeah, my best-cousin was the looker in the family. And I'm hardly a close second. My shoulders always embarrassed me when I was younger. I got teased a lot. And Guermun has a much better ridge-bone."

"Let me see your cousin!" Stares demanded.

Ow'llent chuckled and held up her Dev. Crenkleost glared at her, but she ignored him as she accessed a data file on the illustrious lawyer who was often in the news. "Here you go, Stares, don't get too excited."

Stares peered at the other Strenoi on the Dev. Along with his clothes, Guermun wore a traditional barrister's sash and was staring at the camera with the standard Strenoi posture. However, there was a twinkle in his eye. Stares waved a hand at Ow'llent. "Nah, I like Shoulders here better, right, Kosa? Crenk's cousin's skin is so bright red! I prefer Crenk's wine-coloured scales. If he were wine, I'd drink him right up, right, Kosa?"

"I guess everyone is calling me Crenk, now?" the Strenoi mumbled. Ow'llent also thought it was inappropriate but said nothing. She wanted the Workers to have more rights, but that didn't mean shitting on all Estate traditions. It was an argument she and Corcalla had quite often. By the mystics, she missed her wife.

"Look how tall his ridge bone is!" Kosa added, also ignoring Stares' pointed questions. "How does he not hit his head on doorframes?" She paused. "Wait, is this why you guys have triangular windows? I always wondered …"

Crenkleost let out a laugh. "I suppose so! And this is the first time anyone has said my cousin has any defects! Do you know how many breeding requests Guermun has? And he's always had very attractive partners, too. Every month's end when he'd come back from school and then from work, he'd bring a new partner. It drove my mother crazy, but my uncles and aunts thought it was a riot."

"Is he the lawyer you mentioned before?" Kosa asked.

"Yes."

"Most of that is smooth-talking, I guess." She smiled at him. "No offence, but you don't strike me as the networking type?"

Crenkleost shrugged. "I'm an Estate-head, they call it. When I'm not flying, I prefer to help out at home, to manage the house and help with the kids for my mother, as my uncles and aunts are busy with industry. I check on the produce fields, maintain the home animals, and patrol the desert when the kids are at the academy."

"We Terrans would call you a farm boy, then." Kosa laughed. "Brawny. The outdoors-type."

"Seems to fit." Crenkleost smiled down at her. "As we talked about before, I'm more into the wilderness than the city."

"You and me both." Kosa returned his smile, a full one for once. "Dancing took up a lot of my spare time when I was a teenager, but whenever I had the chance, I was off hiking in the canyons. I had a summer job as a guide one year when I sprained my shoulder and had to take a month off dance."

Ow'llent glanced at Stares. The Rip was studying the two military types with an uncharacteristic quiet as if je were a child trying to make adults forget je was there so they would let jer stay up later than usual. Ow'llent returned her gaze to Crenkleost. His smile at Kosa was not a challenge, as she was accustomed to seeing on his face when he looked at the Terrans. His teeth were partially hidden by his lips, and the corners of his mouth were turned up rather than his mouth opening wide. Crenkleost was *smiling* in the Terran manner, and he was doing it on purpose, for Kosa's benefit. His stance was radiating pleasure, acceptance. And the Terran was looking up at him in the same way, her body relaxed and calm.

Ow'llent's mind reeled. Were they … into each other?

She glanced back at Stares, who had a thin trail of saliva running from jer mouth. Je must be dying to say something risqué or amusing but was holding back. Did the Rip also sense that Kosa and Crenkleost were flirting? Of course, je was, or je wouldn't be so damn quiet right now. Stares, a matchmaker? If it weren't so infuriating, it would be comical. Despite all her studies and vehement argument that the species shared genetic history, Ow'llent felt her lip curl. The corporal and the pilot were both adults, true, and could do what they wanted with their bodies, but a Terran-Strenoi romantic relationship was incredibly distasteful … disgusting even. True, the Terrans shouldn't be wiped out, but to mingle with them, to become emotionally attached? She liked Rammy well enough and Klenni too, but she had no intention of forming a lasting bond with these aliens. She wanted to study the aliens as a scientific endeavour, not live with them … not become involved with them on an emotional and physical level. How could she? They were so different. They were so ugly. The Terrans had fleshy, overly soft skin, lacklustre eyes, small teeth, and the men had no ridge bone to speak off. And the women had two dangling unwieldy breasts, unlike Ow'llent's single, wider one with its gentle curve. Was this why they Crenkleost on this mission with her? Had be been involved with a Terran before? Crenkleost was an emotional person who often acted before he thought – he was from the Equator, the rural wilderness. People there weren't as good at keeping their emotions under control as a proper High Born Strenoi should be since they were less civilized, almost Workers. Crenkleost was clearly letting his emotions cloud his judgement. But what was he thinking would happen with Kosa? Neither of their societies would allow the two of them to stay together if that was their intention. There was no way this was a passing attraction based on looks – a fetish for one another's species – as they had hated each other at the start of the journey. Ow'llent had her fair share of romances in her life; she knew what it was like to learn to care for someone you initially thought you had nothing in common with. But this? Crenkleost deserved a Mindwipe for this. It was disgusting. Abhorrent.

The two people in question broke their gaze from one another and returned it to the ladder. Ow'llent caught eyes with Stares and shook her head as if to say, don't encourage them. Stares blinked innocently, which Ow'llent took to mean the Rip was going to do everything je could to help them along. And Stares was nothing if not persistent.

After ten minutes, Rammy helped Klenni stand, and the group joined the rest at the hatch.

"We're supposed to climb this?" Flugger demanded. "How is Klenni to manage?"

The other Pir-An let out a deep sigh. Flugger's pessimism appeared to be grating on everyone's nerves.

"Perhaps," Wind began, "a sacrifice is all the aliens require to let the rest of us go free. I vote we leave Flugger."

Flugger muttered something under his breath in his own language.

"I will put Klenni on my back," Hynd offered.

"Thank you," Klenni agreed.

"I suppose I can carry Flugger again," Crenkleost suggested.

Flugger's vicious recoil caused laughter to bubble up in Ow'llent throat.

"Oh, come on, bud," Rammy said to the flustered doctor. "The handholds are too far apart for you. Hell, Kosa can barely reach and she's a foot taller than you."

"I don't need help from a Strenoi."

"You know what I think?" Stares asked but didn't wait for anyone to reply. "I think Flugger needs to stop being so racist."

Flugger let out a groan that reverberated up the shaft. "Shells. Fine. I'll ride the Strenoi like a fucking chariot again. Let's go, seahorse."

"Just a second," Rammy began, fiddling with Allie. The net above did not move.

"Give it here, apprentice," Klenni ordered.

Rammy laughed, passing it over.

Ow'llent stood back from the group. Kosa and Crenkleost were speaking in low voices about the ladder, Hynd was staring up at the shaft, Stares had climbed up the ladder's three lower rungs and now hung off the gate like a child at a play center, and the rest hovered around Klenni, watching her work on Allie's interface.

Wind, usually so still, shuffled jer feet and watched Stares intently as the silver-skinned Rip swung like a drying carcass, jer robes billowing gently. Ow'llent rolled her eyes. Was everyone hooking up around here? Were the aliens injecting them secretly with hormones or releasing pheromones into the atmosphere? Was anything here even real? Were her emotions legitimate or a function of the environment? What about her memories? Was this the afterlife? Everything was so mind-bogglingly uncanny that a large part of her was growing convinced she was dead, or at least in some sort of transitory realm wavering between life and death.

Was she in a coma?

She nibbled on the edge of her tongue, then sucked in air sharply when she bit too hard. A Mindwipe of this place would almost be a blessing, but she would die before she let the high Council mess with her head. She had enough experience with that back on Strenovast. Her hand curled around the shaft of her pike. She still couldn't believe that her own people would try to Mindwipe her just because she had discovered something unsavory about their genetic code. How could a civilized people, with multiple worlds and discoveries and successes, do that to one of its citizens that wasn't doing anything wrong?

Four military officers had shown up at her office at the university after her last lecture of the season. She had known they were special forces because they wore the vest but no rank. All the covert units that reported directly to the High Council were considered to have one rank to prevent ambition. Covert soldiers were supposed to be loyal to the High Council and by association, Strenovast. They gave up their estates and family breeding rights to join. They received other perks in return. Their arrival did not surprise Ow'llent; however, it did sadden her. She had expected a terse order to be less passionate about her discoveries, or perhaps a directive to speak only at conferences with older, less impressionable people, not students. Instead, they told her to accompany them, but to where, they refused to say. She had considered protesting but decided it was better to show compliance. Besides, these two wouldn't be the ones making any decisions.

When she stood to follow them, her eyes fell to an etching of her wife, Corcalla, that she kept on her desk. That's what this was about! True, her discoveries likely were something the High Council disliked immensely, but they must have gotten wind of Corcalla's involvement with the Strenoi Liberation Front, the group that was trying to give the Workers upward mobility. Corcalla was the real target here because despite living on Ow'llent's Estate, she was from a much more prestigious bloodline. Her son was an admiral; he would have raised a fuss if his mother were taken, but his aunt? To teach Corcalla a lesson and scare off any other High Born dissidents? Definitely plausible.

They took her by special vehicle to a nondescript office in the industrial sector of her Estate's city, plunking her in a room with another unranked official. This man was of advanced age but still spry, his eyes hard and scales a dull blue. Ow'llent didn't lie. She told the official under no circumstances would she stop her work into the shared genetic history with the Terrans, regardless of how many tenures they rejected her and how many conferences they denied her.

The older man sighed and rapped his claws faintly on the table. He leaned forward, looking Ow'llent in the eye. "Here's our only offer, doctor. You state your retirement. You destroy your data. You undergo a Mindwipe. Then you can move back to your Estate under a generous stipend."

Ow'llent didn't need to think about it. Not only would Corcalla be furious and possibly endanger herself in her anger, but Ow'llent was a scientist first and foremost. There was no way she would compromise her data. Retired? Please. She was barely past breeding age.

"Go fuck yourself," she replied.

They gave her the night to think it over. Perhaps they had wanted her to run, to bolt, or, more likely, implicate Corcalla. She hadn't called her wife. She didn't want to worry her. Or push her to do something rash.

She had spent the night tossing and turning, unable to get comfortable on her pallet in the Worker apartment overlooking the campus. She stayed there when she missed the last train to the Estate, which was often enough as she frequently got drawn into her work and forgot to check the time. She debated going home first thing in the morning. Instead, a few hours before sunrise, she sat on her small verandah, overlooking the empty quad. Would this be the last time she would sit here?

A few hours later, she was at the clinic in the nondescript building in the center of the city. She passed over her Dev to the covert officer who was there to make sure she surrendered her data. He took the device and handed her over to the technician. She was lucky in that they didn't think she would put up a real fight, so they sent her to the closest clinic instead of a military installation. But why would she fight back? A government stipend was something they awarded to top generals or High Council members. It was a generous bribe to keep quiet.

But Ow'llent was a woman of science. A woman of principle. A woman who didn't care about living luxuriously. She gave the officer her Dev, but he was not aware she had ordered another from an off-world trader when the government started poking into her work months ago. She'd hidden that device in the basement of her faculty office, under an old dusty crate that hadn't been moved in years. She had carefully lifted the crate so the dust wouldn't be disturbed and set the Dev under it. As she settled into the chair in the Mindwipe facility, she reached into her pocket and brought out a small disc. She held it out to the technician.

"What's this?" the tech asked, eyeing it sideways.

"A bribe. Untraceable funds are stored in an account on Fabri Station under a fake name. You take this, pretend to 'wipe me, and I'll activate the account as I leave the building."

The technician's uniform had frayed cuffs, her claws were scuffed and needed buffing, and she looked tired. Mindwiping was a thankless job because people were there against their will and didn't remember you when the process was complete. There was no camaraderie like in other places of work. And it offered very little chits. She must have been the bottom of her class at her academy to be given such an unappreciated position.

The tech swallowed hard, then lifted her Dev, inserting the disc. Her eyes widened when she saw the amount.

"What did you do?"

"Nothing. I discovered a shared genetic marker between us and the Terrans. They want me to shut up about it."

"I wondered why they wanted to isolate the last three years. You're not a threat to anyone?"

Ow'llent snorted. "An older person like me?"

The tech sighed. "You know how many bribes I get?"

"I'm guessing none as tempting."

"Sit back."

The tech did not give back the disc. Instead, she approached her screen and entered some data. Ow'llent tightened her grip on the chair. If the tech started up the machine, Ow'llent would fight her. The officer outside would burst in and shoot her, but at least she'd die knowing she tried. She reconsidered. While Corcalla would be proud to die like that, Ow'llent was not so idealistic. There was another way. Ow'llent took a deep breath.

"Please, I'm begging you," Ow'llent pleaded. It was beneath a Strenoi to beg, but she was desperate.

The technician turned, her eyes wide. She turned back to the computer, muttering to herself.

"I've never begged for anything," Ow'llent said. "I'm High Born. I'm a professor. I'm an upstanding citizen."

The tech growled low in her throat. "Just shut up!" She shook her head. "When the officer comes in, act like you're really really hungover. Gag. Blink a lot. Stumble. You don't know the officer or me, but you're so disoriented you let them drive you home. Stay in for the rest of the day – they'll be watching your place. Even when you're inside, just lay low. Anyone you've met recently, you don't know. Anyone you've known for over a year you remember, but not a lot of details. After a few months, they'll stop tailing you."

"Thank you," Ow'llent said. Never in her life had she experienced such relief. Winning her doctoral position had been terrifying, but this was a whole new level of reprieve.

"I'm doing this for the money, not your pathetic begging. You should be ashamed."

"I know. Regardless, I appreciate it."

Ow'llent was brought back to *Misery* when Klenni stopped typing, and the gate slid open with a gentle sucking noise.

CHAPTER 19: CRENK

The Pir-An wasn't nearly as light as carrying one of his young cousins on his back, but Crenk refused to show how much of a burden the surly doctor was.

The shaft was longer than they thought, reaching almost sixty feet. It seemed far longer based on the load Crenk carried. He had to concentrate on putting his one arm up, then his leg, then his arm, then his leg again. The rungs were four feet apart, meaning that everyone except for Hynd and the Rips had to pull to get to the next rung, almost like rock climbing with a thick ledge. Most of them rested their arms on the step above and then pulled up using a combination of upper body strength and attempts to gain purchase with their feet. Crenk also had to contend with the physiology of his legs. They forced him to stick his bottom half out quite far when climbing to avoid knocking his knees against the wall. The first few times he did this, Flugger obnoxiously sucked in a breath, but, finally, the Pir-An had stopped making the annoying noise every step they climbed. Clearly, the aliens running the ship were tall.

Crenk tried to keep his eyes on the task at hand, but every time he looked up, he saw Kosa's ass a rung above him and nearly missed the step. The Strenoi and Terrans shared a similar evolution in how their butts formed, unlike the Rips and Pir-An, who were rather flat-bottomed, and Kosa's was like an upside-down heart. And it didn't help she was wearing what she called her "workout clothes." Every time he glanced up to see the next rung, and subsequently at her butt, which was often, he recalled what it had felt like when said butt had rubbed against his thighs during the drug-induced dance party. The tractor beam that her lower anatomy had on his gaze made him wonder whether the aliens had drugged him again.

As squad leader, Kosa had insisted on taking point, claiming that Rammy and Wind were needed near the bottom in case any creatures came up from behind. Truthfully, she had whispered to Crenk, she didn't want Ow'llent at the top in case they encountered creatures. The older non-combatant shouldn't be the first into the fire. And Stares couldn't be at the top because je would likely get distracted by something and take off. And then they'd have to go and look for jer.

"Crazy that we would go after jer, you know?" Crenk had said.

Kosa's eyes had crinkled in the corners, and she tilted her head to the side. "You're right. At the start of this journey, I never would have thought I'd be looking out for any of you, aside from Delaney."

"Survival situations show you what really matters, don't they?" he'd replied with a chuckle.

"Ah, pilot, is this the first time you've had to fight for your life?" she'd asked with the smallest of grins.

"You can say that to me when we're in a ship, and I'm dodging missiles, and your heart is stuck in your throat."

"It'll take a lot more than that to make it beat any faster."

"Oh really?" he'd said. Kosa had been about to say something else when Ow'llent had barged between them rather rudely. She was in a mood, snapping at Crenk to check the pack for other damaged items, as she was going to wear it for the climb and didn't want to carry anything unnecessary.

Now, the older Strenoi struggled to carry her pike and lift herself to the next rung. The last time any of them had eaten was last night at the party, as they had been too hungover to stomach food this morning. He wanted to reach down and give her a hand, but she would never accept it. Plus, Flugger would freak out, and he was already digging his surprisingly strong fingers into Crenk's collarbone. Thankfully, the Pir-An didn't have fingernails.

After the group had suffered two near falls – one because Stares got cocky, and the other when Rammy slipped after looking down – Kosa reached the top.

"Dammit, I'm a fucking moron," she said, her voice full of defeat and fatigue. The group rested below her, gripping the rungs with tired hands. "I should have sent Wind up here to recon."

"What's the problem?" Klenni called.

"There's another gate!"

"Give me a minute!"

Crenk craned his head to stare past Ow'llent at the female Pir-An. She used one hand to type into Allie while the other gripped Hynd's fur. The Dirge winced every time Klenni readjusted her hold; their neck wounds had opened up on the climb. Crenk often forgot the Dirge was with them – they were so calm and quiet despite their size. Unlike Wind, who radiated misanthropy, Hynd reminded Crenk of a Mystic – the small sect of semi-religious Strenoi who lived in Mount Petillan'it, the coldest area of Strenovast, and the only area not run by an Estate. They lived a reclusive, austere life they claimed brought peace. It was a common threat from House Mothers or guardians to hyperactive youngsters that if they misbehaved, they would be sent to Mount Petillan'it to live with the Mystics in silent contemplation.

"Kosa," Crenk whispered. He felt Ow'llent's stern gaze on him. Why the hell had she become so frosty all of a sudden? He ignored her.

"Yes?" she asked, glancing down at him. She let herself arc backwards slightly with one hand so she could push her wayward hair behind her ear.

His mind went blank. "Uh, never mind."

Ow'llent scoffed behind him.

"Got it!" Klenni called. The strange gate opened with a squelching that ended in a hiss.

Crenk breathed a sigh of relief and followed Kosa up the ladder. He glanced down to see that Ow'llent hadn't moved.

"Just give me a moment," she said, her tone irritated. He assumed it was from the climb.

Kosa was already up and into the room.

When Crenk reached the lip of the floor, a hand extended down to him. He accepted Kosa's offer of assistance so he could get far enough out of the shaft for the corporal to assist the Pir-An off his back.

"Shells," Flugger breathed. *Shells* was right. The room was the same size and shape as the docking bay *Starship 330307* rested in, but this was pulsing with life where that had been sterile. The room had an earthy smell with an undercurrent of cinnamon. The walls were the same material as the shaft and the lower levels, but dark purple tendrils from the ceiling. They reminded Crenk of the stalactites that formed in the desert caves back home, but instead of mineral, these appeared to be biological. Moisture ran off them, but instead of falling to the ground, drops were gently sucked up into the ceiling in a gravity-defying manner Crenk couldn't explain. The ceiling itself was composed of what looked like dark green moss, and the temperature was humid, almost muggy; his increasing temperature in the shaft had not been entirely due to the exertion of the climb. The room stored nearly a dozen ten-by-ten-foot containers in a seemingly random configuration; they appeared to be placed with no order. Other containers were mounted on the ceiling, the tendrils growing around them but not touching them. What they housed was a mystery. The room was dim, darker than the lower levels, though fist-sized glowing purple orbs floated around the room like fireflies, their purpose unknown.

"And I thought Bubble was a weird place," Kosa whispered.

"Oh, ha, ha. Very funny," Flugger grumbled. He looked up at Crenk. "Un, thanks for the assist, Strenoi." Crenk nodded.

"Where do you think we are?" Crenk asked Kosa, keeping his voice low.

Kosa shrugged. "Hells if I know. At least it's something different."

"Little help?" Ow'llent grunted. Both Kosa and Crenk turned to assist. Kosa made it there first, but Ow'llent batted her hand away and took Crenk's instead. Crenk glanced at Kosa, catching a brief hurt expression before the corporal hid it with an aloof gaze.

Crenk was about to ask Ow'llent what her problem was when Kosa spoke. "Let's scout this room before the rest of them get up here."

"Stay here!" Crenk hissed to Ow'llent while taking the pack from her to lessen the load. The older Strenoi nodded, lowering her hands to her knees to take deep breaths.

Crenk held his raptor-like claws off the floor so they wouldn't clack against the ground, putting his weight on his heels. Kosa was walking quieter than usual too, leaning forward onto her toes. They headed towards the large container in front of them.

"What's our plan?" Crenk whispered when they reached it.

"We get out of this weird-ass room," Kosa replied.

As she spoke, they rounded the container, heading to the left. There was an empty zone between two containers into which they moved.

A gentle shushing noise ended their conversation. Kosa's hair whipped with the force of her violent turn towards it. The source was a large door opening fifty feet in front of them. Seven shapes moved into the room. Kosa and Crenk stopped short. These were not the Frankenstein-like creatures from before. They were four-armed, two-legged beings with four eyes, spider-like mouths, and a long exoskeletal carapace on their backs. They were as tall as Hynd but half the width. The aliens stared at the Terran and Strenoi, blinking with all four eyes. Kosa and Crenk froze, unsure if these were their captors or other captives. The aliens raised weapons, pointing them at the pair.

Kosa and Crenk dove towards the closest container in front of them, seeking cover.

"Hostiles in front! Find cover!" Kosa yelled back at the rest of the group as she pulled out her knife. Crenk joined her in bringing out his golok.

Crenk glanced behind him to see Flugger rush to the right to hide behind the closest crate. Ow'llent grabbed Klenni and pulled her to the left, behind another container. Hynd ran towards the forward crate, hands pulled into fists, surely bracing themselves for combat. Wind and Stares joined them, waiting for orders. Wind pulled out jer rifle, leaning around the side. Rammy pulled himself out of the shaft and ran to cover Flugger. Kosa had told him protecting the medic was the Terran's task in battle if they were pinned down.

"What do we do, Koharu?" Crenk asked. For the first time, he saw her fidget, gripping and regripping the hilt of her knife. She bit her lower lip, a furrow appearing between her brows. Her shoulders were hunched. She didn't reply.

"Why aren't they coming?" Kosa asked after a moment.

"Kosa, orders?" Rammy called.

Crenk continued to watch Kosa. Her face was twisted in indecision. She looked down at her knife. No one else in the group had ammo except for Wind, and he couldn't take out all of them. Finally, she exhaled sharply and shook her head as if to clear it.

She looked at him. "You make a break for the others. I'll distract the group, and you lead them the other way, try to find another exit."

Crenk hissed. "No, Kosa, that's suicide."

Kosa's brow furrowed deeper, and her mouth hardened. "That's an order."

Crenk took her arm, a gesture in his culture that meant he was offering support. He was unaware it meant something rather different in Terran terms, that it was an action that suggested reproach or control.

"I don't report to you. I won't let you kill yourself for us."

"Let me go!" she commanded, yanking her arm away. "I'm the one who got us into this mess, so I'm going to get us out of it!"

As she spoke, a loud whoosh hit Crenk's auditory sensors, followed by a large bang, followed further by Stares' cursing. To the right of them, where the Rips and Dirge had stood, a container now rested. Given that Stares was talking and not screaming in pain, the container was bottomless, but it had trapped the three inside.

"Everyone, freeze!" Crenk bellowed. Another whoosh and bang resounded but behind him this time. Ow'llent and Klenni screamed. Another cage was dropped, presumably surrounding Rammy and Flugger, as the male Pir-An began to yell for Klenni.

To stop Kosa from running at the enemy, Crenk did the only thing he could think of: he tackled her. The cage fell.

Kosa was warm beneath him. Her body smelled of blood, Terran sweat, and other less pleasant things, but his arms tightened around her back regardless. He looked up – the edge of the container had missed his ridge bone by an inch. If he hadn't jumped on her, the container's edge would have landed on Kosa's back, undoubtedly breaking it, possibly severing her in half.

For a moment, she lay still, eyes closed. He looked down at her, taking the time to examine her cheekbones, the curve of her eyes so unlike his, the way her hair spread out behind her head like a fan. She opened her eyes, meeting his. He didn't move, and she didn't try to make him. The intense frustration that had marred her face had dissipated, replaced with resignation or perhaps despondency. Her hands slid out from under his arms so they were free. She rested them on his shoulders. He continued to stare at her and cradle her in his arms. What was she doing?

"Get off, you brute!" she exclaimed, pushing at him. Crenk let go of her, backing up so he could stand. He then took two steps back. Kosa glared. "Why did you do that!?"

"I just saved your ass!"

Kosa frowned, looking around her at their apparent cage. She sighed heavily, slumping down to sit against the wall. "Fuck. I made a real mess of that, didn't I?"

Crenk shrugged, sliding down beside her. "I don't –"

Kosa shook her head sharply, letting her hair fall in front of her face. She was quiet for a moment, then pushed strands of hair behind her ears. Her brow was creased so intently her eyebrows were touching above her nose, and her mouth was scrunched so her lips turned white. After a moment in this position, she relaxed, resting her head back against the container wall.

"No, I did mess up. I should have waited for everyone to climb the ladder. I should have sent one person to scout, not break us into small groups. Climbing the shaft was probably a stupid idea anyway – there's no way they didn't know what we were doing. We've been tracked this entire time, I bet. They're probably watching us right now. I fucked up. This is on me to fix. I'll get us out."

Crenk looked at her, unable and unwilling to hide how impressed he was. He'd never seen anyone accept their failings so gallantly. While he didn't entirely agree that it was her fault they were trapped in this cage, she owned the problem to inspire herself to fix it. She had what he thought he had when he'd defended his best-cousin – she had honour, courage. She was what he wanted to be.

He wanted her respect. No, he *craved* her respect. He was the one who wasn't worthy here. Other than follow her orders, what had he done for the group in this horrid situation? Just like in defending his cousin, he had taken a short-sighted, rash way of approaching a problem. Kosa would never have punched out a superior officer; she would have defended her cousin in a better way.

He glanced at her again. How would she react if she knew why he was really here? His orders were simple. There was a strange ship near the edge of known space. The Rips, somehow, had found out about it too. The Terrans and the Pir-An weren't talking about it, but it was likely they knew it was there. Either way, Crenk's job was to take Ow'llent, who was under High Council surveillance, shadow the Rips to the derelict, then kill them or drive them off before they learned anything of value. They didn't tell him what Ow'llent had done, but he was to pretend this was a mission of discovery, then, afterwards, bring her back to military command *if* she survived. The emphasis on the *if* had make Crenk's eyes narrow in suspicion. At the time of getting the mission, he hadn't cared what they had planned for her. All he'd wanted was to fly again, to have his pilot's status reinstated.

Yet after seeing how hard Kosa fought for not only Rammy, but all of them, he was ashamed at how he leapt to clear his dishonour without thinking how it would affect Ow'llent, let alone the Rips. Crenk wasn't an idiot; he knew his government performed unsanctioned Mindwipes on those they considered dissidents. He'd heard the rumours that his government assassinated those that threatened the High Council's control. Less than a week ago, he would have ignored what they were planning to do to Ow'llent to further his own goals. But now … *no*, he decided. He was going to *protect* Ow'llent. He would not take her back to Strenovast, but somewhere else. He would lie and say she was dead. He would not turn her in for a Mindwipe or to be sent to a penal colony or to be *murdered* for whatever crime the government accused her. Military standing be damned – his personal honour was at stake. Yes, they would ground him, but he would not sacrifice Ow'llent for his happiness.

He looked at Kosa. She wouldn't do that to anyone. Neither would he.

CHAPTER 20: RAMMY AND FLUGGER

Neither Terren nor Pir-An were happy to be in this situation. True, no one was delighted to be trapped on the aptly named *Misery* with no food or water, but Rammy and Flugger were even more frustrated to be confined in this strange cage with one another. Rammy thought Flugger was a whiny, suspicious, racist twat. Flugger had no issue with Rammy; in fact, he considered him one of the better aliens of the group because he was easy-going and non-confrontational, but Flugger wanted to be with Klenni. He wanted to work things out with her. He wanted to apologize. He didn't want to die trapped in a shitty cage with a Terran male whose odour was rank with mammal sweat. At least he wasn't trapped with Hynd, whose fur was getting more and more pungent by the hour.

"Is everyone alright?" Rammy had yelled after the reverberations of the last cage had dulled to silence.

Everyone replied in the affirmative, Stares including a complaint about being bored already.

"What do we do, Kosa?" Rammy had asked.

"Sit tight!" Kosa replied. "Unless anyone has any ideas? Where's Allie?"

"It's with us," Hynd replied.

"So, it's useless," Flugger had sighed quietly. The Dirge's fingers were too big to use the machine's controls, and the Rips were unaccustomed to intricate tech.

"OK, well, orders stay the same. Sit tight. I'll get us out," Kosa had called.

While they could hear dull murmurs begin, none of the other conversations were audible. As such, Flugger had sat down against a wall, Rammy across from him.

Rammy fiddled with this rifle, counted the rounds, and wiped it with his sleeve. Finally, he set it aside. Flugger closed his eyes but found he could not sleep. He kept his eyes closed for what felt like ten minutes. He opened them to find Rammy staring at him, pulling gently on his ear lobe.

"What do you want, Terran?" Flugger asked.

Rammy had been watching Flugger because there wasn't much else to do. How had a sweetheart like Klenni ended up with a surly bastard like Flugger? Then again, he had never expected AJ to look his way, and they had dated for almost six months. Dammit, AJ.

"Just bored, I guess. Want to talk about stuff?"

Flugger snorted. "Like what? How we're all going to die?"

Rammy snorted back. "We're not going to die. Kosa will think of something."

"Ah yes, the walking example of the military-industrial complex."

"At least she's not the walking example of a *douchebag*."

Flugger blinked slowly. "What's that?"

"A Terran insult. It means you're a dick."

Flugger's fish lips pressed into a straight line. "Pardon me for being a little upset by being trapped here, my partner being injured, and being forced to play doctor for Rips and other malcontents."

"The only malcontent here is you, man! You need to chill out. Getting stressed makes this entire thing worse."

"Nothing could make this situation worse."

Rammy raised his eyebrows. "There are a number of ways it could be worse! You could be dead. You could be strung up like Hynd was. You could be missing limbs. You could be trapped in a cage with a dickhead, but you're not."

Flugger grunted.

"So," Rammy continued. "Let's work through this. I take it you and Klenni are having trouble because you want kids and she doesn't?"

"How dare you!" Flugger sat up sharply. "That is personal!"

Rammy chuckled. "It's goddamn obvious; that's what it is. Fine, you don't want to talk about that? What do you want to do to pass the time?"

"Let's play what we on Bubble call 'The Quiet Game.'"

"We have that game too, but, nah, that's boring. Do you guys have the same relationship structure we do? Like do you date then commit fully to one another? I always wondered when I worked with Pir-An at school."

Flugger's tendrils whipping black and forth would have put off another Pir-An from further conversation, but the Terran kept staring at him expectantly. Flugger sighed heavily.

"Yes, it's similar. First, we have a less serious relationship to see if we're compatible, then we have a ceremony of unity." Flugger's tendrils slowed to a gentle wave as he recalled his ceremony again. Klenni's beautiful fin would never look the same after that wound. It was the

Terran equivalent of someone having a massive scar on their face.

"I'm assuming you asked Klenni out?" Rammy grinned.

Flugger let out a small laugh. "Actually, no. She pursued me. We met at a, well, you'd call it a bar. From what I understand, your places of socialization aren't split into purpose, correct?"

"I have no idea what you mean."

"We have … bars … for single people looking to have non-reproductive sex. We have bars for committed couples to hang with other committed couples. We have bars for committed couples who want to meet another couple for friendship. We have bars for committed couples who want to meet another couple for sex. We have bars for single people to meet other single people to date, not just sex."

"That's very confusing. What if you walk into the wrong bar?"

"You leave?"

Rammy paused for a moment, then nodded. "That actually does sounds nice. None of that scoping around the bar looking for someone you hope is single."

"Are you committed? You never mentioned anyone." The instant he asked this, Flugger regretted it. He didn't want to know about this Terran's problems! Why had he let this man lure him into a discussion?

Rammy's face tightened around the mouth, and his eyes looked off in the distance. *Oh great, here it comes.*

"Yeah," Rammy sighed. "I had a boyfriend for the last half-year. AJ. He dumped me. That's why I went off with Kosa. She's on leave, and I took an early leave too to get away from him. AJ … he's not in my unit, but we crossed paths a lot at base, and I … I found it hard to interact with him. I had only planned to take a week off, clear my head, then return to finish my stint."

Rammy ran a hand over the curly black beard growing in after days of being unable to shave. Flugger had noticed that everyone appeared a little frayed around the edges. Kosa's armpits and lower legs were growing hair, Ow'llent and Crenk's nails were curling inwards, the Rips were losing bits of skin here and there as if they were snakes, and Hynd shed constantly.

Rammy licked his lips. "AJ and I broke up a couple of weeks ago. He's a heavy gunner – carries a big, belt-fed rail gun into battle or sometimes a rocket launcher." Rammy frowned. "He dumped me because I wouldn't give him a quick answer about applying for a shared bunk at base. I knew he wasn't asking me to marry him; hell, he's the one who insisted on an open relationship with limits! But because I said I wanted to think about it, he flew off the handle and told me not to worry about it, that we were done! I mean, I knew the guy was a bit of a live wire, which is why I liked … like … him so much, but that was insane." Rammy crossed his arms over his chest.

Flugger looked at him. "If you found someone you cared about, why would you hesitate to move forwards with them? What's the big deal?"

Rammy ran his hands through his hair. "I don't know, man, I got cold feet."

"Explain the expression."

"I got nervous! I got freaked out. I'm … I'm not good with …"

"You're indecisive."

Rammy's head snapped up as if Flugger had slapped him. That word. His father called him indecisive his whole life. And sure, Rammy knew he sometimes had trouble making decisions, but he simply liked to take his time to assess all the options. But his father never let him forget when he missed out on things because he was "unable to make up his damn mind." He'd always assumed his father was exaggerating, but now that a completely random person had accused him of the same thing – was it true?

Flugger stared at him, his fish-eyes wide. "What? You only now figured that out about yourself? Are all Terrans so dense?"

"Yes, I mean, no . . . I mean –"

"Bah, you're just a guppy. You'll learn."

"I'm twenty-four years old!"

"That's still a child in Pir-An years."

"Really? How long do you live? How old are you?"

"We live to two hundred if we're lucky. I'm seventy-six." He held up a hand. "I'm in my prime child-bearing years, yes."

Rammy laughed lightly.

"What?"

"Our culture rarely refers to males in regards to their fertility."

"That's because you're barbaric and barely evolved."

Rammy shook his head. "I'm not the one who is pissed at his partner because she won't give up her life to have kids."

Flugger's right eye twitched. "She wouldn't be giving up her life! I gestate for *two years*! That's a long time to fritter around on alien spaceships and do all the drugs she wants. She just doesn't understand how long I've waited for her to be ready. We've been together for twenty years. She doesn't understand what it's like to have to think about your body all the time. Gestation isn't guaranteed! Sometimes things happen to prevent fertilization. I don't want us to be too old to try and end up failing. My protective juices, which harbour the eggs, have a shelf-life."

Rammy blinked. "I've heard this argument before from my sister. She wants to have kids, but the man she's dating doesn't. The last time I talked to her, she was debating whether to dump him and find someone who does want kids or go to a clinic. She's thirty-one and worried about her fertility. It also doesn't help that our mom is a midwife, so babies are a constant source of conversation in our house." Despite the average lifespan for Terrans being over one hundred years, reproduction timelines hadn't changed since the early twenty-first century.

This time it was Flugger who was taken aback. His fin shivered as if he had swum into cold water. "Wait. You think Klenni will leave me if I keep trying to get a definite answer from her?"

Rammy held up his hands. "Dude, I don't know. Maybe don't pester her so much, you know? She obviously loves you, and she's an amazing person. But if you squeeze something too tight, it breaks. Maybe focus on getting out of here rather than on whether she'll . . . or, sorry, you'll . . . have kids soon. First, we have to make it out of this place."

Rammy banged the flat of his hand against the container behind him. Flugger slumped further down.

"Thanks," he grumbled. "And for what it's worth, I think you should move on from this AJ character."

"I think that ship has sailed anyway," Rammy sighed. "I didn't leave as much because seeing him broke my heart, but because when Kosa found out what happened, she paid someone to punch him in the face. She has no idea that I know about that. That's why I follow her, you know? She may be a bit over-the-top at times, but she's damn loyal to her team."

Flugger nodded, sitting back. Finally, sleep came to him.

CHAPTER 21: KLENNI AND OW'LLENT

There were two people Klenni was relieved she wasn't trapped with, and that was Wind and Stares. While she didn't think them capable of harming her out of boredom, if they were trapped here long enough, she wouldn't put it past the Rips to kill her for food. Crenk and Kosa were too honourable to do that to someone who was part of their team, at least she hoped. Hynd was a vegetarian, Rammy was her friend, and Flugger, well, if she let herself admit it, she was happy they weren't together at the moment. But Ow'llent? The other Strenoi was a bit of a wild card. Crenk was bluff and bluster, posturing to and buttering up Kosa because she was the leader, but Ow'llent wasn't military. And aside from the occasional acerbic comment, she kept her gills close to her neck. That was more dangerous than anyone, Klenni believed, being someone who considered herself open and easy to read.

She sat across from the Strenoi as the other female dozed. They'd been in the cage for about an hour. Klenni took the time to dwell on what her parents must be thinking. They knew she had a dangerous job now, but not hearing from her for almost a week would make them worry. This had happened in the war when the comms had been silenced and another time during a science mission when an engine malfunction forced them to run on only impulse power for several days. Hopefully, they weren't too worried. They were in their late 160s now, so retired from work and living at a lagoon for elders. They had time to worry about their youngest guppy, the one who had always been adventurous.

A harsh beeping filled the air.

"What's that?!" Kosa called out. "Prepare for impact!"

Ow'llent roused herself and pressed a button on her Dev. "Just me!" She croaked out, her voice tinged with sleep. "Go back to whatever you were … doing."

"You mean sitting here bored out of my sludging mind!?" Stares screamed.

"How're you faring, Hynd?" Rammy called.

The Dirge released a thwumping groan.

"Trapped with the pair of Rips. I bet they wish they were back up on the wall," Ow'llent muttered.

"What was your Dev doing?" Klenni asked.

"It's an alarm. I have a dentist appointment tomorrow that I'm probably going to miss."

"Dentist?"

"To have my teeth inspected and cleaned. I go to a center, and a little drone flies into my mouth, files my teeth, and makes sure they are healthy. We used to have to file them manually. Unlike yours, ours are like claws – we have to buff them to keep them from growing too long." She sighed. "The newest trend at universities is for the students to grow out certain teeth but keep others short. It looks so Mystics-damned stupid."

Klenni tried to picture Ow'llent or Crenk with a couple of long teeth and it made her laugh. "Kids always do the stupidest things. When I was in university, the style was to pierce your tendrils with little lights. It looked really cool at parties, but they tended to get infected easily and sometimes impacted our ability to converse emotionally. See the scars?" She held out her tendrils.

Ow'llent stared. She had no idea the Pir-An could extend their tendrils straight out, parallel to the floor, like Klenni was doing. They were as flat as a horizon. Ow'llent admired the fleshy red strand, about as thick as her finger and somewhat translucent. In several places were small circular etchings, which must be how the scarring manifested itself.

"I had my nostril pierced when I was young," Ow'llent admitted. "That was a resurrected trend from a few hundred years ago. My wife, Corcalla, had been a cultural historian, and she still studies it as a hobby. She could talk your auditory sensors off about fashion changes in Strenoi history."

"Do you miss her?"

"Of course. Like how I miss oxygen when I'm underwater. But we're used to being apart."

Klenni lowered her tone. "To be honest, I wouldn't mind if Flugger were at home right now. I mean, I would love to be at home too, but despite the circumstances, I'm glad we're not trapped in a cage right now together. He'd probably try to talk about having kids again."

Ow'llent tried not to laugh. She didn't understand these other cultures and their focus on breeding. If a Strenoi didn't want to breed, they didn't breed. No one cared. There were always enough kids on an Estate that it didn't matter. And if you wanted to live on an Estate with no children, either with a collection of adults or just one, it wasn't unheard of. Corcalla had three children. Ow'llent liked the kids well enough, especially now that they were grown, but the raising, discipline, education, and life advice had been up to Corcalla. She had retired from her scholarly path to be the House Mother, and now that her kids and their cousins of that generation were grown, she had turned to the SLF and her Worker's rights mission. The only time people got pissy about breeding was when a man told his issue that he was their father. That was taboo and happened very rarely. She was part of a minority who thought the Fathering Silence, as they called it, was archaic and rather stupid, but then again, she was also trying to argue that Strenoi and Terrans shared DNA.

"Why don't you want kids?" Ow'llent asked, unsure what response Klenni needed.

The Pir-An's tendrils wrapped lazily around themselves as she spoke. "Oh, I do. I just don't want to settle down yet. You know, a clutch ties you down. We don't tend to have one or two kids like Terrans or you Strenoi; we have multiple guppies – we could get eight at once! Of course, Flugger would stay home with them since he's always wanted to, but I couldn't accept any off-world or long-distance missions for about twenty years until they're old enough not to be underfoot. That wouldn't be fair to them or to me. I like guppies; I just don't want to fertilize Flugger like, tomorrow."

Ow'llent nodded.

"But, you've likely heard us fighting about this the whole time we've been trapped here." She looked around at the cage, her tone shifting when she next spoke. "What do you think is going to happen next?"

"Oh, I'm sure the aliens will come to collect us at some point. Either use us for experiments or interrogate us or … something."

Klenni shuddered. "I'd almost rather that than fight those creatures again. They were so disgusting. If … when … we get out of here, I'm booking myself into a solid week of psychological discourse with a professional to work those out of my brain. I wish I could erase it from my memory!"

Ow'llent nodded again, but inside she winced. Klenni didn't know about the attempted Mindwipe, of course.

"I'll bet that Kosa finds a way to rescue us. She's the toughest person I've ever met, you know?" Klenni sighed.

"Yes, she's something," Ow'llent replied noncommittally. At the mention of the corporal, all Ow'llent could think about was whether Crenkleost and the Terran had their hands all over one another. They were trapped together, of course. What if this entire thing was a trap *by* the Terrans? What if they were trying to see if they could manipulate Strenoi to their side using the most basic of instincts? She internally shook her head. No, that was crazy. This was too elaborate a scheme for the Terrans to waste money on. Yet, they *were* sex-maniacs and likely thought the Strenoi were the same, so she wouldn't entirely put it past them.

"I bet she and Crenk find a way to scale the walls of their container!" Klenni looked so hopeful Ow'llent couldn't bring herself to sarcasm. Despite her age, which was likely seventies, Klenni was so exuberant, so optimistic. Ow'llent had never been considered chipper, but there was a time when she was hopeful about her life. Now? Not so much. What was going to happen to her when they got out of here? Should she return home? Was the High Council going to lock her up? Perform another Mindwipe but successfully this time? Was her research worth this stress? But she couldn't abandon it, much as Corcalla could never give up her children or the SLF. Perhaps it was time to tell Corcalla the truth.

Klenni wished she knew which conversations would urge Ow'llent to talk more. As well as distract her from worrying about the aliens, Klenni wanted Ow'llent to like her, so there was less chance she would want to eat her. Thinking about Kosa and Crenk gave her an idea.

"Tell me about your work! Rammy was saying you have a theory about Terran and Strenoi DNA?"

"Yes, well, it's very controversial, apparently," Ow'llent said, her tone dry but considerably more animated. She shifted her weight and groaned when stiffness in her back caused it to contort slightly.

"Ooh, I like controversy!"

"To put it in the simplest of terms, I've discovered that there is a very small but tangible, shared protein in our DNA strands. This could indicate that our primordial soup, so to speak, was generated from the same bacteria. My theory is that there was an asteroid with bacterial life on it. It split or struck something, breaking into other pieces. One of the pieces went to Strenovast, the other to Terra."

Klenni's tendrils twirled up and down. "Ooh, that is exciting! So, you're saying that you and the Terrans are like the same species?"

Ow'llent burst out laughing. "No, no, nothing like that! Terrans share sixty percent of their genes with some *fruit* on their planet. We Strenoi share almost ninety percent of our DNA with a water-dwelling vertebrate animal in our sea that looks nothing like us. This link between Strenoi and Terran is a way to look at the formation of our universe, not trying to argue that us Strenoi and Terran should be …" she grimaced and altered what she was going to say, "… more than allies or, at the most, trading partners."

"You don't think the whole universe, maybe excluding the Rips, can't be harmonious?"

"I forget your people don't have a history of conflict."

"Oh, we've had our conflicts; they're just so far in the past we tend to forget them. I mean, we're all one universe. Can't we live and let live? Can't we accept each others' differences?"

Ow'llent snorted. "Oh, *sodi*, aren't you old enough to have lost any sense of idealism?"

Klenni's expression hardened. "Aren't you too old to be making the same mistakes over and over?"

Ow'llent slowly showed her teeth to Klenni. As much as she didn't mean it, it was fun to watch the Pir-An squirm. Klenni was right, of course; it would be great if everyone got along, but how could Ow'llent believe that was a possibility when her own government was silencing her?

"Why are you out here with Crenk when you're doing such important work?"

Ow'llent hissed. "My government tried to have my mind wiped of this discovery!" She balled her right hand into a fist and smashed it down on her knee. "For years prior, they gaslit and ghosted me from conferences! They blocked funding to my department, tried to have me fired, and denied me tenure and resources. Of course, I realize all this in retrospect."

"That's awful!" Klenni gasped. "They're blocking *science*?!"

"Yes, imagine if you found some … algorithm in computer science that changed everything. And your government tried to hide it."

"I'd kick some shells-damned ass!" Klenni declared.

Ow'llent chuckled. "Yes, well, what I did was bribe a technician to not Mindwipe me. Then I played dumb for a few months. But …" she eyed the Pir-An. "I guess I can tell you this. I managed to save my data and hid it somewhere secure for a few months until I could send it out to a trusted colleague off-world. He released it to the public! I have never in my life witnessed Strenoi do what they did – they protested. Protested! We've never had that kind of public demonstration against the government in Strenoi history, even during the war."

"That's great!" Klenni commented. "But why are you here?"

"The government contacted me. Of course, they knew that if they Mindwiped me or killed me, the people would freak out, or, worse yet, the Terrans and your government might decide they contravened the section of the Accord related to information-sharing and start another war. So, they sent me on this mission as an 'academic study.' Crenkleost doesn't know any of this. He thinks I'm here to do scientific studies. True, I'm taking notes, but I know full well they hope I fail or get killed. I think they just wanted me off the world to let people simmer down. I have no idea why Crenkleost got this crappy assignment."

Klenni shook her head. "I can't believe that happened to you. I'm sorry."

Ow'llent shrugged. "Don't be. Shit happens."

"Do all Strenoi share this fatalism?"

Ow'llent laughed. "Yes, to some degree. We are expected to accept things rather than fight them. Unless our honour is called into question, of course, then we get feisty."

"I bet I could live on Strenovast for a century and still not understand completely."

"Of course not, but we're different species. We'll never truly understand one another. The best we can hope for is polite indifference."

Klenni's tendrils waved slightly. "That I disagree with. Look at Rammy and me! I consider him a friend. And look at Kosa and Crenk: they were all gung-ho to kill one another, and now they're comrades-in-arms!"

"Yes, comrades," Ow'llent replied, trying to hide her frown.

When were they getting out of this damn cage?

CHAPTER 22:
KOSA AND CRENK

Kosa paced. Crenk lay on his back in the centre of the room, staring up at the stalactites. Kosa walked around him. He wasn't watching her, but the shadows from the faint light deepened or lightened as she walked, and she was stomping loud enough he would have been completely deaf not to hear where she was. She paced the cage seven large steps each length, muttering to herself in a pidgin of English and Japanese. Crenk thought it was interesting that he understood the English parts but not the Japanese. How did the aliens' virus, or whatever it was, work? Ow'llent or Hynd might have figured it out by now.

"You gonna help me?" Kosa snarled. Crenk craned his head to look up at her.

"Are you pacing a hole through the floor? Is that your plan? Granted, my claws would work better, but even then, it would take some time."

"No, help me think!"

"I am thinking. I think best when I'm lying down." He paused. "You should try it. Maybe you'll get an idea because your body isn't using so much oxygen stomping about."

"I'm getting my parts moving. It gets my brain moving. How tall are you?"

"What?"

"How tall? You think you could boost me to the top?"

Crenk raised his eyes to look up at the cage. "It's like twenty feet. I could throw you, but you would break an ankle or worse trying to get down."

"We could try."

"Let's leave that as a plan … Z. A last recourse."

"My last recourse was to scream." She stopped walking for a second, as if going to do just that, then began walking again. "I want to do that now, but it's not productive. Let's see. We have our packs. If we removed the straps and tied them to your gun or our knives, we could make a kind of grappling hook?"

"Kosa."

"Then we could scale the wall. You help me to the floor. Then I get Hynd or Ow'llent out to help you down."

"Kosa."

"But would our knives hold our weight? We could damage our only remaining weapons."

"Koharu!" Crenk bellowed.

"Ooh, someone's in trouble!" Stares called over the wall, jer voice tinged with glee. "Punish her, Strenoi. Use those shoulder muscles. Maybe a spanking!"

Kosa faced Crenk, who was trying to hide his embarrassment at Stares' comments by looking concerned. Kosa put her hands on her hips. "Now that you've got Stares all hot and bothered, have you something to input?"

She laughed when she realized what she said could be interpreted as innuendo. "Oh no, I've been hanging around that Rip too long. Everything is a *double entendre.*"

"Koharu, stop for a moment and relax. We're stuck in this cage, yes. It's not your fault."

"No, I –"

"Even if you had an expertly designed plan of clearing and escaping this room when we exited the shaft, things happen. Unexpected things. And if you keep pacing and burning energy, you're going to get hungry. And dehydrated. Maybe that's their plan."

"Shit," she muttered. "You're right. What do you suggest we do?"

"Sit down." He sat down against the wall and patted the space beside him. "Rest. Take a nap. My shoulder isn't the most comfortable, but at least it's warm."

Kosa looked at him for a moment, then sat beside him, her shoulder against his. She ran a hand over her face.

"I'm just frustrated, you know? The only reason I'm in this mess is because I messed up. I'm not on leave; I got suspended."

"Did you kill someone?" Crenk asked, semi-serious.

Kosa laughed. "No! I, well …" She wrapped a tendril of hair around her pointer finger, then looked at it, away from him. "I lost my temper at my CO. I didn't yell or fly off the handle, but I wasn't very polite. He gave a promotion I really wanted to someone else. Someone under-qualified. I waited a few hours, then sent an email accusing the army of nepotism, of favouritism." She frowned. "And they said my reaction was the reason why I wasn't being promoted. It isn't fair. I'm a great soldier. I care about my team. I care about justice. If someone isn't pulling their weight, if someone is unsafe, I get angry. It's not like I am a yeller who freaks at people for moving my coffee thermos. I *deserved* that promotion."

"I can see you yelling at someone for moving your coffee." Crenk grinned.

She narrowed her eyes at him and crinkled her nose as if to say "ha-ha."

"That does sound unfair," Crenk added, not wanting her to think he was dismissive of her issue. "They kicked you out?"

"No, I'm on leave. A week to 'cool my head.' Of course, I'll go back. Can't have Aunt Eiko saying 'I told you so.'"

"Who's that?" He leaned forward expectantly.

Kosa sighed heavily. "Oh, my mom's sister. Her daughter is this big shot in marketing, and her son is on a fast track to a seat on our governing council. Then there's me, who ditched dance, the one thing I was actually good at, to join the military. Yeah, there's recognition in it, but not as much as you'd think, especially now that the war is over. It's stupid, but my aunt is well … a total bitch to my mom. Always has been. She has no ambition but to get her kids rich and famous. Then there's my mom, who tries as hard as she can just to survive. My dad died when I was a kid, and my mom has health problems. She can't work more than a couple of days a week, so I grew up on UBI, for the most part. But did my rich aunt help her out? No. Other than to pay for my dance lessons, which she used to make my mom feel small. And she constantly brags about her own life or does the 'rich-person whining' that I can't stand. When I was a kid, I always wondered why my mom didn't just ditch her, but when I was a teenager, I realized it was my fault … it was the dance lessons. And maybe because she hoped my aunt would help me get a job? Help me make contacts so I wouldn't end up living like her? That's one reason why I joined the military, I guess. I didn't need my aunt's help to do that."

She glanced at Crenk as if checking to see if he were bored. He smiled in the way Terrans showed acceptance: a close-lipped smile. It tugged at the skin on his jaws, but not in a bad way.

"My cousins are actually fine people – likely they take after their dad – but Aunt Eiko is the worst. I guess I feel shitty about fucking up in the Navy because it's another shot she can take at my mom." She put on a hoity-toity accent. "Oh, look, Takane, your daughter can't even make it in the military, where mine is pulling in a six-figure salary before thirty on the *corporate* battlefield." The accent dropped off. "Yeah, because you used your husband's money to pay for her to go to the best university on the planet, you stupid asshole. Ugh."

Kosa looked over at Crenk, suddenly aware she was spilling her guts to an alien. Her cheeks grew hot, and she picked at a new hangnail – every finger was cursed with them, and she couldn't help nibbling. Then again, perhaps it wasn't so much embarrassment but how his fetching eyes made her self-conscious. They were watching her with such understanding. Oh, right, honour was a big deal for his people. This likely made a lot of sense to him. Nice to finally have someone else understand her issues, even if it was a goddamn Strenoi.

"You know why I'm here?" Crenk asked, his voice low. She leaned towards him to hear better. His scent wafted up to her again, the sea after the rain. If this was Strenoi B.O., she was all for it. "My best-cousin Guermun, the big fancy lawyer? Every High Born Strenoi has to serve a stint in the military after they finish at academy. He served his obligatory term doing basic grunt work – the easiest and quickest way to get it done. His team was part of a clean-up on Hgor-ip – you call it New Russia."

"Oh, the Battle of Ferma. You guys were trying to destroy their food producer factory, and it turned into, what, a six-week siege?"

"Yes. The clean-up was much later, only six years ago. He was part of a group assigned to do basic surveillance of our side of the planet."

"Yeah, there's what, four planets we share now?"

"I believe so. Anyway, his team activated a pulse mine."

"Oh. OH." Kosa's eyes grew wide.

"He survived because he was pulling rear guard. But have you seen what one of those can do to a person who steps on it?"

"I'm a marine, Crenk, I know."

"Well, he clammed up. Didn't talk for a week. Refused a Mindwipe – said it was a dishonour to his fellow soldiers. And Mindwipes don't work for emotional trauma; they can make it worse. If you remove the reason from your brain, it's as bad as repressing it because emotions are still there and having a gap sometimes makes you crazy dwelling on what you can't remember you had removed." He sighed, gripping his knees with his hands. Kosa looked at those hands. Not unlike hers, except for the scales and the claws. She placed her hand over his briefly, resting the tips of her fingers between his, squeezing. He turned and looked at her, nodding in thanks. She slid her hand off his, letting it rest against her exposed knee, the fabric having torn long ago. She was resting against him in a way she hoped appeared accidental. Kosa was a physically emotive person, but she didn't know Crenk well enough to nuzzle into him like she would one of her friends or even Rammy. She flicked at the hairs that were sprouting on her knee, self-consciously hoping Crenk didn't find them unattractive, then wondered why she cared.

"He was classified as having PTSD, of course."

"Oh, I'm sorry."

"After treatment, he goes back to law school and graduates and becomes a big shot. A few months ago, I'm in a bar with a few friends from flight school, and he comes on the news – he'd won a monumental case. That picture Ow'llent showed you? Where you made fun of his ridge? That was from that day. Anyway, I overhear another Strenoi telling his buddy how my cousin, my best friend, was a coward and used his PTSD to get out of military duty early. Before I know it, I'm pulling back my fist. We had a pretty good fight. I like to think I won, as he was the one with the broken incisor and burst capillaries in his eyes. But, in the end, he won because he was a captain. I beat up a superior officer."

"Crenk," Kosa began, wishing to squeeze his hand again but deciding against it.

He ran a hand over his ridge. "I know, I'm an idiot. I dishonoured myself and my family and my Estate. I'm an idiot." He repeated this quietly as he let his head droop.

Compassion and understanding made Kosa's heart ache. "No, you're not. I would have done the same."

"No, you would have done something smarter. Like put a laxative in his drink."

Kosa laughed. "Did you not listen to my story? At least you did it for a good cause, not just a job promotion."

Crenk's scales grew warm under Kosa's gaze. She was looking at him with such empathy. Yet, he wanted to impress her, not garner her pity. "The High Council, they want me to bring Ow'llent back for a Mindwipe. She's some sort of political dissident or something; I don't really know. But I'm not going to do it." He decided to leave out the part about him deciding this only an hour ago.

Kosa nodded. It wasn't the reaction he was hoping for, but, if he were true to himself, what had been wanting? An enthusiastic speech on his merits? A list of why she thought he was amazing?

They sat in silence for a few minutes, both deep in thought. After admitting to Crenk what had happened with Command, Kosa wondered whether she would return to the marines if they made it out of here. She couldn't imagine now that the top brass based their promotions on merit rather than connections. And what connections did she have? She signed up as a basic grunt, an NCO from a colony world. True, many NCOs got far, but they were offering honourable discharge packages to most now that the war was over. What Crenk said about his government wanting to wipe Ow'llent's mind because of her political leanings … she could see her people doing the same thing.

Why was she fighting for them? Why was she fighting against the Strenoi anyway? Could she go back to killing them if another war broke out? She supposed she must, but maybe there was something else she could do instead. She used to look down on mercenaries, but perhaps they had a point about having no allegiances.

Her stomach grumbled. Crenk looked over at her and laughed.

"What a weird body you have," he teased.

"I think it's pretty good," she replied, "though I don't have any Rips lusting after my shoulders."

She nudged him in that part of his anatomy, and he jostled her in return.

"Oh, I have something for you!" Crenk explained. He pulled his pack towards him and pulled out some cookies. They were broken and had lint on them but still intact enough to eat. He held them out to her. "I pocketed these last night. I just remembered!"

Kosa laughed. "Aren't they drugged?"

Crenk stared down at them in surprise, then face-palmed with his free hand.

Kosa laughed again and took them from him. "Well, I appreciate that you thought of me."

"Of course!" He blurted, then looked away when her eyes widened. "I mean, um, you've pulled us through this. You've done a lot for us. It's the least I could do to bring you some … useless cookies."

He didn't mention the shotgun pieces in his bag. He also didn't mention that the reason he brought the cookies wasn't solely out of gratitude. He brought them because he liked to see her rare smile, to be the one to inspire that expression. Her grin had a feral-ness to it that reminded him of the spike plants back home in the desert, his favourite flower. Why did he have to hide this from her? Why shouldn't he like to see her smile? So what if he found it attractive? It didn't mean anything. He found certain things attractive on many people. He was simply in tune with her. She was someone he respected. Someone who understood him. Someone who fought well. Someone who was smart, quick, graceful, strong … and had a nice ass.

She nudged his shoulder again and smiled up at him. A compulsion ran through him to touch her again, to nuzzle her neck with his face, to run his hand through her hair. It was different from the party; that was a compulsion he could blame on external forces. This was something else, and it reared up deep inside him, surprising him. His fingers ached to feel her flesh beneath them. Would that another container would crash down, so he could tackle her out of the way again, to have her body beneath him.

What was he doing, looking down at this Terran and having such thoughts? This had to be another alien interference. Maybe the stalactites above exuded more drugs. Even if not, she *was* such a Terran. The way she had looked at him when they first met, the abject repugnance; was that not still inside her? If he told her he liked to see her smile and if he tried to move closer to her, would she shove him away, sneer at him? Was her friendliness, and what he hoped was mutual attraction, simply masking a deep-seated dislike she was hiding due to their situation?

He pulled back from her. Looked away.

Don't be rash, he berated himself. He was working on it.

Kosa tried not to exhale too sharply when Crenk broke their gaze. The way he had been looking at her, like she was the only thing in the entire universe, had halted the synapses in her brain. He looked at her as if he wanted to devour her heart, but in a way that made her want to wrap her arms around his neck.

But how could she forget that he was Strenoi, a goddamn *raptor*. It didn't matter that his shoulders were impressive, his grin infectious, and his devotion to his people relatable. It didn't matter that she had grown to rely on him to have her back, that her hips still felt phantom pressure where his hands had rested, that she would love to teach him to dance properly. None of that mattered. She was on a maze of a spaceship with no way to escape, with murderous aliens having trapped her in a cage. No wonder her libido was firing on all cylinders right now – it was a bodily reaction to having some downtime amidst all the constant stress. Crenk was the closest thing she could get to a viable partner, that's all. And the way he looked at her? She was probably misinterpreting it.

CHAPTER 23: STARES, WIND, AND HYND

Hynd could recall that one of the most lingering of the Terran religions had a very specific idea about the afterlife. They claimed you were thrown into a deep pit filled with fire, where creatures would torment you for the rest of time.

Hynd now believed they understood the concept. Being trapped in a cage with the Rips was Hell. Granted, had it been only Wind, they would have been fine with it, comfortable even, but Stares was … incorrigible. The damn Rip wouldn't or couldn't sit still. It was antithetical to all that the Dirge strove to be: calm, gentle-minded, and logical. Stares was frantic, scathingly emotional, and irrational. Je tried to scale the container. Je rooted through the pack je shared with Wind, looking for something. Je tried to take Wind's Sniper Rifle apart, which resulted in the only time the Dirge had seen Wind lash out; je had grabbed Stares and flung jer away from the gun and into the container wall, which resulted in the Rips hissing and snarling at one another, circling.

Finally, Hynd wearily told them to stop. Afterwards, Stares spent two minutes, the best two minutes of Hynd's day, sulking in the corner. Then je had bounded over and asked Hynd if je could braid their fur. Hynd allowed this, as it was better than some of the other things Stares could start doing. They did not allow Stares to touch their hair, though, worried je would damage it further. The Dirge's one vanity was their hair, and Hynd kept theirs long. Every night back home, Hynd had it treated and curled. They couldn't bear to look at it right now, though they could feel how knotted and greasy it was when it brushed their face.

Stares sat as far away from Hynd as je could, jer long arms and fingers extended to make small braids starting at Hynd's shoulders. Hynd watched the Rip as je concentrated on jer task, jer fingers supple and quick. They leaned back, head against the wall. It was impossible to relax, to imagine Stares was a stylist and Hynd was at their bi-weekly treatment. There was no way Hynd was getting out of this ship. They would never get back to Low, never hold Jurl in their arms, and never see their friends again. They sighed, lips flapping slightly with the exhalation. Jurl had wanted to accompany Hynd on their short assignment, but Hynd had resisted the idea. Not because they didn't want to spend time with Jurl, but because they knew Jurl was only offering to be polite. Jurl hated off-world studies, preferring to stay on Low and work in a lab. That was how the pair had met – at work.

"Hynd, you Dirge aren't like the Terrans, right?" Stares asked.

Hynd opened their eyes. "In what sense?"

"You don't have their overactive sex drives."

"This is true. The Terrans used to think we were asexual for some reason, and while some of us are, just like there are asexual Terrans, Pir-An, and Strenoi, most of us have active sex drives. We just don't do it for reproduction. We haven't for hundreds of years, since the plague."

"A plague destroyed a lot of Rips once," Stares replied.

"This one was created by us. It was an attempt to modify our spawn on the genetic level. Instead, it modified our reproductive organs, sterilizing the entire population. We tried everything, containment, isolation, reverse-engineering, but we've never been able to figure out how to, well, fix it."

"I heard you guys don't fall in love?"

Hynd shook their head. Where do all these rumours about their people come from? "Of course, we do. You Rips are the ones who don't fall in love."

"We do fall in love," Wind corrected, jer voice quiet. "We just don't tend to partner in that way until later in life, after we have kids."

"Then I guess we're all like the Terrans after all," Hynd replied, unwilling to continue this conversation, as it only reminded them of Jurl, who was likely frantic. They smiled grimly. Jurl would be wringing their hands or pacing while their two friends and housemates, and sometimes lovers, Aust and Prou, tried to contact the government or perhaps even find Hynd's ship. At least, Hynd hoped they were. They had been friends with Aust since their emergence. Dirge were born from their gestation pod, nicknamed The Vat, full-grown. They spent three years in a learning centre, developing language and social skills.

Dirge only lived to sixty, but because their "childhood," as the Terrans would call it, was only three years, Hynd didn't feel their twenty-three years in the universe had flown by.

Stares sat back on jer heels. "There! Gorgeous. Look, Wind!"

Hynd glanced down at their shoulders and was pleasantly surprised to see it wasn't as bad as they expected.

The ink-black Rip came over. Je also squatted down, reminding Hynd of a large avian creature. Hynd stared at the Rips. Now that they had been around them for so long, they were starting to see the differences other than skin and eye tone. Wind's jaw was wider, and Stares' mouth was bigger. Stares' cheekbones were more pronounced, and Wind's fingers were longer.

"Hey Wind, think fast!" Stares declared, then shoved Wind so je tottered on jer feet and fell over.

Stares laughed.

Hynd shook their head.

Wind looked up at Stares from where je lay on the surprisingly warm floor. While the braids now adorning the Dirge's shoulders looked more like Hynd was draped in small worms than whatever attempt Stares had been aiming for (presuming Stares hadn't been intending the braids to look like worms), Wind had been unable to concentrate on them. Jer body was simultaneously on fire and experiencing chills. Jer skin was pulled with fishhooks towards wherever Stares was in the room.

This was the first time Wind had experienced the *Thrum*. Of course, jer grandparent had explained what it felt like when je experienced the desire to reproduce, but, as je also said, it was something they couldn't prepare Wind for. The best way to deal with the *Thrum* was to remedy it.

"What's your problem?" Stares asked, staring down at jer. Wind realized je hadn't moved; je had been watching Stares intently since je'd fallen. Je was focused on the way Stares' neck elongated when je laughed, the glinting sparkles of jer silver skin in the dimmed light, the gentle curve of jer back, jer beautiful sharp teeth. Je wanted to run jer tongue up and down Stares' body – je didn't care if je hadn't been able to bathe in the days they had been trapped here.

"I …" Wind began.

"You're shaking," Hynd pointed out, big bovine-eyes staring at Wind in what je was surprised to see was concern. "Are you ok?"

"I … I … I …"

"Dammit, Wind, spit it out!" Stares demanded.

"I want to reproduce with you!" je blurted.

Stares paused for a moment, then laughed. "Yeah, sure."

Wind pushed jerself to jer feet and lunged at Stares, wrapping jer arms around the other Rip. "Can't you feel it?" je demanded, running jer tongue from Stares' chin to jer forehead.

Stares didn't make any effort to move, but, unlike what Wind's grandparent had said would happen, Stares didn't respond by also licking Wind in the face. Je simply stood in jer embrace, annoyed.

Hynd pulled Wind off Stares and flung jer away. Wind landed on all fours, arched jer back like a cat, and hissed.

"It's ok!" Stares protested, putting jer hand on Hynd's chest to stop the Dirge from stomping over to Wind. "It's how we do things."

"There's nothing natural about grabbing someone without their consent!" Hynd declared, glaring at Wind.

Stares blinked as if surprised someone was trying to protect jer. As when je comforted Kosa, jer voice grew soft. "No, no, that's not what je did. We … we can sense things with our tongues. Je was … confirmation."

Wind panted, unable to do anything but breathe. Jer stomach was churning, and jer chest was heaving. This was what reproducing was like? It was torture!

Hynd frowned.

Stares pointed at Wind as if je were an exhibit. "We don't have a sex drive like the other aliens. But certain people can trigger our bodies into reproductive mode – we call it the *Thrum*. It's so hard to explain to a non-Rip, but Wind's body has been reacting to me. I'm assuming it's been since we met, or at least since we arrived on *Misery*. Jer reproductive faculties have been sparked by the pheromones from my body so jer body has been preparing for self-fertilization. Once je reaches sexual climax, jer body will release sperm and an egg from jer different organs, and its possible je will get pregnant."

Air whistled from Wind's nose. Stares was so so so beautiful standing there, the purple lights sparkling on jer skin. Je pushed jerself to jer feet and limped over.

Stares eyed jer warily. "Don't come near me."

Wind stopped. "Why? I can taste it on you!"

Stares crossed her arms over her chest. "No. I don't feel anything for you!"

Wind blinked three times, slowly. "How could you not? We've been in close proximity for almost a week. We slept together in a bundle; you've been flirting with me constantly."

"So what? I'm not risking getting pregnant."

"Wait, so you *do* feel it? You're … we can sense things with our tongues. Je was … confirmation resisting!? That's not possible!"

Stares shook jer head. "No, I'm not. I simply nipped it in the bud earlier on. I suppressed the starting of attraction, so it didn't build."

Wind stared at jer. "You can't do that."

"Oh yes, it's entirely possible with . . . with practice."

"But why would you want to? If we were back on Ripplia, in the bog … we can sense things with our tongues. Je was … confirmation we'd be all alone. We could take the time to really explore one another. Don't you want to see what it's like?"

Stares' expression hardened. "We're not at home, are we? Besides, I don't live in the swamp! I'm not a *roamer*. I'm from a city."

"I knew it! You're Upper Echelon!"

Stares snorted. "That's the only reason you want to reproduce with me. You want to brag about tangling your cilia with someone from the UE!"

"No! That's not true at all! I … I care for you, Stares."

Stares' head cocked to the side, level with jer auditory sensors. "What do you mean?"

"I don't want this to be a one-time reproductive thing. I want to be with you, Stares. I want to follow you wherever you go."

Stares laughed. "What? You can't be serious. Rips our age don't do that. We've been hanging around these aliens too long. Your sexual desire, which I can smell from here, by the way, is clouding your mind."

"But you flirt with me all the time!"

"I flirt with everyone, Wind! It's just for fun."

"I wish you'd considered what effect it would have on me!"

"I can't help it if they don't teach you *roamers* how to ward off the *Thrum*!"

Wind bit jer lower lip so hard blood trickled down jer chin. Stares took a step back, glancing over at Hynd. Despite what Stares had said, Wind's body still ached for jer.

"Can you at least … help me out?"

"No! I may have been able to tamper the *Thrum* down, but if I start engaging with you while your pheromones are flying off the handle, mine *will* react. I told you, I can't risk pregnancy right now. Get back!"

Wind raked jer hands down jer face, leaving indents in his black skin. "Argh, ok, well, then, you guys just … just turn around so I can try and figure this out on my own. I'm … I'm dying here, OK? I've never done this before. If I can't fix this … I'm going to smash my face against the fucking wall!"

Hynd had started out watching the exchange with amusement, but it had drifted into pity. While Wind was acting on natural impulses, it was clear that je also possessed a depth of affection for Stares that was not reciprocated. Hynd had experienced unrequited romance and knew how much it hurt. While Rips, as a people, were sporadic and intense and aggressive, Hynd liked Wind. Je was quiet, contemplative, and serious. Je reminded them of Jurl, just a little bit. And Wind was suffering; jer agony was … distressing.

"I'll help you out," Hynd found themselves saying.

Both Rips spun to face them as Hynd stood up.

"What?" Stares asked.

"Why?" Wind asked.

Hynd shrugged. "I'm bored. And, to be honest, I'm kind of interested. And you need it."

Stares stared at the Dirge after they made their offer. What was the Dirge offering to do for Wind, exactly? Stares glanced at jer fellow Rip. Je liked Wind, but not enough to risk pregnancy. While a term was only three months, Stares didn't have three months. Stares had orders. Stares had plans. What je would do for jer people was monumental. Worth far more than satisfying Wind's desires. And what je'd said about wanting to be with jer? That was the intense need for reproductive release talking. Then again, if jer feelings were true, Stares could use that to jer advantage later.

Wind appeared to be torn. Je was staring at the Dirge, saliva mingling with the blood from jer lip. Je began to shake slightly. *How pedestrian*, Stares thought, *those roamers really need to learn to control their impulses. No wonder the aliens think we're savages.*

"Ah, ok, ok, ok, just be gentle, ok? I've never done this with anyone," Wind agreed.

"I don't generally engage in this kind of thing with … aliens."

"You guys are making history," Stares joked.

Wind didn't turn to look at jer. "Shut up!" je hissed. "You don't know anything about any of this!"

The rage on Wind's face told Stares je had gone too far this time. "Ok, ok, I'll go over here." Je went to the other side of the cage and sat down on the floor, pulling out jer pack. Je retrieved a glowing orb je had snatched from the air earlier after they climbed the ladder. Je whistled a particular three notes, and Allie, conserving energy in the corner, rose and approached. Stares knew the Terran, Strenoi, and Pir-An thought je had no idea how to work any form of technology, and je preferred to let them think je was ignorant.

Je glanced over at Hynd and Wind, who were sitting on the other side of the cage, Hynd's large hand down Wind's undone pants, clearly caressing the Rip's genital cilia. Wind moaned, and Hynd stared at jer, an interested expression on their face.

Stares turned back to the task at hand. Jer fingers flew elegantly over Allie's keyboard, accessing a specific protocol. Stares held up the purple ball with one hand, and Allie flew around it, scanning its components. It looked like rubber, but Stares wanted to know whether it was sentient or A.I. or a combination. Perhaps this was the way for the Rips to differentiate themselves from the other species? What if they created organic but technologically-enhanced weapons and ships? Ripplia did not have many metal deposits, nor did the people have the infrastructure (or freedom from *Borkas*) to mine, and the tariffs or fees the other species would charge for the Rips to mine on their colonialized worlds would be astronomical. But if Rips could instead modify their naturally occurring organic mass, such as the overwhelming number of gelatinous pools in the swamps, to become solid and incorporate tech, it would be cheaper, *and* they could do it on the sly with the Accord species knowing.

This one little purple ball could be what gave jer people the edge they needed to convince the Accord to let them join!

As Allie finished scanning, Wind let out a small scream. Stares looked over – Wind's back was arched, jer knees in the air as if je were some mammal giving birth. Stares turned back to Allie, inserted a small round flash drive from jer pocket into one of its ports, and transferred the results of the scan. Je pocked the ball just as one side of the container opened outwards, like a door.

Klenni, Kosa, Crenk, and Ow'llent stared at the scene in front of them as Wind screamed again and fell backwards, eyes closed. Hynd removed their hand from Wind's cilia.

"No mess," they commented. "Interesting."

Klenni burst into wild giggles. Wind opened jer eyes, saw the four newcomers staring at jer, and covered jer face with jer hands, mortified. Hynd patted jer on the shoulder.

"Things have changed," Kosa said, her mouth twitching.

CHAPTER 24: KLENNI

They let Kosa and Crenk out first. Then Klenni and Ow'llent. Klenni had been explaining to the Strenoi what *at'al'ie*, Bubble's national dish, tasted like when the cage wall behind her shifted, causing Klenni to scramble forwards. Ow'llent had leapt to her feet, pike extended in front of her, but it was Kosa and Crenk at the door. Klenni had expected the Strenoi to be happy to see their leader and her fellow countryperson, but instead, Ow'llent had barely thanked them. Klenni didn't have time to think about it as three beings stepped out behind Crenk.

Aliens. *New* aliens.

"Who in the Aether is this?" Ow'llent had demanded, raising the pike again.

Kosa scratched her eyebrow. "These are the Trychu – at least that's the closest I can get to pronouncing it. They let us out."

If the Rips were terrifying to the other species in the galaxy, these aliens gave them a run for their money. They were as tall as the Rips. They had four arms sprouting from a thorax-shaped torso, each with two skinny fingers and a very long thumb. They walked upright on two thick, elongated femurs that ran parallel to the ground, connected to straight tibias resting on clawed, three-toed feet. Their arms, legs, face, and stomach were composed of skin, a dark blue. They wore a smock-like garment covering their chests and, presumably, reproductive or expulsion orifices. Their backs were lined with a thick carapace, which clicked gently as they walked. Their head was round, like a bumblebee but proportionate to their body. They had no nose, no ears, but four compound eyes and a wide mouth complete with spider-like jaws. Simply put, they looked like bugs mixed with crabs.

"Well, um, thank you," Klenni had said.

The lead Trychu nodded.

"We're going to let everyone out and then regroup," Kosa had ordered, stepping behind the Trychu, who chittered something at its mates.

After the *interesting* discovery in the Rip and Dirge cell, which Klenni was dying to tell Rammy about, they released the remainder of the team. Klenni allowed Flugger to hug her, though anger still coursed through her. Talking with Ow'llent hadn't lessened her frustration.

"Follow us," the lead Trychu said, their voice coming from their wrist and not their mouth. There was a small elongated oval glowing slightly under the skin of their lower left forearm as if it had a Dev inserted inside it. Klenni couldn't help but gape.

"Why are you helping us?" Kosa demanded. "We don't know if we can trust you."

The Trychu stopped walking and turned on Kosa, towering over her. Crenk stepped up beside them, a growl emitting from his throat. Kosa held up a hand to Crenk but didn't take her eyes from the Trychu. The alien's jaws opened wide to show a mouth with pointed teeth. The Trychu was over seven feet tall. Kosa's other hand hung by her side, trembling slightly, though her face remained stoic.

"I squash bugs like you by accident," Kosa added.

The Trychu snapped their jaws together. They chittered, their wrist providing a translation. "We are not here to fight!"

"We're not going anywhere until you give us a little bit of information!" Kosa demanded. Klenni wondered whether you could be confident like Kosa without being intimidating. Probably not. Had Kosa always been this tough, or had life made her this way? Was it a conscious decision? People were always telling Klenni to be a little less nice, but she could never do it. It was much easier to accommodate than argue.

The Trychu looked at their partners briefly, then turned back to Kosa. "We are here to help you escape! We are spies, rebels, on this ship. We don't like the way the Leadership are treating your people. We have time for a few questions as we lead you to safety. Talk fast – Rhinn'o here can only mask our movements for so long." They gestured towards one of the other Trychu, who used three of their hands to type into their implanted Dev.

"Where are you from?" Ow'llent called as they stepped in line behind the Trychu. The bug peered out the door into a hallway resembling the bottom level, but this one was a pale green rather than dull gray.

"We are the Trychu. We are part of a religious fleet that left our homeworld centuries ago to study space and find other life. About ten years ago, our people suffered what we call The Schism. It's more complicated than this, but, for your purposes, our group believes that all sentient life has value, where the others, the ones who run this ship, believe anyone with less technology is a lesser being. As such, these ships want to stop our sacred journey and settle in your galaxy, take over your planets as their own. Our people want to leave you alone, keep travelling. Some of ours have already left. Our Leaderships sent us over from our ships to be informants. We have been in your galaxy for two of your years, gathering resources as the Leadership cements their plans for your galaxy."

Klenni accepted a hand from Rammy to climb up a ladder that the tall Trychu had no trouble ascending with their four arms.

"What are your ships made of?" she asked.

"As you have probably guessed, our ships are both organic and non-organic. When a ship breaks down, we find a suitable planet to gather resources from to repair it. The organic components heal themselves over time."

"How come we only discovered this one ship?"

"I'm assuming they wanted you to find their ship signature to lure you in to do more experiments. The ship had already moved millions of kilometres away from where it was when you arrived. Also, we have very advanced stealth drives."

Hynd's ears flicked upwards at that. From what Klenni knew of Dirge, it meant they were intrigued. Hynd was a mathematician and an engineer, and true stealth tech was something even the Dirge hadn't yet developed.

"Were you watching us the whole time?" Kosa demanded, fists clenched.

"*We* weren't. We don't have spies at a high enough level to do that, but I'm guessing the Leadership's scientists were tracking you or straight up observing. One of our people found out you made it to this level, so we decided to act. We've set up a system failure on this level, but we have to move quickly. If we're caught ..."

"Thank you for risking yourselves for us." Crenk nodded deeply.

The Trychu nodded back.

As they jogged, Klenni watched the creatures' gait. They bobbed slightly, and with each step, their carapace flexed like someone performing a glissando on the piano. Now that she had been around them for a few minutes, they were less horrifying. In fact, she'd argue that the Rips were still far scarier than these aliens. Finally, they entered a small room.

"Watch the door," the Trychu called to Wind, hovering at the back, away from the group, clearly still embarrassed by whatever je had been doing with Hynd.

"Have you been injecting pheromones into the air to experiment with our physiology?" Ow'llent asked.

"I don't think so, though I do know they drugged other captives with various narcotics."

"What was the point?" Ow'llent asked.

"Experimentation. As much as they have designs on your planets and resources, part of our mission is to study. Granted, we on the other ships have strict regulations about beings consenting to such activities, but they have thrown decency away here. For example, with another group, they exposed them to a different drug, and the aliens went crazy and killed one another."

"We haven't been exposed to anything else?" Ow'llent repeated.

"Believe me or not, I don't care."

Klenni, positioned beside Ow'llent, glanced up at her. The Strenoi was staring at Kosa and Crenk, who stood beside one another in front of the female Strenoi. When the Strenoi realized Klenni was observing her eyeing the other two, she turned her gaze back to the Trychu. Klenni looked at Kosa and Crenk. They stood very close, their arms touching. True, the room was small, but there was no reason to press together. Did Ow'llent think … Klenni felt her mouth drop open slightly, and she closed it just as quickly.

"How do you have sex?" Stares asked.

Everyone groaned.

"Stares, really!" Rammy protested.

Stares shrugged. "What? Maybe I'll be the first person in our galaxy to fornicate with a Trychu."

"You wish," one of the Trychu replied. Klenni rolled her eyes when Stares reached forward and tweaked the Trychu's mandible jaws. The Trychu let out a high-pitched chittering that could only be laughter.

"Stop that! You need to get going now!" the lead Trychu urged Kosa.

"One more question!" Rammy called from behind Hynd. "How can we understand one another, but you have to use a wrist translator?"

"I'm assuming the scientists didn't want you able to understand us in the event you did make it to any of the upper levels on your own. Why they found it necessary to allow you to communicate is beyond me. The Leadership's head scientist is … unstable."

"How does it work?"

The Trychu clasped two of their hands together in exasperation. "I don't know. I'm not a scientist."

"Time …" Rhinn'o said.

"Here!" The Trychu slammed a hand to the wall. A symbol appeared, like those in the lower level. As the Trychu pressed it, a box appeared. The wall slid away to reveal a lift.

"What's your name?" Kosa asked, ushering everyone else in before her. Klenni raced in first, not wishing to be anywhere near these new aliens.

"Grukli," the Trychu said. "Here, this will lead you to a new level. Here is a map," they handed her a physical piece of paper that was translucent, like vellum, but sturdier, "and the unlocking code for a Strenoi ship in our bay. Look for this symbol to lead you to the bay. We'll open the bay door when you're inside." They held up their arm, and a hologram was projected that looked like a triangle with another smaller triangle attached to it.

Kosa held out her hand. Grukli stared at it, then stuck out one of their own. Kosa slid her hand into Grukli's and shook briefly, then stepped into the lift.

CHAPTER 25: KOSA

Everyone was crunched together in the lift. The stench of various body odours wafted into Kosa's nose, making her gag. She turned slightly towards Crenk, whose smell of the sea was growing less comforting and more stifling but still better than the rank diffusion of Hynd's fur. She couldn't imagine she smelled that great either, given the B.O. Rammy was emitting. She glanced up at Crenk, admiring the curve of his jaw, despite herself. He looked down at her. Before the Trychu had shown up, they had passed the remainder of their time talking about their childhoods. Kosa, an only child, had always been a little lonely before she started dance at nine years old. She had spent her time after school walking in the woods with her daydreams to keep her company, as her mother hogged the holovision when her *myalgic encephalomyelitis*, or Chronic Fatigue Syndrome, reared its head. Crenk, to escape his hectic Estate, had spent most of his free time in the desert, exploring the caves or taking flying lessons.

After finally accepting that she was attracted to him, Kosa had intended not to talk so much to Crenk, to ward off those confusing and embarrassing feelings, but found she hadn't been able to be cold with him. He was easy to talk to. He was handsome in his strange alien way. Why couldn't he be an asshole? If he were, then standing so close to him in this elevator wouldn't cause her breath to catch in her throat.

Focus on the mission, Koharu, she said to herself. *Redeem yourself.*

"Weapons ready, people," she said. "As much as I liked Grukli, their little rescue could easily have been part of the Trychu's experiments."

"Is that music?" Klenni asked after the shuffling to get into some semblance of preparedness settled down. She was correct – elevator music was indeed playing. It wasn't Muzak, like on Earth, but it was the equivalent.

Kosa refused to comment on the music. "Alright, when the doors open, Crenk and I will exit first. Flugger, stay behind. Stares, Klenni, Rammy – you're second wave. Ow'llent and Hynd, third."

"Someone is grabbing my ass," Stares complained.

"What ass?" Hynd muttered.

"Yeah, we all know Hynd likes to grab other things," Ow'llent sneered.

"Hey!" Kosa exclaimed. "What consenting adults do in their spare time is no concern of yours."

"Yes, I know how you feel about inter-species relationships," Ow'llent replied.

"I thought Dirge didn't have sex?" Klenni saved Kosa from sputtering out a denial. Ow'llent's comment proved that Kosa really needed to control herself when it came to Crenk. It was like when she was twelve all over again. She had been at a sleepover with three other girls. They wanted to play Truth or Dare. Kosa had thought nothing about admitting whom she thought was cute at school, only to receive expressions of disbelief and disgust from her friends. She couldn't even remember the boy's name now, but she had never forgotten the shame. Eventually, she realized the issue the girls had was that he had been poor. Given Kosa's shared economic state, the girls eventually stopped being friends with her, too. Kosa was better off without them, she realized in her late teens, and she had vowed never to let anyone shame her again. But this was different. Ow'llent's reaction made perfect sense. Her attraction to Crenk was wrong. He was an alien. There was something wrong with her.

"Why do people think we don't have sex?" Hynd asked in response to Klenni's question. "We do have sex. My roommates and I –"

"Wait, what are we talking about?" Flugger demanded.

"Wind got all turned on by me, but I didn't have the same reaction, so Hynd offered to help jer get to orgasm," Stares explained.

"Can we not talk about this?" Wind asked, faintly, from the back.

Rammy chuckled, but it faded away when no one else laughed. "Wait, really?" he turned his head to stare at Hynd.

Hynd shrugged, causing a waft of unwashed Dirge fur to plume into the elevator. Everyone gagged.

"Open up, doors," Kosa hissed as Rammy continued to question Stares and Hynd about what had transpired in the Rip/Dirge cage.

"I know what you mean about the smell," Crenk said, his voice low. Kosa resolved to make a noncommittal noise, but upon meeting his gaze, she found herself replying.

"I don't know how you can stand being so close to me. I probably stink like a corpse."

"Perhaps I don't mind the smell of corpses," Crenk replied.

A laugh bubbled out of Kosa as the elevator stopped moving. She turned from Crenk and faced the doors, knife in hand.

The door opened with a hiss followed by a faint squelch, as if the metal was being drawn into place by an octopus' suckers.

Kosa stepped out to the right, the knife held in a ready position. Crenk's sickle claws tapped onto the floor to the left of the doors. They were in a hallway that was approximately fifteen feet wide with a ten-foot ceiling. The lighting was as dim as the room with the crates, with similar, but smaller, stalactites hanging from the ceiling. There was no water reclamation unit, if that's what had been sucking up the water droplets, here. Windows lined the right side of the hall. Unshuttered windows. *Space.* Kosa and Crenk glanced at one another, then bolted to the nearest window, staring out.

Kosa heard the rest of the team exit, making their way to the other windows, but she was mesmerized. She knew she should be setting up a watch, should be scouting, but after days in the bowels of the ship, seeing the darkness of space with its glimmering stars banished her weariness and revitalized her desire to escape. She sighed in relief. Crenk's arm brushed hers.

"What system are we in?" he asked. She turned her head to find that he was not looking out the window but down at her. How could he not be staring out the window, trying, as she was, to absorb the view, to store it in her mind? This could be the last time they were to see it. Instead, he was looking at a stinky, dirty, blood-soaked Terran with matted, stringy hair. One who knew her eyes were too close to her nose, her lips too thin, and her chin too sharp. True, she had a ripped body she worked hard to maintain, but especially in her current state, she couldn't imagine anyone wanting to look at her rather than at the majesty of space.

"I don't know." Kosa shook her head, then glanced back at space again.

"It's Phrasa. A gas giant," Klenni said from the next window. "The asteroid-encircled moon is very distinctive."

They were parked, so to speak, a few million miles from a dark blue planet orbited by four moons, one of which was indeed orbited by asteroids. As Grukli had said, *Misery* was no longer where it was when they had been taken into it.

"Can you navigate us home from here?" Kosa asked.

Klenni nodded. "I've never been this far out, but I can plot us a course."

"Well, then let's stop staring at and get moving," Kosa demanded, more of herself than the others. "Everyone, back into formation. We need to find the room that has a symbol near it that looks like two triangles."

The group fell back into the pattern she had decided on in the lift. Now that she wrenched herself from the windows, Kosa took a more discriminating look at the hallway. Along with the stalactites, there were faint purple and green growths in various places on the walls and in the windows, with no discernible order. It reminded her of lichen.

"Stares," she ordered, knowing the Rip would agree to experiment. "Are these patches organic?" The Rip instantly touched one.

"Ooh, they're kind of warm to the touch. I think they're growing—but very slowly."

"You think they're some kind of infestation?" Rammy asked the group.

"I bet they're not," Hynd replied. "Though I couldn't begin to tell you their purpose."

The group fell silent, unwilling or too tired of unexplained phenomenon or technology to enter into speculation. Kosa's legs tingled, as they always did when she sat in the marine dropship waiting to disembark to battle. The now-building adrenaline had coursed through her several times on this ship already, but now that they were, presumably, so close to their goal of escape, she itched for a fight.

They passed several doors on the left of the hallway, but none had the two triangle symbols. Like in the lower levels, the symbols on the doors were glittering holograms. Unlike below, these holograms had smaller characters running to the right or left of the larger symbols – further designations, perhaps? Kosa glanced back to make sure everyone was accounted for and saw Ow'llent scanning the symbols with her Dev as they passed. Scientists had to study everything.

The hallway took a sharp bend to the left for a few hundred feet, then returned to its original direction. They still hadn't seen a soul. It was entirely unlike a Terran ship, where every hallway was bustling with people. Had the Trychu lied to her? Was their "help" just another experiment?

"There!" Crenk exclaimed, racing past her. A pair of eight-foot-tall doors on the right had the two triangles shape floating before it.

"Yes!" Kosa breathed. She glanced back at everyone. "Alright, people, we can't expect this to go easy-peasy. Rammy, Wind, it's time you used the last of your ammo. Klenni, how's that pistol?"

"Here, Kosa, you have it."

Kosa paused, considering, then shook her head. "No, I'm better served using my knife. You use it."

Klenni nodded.

"Ok, people. We can do this. We're so close to getting the fuck out of here. We've all made it this far, and we can make it a little further. I just want to say it's been an honour working with you." Kosa eyed everyone in turn. Klenni's tendrils wiggled with pride, Flugger made no response, Rammy saluted, Ow'llent gave a grudging nod, Stares smiled, Wind bowed his head, Hynd blinked, and Crenk, who was beside her, placed his first to his temple, then briefly rested his hand on her shoulder. Ow'llent's eyes burned into Kosa. With that glare, the Strenoi would make an excellent CO. Her students were likely terrified of her.

"Alright, move out!" Kosa said, turning towards the symbol and pressing her hand against it. The doors opened with the hiss to which they'd grown accustomed.

They were in a large room. It was not quite as big as the bay where *Starship 330307*'s remains lay, but maybe three-quarters that size. Like the room with the crates, this one was dotted with excellent items to provide cover, but instead of cages, there were what appeared to be pieces of ships sitting on different-coloured sections of the floor. Kosa's head snapped upwards; instead of cages hanging from the ceiling, there were boxes, some the size of couches, others as small as a backpack. Each box was suspended over each ship piece. Did they hold components? Tools?

Rammy's sharp intake of breath caused Kosa to glance towards him. He was edging towards what Kosa presumed to be some sort of engine, clearly entranced by it. *Scientists*. Kosa rolled her eyes.

As the others began to whisper theories about the ship parts, Kosa struggled with telling them to shut up. They were civilians – despite their time in this ship, working at a military unit still didn't come naturally.

Kosa let them ponder as she surveyed the rest of the room. There was no ship in here, but another set of doors, these transparent, likely glass or an alien variant. Through them, she could see large dark shapes that were, hopefully, working ships. This room they were in was some sort of garage, perhaps research and development, and it made sense that the working vessels lay beyond, near the airlock doors.

She smiled, though she knew hope often opened the door for trouble.

"We've made it," Crenk breathed. He, as usual, stood at her side. She was so used to him being there; she now felt his absence when he wasn't next to her. Would she suffer his absence when they got out of *Misery* and parted ways? That's what they were going to do, right?

"So far, so good," Kosa whispered.

"Why are we whispering?"

"I'm still not sure we're in the clear. I don't want us to rush in there to be mown down or captured. We can't get sloppy now, especially after what happened with the cages."

"To be honest," Crenk said, stepping a little closer. "I didn't mind being trapped with you."

"Better than Flugger or the Rips, am I right?"

Crenk smirked. "Especially if Wind had expected my help with jer problem."

Kosa giggled, then cut it off. She hated her giggle. She'd worked hard her adult life to have a mature laugh, the laugh of a woman, not her natural asinine giggle that made her seem like a schoolgirl.

"I enjoy making you laugh," Crenk said. "Being with you, learning about you, has been the only redeeming experience of this entire situation."

"Even when we fought at the start?" she smiled, brushing grimy hair behind her ear.

"Even then."

Her cheeks grew hot. She looked away, looked back. She picked at a hangnail on her thumb with her pointer finger on the opposite hand. "I will admit that your evasive maneuvers were pretty damn cool. For a pilot." She smirked.

Crenk laughed.

Ow'llent appeared. "Are we leaving now? Why are you stalling?"

Kosa bristled. "We're not stalling."

"The ships are right there!" Ow'llent pointed a clawed hand, her elongated toe-claw tapping the ground five clicks per second. "Why are we standing around in this, whatever it is?"

"Settle down." Crenk frowned. "We want to make sure it isn't a trap."

"Then send one of the Rips in there to scout!"

"When did you become a military expert?" Kosa demanded with her hands on her hips.

Ow'llent gripped her pike. "When I wasn't the one delaying us so I could have some more time with Crenkleost."

Kosa frowned. "Look. I get it. We're all tired. We're all filthy. We're all starving and thirsty. But we can't rush in."

Ow'llent shook her head. "Whatever. You two do whatever disgusting things you want to one another. I'm leaving!"

She strode towards the doors and put her hand towards the symbol. It spun, turned green, the doors opened three inches, then slammed back together.

Ow'llent grabbed the horizontal bar that was presumably a handle and pulled. The doors creaked but did not open.

"Gas!" Rammy called. "Kosa! There's gas or smoke coming from the ceiling!"

CHAPTER 26: HYND

Even with their own people, Hynd wasn't the most talkative, so they were especially unsure about what topic to broach with the aliens and thus stood on their own, lost in thought. The rest of the group had known one another longer, hadn't been in the ship as long as Hynd had been, and each of them had another of their species to converse with, even though the doctor and the computer scientist were fighting and something unorthodox was brewing between the corporal and the pilot.

Hynd's people, for the most part, were calmer than the rest of the aliens. They'd been referred to as plodding, as methodical, as too slow; Hynd was considered by many of their peers and friends to be the rash one. All they wanted was to get off this damn ship. All they wanted was to see Jurl and their friends again. To breathe fresh, not recycled, air.

So, when the gas began pouring into the room, Hynd's slow-to-boil rage began to effervesce. How *dare* another culture imprison them for study? How *dare* they attack them over and over with no reprieve? How *dare* they destroy their sources of food and water?

"I can stop it!" Klenni exclaimed. "Flugger, for once, get the fuck off of me and let me work!"

As Hynd looked over, Klenni shoved Flugger and grabbed at Allie, who was floating nearby. She opened up its interface and began typing.

"Everyone, cover your mouths!" Kosa called. Rammy yanked the shirt off his back and further ripped it into strips, handing them to the closest people, Hynd included. Crenk used a claw to rip his own shirt, tearing off strips and giving them to Kosa and Ow'llent. Hynd would have laughed at these displays if it weren't for the direness of the situation. The slowly drifting gas reached their nostrils first, as they were the tallest. They sneezed, and with the next inhale, their throat began to close up. Hynd panicked, began tearing at their neck. The makeshift masks were ineffective.

"Get to the floor!" Kosa called, then coughed violently. Hynd fell to their knees. Would they awaken in the lab, mounted to the wall, only to be taken away again to be divested of their innards? Would they not wake at all? Is this where they would die? Pain overtook their panicked thoughts, and they struggled to bring oxygen into their lungs. Spikes stabbed through their ribcage and throat. Hynd forced their eyes open as they choked, their blurred vision revealing everyone else lying on the ground, some taking small breaths, others beginning to asphyxiate as Hynd was.

The world grew dimmer.

"Klen …" Rammy mumbled as the Pir-An began to cough harder, fingers still typing.

"Just need … to … *cough* … bypass … *cough cough* … one system …" Klenni hacked violently and began to gasp. Her fingers continued to type, despite her face growing a darker blue. "Fuck you … *yurtl-nakers*!" she managed to shout, using the Rip's insult, and Allie's keyboard retracted. The gas stopped hissing from wherever it emitted from. Instead, greasy, purple water misted from different ports in the ceiling.

"Breathe it in!" Kosa croaked. Deep breaths were taken around Hynd, followed by more coughing. Hynd realized they were lying on their side, staring at the room. They took long, laboured breaths, watching as Rammy pushed himself to his feet, then raced to Klenni and wrapped his arms around her shoulders. The Pir-An wrapped her tendrils around his arm. The Terran stared down at it in surprise, then smiled and kissed Klenni on the head.

"Get off her!" Flugger bellowed, coughing.

Klenni glanced up at Rammy, pointedly ignoring her husband. Hynd snorted as they glanced around the room, taking deep breaths of the soothing mist. It began to dissipate but left the machinery in the room coated with slimy dew. The Rips pushed themselves to their feet. Kosa surveyed the room, the water pasting her hair to her head. Crenk extended a hand down to Ow'llent, who was breathing hard. The older Strenoi pushed his hand away.

Rammy approached Hynd, crouched, and extended his own hand. Hynd stared.

"Do you need help?" Rammy asked. Hynd accepted the hand, more as a balance than a counterweight.

"I like your fur," Hynd commented. Water ran in rivets through the curling black hair on the Terran's chest. Fur that dark, and that curly, was very rare in Dirge society, making it the most desired. Dirge spent hours at the salon each week, having their long hair dyed and curled and coiffed. Hynd decided this was the first thing they would do when they got home: a full-body fur treatment and a hair revitalizing session. In an open-air salon, of course.

The hallway doors behind them opened.

"Cover!" Kosa screamed, voice hoarse. Hynd dove behind the nearest engine part. Rammy scooping up his rifle and slid on the slippery floor to join them. The scrambling of feet and claws suggested the others were seeking shelter as well.

"Ow'llent! Cover!" Kosa ordered. Hynd looked behind them to see Ow'llent pulling as hard as she could on the doors to the bay.

"Ow'llent!" Crenk bellowed. "Get to cover!"

The older Strenoi ignored both calls, and for it, projectiles slammed into her back. Her blood splattered the doors she was so desperately trying to open.

"Ow'llent!" Crenk exclaimed again, this time in despair, as the female Strenoi sank to her knees, leaving a red smear on the glass. Her body collapsed sideways to join her pike on the floor.

"Rammy, Wind, open fire!" Kosa ordered. "Klenni, override the bay doors!"

"I can't!" she exclaimed. "They're on a different system or something! Or maybe they figured out my backdoor access and re –"

"Ok, then shoot, goddamn it!"

Shots from Klenni's plasma pistol rang out amidst the clatter of Rammy's rail gun and a sharp crack from Wind's rifle.

Hynd peeked out the other side of the engine. Their assailants were a dozen Trychu, armed with odd-shaped guns. Movement behind them. Hynd turned to see Kosa and Crenk sneaking from ship part to ship part, clearly determining to fight the creatures with their knives. The main problem with their plan was the fifteen-foot gap between the closest engine and the attackers. Unless there were a distraction to draw the Trychu's fire, they'd never make it.

"Are you joining us?" Kosa asked as she arrived beside Hynd. Rammy ceased firing for a moment.

"Last mag, Corporal," he said, face grim.

"OK, you use that to give us some time to get to the Trychu bastards," Kosa said.

"Better idea," Hynd replied, readying themselves to move. "I'll gain us entry to the bay."

"How the –" Crenk began, but Hynd was already running. They burst from behind the engine, hurtling straight for the glass doors already weakened by the bullets that had killed Ow'llent.

Pain blossomed in Hynd's left shoulder, another in their lower back, but they kept running. Hynd lowered their head, tucked it into their shoulder, and slammed their body into the doors. Glass shattered around them as they fell into the bay, onto their injured shoulder, facing their comrades. The pain of landing on the wound overtook anything else, turning the world briefly white.

They could hear Kosa shouting orders, Crenk bellowing, Stares shrieking, and Klenni's little gun retorting, but all Hynd could see was Ow'llent's blank eyes where she lay slumped forwards, her pike beside her, her Dev blinking a dull red pulse.

Hynd took a deep breath, air shuddering into their lungs. Everything hurt. They were certain glass shards were embedded in them in all manner of places. A rivet of blood ran from their forehead down their snout. They wanted to wipe it off before it reached their lips, but their arms wouldn't move. The metallic stench of so much blood burned their nostrils.

Hynd's eyes focused on Kosa on top of a Trychu, stabbing it in the underbelly. Rammy was bludgeoning another in the head with his gun. Crenk was slamming his powerful fists against another Trychu's face. Wind used jer last shot to burst a Trychu's head into bits. Flugger, still in cover, looked at Klenni and then back at Hynd. Stares leapt over two dead Trychu to land on another, legs wrapping around the giant bug as if embracing them. Jer hands grabbed the Trychu's jaws, yanked their head upwards, and je thrust jer teeth deep into the alien's neck. The Trychu let out a scream of anguish as they flailed, trying to dislodge the Rip.

The last thing Hynd saw was Stares spitting out viscera and licking jer fingers as the rest of the team ran towards the shattered glass doors.

CHAPTER 27: RAMMY

The group managed to get Hynd to their feet, though the Dirge wavered in and out of consciousness. Rammy hoisted the large, damp, bleeding Dirge under his one shoulder. Stares and Wind took the other side. Hynd had saved everyone. If they hadn't run towards the doors, attracting the fire of the Trychu, Kosa and Crenk would surely have been mowed down when they attempted to rush the attackers. Granted, the Trychu were terrible fighters. They lacked coordination and had terrible aim, which made Rammy wonder why they used guns at all, but without Hynd, the escapees surely wouldn't be on their way to what was, hopefully, safety.

Kosa was leading the group, and Klenni functioned as rear guard. Flugger shuffled next to her. Crenk had hoisted Ow'llent's body onto his shoulders in a firefighter's carry, determined not to leave her here. As much as Rammy understood that, he had left many comrade's bodies on the field. If the Trychu returned, he hoped the Strenoi would be able to drop Ow'llent's body. They needed Crenk, more than anyone, to fly the ship.

Rammy watched Ow'llent's flaccid hand bump against Crenk's unclothed back. Maybe she was still ok? The Strenoi had different physiology than Terrans. Not drastically different, like the Rips, but perhaps she was simply in a coma. It didn't seem fair that a civilian, an older woman with a lauded career in academia, would die in a firefight. It should have been him. Or Kosa. Or … well, that wasn't fair either.

They were all dropped on this ship against their will. They should count themselves lucky Ow'llent was the only casualty so far. But that didn't make it any easier, did it? Ow'llent wasn't an anonymous prisoner; she had been a friend. He liked and respected her. She always knew when to drop a good joke, and she had that lofty professor vibe he coveted for himself. If he made it out of here, if he got his Ph.D., he'd try to base his demeanour on this brave Strenoi.

"You know why we're called the Dirge, right?" Hynd mumbled, their words barely decipherable due to slurring. Flugger had shot Hynd with his last painkiller.

"No. Why?" Rammy asked, figuring it was good to keep them talking.

"It means lament. A death … lament."

"You're going to be fine," Rammy said, trying to breathe from his mouth. Hynd's blood oozed down his shoulder.

"No … our people. They are dead. We're resurrected again and again."

"Hynd! That's very offensive!" Klenni protested from behind them. "I know lab-grown people, and they are not the living dead. What the fins, Hynd!"

"Shut up back there!" Kosa barked.

"I just want to see the sky once more," Hynd muttered.

Me too, Rammy thought, staring up at the cold, gray ceiling.

Ships packed the room. Most were of unknown design, and therefore presumably Trychu. Some were built for speed and others for transporting large items or people. Rammy wished he could spend time examining these alien vehicles, but who knew whether more of the aliens were going to come down on them at any second. They couldn't spend a single moment inspecting these fascinating machines.

"Where the fuck is it?" Kosa gnashed her teeth as they rounded another ship. Rammy was too tired and hungry to smile. Kosa always hated missions of retrieval because she had no sense of direction.

Crenk, a few feet in front of Rammy, his muscles straining to carry Ow'llent's limp form, stopped walking. A low growl emitted from his throat, but not like when he was angry. This was almost a purr.

"What's the problem?" Rammy asked, glancing behind him, preparing to drop Hynd and grab his combat knife.

"There's no problem," Kosa clarified. Rammy's gut, which he hadn't realized he was clenching, released. "We found the ship."

Rammy looked ahead of him, feeling stupid. Of course, they had; a P-class Strenoi starship rested in front of a pair of bay doors. Rammy had overlooked it in his distraction. The Rips urged the Dirge towards it, past Crenk, who had stopped to shift his grip on Ow'llent's body.

"What's Crenk's deal?" Rammy asked as they approached Kosa, who was examining the piece of paper Grukli had given her.

"I think he's in love," she said, distracted. Stares chortled. Rammy raised an eyebrow until Kosa clarified with a frown. "With the ship. I'm guessing it's like a corvette would be to us."

"Oh! Yeah, it is pretty much a space yacht." Rammy whistled. The Strenoi ship was indeed a first-class craft. Most Strenoi ships he had seen were the typical triangular fighters, warships, or giant barges for transport. Rammy had only seen a few civilian, or P-class, crafts before, and nothing like this. It was nowhere near as tall as the others around it, but it had unnecessary curves and superfluous ornaments to suggest luxury. The hull was a shiny dark purple, a colour the Strenoi seemed to love. Back in the olden days, before the end of fossil fuels, Terrans had loved cars – one of Rammy's best friends was obsessed with them. She watched any old shows she could find that featured them and even paid to drive one at a museum track once. This Strenoi ship was the equivalent of a Bugatti supercar back before self-driving cars took over. Today, Bugatti built spaceship components for Terran P-class corvettes.

Kosa strode up to the door and held out the paper from Grukli. She glanced up and down from paper to ship a few times, then pressed the inside of what looked like a vivisected insect that spanned from doorframe to doorframe. A holographic interface floated before her. She pressed three symbols after one another, and nothing happened. She swore in Japanese, then tried again using the opposite order. Rammy let out a sigh of relief when the insect device retracted its legs and floated away. Rammy stared after it, wondering how it worked and where it was going. These Trychu were assholes, but, man, was their tech amazing. Kosa pressed the entry pad, and the door opened with a gentle hiss. Hopefully, they had enough power to escape, if not make it to a friendly world. At least in space, they could decide to die on their own terms.

"Inside!" Kosa ordered, rushing to help Crenk with Ow'llent. Klenni and Flugger raced up to the door and headed in. Rammy entered after, with Hynd and the Rips. The ship was spacious, designed for entertaining. It had a large living room area as its main entry point after a small airlock that was unlocked. Rammy helped lay Hynd down on a flat piece of furniture, a Strenoi couch, and stood back as Crenk and Kosa lay Ow'llent down on the sofa opposite. Kosa closed the Strenoi's eyes as Crenk stared down at his fallen friend.

"I was supposed to protect her," Crenk whispered. Then, to Rammy's surprise, Kosa took Crenk's hand, weaving her fingers between his.

"You did your best," Kosa replied.

Crenk shook his head, his chin dropping to hit his chest. His grip tightened around Kosa's as she pushed her shoulder into his armpit and briefly rested her head on his shoulder.

As much as Rammy wanted to stare at the unorthodox scene longer, they had more pressing concerns. "I'm sorry, guys, but don't we need to leave?"

"Yeah, we'll –" Stares began, but Klenni shushed whatever the callous Rip was going to say next.

"I'll bring her body home to Strenovast," Crenk said, letting go of Kosa and heading towards the cockpit. Kosa followed shortly after. Flugger knelt in front of Hynd and began to inspect their wounds. Wind took a medical kit off the wall by the airlock and passed it to the doctor.

"Stares, since you are so fond of gore, please assist me," the doctor requested. Stares bounded over.

Wind sat on the only empty couch, fiddling with jer sniper rifle, seemingly lost in thought. Klenni headed towards the cockpit after Crenk and Kosa, and Rammy followed.

Crenk occupied the pilot's chair and Kosa, the co-pilot's seat. Klenni, who had been on Strenoi ships before, found the navigation array to the left of Crenk and settled into the chair much too large for her. Rammy leaned on the back of Kosa's chair as Crenk activated the controls. The viewscreen opened to show the bay and the unopened door in front of them.

"This is Leadership Cheli'cerae," a deep, slightly nasal voice boomed throughout the bay.

"They're speaking Rip!" Stares yelled from the living area. As if they hadn't noticed.

"How you *filth* managed to make your way through my ship is beyond me, but I reluctantly have a deal to make with you. Exit the vessel, disarm, and you can live here, providing information on your cultures. You can eat whatever you want, drink whatever you want, have more drugs. Engage in whatever form of recreational sex you desire. The alternative is I blow you up right now."

"They're bluffing." Kosa scowled, crossing arms over her chest. "They wouldn't destroy all these ships to get to us."

"Wasn't Grukli supposed to open the doors?" Crenk whispered.

"Let's hope they do," Kosa replied. She turned to Rammy and Klenni. "You two fine with going down with the ship?"

Rammy nodded. Klenni's tendrils snapped together briskly. "Yes, ma'am. Fuck these *kringle amers*."

"Engage the engines, Pilot," Kosa said to Crenk. The Strenoi saluted, and the ship hummed to life.

Klenni activated the comm system to the rest of the ship. "I love you, Flugger!"

"Wait, what?" the confused voice of Flugger replied.

"This is your final warning!" Cheli'cerae's voice boomed.

"I like this person. They're commanding," Stares' voice came over the open comm. "Kind of sexy. How about I seduce them to help us escape?"

Rammy imagined Flugger's eyes were rolling if he wasn't too busy freaking out.

The ship began to hover. Crenk looked at Kosa. She looked back at him. They held their gaze for a long moment. Rammy wondered if his last thoughts were going to be about why he hadn't noticed this going on before ten minutes ago.

The bay doors opened in front of them.

"WHAT!?" Cheli'cerae shrieked, then their words dissolved into their chittering language. Crenk accelerated the ship as fast as impulse would go, and they shot out of *Misery* and into the black. Rammy couldn't help whooping. They were free!

"What about missiles?" Kosa asked. Rammy's heart sunk.

"I'm on it!" Crenk declared, opening the port viewscreen. Missiles were indeed screaming towards them. Crenk maintained their speed, heading towards the asteroid-surrounded moon.

Rammy slid into an empty seat and strapped on his harness. Déjà vu hit him, though he knew why he felt like he had experienced this before. He had, less than a week ago, although it felt like decades.

"Hang on back there!" he called to Flugger.

"Can't I have five minutes of peace?" Flugger muttered.

Bright silver dots followed the ship, faint blue trails extending behind them. They were a dangerous beauty in the vacuum of space, as they made no sound as they streaked toward their target. Crenk pressed a button, and a manual steering mechanism popped out of the console. He took the handles as the ship entered the field. He weaved between asteroids, threading them, as missiles struck asteroids behind him. He nibbled on his lip as he glanced at the port screen, flew directly at an asteroid, then dropped sharply. The missile smashed into the rock. He was well beyond the debris as another missile approached, which he avoided by skirting left. It crashed into another asteroid. Three missiles remained. He got rid of the first two by similar maneuvers, one causing Rammy's stomach to lurch. The final rocket refused to give up, tailing them closer and closer. There was nowhere else to go but between two city-sized asteroids very close to one another or into open space, where the missile would surely hit them.

Crenk twisted the ship at the last second; it corkscrewed between the two asteroid pieces. The missile exploded behind them, but Crenk couldn't stop or slow down. Despite being rooted in orbit, the asteroids were constantly in flux. One touch would send their ship irrevocably out of control, slamming them into another asteroid given their propulsion. Crenk deftly weaved the ship over, under, and around divots, out-jutting pieces, and debris until they were at the edge of the field. Crenk brought the vessel to a dead stop and turned off everything but auxiliary power. Gravity kicked out.

"Hey!" Flugger called.

"We have to lay low until Klenni plots a jump," Crenk explained. "The asteroids will block their sensors."

"As long as they're not crazy enough to blast the entire moon," Wind grumbled.

"How long will it take?"

"Hang tight," Klenni mumbled. "I have to translate Strenoi to Pir-An to do it, and you don't want me to mess it up."

They made it. The ship had enough power in the Super Lumen engine to get them to the edge of the Marca system, which would take several hours. At which point they would move to impulse speed which was a day's journey to a thankfully neutral space station, called, predictably, Marca Station.

Once the Super Lumen engine was activated, Crenk no longer needed to "pilot" the ship as the A.I. took over. As such, he headed to the showers and to sleep, so he would be well-rested to pilot at impulse. He waved off any offers of food, heading past Ow'llent with a sorrowful look.

The rest of the crew warily approached the food producer, surprised to find that it catered to Pir-An and Terran at a minimal level.

"I bet this was some diplomat's ship, eh?" Rammy suggested. "Which is why they have some of our food. Maybe it was the ship of the Strenoi diplomat Hynd mentioned?"

Kosa took a sip of her coffee and sighed deeply, not caring in the slightest who owned the ship before.

Flugger finished patching up Hynd and declared that the Dirge would live, at least until they reached Marca Station, where their medics could assess them.

"Good job, Flugger." Kosa nodded. "You kept us alive in there."

Flugger look hard at Kosa. "No, that was you. I may be a surly douchebag, as Rammy accused me, but I do appreciate what you did for us. We would never have made it without you."

"What about me?" Stares demanded.

"What about you?"

"I helped."

Flugger snorted.

They ate the rest of their meal in silence, too drained to talk. Afterwards, they headed to the showers and to sleep. There were more than enough cabins. Rammy spent far longer than was needed scrubbing the grime from his hair and massaging the tangles from his inch-thick beard, then sprawled out on the clean, large bed. Strenoi didn't use sheets or a blanket, at least none he could find, just a fitted cover for what was essentially a very soft mattress. There was no pillow, but Rammy didn't care. He fell into a blissful sleep, his stomach full, his skin clean, and no threat of aliens, hybrid-creatures, or cages dogging his every move.

EPILOGUE

After ten hours of blissful slumber, broken only by a few bad dreams, Klenni woke to find everyone still asleep, including Flugger, who slept beside her like the dead. She crept out of the room to let him continue. Hynd lay on the couch in the common room, chest rising and falling gently, so Klenni snuck into the elaborate entertainment zone and turned on the holovision. Nothing had changed. Strenoi and Terra still had a tense truce. The Pir-An and Dirge carried on as usual. The Rips were demanding attention but were ignored. No one had heard of a mysterious ship in the far reaches of civilized space, nor any missiles near Pharsa's asteroid moon.

Eventually, the rest of the crew, minus Hynd, joined her. By then, Klenni had set out breakfast for everyone.

"Is it drugged?" Stares asked. No one laughed. "Too soon?"

Wind shook jer head. "Sometimes, Stares, I wonder why you ever turned me on."

"Speaking of that, are you still in love with me? Still want to follow me everywhere I go?"

"That was the hormones talking."

Stares shrugged. "I mean, I don't mind your company. You can be my bodyguard if you want."

"For what?"

"When I return to Ripplia. I'm moving up, Wind, and I need someone I can trust to watch my back."

"What is je talking about?" Kosa demanded, though with less ferocity than usual.

"Stares is part of our elite society. We call them Upper Echelon."

"I'm fighting to make Ripplia an independent, self-sustaining, self-governing planet. We Rips deserve the same things you other sapients have."

Kosa and Rammy exchanged glances. To Kosa's surprise, Rammy nodded.

"I agree. Who are we to say that you can't be self-determining? I support you, Stares."

"Our governments elevated you technologically before your time. So they should be prepared to expect you'd want some parity with us," Klenni added.

Stares smiled but kept jer lips from reaching a full grin. As such, je looked less frightening, less aggressive. As much as je rather enjoyed the company of these aliens, je was not going to tell them about the data je had taken from Allie, or the scans je had made of everything. Je did not tell them that je had been implanted with a camera in jer right eye, and je had photos of everything of importance from *Misery*, including the Trychu. Je did not mention that as they all slept, je had hacked into and made a copy of the data from Ow'llent's Dev. Je sat back on the sofa with jer arms behind jer head. Ah, yes, things were going to go very well for Stares At the Stars and Forgets Where Je is From. They'd have to change jer name once je proved how far je was willing to go for jer planet and jer people.

Wind, on the other hand, considered Stares' offer. Je lied when je said jer feelings were hormonal. Wind still couldn't divorce Stares from jer brain. Perhaps because Stares had been the one to begin jer *Thrum*? Or perhaps because Stares was brave, fiercely intelligent despite jer rather absurd actions, made Wind laugh, and had inspired the spawn that was now growing inside of Wind. Unlike Terrans and Strenoi, Rips didn't have a twenty-four-hour process of conception followed by days of implantation. A zygote formed within hours of sex if it were viable. Wind felt … *different*. Je knew je was pregnant. Perhaps if je were Stares' bodyguard, je would allow Wind to leave jer child with the Upper Echelon instead of jer own community? His grandparent would be overjoyed, and Wind's parent would undoubtedly be pleased to raise Wind's child in security and relative luxury. Wind had never had a purpose before now, merely hunted on Ripplia for jer community, sniped for the Strenoi during the war, and never considered jer future. But now … Stares offered something je'd never thought possible before. A change. Status. A purpose. Je had also given jer a child. Wind, to jer surprise, found je was excited to see what the Rip inside jer would look like.

They had moved Ow'llent from the other couch to the cargo bay. The Strenoi ship had a medical station, resembling a coffin in Rammy's opinion, for emergencies. They placed Ow'llent on that gurney, and Crenk wheeled her to the bay himself.

Rammy, unaware that Crenk was still in the room, headed down to search for clothing. His shirt was gone, and his pants were near unwearable. As he rounded the corner, the soft, cork-like Strenoi flooring muffling his steps, he found Kosa and Crenk standing in front of Ow'llent, looking down at her. He slowed and prepared to announce himself, but curiosity stayed his voice. He instead stepped behind a shelving unit and peered out at them.

"She was a good person," Kosa said, looking away from the dead Strenoi to the live one. Crenk nodded.

"I can't believe she's gone. I wish I could tell her partner, Corcalla, what really happened."

"She was a tough old girl." Kosa smiled. She reached down and opened her pack, bringing out Ow'llent's blanket from the first night in the ship.

She handed the blanket out to Crenk. He paused, staring down at it. Rammy wondered what the deal was with the Strenoi's suddenly stricken expression.

"You can't give me this," Crenk said.

"Why?" Kosa demanded. "I'm sure Ow'llent would want –"

"It's a … it's a breeding blanket," Crenk explained. Kosa cocked her head to the side. Crenk ran a hand down his ridge bone, looking away from her, then back. "It means … it means you want me to … provide you with a child. It's as serious a gesture as anything in my culture."

Kosa blinked hard a couple of times. "But *you* gave it to *me*."

Crenk shook his head. "It's not symbolic if I give it to you. Females choose the bloodlines. It's … well, it's ..."

Kosa and Crenk stared at one another, eyes locked. They looked at one another for quite some time, in Rammy's opinion, but that could have been because he was holding his breath.

"Just take it," Kosa finally said.

"No. It's an important part of my culture. If I take it from you, it's an obligation, it means …"

Kosa sighed, but not in frustration. "Take it," she whispered, taking a step towards him, so close they were inches apart. The blanket was pressed between their chests.

Crenk's hands were at his sides. The one facing Rammy twitched. Kosa's eyes were on the Strenoi's face, so she did not notice as his hand moved upwards and his fingers tightened around the hem of the fabric. He hesitated too long. Kosa, unaware he had taken hold of it, frowned and draped the blanket over Ow'llent's medical coffin instead.

"There," she said. "Now it's hers again. And you can decide what's to be done with it."

"Koharu …" Crenk began, his hand taking her arm. Kosa pulled her arm away and whirled on her heel. Rammy stepped further back into the shadows, so she didn't see him as she stalked out, her brows furrowed and mouth tight.

Crenk stared after her, his body still, shoulders slumped.

They arrived at Marca Station less than twenty-four hours after their escape from *Misery*. Klenni had helped Crenk hack the ownership signature of the ship so no one would accuse him of stealing it. Crenk did not tell them whether he planned to keep it or turn it over to the authorities. He was going to drop them off at Marca Station, and Kosa and Rammy would contact the Terran Navy to get back to their base – they had come up with a lie about space pirates abducting them that they would finesse on the way. Klenni and Flugger had a relative in the system who would get them back home. Hynd had woken up at a few hours before, still hurt but no longer dangerously so, and asked if someone would help them shower. No one was surprised when Wind offered jer assistance. Hynd claimed they were capable enough to hobble to the Dirge embassy. The Rips did not tell anyone their plans other than to say they would be fine.

"Stares will probably murder someone for their ship," Crenk joked.

Stares grinned jer feral smile at the Strenoi. "It might be you!"

"I wouldn't put it past you!" Crenk laughed, pushing the Rip on the shoulder. Stares snapped at him but without any real menace.

They docked.

The group stood in the hallway outside the ship, facing one another. Klenni gave everyone, even the Rips, a hug — and they allowed it. Flugger nodded politely at everyone but shook hands with Rammy. The Pir-An headed left, walking together but tendrils not touching. Stares ran a hand down Kosa, Crenk, and Rammy's shoulders, an expression of affection. Wind dipped his head at them all and headed after Stares. Hynd bowed to Rammy, Kosa, and Crenk, then followed the Rips. Wind slowed Stares down to wait for the Dirge, who accepted their company.

Finally, Kosa and Rammy turned to Crenk. Rammy held out his hand. Crenk joined his to the marine's without hesitation.

"You're a badass pilot, Crenkleost," Kosa said as Rammy took a step back to give them space. Given the chill disposition between them the last few hours, they likely hadn't been alone since the blanket incident. Now, Kosa smiled up at the Strenoi, apparently not wishing to leave in bad humour. "If our people are ever friendly enough to one another to allow it, come visit Komorebi. You'd love the planet. I'll give you a tour of the canyons."

Crenk held out his hand. When Kosa slid hers in his, he looked her in the eye. "Koharu, it's been my greatest honour to fight alongside you." He lifted her hand to the height of his chin, slid his grip to her wrist and used his other hand to part her fist, leaving it open. As she stood still, unsure what he was doing, he brought her hand to his mouth and slowly kissed her palm. He let her hand go and bowed low to her, exposing his neck. Rammy knew from the treaty summits this gesture was the way Strenoi showed they trusted someone completely. Kosa was too bewildered to say anything, so Crenk gave her a small Terran-like smile and headed back up to the ship.

Kosa stared after him, absently caressing the palm Crenk had kissed.

Rammy pushed her shoulder. “Go on, chase after him, Corporal. He could be The One.”

Kosa paused for a moment as if considering. She turned to Rammy, her expression inscrutable. “You’re crazy.”

Rammy shook his head. Now that the aliens were gone and they were away from the Trychu, he realized he still had to deal with AJ. But, somehow, the situation didn’t seem so dire. He still cared for AJ, but he knew he’d move on. What he needed was to find a one-night stand. A rash decision he might end up regretting, but why worry about that?

“Once more unto the breach?” Kosa joked, holding out her arm. Rammy slung his between hers as they made their way from the quiet hallway into the Station’s bustling, multi-species crowd.

The crew will return in

The Burnt Ship Trilogy #2: A Threat Revealed

INSPIRATION AND ACKNOWLEDGEMENTS

Thank you, reader, for venturing into this derelict ship with me! I would very much appreciate it if you could drop a review on Amazon or Goodreads; reviews are the lifeblood of indie authors. And if you're on Bookstagram, I'd love if you used the hashtags #NostromoPublications #EscapingFirstContact and #TheBurntShipTrilogy so I don't miss your post! Thank you!

Escaping First Contact owes a lot to 1960s-90s science fiction, some of which has appreciated into the "classic" realm. Most notably, Alan Dean Foster and Tanya Huff's books. If you couldn't tell, I adore books with detailed alien cultures, and Mr. Foster's Commonwealth novels and Ms. Huff's Confederation series were a major inspiration for me in that regard.

There's also Machiko Naguchi, the protagonist of the 1990s *Aliens vs. Predator* series (by Steve Perry and S.D. Perry). Kosa is an homage to her, and a lesser-known heroine called Jade Darcy (of the *Rehumanization of Jade Darcy* duology by Stephen Goldin and Mary Mason). Kosa is her own person, but she takes a few characteristics from these two leading ladies.

The idea for *Escaping First Contact* came to me in the summer of 2018 when I was on the beach reading a novel called *Vector Analysis* (by Jack C. Haldemann II, 1978), which features a space station struck by a deadly disease. The horror elements of the novel owe a great deal to *Alien*, *Virus* (1999), and *Event Horizon*. And Flugger is an ode to one of my favourite obscure classic sci-fis: *The Fluger* by Doris Piserchia.

My deepest gratitude to:

My editor, **Marthese Fenech.** Mar, thank you for your editorial finesse and friendship. You did such an amazing job making my novel so much better. Your kind words and encouragement were the icing on the cake. Check out Marthese's best-selling historical fiction *The Siege of Malta* trilogy. Marthese's attention to detail, fantastic battle scenes, and dedication to her craft are an inspiration to me.

My cover artist, **Jon Stubbington**. Despite my terrible concept drawings, you managed to craft a fantastic trio of covers that I adore. Thank you. Check out Jon's work on Instagram and https://www.jonstubbington.com/

My beta readers, specifically **Stuart**! Thank you for your fantastic feedback.

Rob Gillespie. Thank you so much, Sir, for all your help with the military side of the novel. Any errors are 100% my own. Also, the rail gun was a great suggestion.

My husband, **Rob**, and his willingness to accept that I'm a writer now and putting up with all that entails.

My daughters, **Marceline and Marina**, who dealt with many "mommy is working" moments. Hopefully, you won't remember the neglect when you're older.

My sisters, **Kait and Nikkie**, as always, for their support in everything I do. Beier vs Rest!

My friends **Lindsay and Jeff O'Neill**, who have been nothing but supportive of my writing. Here's to helping a local build a firepit, Ontario-style, in Glenariff! (a little reference to book #3 here).

To everyone who participates in the **#WritingCommunity on Twitter** – you guys are such fun to interact with and bounce ideas off on.

To my family, who are always supportive of my writing, and to everyone who bought a copy of my debut *What Branches Grow*, even if it wasn't your preferred genre.

And, finally, a thank you to all my friends who put up with my wild antics and drunken ramblings about my works in progress. This trilogy, about found friendship, is for all of you.

ABOUT THE AUTHOR

T. (Tina) S. Beier is a science fiction aficionado. Her first novel, the post-apocalyptic adventure *What Branches Grow*, was a Top 5 Category Finalist in the 2020 Kindle Book Awards and (as of this publication), a contestant in High Howey's Self Published Science Fiction Competition. She has a B.A. (Hons.) in English, a graduate certificate in creative writing, a certificate in publishing, and writes for PostApocalypticMedia.com. She is also an entrepreneur and the co-owner of Rising Action Publishing Co., a Canadian-based indie publisher and editing services provider.

You can follow Tina on most socials, but her favourites are Instagram, Twitter, and Booktube. Follow her for giveaways, other bookish content, and updates on her upcoming projects, including *The Burnt Ship Trilogy* #2: *A Threat Revealed* and #3: *Dead in the Water*.

Check out her website, nostromopublications.com, for links to all her work and her socials.

NOSTROMO

Printed in Great Britain
by Amazon

72340388R00187